ALWAYS YOU

AN ADAIR FAMILY NOVEL

SAMANTHA YOUNG

Always You

An Adair Family Novel

By Samantha Young
Copyright © 2022 Samantha Young

ALSO BY SAMANTHA YOUNG

Other Adult Contemporary Novels by Samantha Young

Play On

As Dust Dances

Black Tangled Heart

Hold On: A Play On Novella

Into the Deep

Out of the Shallows

Hero

Villain: A Hero Novella

One Day: A Valentine Novella

Fight or Flight

Much Ado About You

On Dublin Street Series:

On Dublin Street

Down London Road

Before Jamaica Lane

Fall From India Place

Echoes of Scotland Street

Moonlight on Nightingale Way

Until Fountain Bridge (a novella)

Castle Hill (a novella)

Valentine (a novella)

One King's Way (a novella)

War of the Covens Trilogy:

Hunted

Destined

Ascended

The Seven Kings of Jinn Series:

Seven Kings of Jinn

Of Wish and Fury

Queen of Shadow and Ash

The Law of Stars and Sultans

The True Immortality Series:

War of Hearts

Kiss of Vengeance

Kiss of Eternity (a short story)

Bound by Forever

PROLOGUE

ARRO
SIX YEARS AND FOUR MONTHS AGO

Ardnoch Castle, Sutherland
Scottish Highlands

It was strange to see my family home filled to the brim with glamorous people, famous faces, glittering evening gowns, kilts, and tuxedos. Servers in traditional uniforms—coattails, cravats, and white gloves—moved among the crowd, carrying trays of canapés and flutes of champagne. Growing up in our grand castle of a home, it had been a daily overwhelming pile of never-ending repairs. We'd stuck to living in only a few rooms. The rest, along with the hallways, were damp, cold, and grim. During the winter, the castle had been freezing.

But my eldest brother, Lachlan Adair, took some of the megabucks he'd made as a Hollywood action star and convinced a few of his very wealthy friends to take some of theirs, and they invested back in our family's estate. To turn it into this. A private club for the film and television industry's elite.

I won't lie. Part of me hated it. I was territorial and concerned they'd disrespect our home, our history. Yet I knew deep down they wouldn't because Lachlan wouldn't allow it. And I knew that without this club, Ardnoch Castle and Estate would have been taken from the Adairs forever. Lachlan would've had to sell it. This way, at least, it stayed in the family.

"Why do you look so miserable over here on your own?" Thane, my second-eldest brother, sauntered toward me, his wife, Francine, at his side.

I shrugged, giving him a forlorn smile. "You don't think it's strange?"

He glanced around. "Aye, very. But it's a grand building, Arro. This is what it was meant for."

I knew he was right and lifted my glass in acknowledgment.

"At least you look the part." Francine wrapped her arm around my shoulders and gave me a squeeze. "You look stunning and fit right in with all these Hollywood people. I look like a whale."

"You do not," I scoffed. "You're glowing and gorgeous." Fran was five months pregnant with her and Thane's second child, and since I loved being an aunt to my nephew, Lewis, I was extremely excited to welcome a new addition to the family.

Fran patted her dark curls at the same time she smoothed a hand down her rounded stomach. "Thank you, but I don't feel it."

"You're beautiful," Thane countered gruffly, but I noticed he didn't reach for her. My brother and his wife were usually so publicly affectionate, it would send me running in the opposite direction. One, because I didn't want to watch my brother in a lip-lock, and two, because of the envy I felt. I was so happy for Thane, but sometimes I wanted a love like my brother had. Problem was, the likelihood of ever finding it was slim, considering I was already in love with someone, and he didn't love me back, and I was terrified I'd never be able to move on from him.

Still, I wasn't so self-involved that I hadn't noticed things seemed a little strained between Thane and Fran. Or that my brother had been distant with everyone lately. I didn't realize I was staring so intently at him, but as if sensing where my thoughts lay, he took hold of Fran's hand, and she seemed to melt with relief into his side.

"Where're Brodan and Arran?" he asked.

I shrugged, looking around for our brothers. "They're here somewhere. Probably finding someone to kiss at midnight."

"Have you found someone, Arro?" Fran grinned at me.

Yes, yes, I have. I shook my head. Because although I'd found someone I wanted to kiss for all my midnights to come, it was doubtful he'd kiss me back.

Speaking of, "Where's Mac? I haven't seen him all night. He's not working, is he?"

Fran shrugged. "He is head of security."

"No." Thane shook his head. "Lachlan gave him the night off so he could enjoy the New Year with us. One of his team has taken lead for the evening."

"So where is he?"

Fran snorted. "Probably hiding from the many women desperate to get him into bed."

Inwardly, I flinched, while Thane winked at me and said to his wife, "Sweetheart, men don't hide from that."

3

"Och, you." She turned to berate him, but he caught her in a kiss.

I was so happy to see them acting normally around one another, but I did not want to stand there and watch. "Enjoy!" I called over the music before I left to make my way out of the great hall.

Mac definitely wasn't in there, and honestly, his face was the only one I wanted to see.

It always was.

And it had been this way since Dad died.

Or maybe longer. I'd known Mac since I was fourteen, but I had spent little time with him back then since he and Lachlan were always off traveling the world for Lachlan's job as an actor, what with Mac being part of my brother's security team. But I distinctly remembered the Christmas Mac spent with us when I was eighteen years old. I'd just started my first semester at Aberdeen University and was happy to be home with my family. Over the two weeks of that holiday, Mac and Lachlan stayed at Ardnoch, too, and I'd developed a crush on the older man my brother considered his closest friend. Mac was thirty-one at the time, and definitely not interested in his brother's teenage sister. That didn't bother me back then. I just loved having crushes because I enjoyed the butterflies and hyperawareness, the mooning and fantasizing. It was fun!

Love, however, love was not fun.

Love hurt.

And somehow, almost eight years after that crush developed, after Lachlan and Mac had come home to rebuild the estate, I'd fallen in love with Mackennon Galbraith. I was pretty certain he still saw me as Lachlan's wee sister.

Which was why I'd gone all out on my appearance tonight. For once, I'd used a little of the inheritance I'd gotten from Lachlan when he sold land we owned elsewhere, and I bought myself a stupidly expensive dress, but it made me feel sexy. My job as a forest engineer meant I was forever running around the Highlands in jeans or walking trousers and comfy jumpers or T-shirts. For once, I wanted to show off my figure.

I moved through the receiving rooms that Lachlan had transformed for his guests into spaces where they could socialize, smoothing my hands down my dress as I searched for Mac.

Lachlan looked a little annoyed when he saw me earlier, but thankfully, he'd kept his mouth shut. As much as he wanted to keep me a wee girl, I wasn't. I was a woman. Twenty-five years old, almost twenty-six, and capable of making my own decisions. Including wearing a long dress that made me feel a little naked. It was silk, fitted, and a pale icy blue that matched my eyes. If it had been embellished with lace, it could've passed for a negligee.

I wore my hair down and asked my stylist to lighten the blond to platinum. The effect made my eyes bluer, and I decided I loved it so much I'd forego an updo and style it with some waves.

Two Hollywood actors had flirted with me within the first hour of the party.

I rarely needed that kind of attention to bolster my confidence, but Mac wasn't like any man I'd ever wanted before. For a start, I'd never been in love until now.

While Mac wasn't the type of man to settle into a serious relationship, I'd seen the women he casually dated. He was a man of varied taste, so there was absolutely a chance he could be attracted to me. I'd never lacked for confidence or had self-image issues, mostly because of my upbringing. Who cared what anyone else thought? About anything! I'd grown up in a village where everyone knew your business, and the only way to survive it was to not give a damn.

Tonight was a braless night for me, and I gave zero fucks. The dress had thin spaghetti straps, and the silk fabric was so fine, I couldn't wear a bra with it.

Okay. So it was a deliberate choice. I wanted to see if Mac would notice. Sue me.

It was difficult for him to notice, however, if I couldn't bloody find him.

Wondering suddenly if he'd locked himself in his office, I shifted direction, avoided eye contact with guests, and disappeared down the Staff Only corridor.

Mac's office door was shut.

I took a deep breath, rapped my knuckles against it in warning, and pushed inside.

Peeking my head around the door, I found Mac sitting on the armchair in his small office. He looked mammoth in the room that he'd filled with bookshelves. He turned, and my heart melted at the melancholy in his gorgeous eyes.

Without a word, I stepped inside and shut the door behind me. "Mac?"

His gaze drifted down my body, lingering on my breasts, and my breath caught as my stomach flipped with excitement.

But he scowled and looked down at the floor. "What are you doing here? You should be out enjoying the party."

"With a bunch of people I don't know?" I tutted and sat down on the edge of his desk. "No, thanks."

He stared sullenly at the floor, and my chest ached with longing.

Most of the time, Mac was so charming it was difficult not to flirt outrageously with him. He had a wicked smile and always seemed to know just the right thing to say.

However, as I'd gotten to know him well these last two years, I witnessed him go through periods of brooding. Lachlan wouldn't tell me what put Mac in these strange

6

moods, but I desperately wanted to know. So I could comfort him. Soothe whatever hurt him. Like he and Lachlan had soothed me after my father died in my arms.

Tears pricked in my eyes at the memory, and I looked away. "What is it about New Year's Eve that's so depressing?"

A gruff snort drew my gaze back to Mac. Our eyes met, and my pulse throbbed.

Jesus, would I ever be attracted to another man as much as I was attracted to this one?

"New Year is about new beginnings," Mac answered, his deep voice rumbling through me in a way that made me shiver.

Nope. It was highly doubtful I'd ever be attracted to another man as much as I was attracted to Mackennon Galbraith. It was like everything about him had a direct line to my erogenous zones.

"And new beginnings cannot help but remind us of the past and what we're trying to move on from."

I exhaled slowly and forced myself to ask, "And what part of the past are you trying to move on from, Mac?"

I was so afraid it was a woman, selfish as that may be.

He didn't answer. Instead, he pushed up from his chair, and my gaze followed him. Mac was a large man, standing six feet four, broad of shoulder, his waist tapering into that perfect V film superheroes strive for. The first time I'd noticed his biceps in a tight T-shirt, the mere sight turned me to jelly. I hoped I wasn't a deeply shallow person.

I'd never considered myself a woman who cared much about physique—my ex-boyfriends had come in all shapes and sizes—but Mac's strength certainly did it for me. It was the combination of that with his utter ruggedness. He was so far from pretty-boy handsome; it was almost ludicrous how masculine he was. From his bold brow to his aquiline nose to the defined line of his jaw that not even his perpetually unshaven cheeks could hide.

When you looked up the meaning of the word *masculine* in the dictionary, Mac Galbraith's damn picture was right there next to it. As evolved as I liked to believe I was, something about Mac's physicality spoke to something primal within me I couldn't deny.

And maybe I could've gotten past my physical attraction to the potent bloody man, if he hadn't also been the most wonderful and caring friend these past two years.

Mac gave me his back as he crossed the short distance to a sideboard on the opposite wall. His kilt swayed against his muscular calves. I bit my lip, trying not to think about easy access and all that.

Such a perv.

The man was clearly distraught, and I couldn't stop thinking about sex.

Shaking myself, I tried to focus as he pulled a bottle of whisky and two crystal tumblers out of the sideboard. "Drink?"

I'd had two glasses of champagne, and those had made me brave enough to seek out Mac. Who knew what the whisky might make me brave enough to do? "Sure."

As he approached with the drink in hand, I held his stare and commented as I took the glass, "You wear a kilt well, Mac."

The corners of his very kissable mouth quirked up. "Thank you." His gaze flicked over me and then danced quickly away. "You look very nice."

I wrinkled my nose. "Thanks." *I think.* I took a fortifying sip of Clynelish and enjoyed the burn down my throat, spreading warm heat across my chest.

"Why are *you* depressed on New Year's?" he asked.

He remained standing, so I had to tilt my head back a

little to look up at him. I imagined sex with Mac was a little like being conquered, and while I was a fully independent woman outside the bedroom who chafed at the idea of anyone trying to control my choices, I enjoyed the idea of Mac holding me down to conquer me. Mind you, I also fantasized about tying his arms to my bed frame and riding him until we both saw stars, so there was that.

I swallowed a larger gulp of whisky than I'd normally, needing the jolt back to reality.

"Arro?" Mac's brow furrowed.

Remembering his question, I shrugged. "It's just strange seeing the estate like this, filled with people ... none of whom are my dad." Stuart Adair had been a difficult man to get to know, and truth be told, Lachlan had been more of a father figure to me during my early childhood. But I'd known my dad loved me, and since returning to Ardnoch upon graduating from Aberdeen University, we'd grown closer.

It had been almost two years since he'd died of a heart attack. We'd been walking down the beach with his dog, Bram, a big Scottish deerhound he'd adopted while I was at uni.

I couldn't help him.

I couldn't save him.

The powerlessness was ...

I swallowed another drink of whisky, biting back tears of remembrance. Of guilt.

"Hey." Mac reached out to tip my chin up, forcing my eyes to his. His expression was tender. "You need to let the guilt go, Arro."

"Are you a mind reader, Mackennon?"

He released me, his nostrils flaring as his full name echoed around the office. No one called him Mackennon, and it sounded strangely intimate falling from my lips.

I liked it.

Mac searched my face for a second while I stared into his ever-changing eyes. Their color was technically hazel, but they changed dramatically with the light. Under the stark illumination of his office, they looked a dark blue-gray. "No. I just recognize guilt when I see it. I guess we're two guilty people tonight."

"What do you have to feel guilty about?"

He sighed heavily. "If I tell you, you'll think less of me, and I don't think I can cope with that."

I reached out to touch his arm. "I would never think less of you."

The muscle in his jaw twitched before he turned and downed his whisky at the same time. I watched warily as he crossed the room to pour another. His mood was so mercurial, so unpredictable. It wasn't like him, and I was sure I didn't like it.

"Mackennon, please tell me what's going on?"

He cut me a dangerous look over his shoulder. "Why are you calling me Mackennon?"

"Because it's a beautiful name and I enjoy saying it."

I waited for a response and got none. Instead, he poured himself another drink and leaned back against the sideboard. As if he was deliberately putting distance between us.

"You should go out and join the party, Arro."

I slipped off the desk but didn't make a move toward him. "Not until you tell me what's wrong."

"I have a daughter," he blurted out.

I froze in shock.

Mac smirked unhappily. "Oh, aye, you weren't expecting that."

"What?" I huffed out, taking a step closer. "I mean ... when? What? How?" *Was this recent?* I panicked at the thought of some woman coming into his life and taking him from me. Selfish, but true!

"I got a girl pregnant when I was fifteen."

Oh my God.

"I'd not long moved to the States to work with my uncle."

I knew his grandmother had sent him to live with his uncle in Boston to work as a mechanic, and that when he was old enough, he'd joined the Boston Police Department and from there went on to work in security.

But a daughter ... "Mac?"

"Her name is Robyn. She's twenty-three."

Holy ... Mac was only thirty-eight, but he looked like he was still in his early thirties, for Christ's sake, and he had a daughter who was twenty-three? "How did I not know about this?"

"I haven't had a relationship with her since she was fourteen. Her mum made it difficult." Mac ran a hand over his face. "And I didn't fight hard enough. All my letters, my gifts, were returned to me. Now she's a grown woman, a police officer." He shrugged despondently. "Her dad is her stepfather. I'm just the sperm donor." He threw back the rest of his whisky. "The arsehole who abandoned her, just like my mum abandoned me." Tears glittered in his eyes, shocking me. "She doesn't know how much I love her, and honestly, I don't deserve to love her. I don't deserve for her to know."

"Oh, Mac." I crossed the room to him, set my glass down on the table behind him, and hugged him.

He buried his head in my neck, and his arms tightened around me. Feeling him shudder with his emotions, tears thickened my throat.

I had no idea.

Squeezing him close, I held on as tightly as I could.

Finally, he eased, relaxing against me, and he lifted his head from my neck to meet my gaze. The torment in his eyes had softened around the edges. I pressed my palms to his chest, feeling his heart beat fast against my touch. I was so aware of him as a man, of his heat, his strength, his scent ... I tried to force away my awareness because it seemed so inappropriate, but every inch of me tingled and hummed with his proximity.

"I was a good dad," he confessed. "When she was little. Her mum, Stacey, and I split up when Robbie was just a wee thing, but I was always there for her. Stacey was volatile and everything was a war. It was so difficult to be in her life, but I did what I had to, to keep Robyn in mine. Until Stacey married Seth. Things got better again. We all got along. Seth was my friend from the police department. I liked that he was the one who would be in Robyn's life whenever I wasn't. And he never tried to force me out of the picture.

"But when I took the job in security, that meant being away more, and it all changed. Stacey was caustic and argumentative again. Then when Lachlan offered me the job with him, which meant moving across country, she wouldn't even consider sharing custody. I wanted Robyn out in California with me during school holidays. I wanted to come to Boston whenever I had a break in our schedule. But Stacey made it all or nothing.

"And I was a selfish bastard who wanted the job. It paid well. I could give Robyn things she'd never have otherwise. But I didn't just take it for her. I took it for me. And I took it because my pride demanded that Stacey couldn't dictate my life to me. I chose my pride over my kid, and no one can tell me any different."

"If you knew it would mean losing her, would you have chosen the job, your pride?"

"Never," he answered harshly, almost like he was begging me to believe him. "Never, Arro. Robyn has made it clear she wants nothing to do with me. I send letters and gifts every year, but they're always returned to sender. I ... I can't take back what I did." He rubbed his hands up my bare arms as if soothing *me*. He didn't seem to be aware of his caress. "I love Lachlan like a brother, and I love Ardnoch. I wouldn't exchange that for anything ... but her. For her, I would exchange everything that made me happy to have her back in my life. I wish I had never taken the job."

Tears filled my eyes for him. I didn't know he was walking around with this much pain and regret inside him.

"Mackennon," I whispered, reaching for his face, the prickle of his stubble scratching my palm as our gazes held. "You can't take it back. You can only move forward. I wish I could turn back time for you, but it doesn't work that way. This is where we are. But it doesn't mean we're stuck here." I pressed into him unconsciously, and his hands dropped to my hips. "You can change the future."

"I don't deserve a future with her."

Realizing he truly meant it, that he thought so little of himself, hurt. "You are a good man," I said, my voice hoarse with emotion. "The best of men."

He shook his head, but I captured his face in my hands.

"*I'll* decide. And I've decided you're wonderful. And I know I couldn't have gotten through these last two years without you. I wish you could see yourself the way I see you."

Mac squeezed my hips, expression darkening. "Arro ..."

Then some madness came over me. I pulled his head to mine and crushed my mouth to his. Excitement made me tremble as I tasted the whisky on his lips. He grunted, his lips parting in surprise, and I took advantage, touching my tongue to his.

His groan vibrated through me, and he kissed me back.

Just like that, I was on fire, my brain fogged with nothing but lust and need for him. Years of pent-up longing burst forth.

Our kiss was wild, hungry, my fingers tangling through his dark hair, his stubble scratching my skin, his hands fisting in the silk of my dress, pulling it excruciatingly tight across my sensitive breasts.

Yes, yes, YES.

I'd never experienced desire like it.

I wanted his hands everywhere at once.

Mostly, I wanted them between my legs. No, his mouth, I wanted his mouth there.

I moaned at the thought.

Mac curled his hands around my shoulders.

And abruptly pushed me away.

I stumbled, hitting the back of his armchair.

Every inch of my skin flushed, my lips swollen.

Mac gaped at me like he'd never seen me before, his gaze dropping to my chest and darkening. He turned away, his hands clenched at his sides.

A glance down revealed my nipples were visibly hard beneath the silk of my dress.

My cheeks heated, but I refused to hide myself.

Instead, I glared at Mac's back. "Will you look at me?"

He spun around, countenance dark with something I didn't like, as he ran his hands through his hair. "Fuck."

"Mac, it's fine."

"It's not bloody fine." He halted to glower at me. "I just mauled my best friend's wee sister. My boss's wee sister! Christ, you're barely three years older than my daughter."

I winced. "Don't say it like that. You're making it sound worse than it is. You're thirteen years older than me, Mackennon. It's not a big deal."

"It is a big deal." His voice lowered now, his expression softening, pleading almost. "Arro ... Lachlan is the only family I have. I could never hurt him or you. This"—he gestured between us—"darlin', it can't happen. It'll never happen. I ... my mind is in an awful place tonight, and I

14

shouldn't have … we shouldn't have. I don't think of you that way."

Rejection sliced through me.

I didn't want him to see.

I don't think of you that way.

Okay. Well, now I knew for certain, right?

Had I just taken advantage of my friend's vulnerability? The thought scored through me.

I didn't want to lose him over this.

"Mac, I'm sorry. It was a kiss. We both had too much to drink. No one needs to know and it'll never … it'll never happen again. I'll never do that again. I'm sorry. We're fine. We're good, okay?"

His eyes narrowed, studying me. It took everything I had to keep my expression neutral. Finally, he seemed to deflate with relief. "Nothing to be sorry for, darlin'. We're fine. We're good."

"Well"—I mustered up a stoic attitude as I fixed my hair— "I better get back out there for the bells. You should come, Mac. Mingle. Take your mind off Robyn for a while."

He nodded grimly. "I'll be there in a minute."

Leaving him, I felt abruptly cold out in the corridor. Dazed, I strolled back to the great hall, this time nodding at lingering guests. Mac's taste was still on my tongue; my lips still pulsed from his kiss. My body still throbbed from unsatisfied desire.

Shake it off, Arro.

I could hear Lachlan's voice booming as he gave his New Year's speech, and just as I entered the great hall, he shouted from his position on the stairs, "May ye for'er be happy an' yer enemies know it! *Slàinte Mhath!*"

Everyone raised their glasses and shouted back, "*Slàinte Mhath!*"

I waited along the edge as servers appeared with blankets

for the guests. People started wrapping the faux-fur blankets around themselves and suddenly Lachlan was before me. "There you are." He wrapped a blanket around my shoulders. "Time for fireworks before the bells."

I nodded and let him lead me with the guests outside.

"Where were you?"

"I just needed a breather," I lied. "This is all a bit overwhelming."

My big brother cuddled me to his side. "I know, sweetheart. But it'll be worth it, I promise."

I nodded and stood with him in the driveway with the guests as a bagpiper played "Auld Lang Syne" in the distance.

Suddenly, a sharp whistling sound filled the sky seconds before an enormous bang. Golds and silvers and blues and pinks exploded in the dark, and the guests erupted in cheers and applause.

For a while, I was lost in the splendor of the display.

But I felt him before I saw him.

Turning my head, I looked at Mac as he took up position on my other side.

He held my gaze, remorseful, uncertain.

I didn't want him to feel guilty about me.

He was already carrying around enough crap.

I wouldn't be something he regretted too. I'd rather live with the rejection than that.

Reaching down at my side, I slipped my hand into his. "Friends forever," I mouthed.

Mac's gaze brightened, and he squeezed my hand in thanks.

And I looked back up at the sky, watching the fireworks, pretending that my heart wasn't breaking with every single explosion.

1

ARRO

PRESENT DAY

Ardnoch, Sutherland
Scottish Highlands

For seven years, I'd watched the great hall of my family's castle transformed for one event after another. Never before, however, had a moment felt so right as this one. I was walking down the aisle as a bridesmaid in my big brother's wedding. Chairs filled the space on either side of the champagne-gold carpet runner. Old-fashioned lanterns punctuated each row of chairs, leading up and then around to the impressive staircase that led to a landing backlit by the floor-to-ceiling stained glass windows my brother had lovingly restored. On the landing waited Lachlan, Thane, our minister, and my nephew Lewis, who was adorable and handsome in his kilt that matched his father's and uncle's.

Thane's daughter, Eilidh, flounced up the stairs, throwing

the last of her red rose petals, the skirt of the flower girl dress she'd chosen bouncing dramatically to reveal her petticoat. As she'd intended. Lips twitching at my niece's excitement, I watched her beam at her uncle and father, and my chest ached at the loving look both men sent her. Only a few months ago, both Eilidh and Lewis had been in a dark situation no child should ever experience, and I'd worried how we'd get them through it. But children were resilient, and to my everlasting gratitude, they seemed happy and content.

Regan Penhaligon, the younger sister of Lachlan's soon-to-be wife, sashayed ahead of me in her maid of honor gown, and my gratitude extended toward her. I knew she had so much to do with Eil's and Lew's current happiness. She glowed in her silver dress, her hair a copper-red version of mine, styled in elaborately pinned curls. Regan took the stairs with ease, lifting her gown to do so, and envy scored through me at the smoldering look she shared with Thane before taking the position opposite him. As she reached for Eilidh's hand, my niece snuggled into Regan's side, and my brother looked so in love, he might burst with it.

I'd never seen this version of Thane. Not growing up, not when Fran was alive. Regan made him young in a way he never was when he was her age. They'd worried about their thirteen-year-age gap, but not enough to stop them. They'd tumbled headlong into their passionate love story because neither of them could see any other way.

It was a strange feeling, this mixture of joy and relief for my brother, at the same time knowing his love was the catalyst for the destruction of my own.

Stop it, I chided as I took the steps. I shoved away all selfish, melancholy thoughts and grinned at Lachlan, who smiled back tenderly. I shared another smile with Regan as I stood beside her. Today wasn't about me.

I faced the wedding guests who came from all walks of

life—villagers and friends we'd grown up with, actors, singers, athletes, well-known directors, writers, and the not-so-familiar faces of Robyn's friends and family from Boston. And right there in the front row were my brothers Brodan and Arran, both of whom had returned to the family fold for the wedding.

Arran had been gone so long, there was tension among us all. But on such a happy day, I wanted to feel nothing but relief that my brother, closest in age to me, the one I'd chased after as a child, was safe and home. At least for now.

Our eyes met, and Arran gave me that boyish smile so like Lachlan's. Then I lost his attention as it drifted to the bridesmaid walking past him.

Our friend, Eredine Willows, took the stairs elegantly in her silver gown. She had so much hair, the stylist had only pinned up half of her dark brown curls; the rest fell down her back. The silver fabric sparkled against Eredine's golden-brown skin, and the dress molded to her lithe, elegant figure. She looked like a movie star or a supermodel.

It wasn't just Arran who couldn't take his eyes off her. Knowing how much she hated any kind of attention, I moved closer in silent comfort as she stopped beside me. Ery was followed by Robyn's best friend from Boston, Jasmine, or Jaz, as she preferred. Jaz looked regal, the silver of her gown stunning against her umber skin, her braids arranged in an elaborate updo that made mine look boring.

How Robyn had chosen a metallic fabric and silhouette for her bridesmaids' dresses that suited all our body shapes and coloring, I did not know. Maybe it was the photographer in her, and she just understood these things naturally, like she did composition and light.

And then there she was.

Robyn Penhaligon, soon to be Adair.

I'd already seen her, of course. We spent all morning together in a guest suite turned bridal room.

She somehow was the sexiest but classiest bride I'd ever seen in her fit-and-flare white dress. It had a deep sweetheart neckline masked by lace edging, and because of a wee bit of sheer material, it looked as if someone had artfully painted the lace on her skin. The sleeves were lace, skin peeking through here and there. The dress sculpted her body as if it, too, was painted on, and then it flared out from the knee into a train with delicate lace edging. I knew the back was daringly low, with silk button detail that accentuated a round arse perfected by running and MMA training.

She was stunning.

I looked at Lachlan, and tears threatened at the utter awe on his face as she walked toward him, holding his gaze. Had a man ever loved a woman as much as this? My chest tightened with the ache. No one deserved it more. To have this kind of love in his life. Lachlan had been looking after us all for years, for too long, and it was about time he had a partner who made him feel less alone.

Reluctantly, I looked back at Robyn, at the man whose arm she held as they moved down the aisle. I'd avoided him when he'd arrived to collect his daughter to give her away to his best friend and boss.

Mac Galbraith.

No way in hell did he look old enough to give Robyn away, but then he'd fathered her when he was barely sixteen years old. Robyn leaned into him as he murmured something in her ear, and she grinned, looking up at him with love. Mac never would've dreamed this moment would come.

But when Robyn arrived in Ardnoch a year ago, it was to see him. She wanted answers from Mac about his absence in her life, never knowing that her mother had sent back his letters and gifts. I'd been worried at the time that she'd come here to make him feel worse about their estrangement. Yet it had become clear how much Robyn loved Mac, how much she needed him.

Their reconciliation hadn't been easy for many reasons, but they were too alike, too bonded, for it not to happen. No one could've imagined that in reconnecting with her dad, Robyn would fall in love with my eldest brother, or that Lachlan would fall so head over heels for her that he'd propose only months after their meeting, and insist on hurrying her down the aisle within the year.

But when you knew, Lachlan said, you just knew.

Their union provided the bonus for Mac that Robyn was now a permanent resident in Scotland. He wouldn't have to say goodbye to her again. I knew that meant the world to him. He adored her.

For that reason, that love between him and her, between him and the rest of my family, I had a hellish future to look forward to. To pretend anytime we had to share a room that I didn't despise him. Resent him. Wish I'd never laid eyes on him.

He was the source of nothing but pain.

And now humiliation.

I hated him.

Thirteen years between Regan and Thane.

Thirteen years between Mac and me.

If they could do it, so could we, right?

Naively, I'd assumed so.

But Mac had unequivocally shown me the error of my thinking. His reaction to what transpired between us weeks ago had been brutally humiliating, and I'll never forgive him for it.

The memory scalded my throat, and he caught my gaze before I could look away.

The bastard had the audacity to look dejected.

21

I wrenched my attention from him and focused on Lachlan.

I focused on the way he couldn't hide his eagerness to take Robyn from Mac, the way he broke tradition to pull her against him and murmur hoarsely, "You're so beautiful," before brushing his lips over hers.

At least he had his love.

And Thane had his.

If I couldn't have mine, I could be grateful that the people I loved most had theirs.

LACHLAN'S WEDDING planner had transformed the large dining room into a reception hall, filled with round tables, white tablecloths, lantern centerpieces, and twinkle lights galore. The dining room led to one of the club's reception areas, but it, too, had been transformed. They'd installed a temporary dance floor, and while there was a deejay for later, Lachlan had hired a contemporary Scottish fiddle band who journeyed over from Orkney. They'd play after dinner, and I knew the guests would love the fast-paced, energetic folk music. We'd hired the band for an event prior, and they went down a treat.

All guests had been asked to leave their phones in their rooms or estate homes, and the only person allowed to take photographs was the wedding photographer. Lachlan didn't want images of the wedding splashed over the front pages of every tabloid in the country. When he'd quit Hollywood to start the members-only club, he knew he'd always have one foot still in that world, but he was adamant his wedding remain private. The Adair family had been in the news enough these past few months.

I sat on one arm of the U-shaped top table. To Robyn's

right was Mac; Thane sat on Lachlan's left. Regan sat next to Thane, followed by Eilidh, Lewis, and me on the adjoining arm of the table. We'd deliberately put the kids between me, Regan, and Thane because we were three of the four adults they went to most for everything, and weddings could be overwhelming. We wanted them to feel safe and happy after all that had happened to them.

Beside Mac was his ex, Robyn's mum, Stacey. When she smiled, she was attractive, but unfortunately, she'd spent most of the day wearing a scowl. On the opposite arm of the table next to Stacey was Robyn's stepfather and Regan's father, Seth Penhaligon. I liked Seth. He was friendly, down-to-earth, and laid-back.

Robyn had gone through the painful dilemma of deciding which father would walk her down the aisle. After a long conversation with Seth, he told her to ask Mac. She told me Seth said that if she wanted Mac to be her dad for the rest of her life, then she had to treat him like it.

I thought that said a lot about the man Seth Penhaligon was. After all, he'd raised Robyn for most of her life. Unfortunately, since their arrival in Scotland, Stacey couldn't have made it any clearer that it pissed her off Seth wasn't walking Robyn down the aisle.

Everyone, including her husband, had ignored her huffy behavior.

Next to Seth sat Eredine, and next to Eredine was Jaz, and at the round table closest to us, Brodan, Arran, Jaz's husband Autry, and their two daughters, Asia and Jada.

I spent most of the dinner either helping Regan with the kids or turning in my seat to laugh at some joke Brodan threw my way. Not once did I look at Mac.

The volume decreased on the sound system, followed by the tinkle of silverware against glass. My heart leapt as Mac slowly stood to engage the guests. His gaze flickered to me before he looked down at Robyn. She stared up at him with unmasked adoration, and despite everything, despite how much he'd hurt me, happiness leaked through my bitterness. His whole adult life, he'd yearned for that look on her face.

And part of me hated I was happy for him.

I could hear Regan hushing Eilidh's chatter, but I found I couldn't look away from Mac.

He held a mic. "For those of you who don't know, I'm Robyn's father, Mac."

A surprised murmur surged through the guests, and Mac huffed with amusement. "I take it some of you didn't know."

Everyone laughed, and I had to remind myself to force a smile.

"Aye, it comes as a surprise to people." He looked down at Robyn, who grinned knowingly. "I think if Robyn hears one more person react with 'Oh, you can't be old enough to have a daughter this age,' she might put a hit out on me so she doesn't have to deal with it anymore."

The guests laughed again while Robyn smirked. "It's not flattering." I heard her say as Lachlan wrapped an arm around her shoulders to pull her against him. Grinning, he murmured something in her ear that made her laugh before he pressed a kiss to her temple.

There was that pang, that ache in my chest again.

"I was very young when Robyn was born." Mac's tone was sober now as he looked down at her. "Too young. Just a child myself. And I made more mistakes than I can bear to think of."

"Dad," she mouthed, before reaching out to squeeze his arm.

Mac gave her a small smile. "But in my absence, Robyn's mother, Stacey"—he placed a hand on her shoulder, and she looked startled; he then gestured to Seth—"and her stepfather, Seth, raised an extraordinary woman who is a testament to their love and care."

Mac's words brought tears to Stacey's eyes, and I watched her visibly soften, while Seth nodded in gratitude.

Trust Mac. Always fair. Always kind.

Well ... perhaps not always.

He looked back at Robyn, his voice gruff with emotion. "You *are* extraordinary, Robyn. And I say that not as a biased father. It's the truth. You are exceptional in so many ways, inspiring, courageous, kind, loyal, honorable. All the things I ever hoped to be, I now see in you. And that's the greatest gift any parent could ask for. For their child to become so much more than them, to be better."

Robyn's mouth trembled, and I could see her squeezing Lachlan's hand.

Out of the corner of my eye, I saw Regan wipe at tears.

Mine burned in my throat; I refused to let them fall.

"It's my right as your father to believe no one is worthy of you," Mac continued, "but if it had to be anyone, I'm glad it's Lachlan." His attention moved to my brother. "You have been the truest friend of my life, and I trust you with the person I love most in this world."

Lachlan and Mac held each other's gazes, something silent passing between them. Their emotion was palpable, and I struggled to hold back those damn tears.

Mac reached for his champagne flute. His eyes suddenly flickered to me and then back to Robyn and my brother. "If all of us could find a love as strong as yours, the world would be a better place. To Robyn and Lachlan!"

"To Robyn and Lachlan!" The entire wedding party raised their glasses.

I looked to the guests as many dabbed napkins to their eyes at Mac's emotion-filled speech. He had that way about him. Made you love him. Drew you in.

My bitterness rose and I tried to shake it off, but as I turned back to my table, my eyes locked with Mac's. He flinched at whatever he saw on my face, and I looked away, only to meet Regan's gaze.

Hers narrowed as she glanced between me and Mac.

Shit.

I gave her a tight smile and leaned in to ask Lewis if he'd had enough to eat, just as Thane took the mic and stood. The murmur of voices hushed again.

"I'm Thane Adair, one of Lachlan's brothers, and his best man. And I really wished I didn't have to follow Mac's speech," he grumbled, always self-deprecating.

I laughed along with the guests, relaxing now that Mac's speech was over.

"Well, what can I say about my big brother?" He clamped a hand on Lachlan's shoulder as he looked at Robyn. "I guess it's too late to tell you to run, Robyn. Run, run as fast as you can."

More chuckles as Lachlan mock glowered at our brother.

"I'm kidding. Lachlan will be a wonderful husband." Thane nodded. *Now.* But it's a good thing Robyn didn't come along in his twenties because ... well, she would've been underage, so ..." He threw the guests an exaggerated grimace, and they laughed.

"You really want to go there?" Lachlan asked, pointing at Regan.

Most of the guests couldn't hear but could guess what he said and laughed louder.

Thane chuckled, raising his hands to nod. "Fair enough."

It was amazing to hear him joke about their age difference. It wasn't that long ago when he'd had a big problem with it.

"What I mean to say," Thane continued, "is that Lachlan was a different man in his twenties. Someone I'm not sure

Robyn would've found all that tolerable. Though if I remember correctly, she didn't really find you tolerable for the first few months of your acquaintance."

The crowd *oohed* as Robyn nodded, and Lachlan rolled his eyes.

"It raises one's suspicions," Thane mused, eyeing Robyn with a smirk before he whispered into the mic, "If you're here under duress, Robyn, just wink." Thane gave an exaggerated wink. "We'll rescue you."

More laughter as Lachlan somehow concurrently grinned and glared at our brother.

The whole spectacle filled me with joy.

This was the Thane of my childhood. He and Lachlan had always been the serious brothers, but they also had a dry, often mischievous humor. Somewhere along the line, Thane had lost it. Until now. Until Regan.

"No?" Thane asked Robyn again, drawing out the moment.

Robyn laughed, shaking her head.

"*Okay.*" Thane pretended to be unconvinced and shot the guests a wide-eyed look that made them titter harder. My brother, the secret comedian. Then he grinned and turned back to the happy couple. "All joking aside, I couldn't be happier for you both. While Mac worried who on earth could ever be worthy of Robyn, I worried that no woman could match my big brother for spirit, for his sense of loyalty, family, and gregarious thirst for life. And then Robyn Galbraith Penhaligon walked into our lives, and I knew, despite their not so congenial start, that they were each other's match.

"You have been the best brother anyone could ask for." Thane gripped Lachlan's shoulder, and they shared an emotional smile. "And I am so goddamn delighted you found Robyn ..." His grin was wicked now. "For you and for me,

27

because Robyn brought …" He looked down at Regan. "Well, Robyn brought bounty into all our lives, and for that, I am eternally grateful."

Thane seemed to have to force himself to break his stare with Regan, clearing his throat, lifting his champagne. "You've faced the worst life can throw at you and come out stronger together, an inspiration to us all, and a lesson in what love should be. To Robyn and Lachlan!"

By the time Lachlan stood to make his speech, I wasn't sure my heart could take it.

"The actor is going to surprise you all by making this short and sweet," Lachlan said into the mic. "First, thank you to Mac and Thane for your kind words. Though, brother, we could have done without the insinuation I'm forcing my wife to be here."

Everyone laughed.

"My wife," Lachlan murmured, staring down at Robyn adoringly. "Fuck, that feels fantastic to say."

He received some *awws* for that.

"First, thank you all for being with us today. It means a great deal." He gestured with his glass to all the room. "Second, Robyn and I decided we wanted to speak traditional vows at the ceremony, but on reflection, I have to say just this one thing. I've been a blessed man," Lachlan continued, holding Robyn's gaze. "I've traveled the world, I've experienced extraordinary moments, done things only a small percentage of people ever get to do. I have good friends, a family I love more than life."

My heart squeezed.

"And I've known loss. Significant loss. While that might not count as a blessing, it provided the lessons only loss can teach you … that what matters in life are the people you surround yourself with. The people you love are what make it all worthwhile. When you walked into my life, Robyn, you knocked me off my feet. You are *everything*. You're the most courageous person I have ever met, and you astound me every damn day."

Tears welled in my eyes as I watched Robyn fight back her own.

"Your magnificence awes me," Lachlan admitted hoarsely, "and I promise you this, Braveheart—not a day of our lives will pass when I forget it. Know that even during the weeks that are difficult, the days that challenge us, know that I will love you through every minute, every hour until my very last second in this universe."

My tears flowed freely now.

"To Robyn, my wife. My best friend." He raised his glass.

"To Robyn!"

When Lachlan took his seat beside her, Robyn kissed him so long and so deep, only the catcalls from the crowd (i.e., Brodan and Arran) broke them apart.

Their happiness washed over me, suffocating any hint of bitterness, and I felt more like myself again.

2
ARRO

"**Y**ou seem a little happier," Arran observed as we danced to a slow Idlewild track.

"Happier?" I frowned, swaying to the slow rhythm. "Really? Because I was just thinking this song is depressing."

The folk band had finished their set of energetic, enthusiastic music that had gotten everyone on their feet. The deejay then took over and was playing a selection of Robyn and Lachlan's favorite songs.

"Stop avoiding the subject."

"What subject?"

"The subject of your mood. I know things are a wee bit tense between us all since I got home, but something else is going on with you." Arran bent his head to force me to look into his eyes, the same shade of blue as Lachlan's. All my brothers were blond and blue-eyed, but while Lachlan and Thane were a rugged, rough-around-the-edges kind of handsome, Brodan was classically good-looking. Arran was just a younger, smoother version of Lachlan.

While Lachlan and Thane couldn't understand Arran's need to be so far from us all the time, I tried to. Growing up,

Lachlan had been like a father to me, and Thane was a typical overprotective big brother. Brodan and Arran, however, had been my friends as well as my big brothers. Especially Arran. He'd been dreaming of adventures for as long as I could remember. He just didn't seem to have it in him to stand in one place for too long.

Truthfully, though, his prolonged absence had hurt. And it made little sense. Arran was a wanderer, but he'd made it clear, until a few years ago, that his family was still a priority.

"Where have you been?" I turned the tables on him.

His hand tightened in mine. "I'm sorry I stayed away too long."

"Arran," I said, leaning in, not wanting to be overheard, "someone tried to kill Lachlan. A man tied up your niece and nephew and used them to terrorize Regan. Do you understand all that?"

He blanched guiltily and whispered, "I'm sorry."

"Just tell me why," I pleaded. "Why didn't you come back when we needed you?"

Something hardened in his expression. "What's going on with you and Mac?"

I tensed. "Nothing's going on."

Arran smirked unhappily. "Then I guess there's no good reason I didn't come home until now. I'm just a bit of a prick."

"I don't believe that."

"Then your belief is wrong." He looked away, the muscle in his jaw popping with his agitation. His hand tightened in mine again as his eyes narrowed. I followed Arran's gaze, my brows raising to find it had landed on Eredine as she danced with Brodan.

Brodan held Ery awfully close as he murmured things to her that made her smile shyly.

I'd suspected Brodan had a thing for Ery for a while now,

but for whatever reason, he hadn't made a move. Ery was so closed off, I wasn't sure a move would be appreciated, anyway. Yet sometimes I caught her watching him in a way that suggested maybe he fascinated her too.

Frowning, I glanced up at Arran. He didn't know Eredine that well, hadn't been around long enough to get to know her. But it didn't surprise me he'd noticed her. One, she was a knockout, an attractive mix of soft-spoken kindness and dry wit. Not that she showed the latter until she was comfortable with you. Two, the entirety of their youthful romantic lives (i.e., from the time Arran was ten—he and Brodan matured quickly in the girl department), my brothers had vied for the same girls. Their tastes were worryingly similar. They'd put their competitiveness with girls aside; however, when Arran slept with Brodan's best friend, Monroe Sinclair, they'd had a big falling-out after that.

While Brodan insisted he was angry Arran had crossed the line by sleeping with a girl they'd agreed was off-limits, I always believed there was more to it, that perhaps Monroe had meant more to Brodan than he'd acknowledged. Anyway, Monroe left my brothers, Ardnoch, and her family behind after that, and Arran and Brodan finally mended their rift. They never went after the same woman again.

"She's beautiful, kind, witty, guarded, difficult to get to know. I'm her closest friend here, and even I don't really know her."

Arran frowned, his attention still on Ery. "What?"

"Eredine."

He looked at me now. "What about her?"

"She's off-limits," I warned, "to both of you."

Arran's lips quirked. "Dearest, darlin' sister, I have no intentions toward your friend. Can't a man enjoy looking at a woman without ulterior motives?"

"As long as that's all it is, fine."

"You know," he said, swaying me with exaggeration now, "of all the people I expected to be nice to me when I came back, you were the one."

"I am being nice to you. We're dancing, aren't we?"

"A pity dance," he teased, eyes twinkling boyishly. "I can tell."

"Oh, fuck off," I muttered. "I've had to put up with women falling all over my brothers my entire life, and tonight is no exception. I'm surprised someone hasn't clawed our hands apart to get to you."

"It's not our fault we're cursed with good looks and animal magnetism."

I gagged, pretending to vomit, and he laughed.

Something caught his eye behind me, and a look I didn't like entered it. "The Adair men aren't the only ones popular with the guests. Mac is certainly enjoying the attention."

I froze, refusing to look around.

"Oh, aye, I think his speech inspired a few blue beans tonight."

I smacked Arran only half playfully across the head.

"What was that for?" he whined like a little boy.

"Don't talk like that to me. I'm your sister. Show some respect."

"Pfft, I think that was more about Mac than me," he grumbled. "I think you knocked my eye loose."

"It was barely a tap. Stop being a baby."

"Good idea, Arro." Lachlan and Robyn had danced up to us, and he reached out and smacked Arran across the back of the head harder than I had. "That's for making me worry about you for two years."

"Fuck." Arran released me to rub his head. "Was that necessary?"

"Aye. And I feel loads better. Be prepared, I'm telling

Thane how cathartic it is to hit you." He grinned wickedly, dancing Robyn away.

"Is he kidding?" Arran looked around warily, seeming much, much younger than his thirty-five years.

Laughter bubbled on my lips. "I'd stay alert for the rest of the evening if I were you."

"Home sweet home," he muttered.

I'D JUST RETURNED to Eredine's side with a fresh glass of champagne when a man who looked vaguely familiar, and thus I was sure was an actor, approached. He gave us both a nod of hello and me a smile as he held out his hand. "May I have this dance?"

An Adele song played.

"Go." Eredine took my glass and nudged me toward the familiar stranger.

Why not? I thought.

I smiled at the American and put my hand in his. As we strolled across the room, he introduced himself. "I'm Gray. I worked with your brother on a movie about fifteen years ago, and we became friends."

Now that he'd said his name, I knew who he was. He wasn't an overly well-known actor, but I'd heard Lachlan speak of him. "Grayson Evans?"

"That's me." He grinned as he pulled me onto the dance floor, taking my hand in his and placing his other on my waist. "And you're Arrochar. It's weird I've known Lachlan this long, but never met you."

"I'm not in the film industry." Nor would I ever want to be.

"You should be. You have the looks for it."

My answer was a tight smile, my gaze moving over his shoulder.

"Not that ... I mean, obviously you could bring more to acting than that."

I snorted as he realized his error. "I highly doubt it. I'm more suited to forest engineering than acting."

"You're a forest engineer?" He gaped, shocked.

His surprise, unfortunately, was something I'd had to deal with my entire career. I worked in a male-dominated industry as the one in charge on-site, the one responsible for drawing up the maps of topographical features of a timber-harvesting area and planning and directing construction of roads and rail networks needed to transport the logs from the harvest area to a safe storage and loading area. I was the one who ensured the safe and efficient removal of the logs by planning and overseeing the construction of campsites, loading docks, bridges, equipment shelters, and water systems. The one who selected the methods and equipment we'd use for handling the logs, and the one who ordered around a bunch of guys to do it. Let's just say I'd faced my share of battles with misogyny.

"Yes," I answered shortly.

"Sorry." He winced. "I'm not coming across right. I didn't mean it like that. I've just never met a forest engineer before. I don't even know what it is, really."

I softened, a little guilty for being snippy about it, which wasn't like me at all, and explained my job to him.

"Wow. You have an *actual* job."

I laughed softly. "Don't you?"

"Other people don't think it's an actual job."

"It's an actual job," I assured him. "I know from Lachlan how hard you all work."

Gray grinned. "Thanks for saying so."

"I can't believe Galbraith is Robyn's father," a woman said beside me, drawing my focus from my dance partner.

I saw it was the English actor, Angeline Potter. I didn't recognize the man she was with, but they both stared at Mac where he danced with Jasmine. He hadn't been short of partners all night, but at least I knew Jaz was off-limits. The rest had sparked an indignant flare of jealousy I couldn't believe I could still feel.

"I know. No wonder people always tell them he doesn't look old enough," her American partner observed.

"I wonder how old he was when they had her. Thirteen? He can't be much older than forty, right?"

"That would make Robyn only twenty-something, and I'm sure she's thirty."

Twenty-nine, actually, I thought. Thirteen, indeed!

"You're looking at him like you want to fuck him."

"Hush." Angeline smacked his chest. "There are children at this wedding. And yes, believe me, darling, every unattached person at this club so inclined toward the male gender has wanted to climb Galbraith like a monkey since this place opened. I swear Lachlan only hired him because he looks the part. Ever the showman, our Lachlan. I mean, it took Robyn's arrival to figure out it was Lucy Wainwright causing hell here. Doesn't say much for Mac's intelligence that he needed his daughter to uncover the truth."

I danced Gray closer to the actor. "Angeline."

She looked at me, her tight smile widening ever so slightly. "Arrochar, isn't it?"

"Mmm." I glared at her. "While you're a guest at my brother's wedding, I'll ask you to refrain from insulting members of our family where anyone might hear. It's just good manners, you know."

Angeline blanched. "I apologize. I didn't realize—"

"Yes, I'm sure." I danced Gray in the opposite direction, cutting her off.

Gray snorted, his shoulder moving beneath my hand with his amusement, but my anger toward Angeline turned inward.

Why the hell had I defended Mac?

That wasn't my job anymore.

If it ever had been.

NOT LONG LATER, I forced myself to be me again, and that meant forcing Eredine onto the dance floor with me, Lewis, Eilidh, and Jaz and Autry's beautiful daughters, Jada and Asia. While Eredine held Jada's and Asia's hands, creating a circle where they all shimmied to Pharrell Williams' "Happy," I did the same with Eilidh and Lewis. It had taken some convincing to get Lew up because he was such a serious wee guy, so hearing his giggles as his kilt flew around him was the best sound in the world.

I laughed with my niece and nephew, finally feeling nothing but goodness since the day had begun.

"Can I join?" Regan bounced up to us, and I let go of Eilidh's hand so Regan could enter our circle and then took her hand. I watched the way Eils and Lew turned their attention to Regan, their faces lighting up, adoration beaming out of them, and I unconsciously squeezed Regan's hand. She'd brought so much love into their lives.

"You okay?" she mouthed.

"Just grateful for you!" I yelled over the music.

Regan grinned. "We're family for real now!"

"We were before this," I assured her.

She wrapped her arm around my shoulders and hugged me to her side.

Our circle soon merged with Eredine's, and then Robyn was there in her beautiful dress, twirling Jada and Asia. Her interactions with the girls, the way they giggled "Auntie Robbie!" whenever she made a funny face or tickled them, reminded me she'd had a life in Boston. A life she'd partly sacrificed for my brother. That alone was enough to convince me she loved him.

Soon, we drew the attention of the men. First Lachlan, whom Eilidh pounced on. Her uncle hoisted her into his arms. She recently turned six, and I realized it wouldn't be long before the days of being lifted easily into her uncle's or father's embrace would be over. It made me melancholy. I didn't want the kids to grow up too fast.

Then Thane was there, making Lewis giggle harder as he shimmied ridiculously to the music. Brodan sidled up to Eredine to do the robot, and the kids immediately copied him.

Arran appeared and wrapped his arm around Lachlan's shoulders, saying something to Eilidh I couldn't hear over the music. She giggled, and Lachlan grinned at Arran. I missed this. I missed us all being together all the time.

All of us here, happy and safe, after a year of drama worthy of the big screen. We'd had stalking, murder, and kidnapping.

We deserved this moment.

But when Mac joined our circle next to me, holding on to my happiness was so incredibly difficult. His arm brushed mine, once, twice, three times … I tried to edge away, but he seemed closer than ever. To me, it seemed like he was using this moment to do just that. The music blurred into the background, my family's joyful shouts of encouragement and amusement a buzz. All I could sense was him, all I could smell was his aftershave, and the memory of that night less than a month ago wrapped its hand around my throat.

I couldn't breathe.

Breaking away from the circle, I slipped a little in my strappy sandals and had to right my balance. Pushing through the crowded dance floor, I burst into the corridor, trying to think, trying to orient myself.

Calm down, Arro.

Feeling trapped in my stupid heels, I leaned against the wall and practically ripped them off my feet, sighing in relief as my arches sank into the carpeted runner. I then hurried through the castle toward the library.

Unfortunately, a couple of guests occupied the library, so I moved on to Lachlan's office. The door was closed but thankfully not locked. He didn't use this as his actual office. We called it his "stage" office because it looked the part with its fireplace, twin, floor-to-ceiling windows, impressive library desk, and shelves filled with books. His real office resembled Mac's.

Just thinking his name made me flinch, and I stumbled around the chesterfield sofa near the fireplace and slumped into it.

With no fire in the hearth, the room was cold, the hardwood freezing against my bare feet, but the chill cooled my heated skin.

The door clicked open, and I swiveled toward the sound. The room swayed a little as Mac slipped in and closed it behind him.

Nausea shot through me, and I never in my life thought I'd feel that way being alone with him. I pushed up to my feet. "What are you doing here?"

His eyes glittered with a million emotions. "Arro—"

"Get out." I skirted the edges of the room. "Get out, Mac."

He scowled. "Will you please just talk to me?"

"There's nothing to say."

"There are so many things that need to be said."

I didn't want to hear it.

And I didn't want to be alone with him. To be accused, to be humiliated, and rejected again.

"I want out of the room," I demanded, hating that my voice shook. "I want out of this room, so get out of my way."

"For Christ's sake, Arro, talk to—"

"I hate you!" I yelled, my hands shaking, knees trembling.

Mac paled, looking haggard. "Darlin'—"

"I am not your darlin'," I gritted out. "I hate you. I hate how you made me feel that night. I hate I wasted years loving you. But for the sake of our family, I will pretend that the very sight of you doesn't make me want to die inside. Now move out of my way before I scream bloody murder and ruin my brother's wedding."

Squeezing his eyes closed, Mac took a few steps away from the door, and I hurried past him, afraid he'd reach out, afraid that he wouldn't. How fucked up was that?

I yanked open the door and rushed into the corridor, pulling it closed behind me with a slam.

With a shuddering breath, I'd just stepped forward to walk away when I heard Mac bellow, "Fuck!" followed by the sound of something smashing.

I flinched, my heart hammering in my chest.

But I didn't go back to see if he was all right.

I told myself I didn't care.

And I walked away, this time of my own accord.

3

MAC

Shards of light were like sharp needles poking through my eyelids.

My head pounded.

Groaning, I was helpless against the brightness. It pried my heavy, aching lids open, and I muttered a string of curses as I blinked against the sunlight streaming in through the windows in Lachlan's stage office.

What the hell?

The room swayed, nausea roiling within as I sat up from where I'd been sleeping on the couch. The stiff muscles in my neck ached. "How the ... oh, fuck." I swallowed hard and took a deep breath. Elbows to knees, I cradled my head in my hands and tried to remember the night before.

It came back to me in a rush of images. "Fuck, fuck, fuck."

No wonder I felt like hell.

I'd gotten absolutely shit-face blootered at the reception. I couldn't remember the last time I'd drank that much whisky.

Yet it was the only way I knew how to get through my daughter's wedding reception after that scene in this room. I stood up too fast, wondering why I'd returned to the office

41

after that moment with Arro. My gaze narrowed on the shattered paperweight I'd launched at Lachlan's bookshelves. Bloody Nora, I hoped it hadn't been expensive, because it was coming out of my paycheck.

I had to get out of this room. I couldn't think about her.

Her expression—the pain, the fury, the humiliation—flashed across my vision, and I almost threw up right there. Resting a hand on the couch, I drew in a shuddering breath and gathered myself.

I needed aspirin, water, and when I was ready, food.

Focusing on that goal, I made sure my kilt covered everything vital and strode out of the office, forcing myself not to lean into the dizziness.

The castle was awake with activity, staff moving back and forth, guests preparing to leave. A few staff members nodded in greeting, and I nodded back, wondering if I looked as green as I bloody felt.

Then, as if being punished, the first person I saw descending the stairs in the great hall was Grayson Evans.

Not once in the fifteen years I'd known Evans did I have a problem with him. He was Lachlan's mate. He seemed like an all right bloke. But as that fucker's gaze locked with mine and he grinned as he approached, I had to curl my hands into fists to keep from decking him.

"Hey, Mac, how are you this morning? Gotta admit, I'm fighting a hangover."

I took in the small carry-on he rolled beside him, then drifted up the staircase.

No Arro.

Yet I'd watched her leave the reception with this bastard last night. Did her absence mean she'd left already? Grayson looked far too relaxed for my liking. Had this bastard slept with Arro? Jealousy was a tight knot, twisting and twisting in my gut until I couldn't stand it. It was not an unfamiliar feeling. Arro had dated a few men since that New Year's Eve we first kissed, and I'd hated every single one of the arseholes.

"Hey, man, you okay?" Gray frowned when I didn't answer.

I nodded. "Fine."

Gray narrowed his eyes. "Okay. Hungover, I get it. Well, I'll see you around. Stay cool, Mac."

Stay fucking cool? Was he kidding? I tried not to sneer as I nodded again, watching him leave, hoping that he didn't carry Arro's number on his phone.

Sighing, I stepped aside as other guests came downstairs, some walking toward the dining room where breakfast would be served, others heading out the front door to depart. There was no way I could drive myself home, no matter the short distance. I'd have to ask one of my team to drive me.

What an arse. I'd made a right nuisance of myself.

"Mac."

I glanced over as Robyn and Lachlan descended the staircase and strode toward me. My nausea was overtaken with pride and gratitude as I looked at my daughter and friend. Neither of them looked hungover but were fresh-faced and so happy, it was infectious. I couldn't help but smile.

"Dad." Robyn stood on tiptoes to kiss my cheek. "You look a little worse for wear."

"Too much whisky." I blanched, scratching my unshaven cheeks. *Almost a beard now*, I thought absentmindedly. "I didn't do anything embarrassing … right?"

Lachlan snorted. "You flirted so much with Jasmine, I thought Autry would kill you, but other than that, no."

"Fuck," I huffed in disbelief. What a prick. "I'll apologize."

"Don't worry about it," Robyn assured me. "Autry knows you were drunk, and from what I gather, Jasmine enjoyed the fruits of his jealousy."

I grimaced. "Right. Well …" I glanced over their casual

outfits, and realization hit me. Their Hawaiian honeymoon. "Shit, are you leaving now?"

"Aye," Lachlan said just as Wakefield, the estate butler, appeared like magic.

"Sir, your luggage is loaded and your driver is ready."

"Thank you, Wakefield."

"Wakefield—" I caught him before he could leave. "Could you ask one of the men to bring a car around for me? I'm afraid I'm unable to drive myself home."

His expression forever neutral, he nodded. "Of course, sir."

"You should stay and eat something first." Robyn's brows pinched with worry.

I reached for her hand and gave it a gentle squeeze. "It's just a hangover. And I'd prefer to be alone to deal with it."

I'd tried to inject humor into my tone, but my daughter studied my face as if burrowing for secrets. She saw too much.

"Come on." I released her. "You don't want to miss your flight."

The three of us strode across the hall and out onto the gravel driveway where several cars lined up to leave. Lachlan led us to a black Range Rover. It was part of the estate fleet but for his personal use. An estate chauffeur, Richie, was behind the wheel waiting for them.

Robyn suddenly reached for me, and I enveloped her, surprised by how hard she hugged me. I held her closer to reassure her, but still she whispered, "When I get back, we're going to talk about what's going on with you." She kissed my cheek and murmured, "Love you so much."

I swallowed past a lump of emotion. "Love you more than life, wee birdie." The words came out scratchy and hoarse. "Have a wonderful time."

She patted my chest and climbed into the back of the SUV.

I clapped Lachlan on the shoulder. "Take care of her. And by that, I also mean no work. She's the only thing you need to think about while you're away. We've got everything covered here."

My best friend and boss smirked. "You know me too well. But I promise, I will focus on only Robyn."

"You deserve this," I said quietly.

And he did. The Lucy Wainwright trial had been in mid-February and lasted two weeks. After teaming up with Fergus (the estate mechanic and childhood best friend of Brodan and first boyfriend of Arrochar's), former actor Lucy had wrought devastation on the club. She and Lachlan had ended their casual relationship a while ago, but he nor anyone had realized she was in love with him. After she found herself ostracized from Hollywood by the powerful wife of a lover, Lucy grew obsessed with getting Lachlan back. As if somehow he could fix her life. She believed creating a problem for him and then proving she was his greatest support through it all would push him back into her arms.

It started small, with adoring messages scrawled against walls. Then it turned darker, the messages more threatening, a deer's carcass left along with an ominous note. Vandalism. Then I got fucking stabbed, unaware at the time that the perpetrator was Fergus. Only Arro and I knew the reason I was stabbed was because Fergus knew Arro had feelings for me. Thinking he was her friend, she'd confessed it to him. Secretly still in love with Arro, Fergus had tried to wipe out who he viewed as his competition.

Fergus also attacked Robyn in her trailer, but thankfully couldn't best her. Realizing Lachlan was growing increasingly involved with Robyn, Lucy then staged her own attack and had Fergus lock her in the freezer in the club kitchen to garner Lachlan's sympathy and attention. One of my men, a good man, a good friend, Greg McHugh, was killed when he cornered Fergus during the incident. Fergus gutted him. If the bastard weren't already dead, I'd have ended him myself just for that.

Lucy beat me to it. They kidnapped Lachlan and took him to an abandoned shed located on land owned by a local farmer, Collum McCulloch. They lured Robyn there, pretending Lucy was Fergus's victim too. Lucy "freed" herself and shot Fergus point-blank in the head. She was going to do the same to Robyn and Lachlan, all because they'd fallen in love, but Robyn was one of the toughest women I knew, and she overpowered the deranged bitch.

Lucy was charged, and it took awhile, but they finally extradited her to the US. Of course, as she was Hollywood's sweetheart and Lachlan was also famous, it meant the trial was global news. We all flew to the US, since we were witnesses in the case, and I upped security around us, hiring men from an American company I often used to secure my family. The paparazzi were all over us, but we got through it.

Lucy's defense team entered a plea of insanity, but she'd been independently diagnosed by a handful of psychologists who all agreed Lucy was not insane but suffered from narcissistic and antisocial personality disorders. For the murder of Fergus, being an accessory to the murder of Greg, and for the attempted murder of Lachlan and Robyn, she was sentenced to thirty-five years without the possibility of parole. While incarcerated, she was to receive rehabilitation, but I knew enough about the prison system to know resources like that weren't always available. Only time would tell.

"Aye." Lachlan nodded. "We all do. We can all move on now. Dad."

I glowered. "Don't even—"

46

Lachlan burst into laughter. "It's bloody weird, right? I am now your son-in-law."

"Maybe so, but call me Dad again, and I'll deck you."

He laughed harder and drew me into a hug where we pounded our fists against each other's backs to make the display of affection seem more manly. "As long as you never call me 'son.'"

Grinning, I shoved him toward the car. "A promise I can keep, I assure you."

I watched Robyn and Lachlan drive away, heading toward paradise and peace, and a deep bloody melancholy fell over me like a shroud.

It was supposed to be a happy time for us as a family. The victory of justice. Moving on. Robyn and Lachlan getting married. All of us closer than ever.

But I'd gone and fucked it up royally only a few weeks after Lucy's trial ended.

Arro hated me.

Truly.

Abruptly, my stomach turned, and I hurried around the corner of the castle, out of sight.

It was just in time as the vomit rose up and out. After a few seconds of upchucking, I leaned on the wall, wiped my mouth with a shaking hand, and forced back the sting of tears. "Fucking get yourself together, man," I whispered bitterly and pushed away from the wall to find something to clean up my mess.

4

ARRO

"**T**hanks for the invite," I said as I slid onto a stool at Thane and Regan's kitchen island. The kids' laughter floated into the house from the garden where they played football with Eredine. There was a good distance between the house and the edge of the cliff, but Thane had fenced it off to protect Lewis and Eilidh. Thank God, or I'd be a constant nervous wreck when they were out there.

They were safe with Ery, though, who watched them like a hawk. Ever since Regan's crazy stalker, Austin Vale, had knocked Ery unconscious while she was babysitting, she'd been extra protective of them. I'd tried to tell her so many times that Austin tying up the kids and hiding them in Thane's annex was not her fault. Unfortunately, I had a horrible suspicion she didn't believe me.

If being around the kids helped her feel better about it all, that was something Thane, and now Regan, would give her.

"No problem. I drank so much at the wedding, I'm still a little fragile, so I thought I'd make us all a big Scottish breakfast for lunch," Regan said as she moved around the kitchen.

The morning after the wedding, I'd suffered a pretty

terrible hangover myself, but I was feeling fine today. Still, I wouldn't pass up a free lunch, and Regan was handy in the kitchen. She'd learned how to cook local cuisines quickly too. "Are you sure I can't help?" I wasn't too shabby in the kitchen either.

"Nah, it's fine."

"Where's Thane?"

"I told him I'm using most of our essentials to make all this, so he drove into the village for groceries."

"I could've done that, saved him the trip."

She shrugged. "It's cool. We needed the space this morning, anyway."

I didn't like the sound of that. "Uh-oh."

Regan glanced over her shoulder at me from her spot by the hob and rolled her eyes. "It's my fault. I got jealous. I'm cranky from this hangover from hell and took it out on him. I apologized, but I think he's still pissed, and I don't blame him."

I wondered what she'd done. "Jealous? That doesn't sound like you. Thane told me about the picture gallery." I nodded to the wall opposite the kitchen where photographs of our family were artfully displayed in black and white. Thane had told me that just a few weeks ago, he'd replaced the photo of him and Fran on their wedding day with a more recent photo of the kids and Regan at Dunrobin Castle.

The next time he passed the hall, however, he'd noted the wedding photo was back in its place. When he asked Regan about it, she said that Fran was the children's mother, a part of them, a part of their history, and keeping their wedding photo on the wall honored her and didn't diminish Thane and Regan's relationship. I thought it was just about the loveliest thing I'd ever heard. He told me he'd fallen in love with her all over again at that moment.

So jealousy seemed uncharacteristic of Robyn's kind-hearted sister.

Regan huffed. "Do you remember when Thane went out on a date with some woman who worked in his building?"

"Vaguely."

"Keelie." Regan curled her upper lip. "We fought about it at the time because he deliberately went out with her to push me away."

I hadn't known the entire story while their romance was unfolding, but Regan had shared plenty of details since. Now that she mentioned it, I did remember. My big brother was having a difficult time accepting his attraction to Regan, and when Keelie asked him out, he'd said yes. It hurt Regan a lot. "I remember now."

"Thane got a text this morning while he was in the shower, and I swear"—she waved her spatula—"I just happened to be passing his phone when it went off, so I saw the text box come up on the screen. I do not look at his texts, and he knows it."

"It was a text from Keelie?" I guessed.

Regan nodded, frowning. "I'm not a jealous person, but ... I'm so afraid this will go away." She gestured around her, clearly indicating her life with Thane and the kids. "And it's just *her*. Other women come on to him all the time, and it doesn't bother me. Did you see them at the wedding?" She made a comical face. "But I think it's just ... Keelie represents this moment in our burgeoning relationship where I thought I wouldn't get to be with the person I wanted most in this world. And when I'm hungover, I'm as emotional as when I have my period, you know? I think because I'm not a jealous person, it took Thane aback this morning."

I grimaced. "You flipped your lid?"

"I didn't flip my lid, as you all say." She smirked unhappily. "But I certainly had a tone when I asked him, 'What the hell is Keelie Tanner doing texting you on a Sunday morning?'"

"Yeesh."

"Yeah," she huffed, turning back to the hob. "He asked, 'What the hell are you insinuating?' and the fact that he wouldn't just give me a straight answer made me even more jealous and irritated, and before you know it, we were arguing. And he was *mad*." Regan moved poached eggs onto the plates she had set out. "After what Fran did to him, even hinting that Thane might do something shady behind my back is a trigger for him."

I sighed with sympathy. "Sounds like you two had quite the morning."

"It wasn't great." Regan's expression was strained. "But I apologized and didn't even ask him to explain the text as proof of my trust."

"But it's bugging the shit out of you, isn't it?" I tried to hide my grin.

She cut me a dark look. "Seriously, what the fuck is she doing texting him?"

I threw my head back in laughter.

"Hey, you can laugh"—she pointed her spatula at me—"but wait until you love a guy this much and see how crazy it makes you."

My amusement abruptly dried up.

Regan frowned. "I'm sorry, Arro. I didn't mean to upset you."

"I'm not upset," I lied. "I just don't think that kind of love is in the cards for me."

There was a moment of silence and then, "Or maybe you already *do* love someone like that, and something is standing in your way?"

I couldn't look at her. Instead, I looked outside. Thane's living space was open plan with floor-to-ceiling bifold doors opening onto a deck that led down to the garden. I caught flashes of the kids and Ery as they chased a football. "They seem in good spirits. I take it they don't know you and Thane are fighting?"

"We're not fighting now—I think—and no. We kept our angry voices down. I noticed you left the reception with a cute guy on Friday."

At her change of subject, I asked, "So?"

"Well ..." She grinned, revealing her adorable dimples. "Who is he? What happened?"

"Gray." I shrugged, not really wanting to discuss the fact that I'd led a guy on, let him take me to his room, and then freaked out as soon as he tried to undress me. Gray had been kind about it, even though he was pretty drunk, and we'd fallen asleep on his bed without doing anything. I'd snuck out before everyone else woke up, and Wakefield, whom I was quite certain never slept, had a driver take me home. "Nothing happened."

"Oh. Did you want something to happen?"

"Nope."

Regan exhaled in exasperation. "Arro, what is going on with you? It's like pulling teeth to get anything out of you these days. You've been off for weeks."

Scowling, I gestured to the half-ready plates. "Did I come here for lunch or to be interrogated?"

"See? That"—she pointed at me indignantly—"that tone, that whole attitude, this bitchiness, is just not you."

Stunned by her honesty, I slumped.

Because she was right.

This evasive snarkiness was not me.

"I'm sorry."

"Don't be sorry—just tell me what's going on."

I wanted to. I wanted to tell someone so much, and maybe that was the problem. Maybe this anger and pain and

52

resentment simmering inside all the time would never go away if I kept it to myself forever.

But even after everything ... I couldn't turn this family against Mac.

"I'm just being selfish." I couldn't meet Regan's gaze. "Watching Lachlan and Thane meet the loves of their lives makes me wish I could too. It seems impossible living in a tiny place like this." Lately, as much as it physically hurt to think about separating from my family, I wondered if it might not be worth considering a job in the Lowlands, closer to Glasgow and Edinburgh. I'd have a better chance of meeting someone there.

"Why don't you try online dating? Even if you had to travel a little farther to meet someone, it would be worth it, right?"

"I've tried online dating," I murmured.

"Try again. I mean, when was the last time you were in a relationship? When was the last time you had sex?"

I groaned, remembering. "Almost a year ago."

"That's not too bad."

"Says the woman getting it on the regular." I winced, thinking about who was giving it to her on the regular. At her sly look, I warned, "Don't say a word."

Regan snorted. "Would I do that to you?"

"Yes, you would."

She chuckled and bent to pull the bacon, sausages, black pudding, and haggis out from under the grill. Rotating them as she spoke, Regan continued, "How did you meet the last man you dated?"

The thought of Guy made my stomach churn. "He worked for Lachlan."

Realization dawned on her face. "The chef guy?"

"His name was *Guy*." I noted the flash of anger in her eyes and sighed. "Thane told you."

"Is that okay?"

"I guess he tells you everything now, right?"

"I would never tell anyone else," she promised.

"Good. Because some *people* don't know, and I don't want them to."

"Mac."

I didn't reply in the affirmative, but I was indeed referring to Mac. Guy had been Lachlan's chef at the estate. The night he attacked me, I felt ashamed for so many reasons. Mostly for being blind to who he really was. Mac didn't know about it. He didn't know *he* was the reason Guy assaulted me in a jealous rage. He didn't know he was the reason I even said yes to a date with Guy in the first place, even though my feelings for him were lukewarm at best ...

FIFTEEN MONTHS ago

AS I PULLED up to the sports center in Inverness, my phone beeped in my purse on the passenger seat. Switching off the engine, I rummaged through my bag and saw it was a text from Guy.

I frowned.

Maybe I shouldn't have given him my number that night we met at the Gloaming, Gordon's pub and hotel in the village. Our local.

Just one date.

That was all the text said. Guy had been pestering me to go on a date with him for weeks. He'd been the chef at Ardnoch for six months, and he'd flirted with me since his arrival. He was good-looking and had this sexy Australian accent. But he wasn't who I wanted to be with.

Yet the man was nothing if not persistent.

I sighed, not sure how to respond. I decided to think about it later.

Instead, I looked up at the entrance of the sports center and smiled to myself.

Mac taught a jujitsu class in Inverness every Thursday evening. When he lived in the States, he'd won the US Jujitsu Championships three years in a row. I was considering learning just so I could be close to him. Not that we weren't close. A secret smile prodded my lips. One reason I didn't want to say yes to a date with Guy was because Mac and I were growing closer.

Despite my vow to him all those years ago that we would be nothing but friends, something had changed in the past year. We found excuses to spend time together more often. We talked about things that worried us. He confided more about his daughter, Robyn, who was a police officer in Boston. They hadn't been in contact for years, but I continued to prod him to do something about it. Gently, though. Mac was not an easily offended man, but Robyn was a button I knew not to push.

Out of the blue, two days ago, Mac dropped by my work site with a packed lunch for us. He'd taken time out of his busy schedule as head of security on the estate to sit in his SUV with me, laughing and eating sandwiches he'd bought from Morag's deli counter in the village.

His gaze kept dropping to my mouth, something he couldn't seem to stop doing lately. There was always an underlying tension between us. Had been ever since that New Year's Eve all those years ago. But lately, it had intensified.

It gave me hope.

After all, I was thirty now, thirty-one next month. Maybe Mac realized our thirteen-year age gap didn't feel so big now that I was older. Maybe he realized he was the reason none of my relationships lasted. That those guys would never be right for me because they weren't him.

I was wearing Mac down. I grinned giddily, thinking about a future of waking up in his bed, of being free to love and touch him, to reach for him whenever I needed him. I could almost taste that future on my tongue.

So I decided to ramp things up a little, to make sure we spent as much time as possible together. Feeling emboldened by his surprise lunch at my work, as my own surprise, I'd driven to Inverness to meet him after his class. I'd talk him into grabbing dinner in the city, and I'd flirt my arse off until he couldn't resist me. The payoff might not be tonight, but I had patience. I could keep this up until Mac admitted he loved me too.

Just as my fingers touched the handle on the car's door, the entrance to the sports center burst open and Mac strolled out, laughing over his shoulder, the sight of his gloriously tall, broadshouldered body exciting me as much as the sound of his joy. I was obsessed. Seriously obsessed.

Snorting to myself, I had just opened the car door when the person responsible for Mac's laughter walked out behind him and reached for his hand.

A woman.

A brunette who looked younger than me in her yoga pants and racer-back tank top. She was everything I wasn't. Petite, curvy, tits for days.

My heart plummeted as Mac pulled her into his side, and she wrapped an arm around his waist as they strolled across the car park.

I sank down in my seat, cursing the bloody Defender I drove and loved for being so conspicuous. My pulse throbbed, sweat dampening my palms.

Mac was too engrossed in his younger woman to notice me. They stopped at an unfamiliar car, and the brunette pulled his head down to hers to kiss him. He pressed her up against the passenger door and kissed her hungrily.

Like he'd kissed me all those years ago.

Tears I despised filled my eyes as I watched the couple get into her car and drive away.

I noted Mac's SUV left behind in the lot.

I let myself cry in the car park.

He didn't love me.

He'd been telling the truth all those years ago.

My age wasn't the reason Mac didn't want me. Clearly not if he was fucking his younger students. I glowered at his SUV. What did he want with me, then?

To be his friend? His confidant?

She was his sexual release. Just as I was now sure many women before her had been.

I was his emotional release.

This way, we saw to all his needs without him ever having to commit to one woman.

"Well, fuck that," I spat angrily, swiping at my tears.

Fuck that!

I fumbled for my phone and swiped the screen to bring up Guy's text.

Okay, I texted back, I'll go on a date with you.

"ARRO?"

Regan's voice brought me out of the past.

I blinked to find her staring at me in concern.

"I'm sorry for bringing it up."

I shook my head and gave her a reassuring smile. "It's fine, really. And *I'm* fine."

Regan didn't look convinced. "You know you can tell me anything. I won't tell anyone. Not even Thane."

"I wouldn't do that to you—make you keep secrets from him. And anyway, there's nothing to tell."

She seemed frustrated. "Arro ... I am the greatest bull-shitter in the world. I even bullshitted myself when it came

57

to Austin. I convinced myself that what he'd done wasn't as bad as it really was because it was easier than facing reality."

"Regan," I whispered her name in sorrow, hating what that son of a bitch had put her through.

"So I know a fellow bullshitter when I see one. I know when someone is in pain and bottling it up. If you won't talk to me … please, please talk to someone."

Eyes wide, my emotions bubbled to the surface, and I could only nod.

She started to say something else, but the front door opened and shut and Regan's lips pressed together. Thane sauntered into the kitchen carrying two shopping bags.

"Arro." He smiled.

"Hi."

"Just in time." Regan grinned at him. "Lunch is almost ready."

"Smells great." He leaned in to press a quick kiss to her lips, and I watched her relax and reach for another. Thane smiled happily at her eagerness, kissed her, and moved around her to put the groceries away. "Oh, by the way, the reason Keelie texted is that her sister has bought a plot of land and is looking for an architect. She wondered if she could send her my way."

Regan grinned at me where Thane couldn't see, and I loved my brother for giving her that, despite his earlier irritation. "Ah, okay. That makes sense."

Thane shot a smirk at her back. "Aye, imagine that."

Regan made a face at me, and I struggled not to laugh.

"Are you going to take the job?" I asked him.

"Too busy." He shook his head. "I'll refer her to a colleague."

I wondered if that was true, or if Thane just wanted to distance himself from Keelie for Regan's sake. He would never cheat, but Keelie was a reminder of a time when he'd hurt Regan. I knew my brother well enough to know that no matter what, he'd protect Regan from anything, big or small, that hurt her.

She looked over her shoulder at him, and their eyes met. Something passed between them. Something intimate.

They were good.

Minor argument forgiven and forgotten.

But I couldn't forget Regan's words of wisdom before Thane had walked in.

Because I knew she was right.

I'd kept so many feelings locked up for so long to protect Mac, and while I knew myself well enough to know I wouldn't betray him, I had to find an outlet. I had to let go of the hurt, or I'd be swallowed by a pit of depression. It was so much easier to avoid it altogether rather than try to pull myself out of that darkness once I was in it.

5

MAC

T he last place I wanted to be was Lachlan's stage office, but we'd agreed as head of security, I'd work with Wakefield, the estate butler, and Agnes, the head housekeeper, to run Ardnoch while Lachlan was on his honeymoon. Playing Lachlan's part meant being available to club members. They knew if they had any issues to come to Lachlan in his stage office.

Spring rain battered the grounds outside the tall windows. Without a lit fire, the room was chilly, but I was too focused on the pile of work Lachlan had left me. My brows creased as a headache throbbed behind my right eye. Christ, I'd known there was a lot involved in his job, but the minutiae of it was unbelievable.

I read the email from the head groundskeeper, coordinating with the land estate manager about the plans for summer and the quantities of materials he planned on ordering for daily maintenance and special events we staged through now until autumn and decided this one would have to wait. I did not know if Lachlan would approve of the groundskeeper's plans. The only time I consulted on estate groundskeeping was when I was concerned any additions might interfere with security cameras, anti-intruder alarms, and our anti-drone perimeter.

The desk phone ringing brought my head up. The light over the security tab on the phone set blinked. "Galbraith," I answered gruffly.

"Mac, it's Pete." One of my security guards. "There's a man at the gates claiming to be a friend of yours. Billy Carson."

Shock moved through me. What the hell was Billy doing all the way up here?

"ID?"

"Aye. Jock sent us a photo if you want to log on to the system."

"Doing it," I confirmed as I pulled up our security system on Lachlan's computer. Moving through the portal, I opened the photo Jock had logged.

It was a photo of a driving license. And sure enough, it was my old pal Billy Carson.

"Let him in." I hung up, standing from the desk, my mind racing. I couldn't imagine what had brought Billy to my doorstep. Though we had kept tabs on each other over the decades, we hadn't spoken in a few years.

Members lounged in the great hall as I strolled in. I nodded at them, striding past, not inviting conversation as Stephen, the underbutler, pulled open the main door for me. I murmured my thanks and stepped outside. Remaining beneath the sheltered portico, I watched as one of the estate's new hybrid Range Rovers led a silver Volvo up the long driveway to the castle. Jock passed slowly, and I nodded at him in thanks. He'd take the SUV back to the castle mews, assured now I had everything in hand.

The Volvo stopped, and Billy got out, his gaze locked on mine, expression grim.

Fuck.

Billy sat in my office in the staff quarters, bemused by the small space crowded with packed bookshelves. When we were boys, neither of us would've been caught dead reading. What a crushing blow that would have been to our thuggish reputations.

My old pal looked older. Much older. Lines bracketed his eyes, his mouth, and deep grooves scored his forehead. While my dark hair was peppered with gray here and there, he'd gone gray all over.

"Fuck, Mac, dae ye no age, man? Ye make the rest o' us feel fuckin' auld, so ye dae," Billy grumbled, as if reading my thoughts. It was nice hearing the thick Glaswegian brogue I'd left behind when I was fifteen. Thirty years ago.

Jesus Christ, had it really been that long?

It didn't feel it.

I didn't feel forty-five, though my friend's appearance reminded me of it. Billy was older by two years.

Smirking, I replied, "I eat well and I work out."

"Aye, so dae I. But I dinnae look like I've dipped ma fuckin' face in the fountain o' youth."

Laughing, I asked, "Did you just come here to shower me with compliments, Bill, or are you here for another reason?"

Before he could answer, Stephen entered the office with a tray of refreshments. Coffee and some homemade Madeira cake. Once the underbutler was gone, Billy raised an eyebrow. "This is quite the life."

I shrugged, pushing a cup of coffee across my desk toward him.

He took it and settled back in the chair opposite me. "I wish I wis here on pleasanter business, Mac."

Alerted, I nodded for him to continue.

Billy exhaled heavily. "The wife and I head tae Australia in a few days. We're gonnae stay wi' ma brother until we can set oorsels up there permanently."

"Okay?"

"We're ... ye see, we're worried aboot staying here, Mac."

"What's going on? What are you afraid of?"

My old pal scowled but didn't deny his fear. "We're the only wans left who were there the day Craig Kilmany wis murdered."

Two words. A name. One I'd never forgotten. And truly the reason Billy and I, while keeping in touch, had never been close. Each was the reminder of a day that changed us forever. "What do you mean?"

"In the last twa years, every wan o' us who were there that day, except you and me, are deid."

"Dead?" I frowned, my heart picking up pace a little. Seven of us were there that night. "In what manner?"

"Strange fuckin' ways, Mac," Billy said, exasperated. "Nairn got sent doon fur Craig's murder, as ye ken. Left us six. You and me are here. Kenny overdosed on heroin last year, despite his entire fuckin' family sayin' he never touched the stuff in his life. Even when we were bairns, Mac, Kenny didnae touch the stuff. We did what we did, but he didnae use."

It was true enough. We all thought we were wee hard men. Aged between fifteen and eighteen, me being the youngest but ironically, the biggest, we'd swaggered about the streets of Govan in Glasgow like we owned it. Unfortunately, there were other groups of youths who believed we were wrong.

One gang worked for the big man of Govan at the time, Frank Ricci, or Big Frank, as he was known then: drug dealer, racketeer, and car chop shop owner. He paid kids to infest the local schools with his product. His wee gang-bangers thought we were trying to encroach on their territory, to take over their jobs for Big Frank, because one of my mates was stupid enough to take a meeting with him. From that moment on, we were at war with the fuckers.

Then one night, we spotted one of them on their own. Craig.

I thought Nairn, the eldest of our group and our leader of sorts, just wanted to scare him. But before we knew it, Craig was on the ground, and they were all beating the utter shit out of him. Billy and I tried to stop it. We even fought them, our own mates, but we were too late.

While we were preoccupied with the others, Nairn took out his pocketknife and gutted Craig.

We all fled.

Billy and I found a pay phone and made an anonymous emergency call.

But the shame of that night will never leave me.

A brave witness informed on us to the police, but it was also that witness who exonerated me and Billy by vouching that we attempted to stop the attack. Billy and I had little choice but to admit it was Nairn who'd done it because of the witness testimony. The police found Craig's blood on Nairn's clothes. It was enough to send him away for fifteen years. He died in prison six years later during a fight with another prisoner.

While Billy and I never faced formal charges, the whole ugly, horrific incident had scared my gran enough that she sent me to the States, to Boston, to live with my uncle. And I went willingly, desperate to get away from a life I knew deep down I did not want. Billy got into some trouble in his youth, but a short stint in prison set him straight, and he trained to become an electrician. He and his wife moved out of Govan to the other side of Glasgow. They'd never had kids, but he'd seemed happy with his lot in life.

"Ye cannae say it's no fuckin' weird Kenny died that way, Mac."

"Aye, it's strange," I agreed.

"Twa months later, Wee Frickle wis stabbed ootside his local. Nae witnesses. They still havenae caught the bastard. New Year's Eve, Jamie fell aff the roof o' his tenement. There wis three times the legal limit o' alcohol in his blood. Recorded as an accidental death. Then three weeks ago, I get a call from Bryan McNab's mam. Deid. Hit by a car ootside his flat. It wisnae accidental because witnesses saw a car wi' blacked-oot windaes reverse 'er his body and then drive back 'er him again tae make sure the job wis done."

"Fuck," I bit out, shock thrumming through me.

"Ye gonnae tell me that's aw coincidental, Mac?"

Shaking my head, I looked out the shallow window of my office, seeing nothing but rain lashing the windows. "You came here to warn me?"

"Aye. Then I'm gettin' the fuck oot o' Scotland. I'm glad, being here, I can see how safe this place is. It's a fortress. Maybe ye shouldnae leave the grounds for a while."

No way would I wait like a sitting duck trapped on the estate. "I have means to look into their deaths." I looked back at Billy. "Go to Australia. Stay safe. I'll have my contacts dig into this. If this isn't a strange bloody coincidence, then I'll find out who's behind it. How can I reach you so I can let you know what I uncover?"

Billy gave me his brother's number, and we finished our coffees in strained conversation. The knowledge that someone might be after Craig's attackers hung over us like an omen.

Before he left, Billy admitted gruffly, "I ken this isnae the kind o' stuff we ever could get away wi' talkin' aboot back then, but I hud a hard time gettin' 'er it. Whit happened that night. Whit I didnae stop fae happenin'. I doubt I'll ever really be 'er it. But the wife made me talk tae someone, a professional like." He shrugged, clearly a bit embarrassed. "It helped a lot, Mac."

I knew what he was telling me. What he was recommending. "I'll think about it. I'm glad for you, Bill."

When he left, I was admittedly relieved to see him go. I told him to let me know when he arrived in Australia. I wanted to know that if we were in danger, he was somewhere someone was less likely to follow. Billy's safety meant something to me, but that didn't mean I wasn't glad to be rid of the messenger.

The Adairs had only just gotten over the last storm that tried to devastate their family.

I couldn't bring more danger into their lives.

Into *her* life.

I could only hope we were being paranoid.

Determined to know for certain, I pulled out my phone as I marched down the corridor back to my office. Hitting the number in my contacts, I only had to wait a few rings before Lisa Renfrew answered. She was Assistant Chief Constable, Local Police West. Meaning she was one of the highest-ranking officers in Police Scotland, and the city of Glasgow was under her purview.

"Mac Galbraith, as I live and breathe," Lisa answered. "I haven't heard from you in a while."

Lisa and I met when she was a young police officer. She helped coordinate security measures at one of Lachlan's only film premieres in Glasgow many moons ago. We'd had a fling but enjoyed each other's company, so we stayed in touch over the years. Unsurprisingly, she'd risen through the ranks, which was extremely convenient for me right now.

"Sorry to cut past the pleasantries, Lise, but I might have a big problem on my hands. I need some information."

"Tell me and I'll do what I can to help."

A small measure of tightness eased from my chest. Sometimes it was good to have friends in high places.

6
ARRO

The Scottish government, working in conjunction with us, Forestry and Land Scotland, had a goal of planting twenty-five million new trees every year.

As a forest engineer, that goal kept me extremely busy.

After all, this was the twenty-first century. Timber harvesting and planting all had to be planned with renewable energy and biodiversity at the forefront of our minds.

Currently, I was working on two projects with Marcello, project manager and my partner in crime. We worked on nearly all the same projects. I was lucky to be working close to home again—harvesting trees in a forest near Lairg and replanting outside Caelmore, where Lachlan and Thane lived.

It was a big day for me at our Lairg project. As the engineer, it was my responsibility to plan the logistics of safely maneuvering timber lorries and harvesters in and out of the area. Today we'd find out if all my planning was a success.

For the last four years, my record had been solid. The only issues we'd ever come across were ones caused by weather.

I was *good* at my job.

Pulling up behind Marcello's SUV, I jumped out of my Defender in my usual uniform of hiking trousers, hiking boots, T-shirt, and lightweight waterproof jacket. My helmet and safety gear were on my passenger seat. Thankfully, the forecast was for dry weather for the next two days. Enough time to get started before we had to worry about working around wet, soft ground.

"There she is." Marcello looked up from his tablet as I approached the entrance to the site. He stood with a young man I didn't recognize.

Marcello Pernice had lived in Scotland since university. We'd worked together for years, and I considered him and his wife friends.

"Morning." I beamed at him. "Vehicles on their way?"

"They are indeed," he said in his wonderful jumbled Italian and Scottish accent. He indicated his companion. "Arro, this is my new project assistant, Duncan Menzie. Duncan, this is Arrochar Adair. She is our forest engineer. If I'm not around, Arro is in charge, yes."

Duncan frowned as he gave me a rather thorough and irritating once-over. "Nice to meet you," he said in a tone that suggested the opposite.

Warning bells rang in my head, but I took a calming breath and tried not to get ahead of myself. "You too."

As Marcello and I, however, discussed today's schedule, I noted Duncan aimed all his questions at Marcello.

"That is a question for Arro," Marcello replied when Duncan asked about the construction of the road into the site and why the log storage loading area was where it was. All things *I* planned and decided.

Again, when he asked about the temporary bridge we'd constructed over the River Shin in order to use a nonpublic route for access and transport, he asked Marcello.

"Look," Marcello said with a hint of impatience, "you understand everyone's role here, so you know these are questions for Arro, okay?" There was a warning in his tone; I was not to be undermined. His solid, no-nonsense presence made life on site for a woman in a male-oriented industry a smoother ride. That it took the presence of a fair-minded male to make a female's job easier was evidence of just how far we still had to go as a society.

Duncan sullenly nodded at the slight reprimand, but his attitude tried to pierce through my nervous excitement. After months of planning, this was the day I'd been looking forward to. To see if all our hard work would pay off so we could harvest smoothly and safely. It was satisfying to see the plans unfold in real time. The thought of having to deal with a misogynistic employee barely out of college was irritating at best.

I shrugged off Duncan's attitude and attempted not to let it get to me. With everything going on (or not going on) in my personal life, work was my escape. People's lives depended on my accuracy and attention to detail. It allowed me to funnel my entire focus into it, and everything else disappeared. Mac disappeared. For a little while.

Marcello's phone rang. "Driver," he said before answering. They had a brief conversation, and I garnered from Marcello's side of it that the timber lorry driver was unsure which road to take.

"I'm coming, I'm coming," Marcello said hurriedly, hanging up. "I thought we had signposted this well enough, no?" he threw over his shoulder as he marched to his SUV.

"Do you want me to go?"

"No, you stay here to direct him further. If we have more issues, we'll need to reconsider the signage!"

I nodded and watched as he drove off.

"Hmm," Duncan muttered under his breath, looking at the tablet Marcello had handed to him.

"What is it?" I asked, a little sharper than usual.

"Nothing. I'll ask Marcello when he gets back."

My hackles rose. "Is it an engineering question?"

Duncan looked me straight in the eyes. "Yes."

A four-year Bachelor's degree in environmental engineering. A master's degree in environmental and forest management. Throughout it all, I worked as a part-time apprentice with Forestry and Land Scotland, which enabled me to secure a job as an engineer with them straight out of university. I'd experienced zero misogynism during my apprenticeship and walked into my job a little naive.

My first job as a woman in charge of a site roaming with men was eye-opening. They constantly deferred to the project manager, and unlike Marcello, this guy quite enjoyed undermining the hell out of me. One day, I was depressed and at a breaking point, and Mac had taken me for a long walk along the beach. After confessing what bothered me, he gave me a stern pep talk about standing up for myself, no matter how scared or outnumbered I felt. He said many men weren't (frustratingly) even aware they were being sexist and were just mimicking the behavior of those in charge.

But the manager, he said, knew exactly what he was doing. He was a bully, and the only way to beat him was to show him I couldn't be bullied. Mac said, "They'll try to label you as the angry woman when you stand up for yourself. He'll try to make it seem as if you're blowing things out of proportion, but don't let him. Take charge, because if anything under your purview goes wrong, you're responsible, no matter if he made the decisions. And he'll let you swing for his mistakes."

So I took Mac's advice to heart, returned to the office, and made it clear no plans would be made unless I'd signed off on them. The project manager pushed back, but I warned him I wouldn't stand for it, that my arse was on the line, and if he didn't stop undermining my decisions, I would take the issue all the way to the top—and I'd be loud about it.

He didn't listen.

So I took it to the top.

As a company that prided themselves on diversity, they reprimanded the project manager. He was furious. But we finished the project with me in charge of my own decisions. We never worked together again.

I'd been lucky over the years to gather a solid team. Few new people came and went, and those who did were amazing. It was a great industry to work in. And I didn't want anyone upsetting the status quo.

"Duncan." I faced him. "Let me make this clear so there's no confusion: I am the project engineer. You are an assistant. I am your boss as much as Marcello is. If you have engineering questions regarding the project, I'll have the answer, since I implemented the plans. So, if you have a question, ask me. If I give you a task, you do it. Simple as that. We clear?"

The little shit had the audacity to sneer, but he nodded slowly.

"I have influence over who stays on this team, so be careful," I warned gently, and his eyes widened ever so slightly, as if he hadn't expected me to call him on his bullshit.

IT WAS MIDAFTERNOON. We'd taken a break for lunch after Jim and his timber harvester had made swift progress. The tricky part of the day arrived right on schedule. We'd reached the river banks, thankfully far away from the tourist attraction that was the Wee Hoose (a tiny house on a tiny island in the middle of Loch Shin), which made felling more dangerous. Anytime we had a sticky spot on our site or were near houses or power lines, we brought in highly skilled fellers who used chainsaws. My feller was Kelly Wright. I'd made it my mission to make sure women who wanted to work in this industry were given that chance.

Marcello was nowhere in sight as I finished the last of my sandwich while reading an email on my phone regarding my Caelmore project.

"Hey, boss."

I looked up to find Kelly standing in front of me. She wore a T-shirt, hiking trousers, boots, and a safety helmet. "Hey, you, how are you?"

"Good." She grinned. "Danny proposed on Saturday."

"Congratulations." I hugged her.

She laughed. "Thanks, thanks. Aye, it was a surprise, but obviously, a good one."

I studied her face. "You're practically glowing."

"Aye, that's called sweat." She nodded to the supply shed. "Got my gear ready?"

"Always."

She jerked a chin over her shoulder. "Will we go over which trees first?"

"Yeah, yeah, just let me finish replying to this email, and I'll be right over."

I was typing on my phone, head down a moment later, when I heard a man shout, "Hey, hey!" I glanced up from where I stood near the loading area to see Duncan intercepting Kelly. "Where do you think you're going?" he asked loudly, belligerently. "This is a live site."

Kelly crossed her arms over her chest, and I couldn't hear her response as I marched toward the pair. She looked over at my approach, anger glittering in her dark eyes. "Who is this guy?"

"Who am I? Who are you, more like it?" Duncan huffed.

"Excuse me," I snapped at him, and he scowled at me. "Never accost a member of my team in that manner again. Kelly is our feller and has a right to survey the area. Who are you to intercept her?"

He shifted in agitation. "I thought she was a member of the public."

"In a safety helmet?"

Duncan huffed. "How was I to know *she* was a feller?"

I heard the emphasis on the word *she* and felt weary. "Because she's a woman? Kelly is one of the most highly skilled fellers in this country. She also knows the safety protocols on site, and you never cross this line"—I indicated where the live site began—"without a safety helmet." I pointed to his helmet-free head. "Now get off my site without one, and never get in my team's way again."

Looking as if he'd like to waste me, he marched off, and I turned back to Kelly with an exasperated shake of my head.

"I'd watch that one, boss," she warned. "I don't think he likes taking orders from a woman."

"You get them." I shrugged. "They're usually of a certain generation, though."

"Sexist morons come in all ages, everywhere. You and I know that better than anyone." She flicked a look over my shoulder and joked, "Funny thing is, I can already tell that one would piss his pants if I revved my chainsaw at him."

I threw my head back in laughter at the imagery. "Don't you dare."

"It would be funny, though, right?" She grinned wickedly.

My delighted cackle said it all.

A while later, as the team worked around Kelly while she felled the trees by the river, I told Marcello what happened with Duncan. He promised to give his assistant a stern warning and hopefully, that would be the end of it.

I didn't know what was going on with this upcoming

generation, but so many of them seemed to have this unearned confidence and disdain for authority. Maybe I was generalizing too much. Maybe that's what the generation before me thought of mine.

All I knew was that I wouldn't take many more days of a babe fresh out of college questioning me on my own site, or any other woman who crossed his path, before kicking him off the project entirely.

Satisfied with the day's progress, though wearied by Duncan's attitude, I was at least glad for the distraction. That night, I got home late, ate, then fell asleep as soon as my head hit the pillow.

The next day, the adrenaline of the project wore off, but Duncan's attitude did not abate. It wasn't as overt, but he still kept going to Marcello with questions instead of dealing with me. The project itself was going well. In fact, I got home on time, in the late afternoon.

Problem with that was, I had time to think. As I returned home, punching in the security code that disarmed the system Lachlan installed last year, I felt melancholy.

It covered me like a scratchy blanket, and already I planned to call Thane later and ask if I could take the kids somewhere this weekend. The thought of two whole days of having nothing but my own thoughts and emotions to deal with frightened me.

That realization struck hard.

"I know when someone is in pain and bottling it up. If you won't talk to me ... please, please talk to someone."

Maybe Regan was right. I couldn't go on like this. I thought of Eredine and how much I trusted her. If there was anyone in my life who could keep a secret ... I just hadn't wanted to burden her with my Mac relationship stuff for fear she'd feel put in the middle by having to keep it from Lachlan. But maybe she wouldn't. Maybe I should ask her first.

Grabbing my mail, I opened each envelope, thinking about calling Ery. I absentmindedly laid bills aside on one pile and junk mail on the other. Then I opened a plain white envelope and pulled out a single piece of paper.

My blood chilled at the message typed across it:

You're everything to me
I have to be everything to you

ADRENALINE BURST THROUGH ME, my heart raced, and my hands trembled as I checked the envelope to see if there was anything else inside it.

Nothing but this note.

There was no return address.

The evidence from Lucy's trial was branded on my mind.

Lucy had Fergus do her dirty work, including writing the creepy notes left for Lachlan.

I knew those notes by heart.

Lachlan had received this very message. It was the first message they'd left for him.

Was this someone's idea of a sick joke? The media had leaked all the evidence to the press, so it was easy enough for people to find out what Lucy had written in her stalker messages to Lachlan.

I felt nauseated, knowing after everything we'd all been through this past year, I couldn't ignore this. I rummaged through my purse for my phone. The thought of Mac finding out made my pulse leap, but all I could do was make sure he wasn't welcome in my life, no matter the circumstances.

It was something to worry about when the time came. For now, being alone in my house made me feel vulnerable, and I hated it. It pissed me off! Hurrying to the security box, I armed the windows and doors. Then I called my big brother.

"Arro," Thane answered, "can I call you back? We're about to sit down to dinner."

I swallowed hard against the fluttering in my neck. "Thane."

He hesitated and then practically barked, "What's wrong?"

Trying to sound calm, I told him about the note.

"Call the police right now," Thane ordered, fury—but not at me—in his words. "I'm on my way, sweetheart."

7

MAC

A rro.

    Her name roared in my head as I grabbed my keys off Dave, one of the estate chauffeurs, and jumped into my waiting SUV. After receiving an angry call from Thane that Arro had been sent a threatening note that mimicked Lucy's, I'd barked a bunch of orders at my team and rushed from the castle.

All my training, everything I knew about keeping calm in a dangerous situation, fled me.

Because it was her.

Arro.

If anything happened to her …

My hands wrapped tight around the steering wheel as I tore down the estate driveway. Was this how she felt when she heard I'd been stabbed? As the gates to the estate opened to allow my exit, her face flashed before my eyes from that morning last year …

. . .

WHATEVER THEY WERE PUMPING into me helped with the pain, but there was more than a twinge of discomfort anytime I tried to move. I'd been in the hospital for a week, and I couldn't be more desperate to leave. To get to Robyn. Thankfully, they were discharging me tomorrow. It couldn't come soon enough. I'd let my daughter down again. Missed our dinner date. Aye, my excuse wasn't a bad one, but I wondered what she'd thought sitting at the table, counting the minutes I didn't show up. Had I hurt her again?

I winced, angrily. For that alone, the motherfucker who gutted me was going to wish he'd never been born, once I figured out who was behind the purple eyes I saw peeping through the ski mask.

Contacts. To disguise himself. The fucker had come out of nowhere as I stepped out of my house to go meet Robyn for our first dinner together since she was a child.

As Robyn and I had discussed, the contacts probably meant I knew him. I flinched, remembering the sensation of the knife going in. Three times. Renewed frustration filled me. How had I let that happen? I felt like a fool. A failure. All my training, and I'd let someone gut me.

But I couldn't let it consume me. I had to shrug it off and concentrate on finding the bastard. Robyn was sticking around to help me do it, but the thought of any harm coming to her made me even more eager to get out of this hospital bed.

"You're awake."

The voice soothed something so deep inside, no one knew it existed. Something dark, twisted, and full of self-loathing. Like an angry beast, a dragon, buried in the pits of my soul. Only she had the power to quiet its fiery stirring.

Arro.

I smiled tenderly at her as she strode into my hospital room. A glance at the wall clock told me visiting hours had just begun.

"You do know they discharge me tomorrow," I teased. "There's no need to keep checking on me." God, but I was so fucking thankful she'd visited every day.

Arro's sweet smile caused a wave of longing as she took the chair by my bedside and dragged it close. "I want to visit. You look so much better today. The color is back in your cheeks."

"Good," I muttered, studying every feature of her beautiful face. "Won't you be late for work?"

She shrugged. "Marcello is handling things until I get there. How are you feeling?"

"I'm fine."

"Mac." Arro stared me down.

My lips quirked. "I hurt a bit when I move," I confessed.

Those gorgeous pale-blue eyes moved to where my wounds laid beneath my pajama T-shirt. "I'm going to kill the bastard," she muttered, sounding more bloodthirsty than I'd ever heard her.

It made me smile until her gaze returned to mine, and I saw how tormented her expression had become.

"If I'd lost you ..." Her eyes filled with tears, and she lowered them, trying to shield herself from me.

The tortured croak of her voice revealed everything we'd been too afraid to admit out loud. And even though it made me a selfish arsehole, I exulted at the idea of being loved by Arrochar Adair.

I reached for her hand, and she clasped onto me, fingers curling tightly around mine. "I'm fine," I replied hoarsely. "I'm alive and I'm here. Robyn and I will find out who is behind all this."

Arro nodded and seemed to shake herself, blinking rapidly to push back the tears. Our gazes met again, and she gave me a soft smile. "Robyn stayed."

I nodded. "She stayed."

"I'm so happy for you, Mac."

I flinched and tried to pull my hand away, but Arro clung to me. "We're not ... nothing has been... we haven't talked things through. We've just been talking about the case, really."

"But she's here," Arro insisted. "Mac, if she didn't want a relationship with you, she would have left already. And you didn't see her face when I told her about your attack. Robyn was terrified."

I flinched at that too.

"I'm sorry." Arro sighed. "I didn't mean ... I just wanted you to know that Robyn loves you. There might be a lot of hurt between you and many things to discuss, but I believe you and she will work this out. That you'll have a relationship with her again."

Hope, that torturous wee bastard of an emotion, rose inside me.

Fuck, I hoped Arro was right, even as I told myself I didn't deserve the chance. For Robyn's sake, however, I would tell her whatever she needed to know.

She sighed, her eyes drifting over me again. "I bet you're glad you're out of here tomorrow."

"You have no idea."

"I wish I could kidnap you now," Arro teased. "We could just get in the car and drive somewhere, away from all this, just for a bit. Just the two of us."

Her words and the way she looked at me leaned dangerously toward bringing our feelings out into the open. Feelings that were awakened on a New Year's Eve a few years ago. Feelings, I had to admit, might have been developing for months before that.

Now those feelings were locked down in that dark pit with all my demons. They tried to creep out, to escape, but I knew I couldn't let them.

Looking at her now, though ... sometimes it was hard to remember why that was.

Why I couldn't just bridge the distance between us and kiss her pretty mouth?

Arro Adair had given me the best fucking kiss of my life that night, and she didn't know it. She didn't know that kiss plagued my dreams. That in my dreams it went further, that I peeled the silver dress that sculpted her body like a second skin from her perfect tits, that I pushed the hem up past her thighs and sank into her tight heat.

"What are you thinking about?" Her voice was husky, drawing me from the fantasy.

She knew. Her eyes were smoky, cheeks flushed. She was visibly turned on.

Arro knew where my thoughts had gone.

That I dreamed of looking into those beautiful eyes, watching them grow hazy with need as I moved inside her. Sometimes it was slow and loving. Sometimes I fucked her in desperation, her nails biting into my back.

I could feel my body stirring, my mouth dry.

"I don't think you want to know." The words fell from my lips before I could stop them, my voice thick, hoarse.

Arro's breath caught, her fingers tightening around mine. "I think if you weren't currently covered in stitches, I'd very much want to know. Perhaps even indulge in a demonstration or two."

Despite the danger in her flirting, I couldn't help but laugh. She laughed too. But I saw the pain in her expression, the sadness, and even the fear. I hated it. I hated I wasn't free to love her. To promise I'd never leave her.

She bowed her head and pressed a kiss to the top of my hand, and I felt every ounce of her in it.

It hurt.

Fuck, it tore me apart worse than the three knife wounds in my abdomen.

I pulled my hand from hers, needing the distance.

Arro gave me a knowing smirk and murmured, "It's not going anywhere, Mac. What we feel. It's not going anywhere. It just keeps growing. I think Guy can tell."

The temptation of her was agony. And I didn't even want to think about the bloody chef who warmed her bed whenever he liked. Ever since he'd started dating Arro, I couldn't look at him. I'd avoided the estate kitchens for weeks.

But if she, the most loyal and steadfast woman I'd ever met, could look at me like this and say these things, then Guy wasn't the one for her. I didn't see it lasting between them, and that relieved me, selfish bugger that I was.

My gaze dropped to her mouth. I couldn't. But I wanted so badly to pull her to me, even just to feel the brush of her lips on mine. To soothe me.

The door to the room flew open, breaking the moment. Robyn walked in, her expression suspicious as she glanced between me and Arro. I braced myself, but my daughter merely smiled as she walked toward the bed. Her attention on Arro, she said, "Hey, it's nice to see you again."

Arro looked flushed, guilty, and she stood up too quickly. "You too. I was just leaving. I have to return to work."

"I'll walk you out," Robyn said, surprising me.

I tensed, wondering what she'd seen, what she suspected, and what the hell she would say to Arro once she had her alone.

Keeping my face blank, I looked at Arro as she told me she'd see me later.

Whatever she saw in my expression made the light I wanted to protect so badly flicker out of her eyes. She walked away.

My demons bayed from the darkest place inside me, and I closed my eyes to drown out their mournful roars.

BEFORE I KNEW IT, I was pulling up outside Arro's bungalow, parking behind the patrol car that was already there. Thane's SUV was behind Arro's car. Thrust from my memories, I jumped out of my Rover and marched up her front walk to bang on the door.

A few seconds later, Thane opened it.

"Is she okay?" I asked with steely quietness as I entered without an invitation.

Thane's face was hard with fury. "She will be," he promised, and then gestured for me to go into the living room.

Some worry eased at the sight of Arro sitting in her armchair across from the two police constables on her couch. But when she didn't look up at me, that crack inside me grew. Expression carefully controlled, I introduced myself to the police. Thane and I stood as Arro recounted returning home to find the note.

PC Anders, a police officer around my age, held the note in her gloved hands and allowed Thane and me to look at it.

My gut tightened. "It's the exact same wording," I confirmed. "From the Lucy Wainwright and Fergus McBride case. This is the same thing Lucy had Fergus write on the first message to Lachlan. It was painted on the wall behind his bed, though, so whoever sent this couldn't access Arro's home." The thought made my hands curl into fists.

"If that's the situation, we'll process the note for prints, but we'll need to pass your case to the detective inspectors involved in Lucy's case, which means they'll need to speak with you again, Ms. Adair," PC Anders said.

Arro nodded. "That's fine."

The police departed with evidence in hand, leaving me and Thane alone with Arro.

She still wouldn't look at me.

"Possibilities?" Thane broke the silence. "People who hate us?"

"Could be a Lucy Wainwright fan, unhappy with the results of the trial," I suggested. There had been more than a few conspiracy theorists who believed she was innocent and was set up. For what cause, fuck knows. There was no talking sense with blind, infatuated morons.

Thane nodded, but his eyes narrowed on Arro before turning back to me. "What's going on with you two?"

"Nothing," Arro and I said in unison. Too quickly. Guiltily.

Her brother looked aggravated by our answer, but sighed and said, "We need to come up with a list of suspects to give to the police."

"Is there anyone you've had an issue with, Arro?" I asked.

Still not meeting my gaze, she shook her head. "No one I can think of."

"I reckon we get everyone to check their mail. This could be targeted at anyone involved in the case. We should also send someone to the prison to question Lucy."

Thane's brow furrowed. "Won't the DIs do all that?"

"Aye, but I want to make sure we're on top of it too. I have contacts with the police in California. I'll get someone to go speak with Lucy."

"I can't imagine her talking, even if she knows anything."

"We have to cover our bases." I looked back at Arro. Her face was pale, her shoulders hunched over. She looked exhausted.

I wanted to pull her into my arms.

Swallowing hard against the urge, I said, "You can't stay here alone."

"Agreed." Thane nodded.

"I won't let this person chase me out of my home," Arro bristled, standing to pace the living room in agitation. My eyes followed her every move.

"I'll sleep on the couch," I offered, determined to do just that. It wouldn't be the first time. Though it would be since our ... falling-out.

Arro shook her head adamantly. "Like hell. I'm fine."

I tried not to flinch at her vehement rejection.

"You'll stay in my guest room," Thane commanded. "Just for the night. For me," he added.

His sister looked at him and paused, seeing the worry on his face. Her shoulders dropped. "Fine. Let me pack some things." Arro brushed past me, her perfume teasing my nose. "You can leave, Mac," she threw over her shoulder before disappearing into the hallway.

The crack widened.

A few seconds later, Thane stepped into my path, suspicion on his face. "What the hell did you do?"

I was ashamed to admit it, would never admit it out loud, but fear had driven my relationship with Arro. It had kept us apart. It had destroyed us. And now it might ruin everything, all the things I'd feared losing in the first place, all the things my fear had pushed Arro away to protect.

"It's just a disagreement," I hedged, no emotion, no guilt in my voice.

Thane saw through me.

He took a menacing step closer and looked at me in a way he'd never looked at me before.

Like I was the enemy.

"I love you like a brother, Mac." His words did nothing to temper my rising panic. "But don't think I've been blind these past few years. If I find out you've hurt Arro ... I'll fucking kill you."

And he meant every word.

I looked away, my chest feeling shredded. "Keep her safe," I bit out gruffly. "I'll see what I can learn from the police. I ... I will find out who sent that note and end this," I promised before I stormed out of her house.

I stuttered to a stop on her porch, wanting to turn back, to stride back inside and pull her into my arms and feel her breathe against me, alive and well and ... loved.

Even if Arrochar Adair hated me now, I still loved her.

And no fucker would harm a single hair on her head.

They'd have to go through me first, and I was a six-foot-four wall of writhing, contained, cold fury.

The sadistic little fuck who did this was going to regret it for the rest of their life.

8

ARRO

LAST CHRISTMAS

My chest ached with a longing I was well familiar with as I watched Mac with the kids. He worked with them at my kitchen table, helping them roll the cookie dough and cut out shapes with Christmas cookie cutters. Mac had flour in his hair, even some in the scruff on his cheeks.

"Look, Uncle Mac, I did it purrrfectly!" Eilidh raised her arms in a wide V of triumph.

Mac looked down at the wobbly Christmas tree cookie and grinned. "So you did." His attention moved to Lewis, methodically cutting out snowman-shaped cookies. "Looking good, Lew."

Lewis gave him a small smile. "Can I make him blue?"

My lips twitched.

"Well, he is made of snow, and people tend to turn blue when they're cold, so I don't see why not."

I chuckled, drawing Mac's gaze, and he flashed that sexy grin at me.

"Am I wrong?"

"No." I smiled so hard, my cheeks hurt.

I'd been like this since Thane dropped off the kids. It was our tradition that Eilidh and Lewis spent the first weekend in December with me baking cookies, putting up decorations, and watching Christmas movies. This year was different, however, because only days ago, some drunk, grief-stricken bastard (and he was a bastard no matter his circumstances) had tried to kidnap Eilidh outside the school. Thanks to Regan and other parents, Sean McClintock (said bastard) was apprehended. But he'd hit Regan and terrified my niece and nephew. For that reason, Thane was reluctant to let the kids out of his sight while McClintock was out on bail. He'd only agreed to let them stay once I volunteered Mac to be here with us and sleep on the couch. As I knew he would, Mac had said it was no problem.

Watching him put up the Christmas tree, laughing with the kids, his unending patience with them as they helped bake and decorate cookies, I couldn't stop my mind from wandering. The fantasy that unfolded in my head of a future of Christmases together with our own kids.

Mackennon never talked about wanting more children, but I knew of men who hadn't become fathers until they were in their forties. Lachlan would be one of them if Robyn fell pregnant in the future. There was still time. And I knew I wanted kids. I'd known it from the first moment Thane placed newborn Lewis in my arms. I knew it the first time he called me Aunt Arro.

But there was only one man I wanted those children with.

I wanted that future with Mac so badly, it was a physical ache.

"Can we watch *Nightmare of Christmas* now?" Eilidh asked suddenly.

"It's *The Nightmare Before Christmas*," Lewis corrected her.

"No, your dad doesn't want you watching it," Mac replied before I could.

Disgruntled, I placed their cutout cookies on the tray. I wanted to share one of my favorite Christmas movies with the kids, but Thane thought it was too scary for Eilidh. "We'll watch *The Christmas Chronicles* instead."

"But we watched that last year," she said, pouting.

I smiled as I slid the tray into the oven and set the timer. "That's the point, sweetheart. You rewatch your favorite Christmas films every year."

"I wanna watch *Elf*, then!"

"We watched *Elf* yesterday," Lewis grumbled and turned to me. "Please, Aunt Arro, I don't want to watch it again."

I nodded and walked around the table to my niece. "We'll watch something everyone wants to watch, okay?"

She nodded rapidly. "Uncle Mac gets to choose, too, then."

Mac grinned at her. "Thanks, darlin'."

"Whatcha wanna watch?"

"What do you want to watch?" His lips twitched.

"Uh ... *Frozen*!"

Lewis scowled. "That's not a Christmas movie."

"Is so!"

"Is not!"

"Is so!"

"Okay," I raised my voice a little and held out a hand to both of them. "There will be no Christmas movie or cookie decorating if you're going to argue."

"Here's what we'll do." Mac stood, towering over us in the kitchen like the big, friendly bodyguard he was. "We'll each choose a film we'd like to watch, we'll write them down on a wee bit of paper, mix them up in a bowl, and then Aunt Arro will choose a paper from it. Whichever film is written on it is the first film we watch. Plan?"

The kids nodded, happy with that solution.

Me? I inappropriately wanted to jump the man.

IN THE END, we watched *Frozen* and *Frozen II*. Lewis didn't complain. He was just as engrossed in the movies, even though he'd seen them a million times. Eilidh sang along to the songs. We paused to decorate the cookies, and I'd allowed them a few each before putting the rest away. They'd then changed into their Christmas pjs (I had too—it was part of the deal) before we returned to watch the films, each with a mug of hot chocolate.

The kids fell asleep before the second movie finished.

Mac lifted Lewis into his arms, and I followed with Eilidh into the guest room. Neither of the kids woke up as we tiptoed out, closing the door just enough to allow in a crack of light from the hallway.

"Thane will be mad I didn't brush their teeth," I whispered as we walked away.

"It's just this once," Mac assured me. "Make sure they scrub them in the morning."

"Coffee?" I asked as he followed me into the kitchen.

"You got decaf?"

"Of course."

I set about making us both a cup of decaf, but I could sense his attention. Glancing over my shoulder as I filled the machine with water, I caught Mac looking at my arse.

Once upon a time, he would have looked away, irritated to have been caught checking me out, but now he raised his eyes to mine and asked gruffly, "What the hell are you wearing?"

Earlier that night, when I'd appeared from my bedroom dressed in a Christmas onesie, I'd delighted at the thorough once-over Mac had given me. I hadn't bought the onesie with anything but my Christmas weekend with the kids in mind, but feeling his eyes on me, I felt rather smug about the purchase. It was red and white with reindeer printed on it, and it clung to every inch of my body.

"It's a onesie." I bit back a smile as I put the machine on its base and settled the decaf pod within.

"I thought a onesie was supposed to be oversized. This one doesn't leave much to the imagination."

It was rather a sexy onesie, though that hadn't been my intent. I looked over my shoulder again. His dark eyes glinted with more than a hint of desire. My skin tingled and my stomach flipped, low, deep. "Then you must have a dirty imagination because I'm barely showing any skin."

Mac swallowed hard, and to my frustration, looked away. "I meant the style of it."

Staring back at the coffee machine, I reined in my impatience. "I know what you meant."

Hearing movement, I turned to watch him walk into the living room and sighed heavily.

A few minutes later, I followed with mugs in hand, enjoying the glow of the Christmas tree lights. We'd switched off all other lamps in the living room and put on the fire, and what had been cozy for the kids was now something a wee bit more intimate for me and Mac.

I piled blankets and pillows on the armchair for him to use for sleeping. He was on the sofa, staring broodingly into the fire.

"Thanks again," I said, handing him a mug as I snuggled into his side.

He raised an eyebrow at my proximity but merely asked, "For what?"

"For sleeping on my bloody uncomfortable couch just so I could have my weekend with the kids."

"You know I don't mind."

Our gazes held for a second, and then we both took a sip of coffee.

"Even after watching *Frozen* and *Frozen II*?" I teased.

Mac chuckled softly. "Ach, it reminds me of when Robyn was wee. I was the one who took her to see all the latest Disney films because Stacey hated going to the movies."

I wrinkled my nose. "Who hates going to the cinema?"

"She did. Claustrophobic."

"Ah. That's a bit shit for her," I said reluctantly. Even though I'd never met the woman, I wasn't a fan. I now knew that Mac had tried for years to contact Robyn, had sent letters and gifts. He'd even sent gifts to Regan. Stacey had returned all of them and hadn't told Robyn. When Mac showed Robyn all the returned letters, it went a long way toward helping mend their relationship. I think that's all she'd really wanted—to know he loved her.

Funny how we had that in common.

"Finished?" I asked after a while, nodding to his mug.

He handed it to me, and I got up to dump the mugs in the sink. When I came back, Mac still stared into the fire, but he looked a little more relaxed than before.

When I sat back down, I made sure our bodies touched.

He flicked me a dark look. "There's a whole lot of couch here, you know."

My lips twitched with amusement. Sometimes with Mac, I felt like a naughty rogue trying to seduce an innocent maiden. "I enjoy being near you. How are your wounds?"

He raised an eyebrow at the subject change, but shrugged. "It's been months. They're all healed up."

"Let me see." I reached for the hem of his shirt before he could protest and slid it up his torso. Mac sucked in a breath. For once, I wasn't distracted by his well-formed abs.

All I could see were the white scars. Three of them, clustered together.

Fury filled me at the thought of Fergus.

He'd been Brodan's closest friend at school. Then, when I was sixteen, he noticed me. I thought he was cute and kind, and I liked that an older guy was interested in me. My brothers, except for Lachlan, who was in Hollywood, were at university. Brodan was no longer there to keep an eye on Fergus, and my dad was clueless about what I got up to. I was lonely. And Fergus was this handsome, twenty-year-old my brothers all liked. It never even occurred to me he shouldn't have been taking an interest.

By the time my brothers realized we were dating, it was too late. We'd slept together. Brodan eventually forgave Fergus after I broke up with him. I'd decided I didn't want to go to university while in a relationship, and I realized that what I'd felt for Fergus was more familial than romantic. Having sex with him had made me feel weird. According to Brodan, Fergus was heartbroken, and he'd felt bad enough to forgive him for dating me in the first place.

While I'd been feeling guilty about hurting Fergus, I never knew he hadn't gotten over me. In fact, I'd believed we'd become friends. Extremely good friends. Good enough friends for me to break down one night when I was drunk and confide that I was in love with Mac.

So when he'd joined forces behind our backs with Lucy Wainwright, he'd gone off-script on Lucy's arse and attacked Mac.

All because I loved him.

Despite my history with Fergus, I was relieved to know he was dead. Sadness. Unbelievable sadness, but relief. He'd almost killed Mac. Tried to kill Robyn. And he'd murdered Greg McHugh. I didn't want to be loved by someone like that. I didn't want to be the reason other people were hurt.

Tears filled my eyes as I reached out to trace Mac's scars. "I'm sorry, Mackennon."

His stomach muscles flexed at my touch. "You have nothing to be sorry for," he said gruffly.

I looked up, still caressing him. "This was my fault."

"No." His expression darkened. "Fergus was unwell, Arro."

"I shouldn't have told him how I felt about you."

"Not your fault." Mac's voice was so hoarse, it was almost a whisper.

Suddenly, the feel of him under my fingers, the heat of him, his scent, the way his eyes blazed into mine, made the air too thick. It was hard to breathe. And all I could think was, if I wanted air in my lungs again, I needed to kiss him.

His head dipped to mine as mine moved upward.

Our lips crashed together, and it was a frantic, hungry kiss. His arms wound around me, clutching the fabric of the onesie at my back, drawing it tight as we devoured each other. Just the feel of his tongue dancing against mine was enough to thrill my whole body. Needing him between my legs, I straddled him and rolled my hips against his erection.

His growl vibrated down my throat, and my fingers slid through his silky hair to hold him even closer. It was the deepest kiss of my life, and yet I needed deeper. I needed more.

I needed every inch of him to fuse with me until we couldn't tell where I ended and where he began.

His hands smoothed down my waist to grip my hips, and I felt the pressure of him holding me down on his arousal as I rolled my hips again and again until we were panting so hard, we broke the kiss.

I gasped for breath as the coil of need spiraled taut

between my legs, holding Mac's lust-darkened gaze as I rode him. His grip tightened, and he arched beneath me to increase the pressure. We panted as I rubbed against him, growing wetter, more needful. I wanted his fingers. I wanted to rip off the fabric of this stupid onesie so there was nothing between us.

"I need to come," I murmured against his lips.

His nostrils flared, and then he kissed me again, his grip bruising as he moved my hips over him. Oh, God, could I come like this? I thought in wonder as that coil inside me tightened, tightened. "Mackennon ..." I gasped for breath, arching my back to grind deeper. But satisfaction was just out of reach. I needed more. I needed his thumb or his tongue on my clit. I needed his thick length inside me. "Mackennon." I pressed my cheek to his, loving the scrape of his scruff on my skin. "I need you inside me. I need you. I lo—"

"Aunt Arro!"

I bit off the confession that had almost spilled out in mindless desire as my niece's frightened cry filled the house.

"Aunt Arro!"

Mac released his hold on my hips as I scrambled off him. I couldn't bear to register the sudden panic on his face as lust lifted its spell. Without looking at him, ignoring my throbbing, unsatisfied body, I hurried into the guest room to find Eilidh sitting up in bed.

"She had a nightmare," Lewis whispered from the other bed, still wrapped in a cocoon of blankets.

Concern doused my unspent desire. "Oh, sweetheart." I got into bed beside her, and she curled into me. "Do you want to tell me about it?"

"No." She sniffled. "Tell me a story."

I launched into the story of Disney's *Brave*, because it was her favorite. It took less than ten minutes for Eils to fall back to sleep. Sliding her gently off me, I got out and tucked the covers around her. A quick check proved Lewis was already asleep again, and I tiptoed into the hall.

My pulse raced as I hurried back to the living room to face the man I'd almost confessed my love to while I dry-humped him on my couch.

I couldn't believe that had actually happened. That Mac hadn't resisted. What did that mean?

Hope blossomed—

And deflated like a popped balloon as soon as I walked into the living room. Something like resentment filled me to find the Christmas tree lights out and the fire off. In the spill of light from the hallway, I saw Mac lying on the couch, blankets over him, either asleep or pretending to be.

PRESENT DAY

I COULDN'T STOP THINKING about that night with Mac last Christmas. The reason I couldn't stop thinking of it was because I'd dreamed about it last night. Not of the scary, threatening copycat note. Not a nightmare.

But of Mac.

Again.

He'd toyed with me, whether he meant to or not.

I blinked out of the bitter thought to find Lewis and Eilidh grinning at me over their cereal bowls.

"Where did you go, Aunt Arro?" Eilidh asked, genuinely curious.

"I was thinking of next Christmas, and how I can't wait for our weekend together."

"But it's so far away." Lewis frowned.

I supposed to a kid, it did seem far away.

"It'll be here before you know it," Regan said. "But for now, eat up."

"How long are you staying, Aunt Arro?" Eilidh asked. Her face glowed with happiness. "Is it forever? Are you and Uncle Arran staying forever?"

That the thought filled her with such excitement melted my heart, and I hated to disappoint her. "No, sweetie. It was just for one night. As for Uncle Arran—"

"I'm staying until we know more about the note." My brother's voice filled the space as he walked out of the utility room and into the open-plan kitchen. He was staying in Thane's annex while I slept in the guest suite upstairs.

Eilidh cheered at the thought, and I raised an eyebrow, noticing Regan's surprise too.

"You're staying?"

Arran gave me a serious look as he wrapped an arm around my shoulders. "Until I know everyone's going to be okay."

It meant a lot to have him back, and I couldn't help the sting of tears. While I was trying not to panic about the note, and I didn't want to change my life because of it, I had to admit—it was more than nice to have Arran home, that he was willing to stay for me.

Arran saw and hugged me harder into his side, something a lot like guilt filling his expression.

"Thanks," I whispered.

He shook his head. "You don't need to thank me for staying."

9

MAC

The phone rang, the noise filling my office and stretching my nerves to a breaking point.

Then her voice mail. I closed my eyes. "Hi, you've reached Arrochar. I'm probably in a forest somewhere with no signal, so please leave a message and I'll get back to you."

I hadn't heard that teasing, light tone for what seemed like forever. But it wasn't. It had been mere weeks. Every day our estrangement continued, however, felt like a year. It was only through Thane I heard the detective inspectors from Lucy's case had spoken with Arro. There was nothing anyone could do for now because the note was clean of prints, the envelope hadn't been hand delivered, and no other note had shown up so far.

With Billy's warning hanging over my head, I worried I was the reason for all this. My rational mind told me it wasn't possible. I'd investigated the deaths surrounding the others, and no one else had been hurt—just the men who'd been there the day of Craig Kilmany's murder. It made little sense that if these notes were about Craig that they'd target Arro instead of me, so I didn't mention it.

Still, I wished like hell she'd let me near her so I could be there to protect her.

A week had passed since the first note, and I'd tried calling Arro every day.

She never called back.

"Arro, it's me. Call me." I hung up and winced at how belligerent I'd sounded. Why could I never find the right bloody words to say to her?

She always had the right words for me.

Always.

My memories drifted to the night I fell in love with her ...

THESE KINDS of nights were my favorite on the beach. Cold, but not Baltic, because spring was nearing its end and summer drew closer. The days were growing longer, and the sun still glowed where it met the horizon. The skies above it darkened, bleeding orange into pink to mauve and then to a purple that was almost black.

It was a calm night, so the waves merely lapped at the shore, and it was all I could hear.

All I could feel was the chilly breeze and the wet, cool sand squeezing between my bare toes as I carried my boots.

I thought that missing Robyn would grow easier with time, but these past six months, I'd struggled. I didn't know what had prompted the dark spiral of thoughts, but every day was a fight to keep myself from going under.

The feeling had worsened since New Year's Eve. I wanted to tell myself it was because I'd kissed Arrochar, who, as Lachlan's wee sister and thirteen years my junior, was well and truly off-limits. But the truth was, it was because I'd hardly seen her since the kiss.

I missed her.

And that scared the shit out of me, even more than the fact that she'd given me the best kiss of my life.

As if my thoughts had produced her, a figure in the distance walked down the beach toward the shore. The sway of her hips, her build, the light hair in the last glow of the sun, told me it was Arrochar.

Anger flushed through me when I realized she was alone.

The sun was about to go down, and she was at this beach on her own?

Was she mad?

I picked up my stride, and as I neared her, she neared the shore. She waded in barefoot and placed a bunch of flowers in the water. Realization dawned as she watched the bouquet float out to sea.

Today was the anniversary of Stuart Adair's death.

My fear for her safety and subsequent anger dimmed. I couldn't lecture her about coming out here alone.

"Arro."

She startled, her eyes round with surprise as she glanced over her shoulder at me. "Mackennon?"

My heart lurched at hearing my name on her lips. No one called me Mackennon. The last person who ever had was my gran, and she was long gone.

I didn't understand why Arro using my full name pleased me so much. I didn't want to analyze it.

"Are you okay?" I held out my free hand to help her from the water.

Arro glanced down at my palm, and for a moment, I was afraid she wouldn't take it. While nothing romantic could ever happen between us, I couldn't stand the thought of us no longer being friends.

To my relief, she took my hand, and I helped her out. I released her as soon as she was free and followed her back up the beach to where she'd left her shoes. She sat down and didn't bother to reach for them. Instead, she drew her knees to her chest and locked her arms around them. Strands of loose hair danced on the breeze around her face, and as I sat beside her, I noted how the lighter color she'd dyed it made her eyes so much bluer.

To be honest, I rarely noticed changes in a woman unless she pointed them out. I never noticed when Stacey did something different to her hair, not because I didn't care, but because I was a bloke. The kind of bloke who didn't pay attention to things I didn't think mattered.

But I noticed when Arro lightened her hair.

I mirrored her pose and stared out at the water, not wanting to ponder my reasons for that. I still couldn't work out when she'd gone from Lachlan's wee sister to a woman I was so aware of.

"I've never told anyone this ..." Her soft, lilting voice carried. "But I blamed myself for my mother's death."

Pain, sharp and surprising, knifed through my chest at the confession. "Arro, no," I said gruffly, wanting to reach for her but forcing myself not to. I studied her stunning face until she finally looked up. Another sharp pang of pain buffeted into me at the torment in her expression. "You are not to blame."

Vivien Adair, her mother, had died in childbirth. Lachlan told me the doctors had warned the Adairs another birth might be difficult, but he said his mum was determined to have a wee girl.

Arro shrugged unhappily. "I know that rationally. But for the longest time, I thought the reason my dad was so distant with me was because he blamed me too. And I think I was right." Tears brightened her eyes as she gazed back out at the water. "He resented me and hated himself for it. I think it took me going away to university for him to finally make peace with it all. To try to be a better father.

"You know, for so long, every time I was in a room with him, I hated myself. And when he was gone, when it was just Lachlan and the boys, that self-hatred fell away because they made damn sure I knew I was loved. It got to the point where I never wanted to see Dad because he could so easily take that away from me. When I was at university, it was like I was who I was always meant to be."

She bit her lip, nostrils flaring against tears. Blinking rapidly, however, she fought them back and took a deep breath. "I was confident and a bit cocky and flirty in Aberdeen. But I'd come home to just him and was reminded of my guilt, that just by being here, I'd killed a mum I never got the chance to know. The Arro from Aberdeen disappeared in an instant, and I hated myself all over again."

I squeezed my eyes closed.

Knowing more than a little something about self-loathing, I fucking despised that Arro felt that way. I wanted to rail at the universe for it. "I'm sorry."

She nudged me with her shoulder, her voice catching as she said, "It got better. I graduated, and despite everything, I decided I didn't want to leave Ardnoch, so I moved back home with plans to rent somewhere in the village, if I could. But Dad was different. He wanted to spend time with me and asked me about my life, my day, my opinions. And I ate up every second, desperate for him to love me. We'd come out here"—she gestured to the beach—"every night with Bram, my dad's dog. Dad was Bram's everything. He died weeks after him. Did you know that?"

I shook my head.

"A broken heart." Her breath hitched. "Bram died of a broken heart, just like his master. Dad started talking to me about Mum on those walks. Telling me all the things I'd longed to know about her. He loved her so much." Arro shook her head as if in amazement. "So much that losing her broke him in a way he never recovered from. Part of me envied him for having loved someone that much, and another part of me was destroyed for him, and then yet another, darker part hated him for it. I wanted him to be stronger. As cruel as that sounds. My whole life, I'd just wanted him to be strong enough to be a good dad to me, and it had taken him until I was an adult to get there.

"But I made a conscious decision not to be bitter and to do my best to make sure our relationship was a good one going forward. And we were getting somewhere, Mackennon. We were growing toward something better. Then that night happened." Her breath hitched again, and when I looked at her, the tears escaped, falling quickly down her cheeks. "All I could do was hold him in my arms while we waited for the ambulance." Arro swiped at her tears. "But he knew he was dying. And he told me—" She sobbed, and I reached for her, pulling her hand into mine. "He told me he loved me. It was the first time he'd ever said those words to me. I never got to live a life with him with that sentiment between us."

Arro's expression made my heart thump as she squeezed my hand. "You should go to Robyn, Mackennon."

I jerked back like I'd been hit, surprised by the turn of her thoughts.

"You should tell her you love her in case you never get the chance."

My heart raced, that Arro would care enough about it when her heart was filled with grief. "I ... I don't deserve it. I won't barge into Robbie's life like that. If she comes to me, then I'll make sure she knows I love her."

"You shouldn't wait for those moments to come to you. You should make them happen. I promised myself after Dad said those words, seconds before he died, that I'd never wait to say those words again when I feel them." Arro turned in the sand now, her tear-streaked face filled with a mixture of what seemed like determination and apprehension.

My heart was ready to jump out of my chest.

Because I knew what she was going to say.

"Mackennon, I—"

"Don't." The word whistled sharply through the air like a goddamn bullet and hit her with the impact of one. Remorse filled me, but my fear was greater. "Arro ... don't."

Her shock and hurt dissipated as she studied me. Sadness remained.

I expected anger, bitterness, but Arro leaned into me and reached up to press a sweet kiss to my cheek. Without another word, she pulled on her boots and stood.

For a few seconds, I watched her walk away, still feeling her lips on my skin.

There was no reproach from her. No fury that I couldn't return her feelings.

And suddenly, I was more terrified than I'd ever been.

Because I knew at that moment that I loved her back, but I was just another man in her life who would never say the words. At least her father had said them before he left her. I wouldn't even be able to give her that.

I could give her something, though.

My friendship and my protection.

Standing, I followed Arro from a distance, making sure she returned safely to her car in the beach car park. Knowing that's how it would always be between us.

Me, loving her, from a distance.

Constant rain for two days had transformed the site
into a mud-ravaged mess. The downpour finally
stopped, and after assessing the situation this morning,
Marcello had gone ahead with sending the machinery in to
finish the job since we were so close to being done.

Now our damn timber harvester was stuck, and we'd
spent most of our last hours in the workday trying to get
it out.

The truck on the flat revved its engine one more time and
drove forward against the mud. With great relief, the
harvester pulled free.

A cheer went up around the crew, and I smirked unhappily. We were definitely off schedule now, something I'd
usually be able to handle with little stress, but now it seemed
like a massive deal on top of everything else on my mind. For
example, my brother had only just let me return to my own
house; the mysterious note sender hadn't made another
move, and thus the police couldn't do a thing about it; oh,
and Mac—the cause of this constant, piercing ache in my
chest—kept calling and leaving messages every bloody day.

"Isn't it your job to make sure something like this *doesn't* happen?"

I looked at the asker of the snide question.

Duncan.

Of course.

It was more than sexism here. The little prick did not like me.

And today I was not in the mood to deal with his shit. Everyone knew Marcello had made the decision to go ahead, even though I'd been apprehensive about it. But we'd worked in muddier conditions, so I could see why he thought we might get away with it, and we *were* behind because of the weather. So I backed him. And I wouldn't shift the blame to him because we were a team, and I wouldn't undermine him.

"Excuse me?" I narrowed my eyes in warning at the assistant.

He shrugged, watching as the others parked the timber harvester, securing it for overnight. "Any moron could see this was going to happen."

"Oh. Do you have a crystal ball?"

Duncan sneered. "No, just brains in my head."

And just like that, I snapped. "Speak to me like that again, and you'll find yourself back in the unemployment line."

His eyes flashed in surprise. "You can't fire me."

"Oh, I can and I will."

"Just because you're some daughter of an aristocrat and a movie star's sister doesn't mean you can do anything you like."

I felt true rage in that moment.

This little fucker had looked into me.

"First, my family aren't aristocracy, but you'd know that if you'd dug a little deeper when you were obviously investigating me." Our ancestors had been landed gentry. No titles or ranks like the aristocracy. "And second, what you just said is so far out of line, it is a firing offense. I'm noting this interaction, Duncan, and putting a complaint into Marcello about you. But make no mistake, if this happens again, I won't need Marcello's go-ahead to fire you. You think I haven't dealt with misogynists like you before? You're wrong. And guess what? I'm still here, despite their efforts to get rid of me. So this is your last warning. Give me attitude, make my working environment unpleasant"—I leaned in, despite the stark fury in his expression—"I will not only fire you, I'll make sure you never work in this industry again."

To my shock, he made a move toward me, teeth gritted, and was only stopped by Marcello's voice. "Problemo here?"

"No." Duncan stepped back.

"Yes," I snapped. "Your assistant's attitude is out of line. I'll be emailing you a written account of what was just said to make a formal complaint."

Marcello's countenance darkened as he looked at Duncan. "I would say this is your second strike. One more, and you're out."

"But—"

"No buts. Go home. We're done here for today."

Duncan looked between us, glaring furiously at me, before he stormed off, his attempt at a stomping exit hampered by the mud.

"I may have threatened his job," I admitted.

Marcello raised an eyebrow.

"I know. I'm sorry. He just … he brought up my family. He's looked into me. And he's had it out for me since he got here." Suddenly, the note came to mind, and more than a fissure of apprehension ran through me. Duncan had shown up on-site just before I received it, and his attitude seemed to go beyond misogynism. It was like he had a problem with me, Arrochar Adair, not just that I was a woman.

Shit. No. Now I was being paranoid. This whole note situation had me freaked out.

"Hmm. He's a good worker otherwise too. Shame. But I won't have him around if he's causing you problems. Email me everything that was said."

I nodded. "Are we done here?"

Marcello gave me a worried once-over. "You sure you're okay? It isn't like you to threaten your coworkers, no matter the provocation."

No, it wasn't.

I stewed over that as I drove away from the site ten minutes later. I'd changed out of my muddy boots and into clean ones to drive home, and then I was on my way.

Yes, Duncan had pissed me off, but the anger already in me had burst out in our confrontation. All this resentment.

Remembering Regan's words, I didn't drive back to Ardnoch. Instead, I took the road that would lead me to Eredine's lodge. She'd be home from the estate by now. It was about fifteen minutes northwest of Ardnoch, in the middle of the woods. The lodge was built on stilts, for some reason—it wasn't like there was a lot of flooding here. I could only assume the grounds were too unstable for foundations. Eredine's wraparound porch was brightened by colorful plant pots filled with spring blooms.

Like something from a fairy tale, the home was remote and idyllic, until a person considered what it might be like to live out here in the woods at night. But someone with sharp eyes might note the security cameras in the surrounding trees. They were courtesy of Lachlan, who had insisted on installing them after Austin Vale, Regan's stalker, had attacked Eredine while she was babysitting the kids. The attack had caused Eredine to withdraw emotionally from us, and I wished I knew why. I wished I knew her story.

Maybe she'd tell me once I told her mine.

Her car was parked outside, so she was home. I jumped out of my Defender, my heart racing, because I'd come here to do just that—tell Eredine my story. If she wanted to hear it.

The front door opened before I even made it to the porch steps.

Eredine stepped out, her eyes wide with surprise. She wore sports leggings and an oversized sweater. Her pretty face was clean of makeup, not that she wore much, anyway, and she'd piled her gorgeous dark curls on top of her head in a messy bun that couldn't contain it. She offered a kind smile. "What brings you to my door?"

I'd tried to place her accent, as if I were a master of American dialects, but I couldn't detect anything in her inflections that might point to her state of origin. My sweet friend's background was an utter mystery. "I needed someone to talk to, and you were the first person I thought of."

A mixture of gratitude and concern filled her expression, and she stepped back to gesture me inside.

Her home was small but chic, the living area open plan with a sitting room and kitchen. She had a woodstove and comfortable furnishings around it, the perfect spot to read one of the many books I knew could be found in her guest room.

We'd bonded over our love of reading. Regan was a reader, too, and we'd discussed creating a book club, but nothing had come of it. I'd probably have to be the one to organize it. What seemed like many moons ago, I would've invited Mac to join our book club—few people knew that he was a voracious reader. Melancholy doused me at the realization he'd never get an invitation now. Robyn might join us, though she wasn't much of a book lover. I enjoyed converting people into readers, so I might just keep asking until she gives in.

"Drink?"

"Tea would be lovely." It had been a cold, wet day in the mud, after all. "How are you?"

"I'm good." Eredine shot over her shoulder as she made her way into the kitchen. "Curious now."

I nodded. "How are classes going?" Ery was the Pilates, yoga, and mindfulness instructor for the estate.

"Good." She shrugged as she set about making the tea. "I never have any issues. I think it's the whole Zen vibe of what I do. But you should hear the stories the girls and guys in the spa tell me."

I frowned. "Not members being arseholes?"

"Kind of, yeah. Nothing serious that would concern Lachlan. Just the usual entitled diva shit. Plus"—she grinned mischievously—"they tell all these private stories in front of us. It doesn't go further than staff room chat, I promise," she hurried to assure me, "but I can't believe the things these people have done and are happy to talk about in front of the staff."

"It's because *they* know it won't go any further." All of Lachlan's staff had signed nondisclosure agreements and would find themselves sued thrice over whatever a newspaper might pay them for the juicy details.

Eredine nodded, walking to me with tea in hand. I gratefully accepted a hot mug as she joined me on the couch, curling her feet under her. "This one actor had a three-way with a Hollywood golden couple. Like … my mind is blown by who this couple is."

I chuckled at the twinkle of amusement in her eyes. It was good to see Ery amused and lighthearted again. She'd been so despondent lately. "Now *I* want to know."

She bit her lip. "Sorry, can't."

I shrugged. "I'll just ask Lachlan. He probably already knows."

We laughed, but there was a slight edge of hysteria to mine, and I wondered if Ery heard it. I sipped my tea, trying to calm my nerves.

"What did you want to talk about?" my friend asked quietly.

Taking a deep breath, I answered, "Something I need to tell someone or I might explode ... but it doesn't have to be you, Ery. If I tell you this, I'm essentially putting you in the middle, because I'd be asking you to keep a secret from Lachlan and basically everyone else you care about."

Eredine's brows rose. "And who would you tell if you didn't tell me?"

I didn't know.

There truly wasn't anyone I trusted as much as I trusted my reserved friend.

"Arro ... you're my friend too." Ery leaned over to place a hand over mine. "If you need me, I'm here, even if that means keeping something from Lachlan and the others. I can't imagine you'd ask me to keep something from them they *need* to know."

"No, none of them need to know. I don't think."

"Then tell me. You obviously need to talk about it, whatever it is."

I nodded quickly, my pulse throbbing. "I do."

"I'm all ears."

Settling back against her couch, I stared at the lit fireplace, deciding where to begin. "I'm in love with Mac," I blurted out and looked at her.

Ery did not look surprised.

Shit.

Had I been that obvious?

"I mean, I *was* in love with him. For years. And I thought for the longest time that the reason we weren't together was because of the age difference and because of Lachlan. But after Mac got stabbed, things changed between us. We grew closer. He ... he was always coming around, spending time with me. Then Thane and Regan got together. Do you know there are thirteen years between them, and there are thirteen years between me and Mac?"

"I didn't realize that, no," she murmured.

"I was stupid," I whispered harshly, the memories of that night like fire in my throat. "I thought that because Lachlan was fine about their relationship, that the thirteen years didn't seem to matter to him or to anyone, that it set a precedent. All barriers between me and Mac were out of the way. The night of my birthday, I thought he thought the same thing."

"What happened? I don't remember anything happening."

We'd all gotten together at North Star, my favorite restaurant, some miles up the coast from Ardnoch, to celebrate my thirty-second birthday.

"Do you remember Mac drove me home?" I'd had a few glasses of champagne with dinner, so I'd needed someone else to take me home.

"Yeah. Did something happen then?"

"While I was tipsy?" I shook my head. "Never. I mean, things have happened between us. Kissing, a little more than kissing, never sex, though. And he'd never do anything if I'd had a drink. He's wonderfully and irritatingly old-fashioned that way." Pain ached near my heart. The memory of loving someone I now hated tormented me. "But when we pulled up to my house, he gave me a gift he hadn't wanted to give me in front of everyone else."

I squeezed my eyes closed, my breathing increasing as something like panic fluttered in my chest. "It was a tennis bracelet. A diamond tennis bracelet."

"Holy shit."

I nodded. "Right?"

"What did you do?"

I took a deep, calming inhalation.

"Arro, are you okay?" Ery placed a comforting hand on my arm, and I nodded.

Was I overreacting? Was my body overreacting to what happened? Why did I still feel this way? Why couldn't I just get over it? It wasn't as bad as my body was making it out to be. Right?

"I misinterpreted the diamond bracelet."

11

ARRO

SEVERAL WEEKS AGO

Y ears ago, when Mac traveled more for estate business, he'd given me a spare key to his row house in the middle of the village in case there was an emergency while he was away. His was a narrow, masculine home I'd sneakily made cozier by adding soft furnishings that still felt like Mac might have chosen them. He'd always give me this tender look when we'd meet each other again after his return upon finding something new in his house. He never complained, so I kept doing it.

It was Friday night, two days after my birthday dinner and the surprise gift of jewelry from Mac. The diamond bracelet glittered on my wrist as I let myself into his house. He'd still be at the estate just now, so I had time to get ready. Butterflies fluttered wildly in my stomach. The bracelet had been a message. I just knew it.

Now that Mac realized Lachlan had no problem with

Thane dating Robyn's younger sister, we both knew that we could do this and keep our families intact. The bracelet was Mac's way of saying he understood that. It had to be because he'd never given me anything so expensive or romantic before. But it was clear he needed me to signal I still wanted him romantically.

And I was ready to give the signal all right. I was so done waiting around for the man I loved.

I kicked off my shoes and dumped my large bag on Mac's couch and started pulling items from it. Sexy high heels, check. Silk robe, check. Wine, check. Once that was done, I grabbed matches out of a drawer in Mac's tiny galley kitchen and returned to light the candles I'd placed around his fireplace. He never lit them, but he also hadn't gotten rid of them.

Their soft glow bounced around the room as I switched off all the lights except for a small table lamp in the corner that gave off an amber hue.

Next, I poured two glasses of wine and placed them on his coffee table.

Finally, I undressed, folding my clothes and tucking them into my bag.

I was totally naked in Mac's house.

My breasts swelled, my nipples tightening against the cool air as I thought about Mac's reaction when he came home. Desire flushed my skin as I shrugged into my silk robe, slipped on the sexy shoes, and started the playlist of romantic music on my phone. This was a surefire plan for getting Mac to give in to his feelings for me. The bracelet told me he wanted to, but just in case he still had reservations, I wanted to make it as difficult as possible for him to say no.

Taking a deep breath, I sat down on the couch facing the

door and waited, my knees bouncing with anticipation and nerves.

My life was about to change.

Our lives were about to change.

At the sound of his key turning in the lock, I untied my robe so it was ready to drop and crossed one leg over the other so he could see nothing but my naked legs and fuck-me shoes.

Blood whooshed in my ears, and my palms felt a little sweaty.

He was the only man who excited me like this.

Mac stepped inside, staring down at the floor as he did.

He looked up as he shut the door behind him, and he startled, frozen in wide-eyed shock. Something dark, most definitely lust, flickered in his expression, and his nostrils flared. He scanned the room, taking in the mood lighting and music, before returning to me.

That was my cue.

I stood up, my robe falling open, and shrugged my shoulders so that it fell to the floor at my feet.

Mac's lips parted, and I heard the rough inhalation of breath as his gaze drifted down my naked body and moved back up again, lingering between my legs and then again at my breasts.

My belly squeezed at the unadulterated need in his expression, and I grew slick, ready for him.

"What are you doing?" he asked, his voice so hoarse, it was like he could barely get the words out.

Thinking I really needed no words to explain what was happening, I walked toward him, my hips moving with exaggerated sway because of the high heels, and Mac's eyes followed their rhythmic movement. Then he was close enough I could smell his aftershave, could feel the heat of him.

I reached him, saw the bafflement in his gaze and ignored it, and pressed my body to his, thrilling at the erotic sensation of his fully clothed body against my nakedness. I reached for him, the diamond bracelet on my wrist sparkling in the soft candlelight.

Suddenly, however, my heart jumped unpleasantly as Mac gripped my forearms and pushed me away. He skirted around me, backing up into the living room.

"Mackennon—"

"What the fuck are you doing?" he bit out, not looking at me as he reached for my robe and threw it in my direction. "Put that on now."

How could he still be frightened of this? "Mac … we don't need to hide anymore. Look at Regan and Thane! Jesus, look at Lachlan. He went after Robyn, even though she's your daughter. Why should we stay away from each other when my brothers get to be with who they want, everyone else be damned?"

He wouldn't answer me, wouldn't look at me. "Where are your clothes?" He searched the living room for them.

Furious because it was so much better than being hurt, I hurried over and grabbed hold of him, pressing myself to him. "Stop it," I demanded as he tensed against me, his eyes spearing through mine. "Stop fighting this. I know you want me. I know you *more* than want me." I moved to kiss him, but he jerked his face away. Rejection burned, which only made me more determined to kiss him. I knew if I kissed him, he'd be lost to it.

"For fuck's sake!" Mac shoved me away from him so hard, I tripped over my heels and bounced down onto the couch.

Horrified, I could only stare up at him.

He looked equally horrified as his hands flexed into fists, as if he wanted to reach out.

But didn't.

Humiliation crawled over me. "I don't understand … the bracelet." I waved my wrist at him. "I thought it meant—"

"What?" he snapped, looking pointedly away, the muscle in his jaw ticking with anger. "Meant what?"

I sat forward, searching the floor blindly for my clothes. Where had I put them?

"Meant what, Arro?"

"You've never given me a gift like that before. Something so romantic. I thought it was a sign that you wanted …"

"You admired the one I bought for Robyn's twenty-ninth birthday so much that I made a note to buy one for your birthday too. It's been such a shit year for everyone. I thought you deserved something nicer for this birthday."

Oh my God.

I covered my face with my hands, my skin hot with mortification.

How had I totally forgotten that he'd bought Robyn the same bracelet?

Oh, fuck.

I looked up at him and studied the way he glowered at the fireplace, adamantly avoiding my gaze.

But the memory of that night when Eils and Lew stayed over for Christmas decorating filled my mind. Followed by our kiss on New Year's Eve. Not to mention all the times we'd flirted, including at the village anniversary ceilidh last year. Damn it, the way his eyes had followed me all night was the reason Guy had exploded with jealousy and beat the hell out of me for it.

Newly determined, I stood up again, uncaring of my nakedness. This bullshit between us had to stop one way or another.

I pulled on his arm, forcing him to look at me. "I'm not imagining this." I slipped my hand under his shirt, feeling his stomach muscles flex beneath my touch. Caressing him, slowly moving downward, I whispered, "We love each other, and touching the person you love, making love to the person you love, is allowed, Mackennon. So let me love you."

His chest heaved with shallow breaths as my other hand slipped under his shirt and moved upward to explore his chest, my thumb rolling over his nipple. The fingertips of my other hand pushed beneath his underwear—

"Jesus Christ, Arro," Mac bit out, this time retreating instead of shoving me away.

I moved to follow him, and he held up his hands like warding off an opponent.

"No means fucking no," he snarled.

The words sliced through me, and I froze.

But he wasn't done.

"I don't feel that way about you." He glowered over my shoulder. "End of fucking discussion. Now I need you to get dressed and leave."

"You can't really mean that," I whispered, betrayal washing through me.

Mac's eyes flared a second before his expression turned blank.

He'd never looked at me like that.

Like he was staring right through me.

His tone cold, he said, "This will never happen again. Get dressed and get out, and I'll pretend like it never happened."

Nausea rolled upward and I fought to keep it down as tears blinded me. I needed my clothes. "I'm sorry," I whispered.

I needed to cover the skin that now felt covered in dirt. Only a few minutes ago, I was powerful and sexy in my nakedness. Now it was as though someone had stripped me and tied me up outside for strangers to gawk at.

Guilt and dread, the cause of the sick feeling in the pit of my stomach, carried me as I hurried to dress, forgoing underwear to get my clothes on as quickly as possible. "I'm sorry," I muttered hollowly again as I moved toward his front door.

"Arro—"

I hurried out, slamming it behind me, and then I was running and crying, sobs racking my whole body as I sped toward my car parked around the corner, out of sight.

I didn't know if anyone saw me.

I had one goal: to get as far away from Mackennon Galbraith as possible.

PRESENT DAY

I THOUGHT I'd cry retelling the scene to Ery, but I'd cried myself out weeks ago. That whole night I'd cried so much, I thought I might die from it.

"For a few days, I was so humiliated and wrecked by what happened, I could only feel guilt. For doing that to us." I met Ery's sad gaze and shrugged miserably. "But I realized after those first few days that the only reason I thought he'd want that from me was because everything he'd done in this past year suggested he loved me, that he wanted me. I didn't imagine those kisses, his touch, the long phone calls and flirty texts. I didn't imagine that, Ery."

Tears finally burned my eyes, furious fucking tears. "Was I in the wrong that night? Yes. Maybe I was blinded by my desperation for him, and I tried to manipulate everything. I should've listened instead of trying to seduce him. For that, I'm sorry.

"But this wasn't that simple or straightforward. It's complicated between us, and I deserved better than to be treated like a stranger, to be humiliated and made to feel like … I can't even describe how I felt at that moment. Like I wanted to disappear. I just wanted to disappear."

The sob broke out between my lips, taking me aback. "I hate him! I hate that I lost myself so much in wanting him. That I did that to him. And that he humiliated me for it. I feel sick every time I see him, like I want to crawl out of my skin, and I'm so angry, Ery." I sobbed harder, and she pulled me into her arms. I clawed at her, holding on as she rocked me and whispered soothing words against my hair. "I'm angry at everything, and I'm so tired. I'm so tired. I don't want to be angry anymore."

Eredine's arm tightened around me, and I could hear the tears in her voice as she promised me it was okay, that everything would be okay.

But I wasn't sure it was a promise she could keep.

12

MAC

L isa, my friend and chief constable in Glasgow, could provide me with no leads, no useful information into the deaths of Kenny, Frickle, and Bryan. The car that ran over Bryan was reported stolen days before, though she did agree it was a little too coincidental and the circumstances for each case seemed odd. She'd asked two of her detective sergeants to reopen the investigations into their deaths and asked me to stay out of it.

But I couldn't. No DSs were going to be as invested in discovering the truth as someone potentially in the firing line. Billy made it to Australia with his wife, and I hoped that would keep him safe for now.

I did my own digging. First, I looked into Craig Kilmany's family because these were the people who had the motive to kill the boys involved in Craig's murder. Craig had two brothers: Jimmy, in prison, and Lee, who'd gotten out of prison a year ago. Craig's parents were deceased; his father died of cancer not long after Craig's death. His mother died of an overdose some years later.

The brothers interested me—I remembered they were as

thick as thieves growing up, all part of the same gang. And since Lee was out of prison, I focused on him. I called up the private investigator, Daniel Ludlaw, whom Lachlan and I had employed sporadically over the last decade, and asked him to look into Lee Kilmany. I wanted to know what he'd been up to this past year.

With this weighing on my mind, I was glad Robyn and Lachlan were returning from their honeymoon soon. Not just for the peace of mind of having them close to home, but because I would be glad to hand the estate reins back to Lachlan. Managing it was wearing on me. *Everything* was wearing on me.

Mostly the estrangement between me and Arro was wearing on me.

For the millionth time since that night, I wished I could go back and change the way I'd reacted. That I hadn't let my fear lash out in anger. Even after she'd fled, I'd convinced myself we'd be okay. That we'd get over the horrific moment. It wouldn't be too long before I realized how fucking naive I'd been ...

ARRO WASN'T ANSWERING *her phone. I'd have to go to her. Maybe give her a few days. Last night had been a hellish scene.*

Upon unlocking my front door, I had a flashback as I stepped into my now dark and cold living room—Arro walking toward me, wearing nothing but high heels and the bracelet I'd bought her.

"Fuck," I muttered, closing the door behind me as my body responded to the memory. If only she knew the strength of will it had taken to push her away.

Was it strength of will, though? *I thought bitterly as I threw my keys in the dish on the side table and switched on a lamp. Shrugging out of my jacket, I flinched remembering the look on*

Arro's face as she scrambled to dress. Not for the first time in my life, I truly hated myself.

I was a fucking coward.

Swallowing hard, I wandered into the kitchen and stared at the bottle of whisky on the counter. It would be so easy to drown in it. Make her fade out. But I'd always been aware that I was the son of an addict, and there were a few times in my life where I'd come close to disappearing into the oblivion alcohol could bring. I always stopped myself. Never went down that road. Desperate to prove I wasn't my dad. But I was. I was just self-destructive in other ways.

Ignoring the whisky, I filled a glass with tap water.

I could have had her last night. The insidious thought crept into my mind as I stood in the kitchen. My body stirred at the thought. I'd wanted her for so long, and the thought of coming home to her every night was such a painful goddamn longing. And there she'd been, so beautiful, so sexy and confident.

Until I destroyed her.

"You haven't destroyed her," I muttered, shaking my head. It was just an awkward, horrible moment, but we'd get past it. We were Mac and Arro.

I'd go talk to her and finally have an honest conversation about why we could never be together like that. No matter how much we wanted it. The memory of that night on her couch last December still haunted my dreams. Still made me wake up hard. It was one of the sexiest moments of my life, and we didn't even fuck.

I would tell her that I hadn't had sex in too long, and perhaps that was a factor. But it wasn't the overlying factor, and I was old enough to know better. I wasn't a young man who believed he could drown out the woman he really wanted by sleeping with another. I knew from experience that it didn't work, and sometime over the past few years, I'd lost the appetite for casual sex. It would never satisfy me now. Nothing but Arro could satisfy me.

So I was fucked since I refused to go there with her. Maybe that was my punishment for standing by while a boy was murdered, for *never loving the mother of my child the way she wanted me to, for abandoning my daughter, and for loving a woman younger, kinder, and far too good for me.*

Sighing heavily, I walked back into the living room, and my eye caught on the large envelope that had been pushed through my letter box.

That hadn't been there when I'd gotten home. I strode over and picked it up. It held a long, narrow object. Flipping the envelope over, I saw it was blank.

What the ...

I tipped the contents out on my sideboard and froze.

The spare key to my house and a black velvet box. Placing my glass down, I used both hands to open the box and found Arro's diamond bracelet inside.

A wave of dread crashed over me. My heart raced and my palms were suddenly slick as I braced on the sideboard to catch my breath. The room spun as panic clawed at me.

I'd been kidding myself, pretending like last night wasn't as bad as it had been.

I'd fucked up.

For years, I'd been so afraid of hurting her that my fear had done just that.

This was a good thing, I said to myself. I pushed her away to protect her from me because look what I could do to her. I humiliated her. I didn't deserve her.

I hurt the people I loved.

SLIDING open my office desk drawer, I stared down at the black velvet box. For some stupid reason, I couldn't get rid of the bloody bracelet. Arro had wrapped up all her hopes in that gift, a gift I never should've given her. Because I'd lied. Yes, I'd seen how much she admired Robyn's bracelet, an extravagant gift I'd given to somehow make up for lost time.

But that wasn't the real reason I'd given Arro the piece of jewelry.

For just a second, I'd wanted to pretend that she was mine to give diamonds to.

To feel some kind of claim on her whenever I saw her wearing it.

And that made me a bigger bastard than she even knew.

All these years, I'd kept Arro at bay to protect her from me, and I'd hurt her anyway with my mixed signals.

I slammed the drawer and reached for my phone. I had to talk to her. Had to fix things.

I couldn't give up hope we could be friends again.

I'd never been one to say someone was a "best" friend, but Arro … she was my best friend.

Like always, however, the call rang out.

I hung up, glaring at my computer screen.

She had until Robyn and Lachlan returned in a few days, and if she didn't pick up any of my calls in that time, I'd go to her. We needed to have this out once and for all.

13

ARRO

I'd woken early to a text from Eredine asking me to breakfast the Sunday after our talk. I'd gotten calls and texts from Ery all week, and it was lovely. She was acting very protective of me, but the truth was, I felt a million times better after confiding in her. It was a massive weight off my shoulders. Ery didn't judge me for my wrongdoing in the whole situation, and she didn't judge Mac either. She just let me feel what I wanted to feel about it and made it clear she was there for me.

It was a special friend who kept her opinions and bias out of an emotional situation. I was grateful to her.

For the first time since that night, I was looking forward to a social situation—breakfast at An Sealladh, a roadside café fifteen minutes outside the village with a view across Ardnoch Firth. It was called the View in Gaelic, and they cooked the best Scottish breakfasts. Hoping it wouldn't be too busy that morning, I hurried to dress to pick up Ery on my way. There was no point in taking two cars.

I'd just stepped out of the house when a Range Rover pulled into the driveway with Arran at the wheel. He must've borrowed one from Lachlan's new fleet. What was he doing here?

My brother got out of the SUV and bleeped it shut behind him with a point of the fob. "Where are you off to?" he asked before I could question him.

"Breakfast with Ery. What brings you to my door, especially at this hour?"

His face brightened suspiciously at the mention of Eredine. "I was coming to take you for breakfast myself. How fortuitous. Shall I drive or …?"

Rolling my eyes at his boyish smile, I answered by walking to my Defender. He followed like a happy puppy, and while it thrilled me to have him home, I felt the need to repeat myself. "Ery's off-limits."

"You can't make people off-limits, Arro," Arran replied humorlessly as he pulled on his seat belt.

I did the same thing but glowered at him. "I can make her off-limits. She's my friend. And she doesn't need you blowing into town, devastating her, and then blowing back out."

He shot me a dark look. "Not everything has to be taken so seriously, wee sister. Frankly, Eredine needs to indulge in a wee bit o' lighthearted flirting."

"What do you know about it?" I huffed, pulling away from the house.

"I know Lachlan and Mac won't tell anyone a damn thing about where they found her, and that in itself means something potentially bad happened." He shrugged. "I'm not looking to uncover her secrets. I just want to make her smile."

"Well, that's about the sweetest thing I've ever heard," I teased.

"Fuck off."

I laughed, but as my amusement died, I warned, "Don't lead her on. Brodan flirts with her any chance he gets, but he always buggers off and leaves her behind without a thought. I don't know if Ery takes him seriously, but she doesn't need another Adair man messing with her emotions."

Arran didn't respond, and we didn't mention her again until we pulled up to her house in the woods.

"This is where she lives?" Arran scowled, his head dipping to look out the windshield. "Alone?"

"Yup."

"And Lachlan allows this?"

At his belligerent tone, I sighed heavily. "It's not really up to Lachlan. Believe it or not, Arran, as a thirty-one-year-old woman living in the twenty-first century, it's entirely up to Eredine where she lives."

"Funny."

"I was being perfectly serious." I hit my horn gently to let Ery know we were there, but she'd already know because of the cameras. "And Lachlan has cameras everywhere in the woods around her house."

Arran relaxed at that.

"Caveman," I murmured under my breath.

"What was that?"

"Caveman," I said louder.

Arran grunted and I smirked because, well, point made.

The front door opened, and Ery appeared. My attention flicked to Arran, who watched her with a troubling fascination. It troubled me because Brodan looked at her the same way.

My bloody brothers and their similar taste in women. I'll kill them if Ery ever ends up in the middle of their shenanigans.

Her beautiful smile froze with surprise when she saw Arran beside me. He unclipped his belt and got out, holding the door open for her.

"I can sit in the back," Ery said.

But Arran, ever the gentleman, insisted she take the front passenger seat.

"Just do it, Ery," I said, "or we'll be here all day."

"Someone got up on the wrong side of the bed this morning," Arran whispered loudly in Ery's ear.

She seemed to flush at his proximity, a tinge of red beneath her smooth, golden-brown skin, before she gracefully slid onto the front seat. Every move Ery made was graceful. She reminded me of a ballerina.

Catching the smug expression on Arran's face, I shot him a warning look, and he laughed before he got into the back.

"Sorry, I didn't know he was coming," I said to Ery as I did a three-point turn in her gravel driveway.

"It's fine. The more, the merrier."

"I don't know about that."

Arran slid forward to rest his chin on my shoulder. "I thought my wee sister was happy to have me home?"

Though he was teasing, I heard something, a note of disquiet, that disturbed me. I glanced in the rearview mirror, meeting his gaze. "I am happy. I just wish you'd stay."

Something sad, troubled, entered his eyes, and I wanted to ask him what the hell was going on. Why had he stayed away so long?

Just like that, the look was gone, and he sat back in his seat. "So, where are we off to for breakfast?"

"An Sealladh," Ery answered.

"Excellent choice, ladies. Glad to hear the old place is still going strong. I wouldn't have thought you were a fry-up kind of woman, Eredine." He leaned against her seat now.

I flicked a look at her and saw she was ignoring his face propped on the edge of her headrest.

"Why would you think anything about me? You don't know me." Her sassy assertion was surprising.

I snorted, glancing at Arran only to find him grinning.

"It's a good thing we're about to have breakfast together, then." He leaned in close to her ear again and said in a deep, throaty voice I'd seen melt many a girl, "A man can tell a lot of things about a woman from the way she eats."

I made a gagging noise.

"Oh?" Ery asked with quiet primness. "Can he tell when a woman would like him to stop purring in her ear like a tomcat?"

It took everything I had not to burst into laughter.

"Fair enough." Arran chuckled and sat back again.

"How was work yesterday?" I tried to commandeer the conversation.

Ery shrugged. "It was fine. It'll be good when Lachlan's back. The place just isn't the same without him."

It was on the tip of my tongue to ask her how Mac was, but I stopped. Sometimes I had to remind myself that I hated him and didn't care how he fared. I'd even caught myself being mad at him for not phoning me in days, until I remembered I'd blocked his bloody number, because every time his name came up on my screen, I wanted to curl up in a dark room and cry.

Ery spoke a little more about the estate and asked about my work. I told Arran and her about Duncan, and Arran, serious for once, said we should tell my brothers and Mac about it. We already told Robyn and Lachlan about the ominous note for their own safety, and I had to convince them to finish out their honeymoon. I had a feeling it had ruined it, anyway, and that they'd be glad to get home to us.

"I suppose we should," I murmured, uneasy about adding Duncan to my nonexistent list of suspects. It didn't seem right to accuse him of this when it was more than likely his behavior at work was unconnected. Still, Lucy had taught me caution, and admittedly, paranoia.

An Sealladh wasn't busy at this time of the morning.

They'd just opened, so we had our pick of tables. Arran took the seat opposite Eredine, studying her in a way that made her squirm. I wanted to tell him to stop making her uncomfortable, but I knew that wasn't his intention. I didn't think he realized he was staring so much, and I didn't want to embarrass him by pointing it out.

"You have the most astonishing eyes," Arran said as we waited for our server.

Or maybe he did know he was staring.

For fuck's sake, was I to endure his flirting with Ery all morning?

Rather than looking embarrassed, Ery stared at him with surprising forthrightness. "So I've been told."

Arran's blue eyes twinkled at her unimpressed response.

Me? I was impressed. I'd only ever seen this assertive side to Eredine among her friends.

When Brodan paid attention to her, she clammed up, impossibly shy around him. Around most men, in fact.

"Aren't you going to compliment me in return?" my brother teased.

"Why? Do you have self-esteem issues that require women to stroke your ego?"

"Ha!" I couldn't help myself. Who was this woman with the tart responses, and where had she come from?

Unfortunately, Ery's dry wit only seemed to spur Arran on.

Thankfully, the waitress interrupted him mid flirt, and we ordered a full Scottish breakfast.

"See, I definitely would have taken you for an omelet kind of woman, or maybe eggs Benedict," Arran mused, studying Ery's face in a manner that was making *me* uncomfortable.

I was a bloody third wheel.

"Proof that you don't know me."

Arran leaned over the table toward her. "But I'd like to."

"I'm going to shoot you if you don't stop flirting right this second." I sighed. "Please, I just want to eat my breakfast without feeling the need to run to a bathroom and vomit."

"My flirting isn't that bad." Arran settled back in his seat. "Is it, Eredine?"

"Oh, was that flirting? I thought you just had a staring problem."

I snorted and she looked at me, her mouth twitching against a grin.

"I do have a staring problem, but only around you. It's impossible not to look at you." Arran smoldered, and I shuddered at witnessing him in seduction mode.

Eredine stared impassively at him for a second before she looked past me and out the window to the firth. "Sometimes I forget how beautiful it is here. I could stare at that view all day."

"So could I," Arran murmured, seeming to memorize her profile.

I scoffed, and he raised his hands defensively. "It slipped out. Just an honest response to a spectacular view."

"Oh my God, do they serve Macallan here? I think I'm going to need it."

THEY DIDN'T SERVE WHISKY, and I didn't need it because Arran mostly behaved himself. He slipped flirtations into his interactions with Eredine, but we actually enjoyed a pleasant breakfast together. My brother was cagey about his time in Thailand, where he was supposed to have been bartending for the past two years, but I hoped he'd open up a little when it was just the two of us.

Arran insisted on paying for breakfast, and Ery and I waited by the door. She was fixing her hair, the heavy mass of it slipping from its tie, when Arran sauntered over. His gaze fixed on her hair as she pulled it with effort into a high ponytail. "Christ, you've got gorgeous hair," he said, his voice a little hoarse for my liking.

Eredine raised an eyebrow and asked as I pushed open the door, "When are you leaving again?"

My smirk dropped as soon as I spotted my Defender where I'd parked it in the distance. I could see the spray paint from here.

Hurrying into a run, I heard my brother utter a muffled curse, and his footsteps and Ery's picked up pace.

I skidded to a halt by my car. Fear thrummed through me. Spray-painted across its side:

You aren't you without me

THEY WERE the same words Fergus spray-painted across a Range Rover on Lachlan's estate last year at Lucy's bidding.

"When am I leaving?" Arran growled. "Not anytime soon, by the looks of this."

THE POLICE CHECKED the security cameras at An Sealladh, but my Defender was parked too far from the building. They checked with people who'd come into the café after us, but no one saw anything or had dash cams that might have caught the culprit. The car park was at the windowless front of the building, with all other windows facing the view across the loch and either side of the café.

We had nothing.

And the bastard was now doing an excellent job of frightening me.

I'd gotten lulled into a false sense of security since nothing had come of the first note. The constables who'd arrived to check the car had called it in and had been advised to confiscate the vehicle. They said there wasn't much else they could do but turn it over to the detective inspectors from the original case. I felt helpless. Powerless.

Gravel kicked up behind me, and I spun from watching the police confiscate my Defender for prints to find two SUVs pulling into the car park.

Thane and Mac.

My attention moved to Mac as he jumped out of his vehicle, his face dark with thunderous rage.

And while there was still anger inside me when I looked at him, it wasn't as volcanic. In fact, it had been diluted with utter sadness because I was pretty sure I could never forgive myself for putting us in that situation, and I'd never forgive him for his reaction to it.

Looking away, I turned to Thane as my big brother pulled me into his embrace. "Are you okay?" he asked gruffly.

I nodded, giving him a reassuring squeeze. God, our family needed a break from all this crap. When would it stop?

Mac's eyes bored through me as he gathered with us to watch the police load my Defender onto a recovery truck. "When do you think I'll get it back? They just said 'as soon as possible.'"

"I'll see if I can get a bit more information," Thane said, already moving away. "I want to talk to the police, anyway."

Mac hurried to follow him.

A few minutes later, the police got in their car and followed the recovery vehicle out of the car park while my brother and Mac returned to us.

"Well?"

"They said they'd contact you, right?" Thane asked.

"Yes, but I was hoping they might give a specific day." How the hell was I going to cope without a car? I needed a vehicle to get to work.

Thane shook his head. "They said as soon as possible, and I believe them. For now, let's get away from here. I can get everyone in my car. We'll head back to mine to discuss."

"I'm actually kind of tired." Ery gave me an apologetic smile. "I can stay if you need me, but I thought maybe Mac could drop me off since I'm in the opposite direction from you all."

I was surprised, but not upset. Whatever had gone on in Ery's past, I had a feeling all this brought it back up for her. I didn't want her to be alone to deal with it, though. "Do you need company?"

She shook her head. "I think I'm going to take a nap. Call me if you need me, though."

"I will." I hugged her and whispered, "I'm sorry about all this."

"Hey, not your fault." She stepped back, her next words directed at Mac. "Do you mind?"

Mac flicked me a look but said, "Of course not."

Arran and I piled into Thane's SUV, and the first words out of Arran's mouth were, "That's it, you're moving back in with us."

"Us?" I asked, my hackles rising at his bossy tone.

"Thane's."

"No way. Thane already has you. He's not putting up with me indefinitely."

"I'm right here," Thane cut in as we pulled out onto the road. "And Arran's right. You can't stay on your own while we're in the dark here."

"No."

136

"Then move onto the estate," Arran pushed. "It's guarded."

"That helped Greg McHugh, didn't it?" I flinched at my bitter sarcasm. "I'm perfectly safe at my home with my very expensive security system."

"You don't have a car right now," Thane reminded me. "Come stay with us for a bit, and you can borrow mine. We'll make do with one for now."

"No," I repeated stubbornly. "I'll borrow a car from Lachlan's fleet. But I'm not changing my life because of this moron who's just trying to scare me. Me. No. Take me back to my house. Arran's left a borrowed Range Rover there, anyway, that he needs to collect."

"Oh, shit, yeah, I forgot about that," he muttered.

"I hate this." Thane's voice rose with anger. "I hate we don't know who is behind this, and that I have to leave you alone. Don't make me."

Despite my fear, despite my need to please my family, I couldn't give in on this. Inside I was shaken more than I could say. Why was I being targeted because of Lucy's case? I'd had very little to do with the whole thing. But I couldn't let my brothers see how scared I was. I needed them to think I was okay because I needed them to let me deal with this in my own way. No one was chasing me out of my own home.

"I'm fine, Thane. And for all we know, this is just some wee prick playing a prank. I feel safe at home. Don't take *that* away from *me*."

My brothers grunted in unison. I knew what that meant. They'd take me home, but they weren't happy about it.

MAC

137

WHILE I WAS desperate to get back to Arro, to ascertain how she was feeling, furious at the thought of her being afraid, I'd also do just about anything for Eredine Willows, so there was no chance of me saying no on the rare occasion she asked for a favor. Not that I knew her all that well. And yet, I probably knew more about her than most. I'd known her when she answered to a different name, was there when she picked the new one after looking at a map of Scotland, and I'd helped Lachlan protect her all these years. Despite not sharing a close friendship with her, she was my family. Because she felt a deep loyalty to Lachlan.

"Are you all right?" I finally asked as we drove down the road that led to her home in the woods. "This whole situation ... is it bringing things up you don't want to remember?" I knew from Lachlan that Lucy's stalking had shaken Eredine.

"I'm fine." She gave me a toothless smile. "Just worried about Arro."

There was something in her voice, something pointed.

I pulled to a stop behind her car outside her idyllic home. Switching off the engine, I looked at her, and she studied me in a way that made me feel seen. And I was sure I didn't like it.

"I know, Mac. About you and Arro. Arro needed a friend to confide in. I know about the past few years, and I know what happened at your house a few weeks ago."

Every muscle in my body locked as I waited for Eredine's censure. For her to voice out loud every awful thing I already knew about myself.

To my shock, she offered me a weary smile. "I don't think Arro knows Lachlan is aware of what's between you and her ... but you know he knows, don't you, Mac?"

Fuck.

How the hell did Eredine know that?

"Lachlan told me." She shrugged, answering my question.

Seems everyone told Eredine their secrets.

"And after he just married your daughter, we all know he doesn't have the moral high ground when it comes to standing in your way of being with Arro. He wouldn't, anyway. You know that, too, don't you?"

I did know that.

My pulse throbbed in my neck. My face was too warm.

"Arro thinks you pushed her away because of Lachlan, but we both know differently. We both know why you really pushed her away. At least I can guess. Probably the same reason I push everyone away." Eredine's expression turned stark as she looked out the windscreen. "Not deserving of them," she whispered.

My throat thickened at her unnerving perception.

At my silence, she looked at me again. "I'd be a hypocrite to tell you to get over yourself. But I will say this ... you don't see yourself the way others see you, Mac. People truly depend on you because you make us feel safe. We see the good in you. The protector. You are good enough. More than."

Unexpected emotion filled me, and I resented her a little for the immensity of the feeling. Pushing through it, unwilling to hurt another woman I cared about, I replied, "If I'm good enough, Eredine, then you're an angel. I don't like that you think ill of yourself."

In answer, she gave me an exhausted shrug and opened the car door. I wanted to say more, to find the right words to understand why she felt unworthy, but I already knew I wasn't the right person for that job. How could I be when apparently, we were cut from the same cloth?

Before she closed the door, she leaned back into the car and said, "Don't stay away because you think that's what Arro wants. Don't wait for her to come to you, Mac, because she won't. She won't ever again." Her words ignited my panic. "It has to be you." Eredine's smile was encouraging, sweet, and it made me pause. As I watched her climb the steps to her house, waiting to make sure she got safely inside, I reeled.

Arro had told Eredine everything about my reaction to her a few weeks back, and Eredine hadn't judged me for it. She hadn't raged at me to stay away from Arro.

She'd understood as no one could.

I hated the reason she understood.

But she did.

And she believed I shouldn't give up on Arro.

Years ago, I'd left it up to Robyn to come to me, and once we discussed our past, I realized quickly that I should've gone to her. I shouldn't have given her the space to come to me if she wanted to, because that wasn't what she needed. Robyn had needed to know I loved her and wanted to be in her life. I'd let my guilt and self-loathing cloud my judgment.

And when I hurt Arro, I'd done the same thing again. I'd stayed away because I thought that was what she needed.

What if I was wrong again?

What if Eredine was right?

14

ARRO

Sunday afternoon, I convinced my brothers to drop me off at my place when Thane took Arran to collect his borrowed SUV. I needed to be alone to figure out my feelings about these notes, and I knew if I went back to Thane's, Mac would show up after dropping off Eredine.

It was just as well we didn't have a family meeting to discuss what the hell was going on because Robyn and Lachlan returned from their honeymoon the following day and, despite being jet-lagged had insisted everyone meet at their house after work that night.

Marcello took me to the work site and then dropped me off at home that afternoon, so Eredine picked me up to go to my brother's. And curiosity got the better of me. I'd asked her if she and Mac talked about anything when he drove her home, but she shrugged and said, "Not really." Prying would suggest I cared what Mac did or said, so I didn't pursue the questioning, even though something in her demeanor made me feel like she wasn't quite telling the truth.

Lachlan and Thane lived in Caelmore in almost identical homes Thane had designed. The small estate on the outskirts of Ardnoch had no other houses around because the surrounding land belonged to me, Arran, and Brodan. It waited there for us to build our homes on it if we so wished. And with a view out over the firth, I had to admit, I saw my future here, with a husband and family, living close to my brothers. Not that I'd admit that to Lachlan and Thane, because they'd start building the bloody house right away. Overprotective as they were, they wanted me closer.

Now more than ever, and I didn't blame them one bit.

Ery pulled up outside Thane's house, and I knew by the many cars in both of my brothers' driveways that we were likely the last to arrive. As I got out of the car, I noted a new black Defender that I didn't recognize, and wondered who it belonged to. Before I could ask Ery if she knew, Regan opened the door to her and Thane's place.

"Hey, you okay?" Regan asked as I reached her.

I gave her a hug and lied, telling her I was fine.

"Bullshit," she murmured but gave me an understanding smile, her dimples barely indenting her pretty cheeks before disappearing again.

"Where are the kids?" I asked as we stepped inside the hallway.

"Watching a little TV before bath time." Regan gestured toward Lachlan's. "I just wanted to pop my head out and say hey, but everyone is next door. Thane's already there."

"You go be with them." Eredine shrugged out of her jacket. "I'll watch the kids."

"You don't have to do that."

"I want to."

Suspecting Ery was evading anything to do with the investigation, I gave Regan a pointed look. "Let her."

Regan studied Ery for a second, mulling something over in her intelligent gaze. I remembered before she first arrived in Ardnoch, Lachlan had called her a vapid princess. It wouldn't be the first time my brother was one hundred percent wrong about a person. He'd been wrong about Robyn in the beginning too.

"Okay," Regan decided. "Arro, why don't you head next door? If the kids see you, you'll never get away."

I laughed under my breath, knowing it was true, wishing I could see them. Eilidh and Lewis always brightened my day. But I decided to wait for Regan outside, wanting someone with me when I walked through my big brother's door.

A few minutes later, after Regan had left Ery with the kids, the two of us let ourselves into Lachlan and Robyn's.

"In here!" I heard Lachlan call.

I'd missed him.

Kicking off our shoes, Regan and I strolled into the open-plan living space, much like Thane's in architecture but different in style. While Thane's had a more traditional feel to the kitchen, Lachlan's kitchen was ultramodern, with clean lines, hidden handles, and all.

My family gathered in his living room, and my gaze zeroed in on Mac. He watched me, almost predatory, from his seat on the recliner, and I quickly looked away as Lachlan and Robyn stood to greet me. They'd already seen Regan, so I was lucky enough to be showered with all their affection.

"I hope you enjoyed your honeymoon, despite all this crap," I said apologetically.

"Don't worry about it," Robyn assured me. "We had a great time."

"Though we were eager to get home by the time we found out what was happening here," Lachlan admitted. "Robyn plagued me about five times a day to change our flight, and nothing but sex would shut her up. It was exhausting."

Robyn shot him a dirty look, and he flashed her a wicked grin.

"It sounds like you were very worried," I observed dryly.

My brother's wife was serious as she said, "We really were. I'm glad we're home. Let's talk about it." She gestured to the massive corner sofa occupied by Thane, Regan, and Arran.

"Can I get you a drink, Arro?" Lachlan offered.

"I'm all right, thanks."

Ignoring Mac's penetrating gaze, I sat down on the sofa and was joined by Robyn. Lachlan took the armchair next to Mac's recliner.

"Oh." My eldest brother got up again and reached into his back pocket, pulling out a fob. "Before I forget." He handed it to me, and I took it as he explained, "Black Defender outside is yours to use until you get yours back from the police."

"Thanks." I smiled gratefully. "They said by the end of the week, so I can return this to you then."

"Maybe see how you like driving it first." Lachlan sat back down. "It's safer than your old one."

I had a sentimental attachment to my Defender, which we both knew. "I can't get rid of Dad's car."

Lachlan gave me a smile that didn't quite reach his eyes. "We'd put it in storage. I just want you safe."

"It is safe," I insisted gently.

"This one is *safer* and it would make your big brother sleep better at night knowing you're in a safe vehicle."

Damn him. He pulled out the big guns there.

"We'll talk about that later," Robyn said, drawing my focus. Her expression was hard, determined, and I recognized it from when she was investigating Mac's stabbing. "Any word from the police regarding prints?"

"No prints so far. They want to do a few more interior checks, but I don't think whoever did this broke into my car."

"We need to think about where this is going next," Mac put in, and I forced myself to look at him. Our eyes met and held, his roiling with emotion I didn't want to contemplate. "The next note," he continued, his voice a wee bit gruffer than before, "was WHY WON'T YOU SEE ME? It was written on Post-it notes all over Lachlan's stage office. It's when the tone of the notes changed."

"But should we be looking at this from the same perspective as before?" Regan asked. "I mean, this could just be some asshole playing a prank."

"That's true," Arran agreed.

"Yeah, it could be." Robyn nodded. "But considering what this family has been through this past year, we need to be extra cautious. For now, we're taking this seriously, so I want suspects."

"I'm with Robyn," Mac said.

I didn't look at him this time. It was too difficult to stay numb when I looked at him.

"Suspects, then?" Lachlan asked. "Thoughts, Arro?"

"I can't think of anyone specific."

"There's that Duncan guy," Arran said.

"Duncan?" Mac's voice was like a whip.

"A guy at work." I glowered at Arran. "But not someone I suspect. He's a bit of a misogynistic dick, but that's a personality flaw, not an excuse to indict him."

"But you said he'd looked into you," Arran argued, and then turned to Mac and Lachlan. "He made a comment about her thinking she was above everything because of her family, because of you and Brodan being movie stars."

"I'm adding him to the list." Robyn produced a tablet as if out of nowhere and scrawled his name across the screen. "Surname?"

I reluctantly gave it to her but added, "I don't think he's a strong suspect at all."

"Duly noted."

"I'm leaning toward a crazed fan of Lucy's," Mac continued. "I've already got our PI investigating any known or obsessive Wainwright fans. We're still trying to get someone to go in and speak with her to see if she'll tell us anything useful, but she's denying visitation."

Robyn noted all this and mused, "Why you, Arro? I think we should talk about that as a starting point. No one else has received notes, so our clue to who this is lies with you."

Thane sighed. "If it is a crazy stalker fan of Lucy's, it could just be that they've fixated on Arro because she's the only adult female Adair. Or was until recently."

"She's also gorgeous," Regan added. "Could be fixated on her because of her looks, as sad and shallow as that is."

I smirked unhappily. "As much as I appreciate the compliment, I think it's more likely that they saw me as the weak link. Perhaps a man who sees women as the weaker sex but recognizes Robyn isn't an easy target, considering she's the reason Lucy failed to kill her and Lachlan." I flinched just thinking about how close I'd come to losing my big brother. How close Mac had come to losing his daughter.

Our eyes met like two magnets, and I saw the fear roil in his beautiful, dark gaze. He remembered too.

I looked quickly away before he pierced my numbness.

"Why not Regan or Eredine, then?" Robyn prodded the theory.

"We're not family," Regan answered, and Thane could've gotten whiplash with how fast he jerked his head to glare at her. She hurried to explain, "I mean, not officially Adairs."

He grimaced and glanced around at us all. "We're psychoanalyzing a ghost. All this is just guessing. We need more information."

"Working on it," Mac replied through gritted teeth. "Believe me."

"What if we stop looking at it from the Lucy perspective?" Arran offered quietly. "What if it's nothing to do with her?

The notes from the case were well publicized, thanks to the media. This could just be someone terrorizing Arro because she is …" His worried gaze met mine. "Because she *is* the target."

A horrible silence filled the room at the thought, and I couldn't hold back a shiver or the way my heart raced with fear. Thane reached out to squeeze my hand, and I held it, grateful.

Finally, Robyn cleared her throat. "Okay, say worst-case scenario, this is about Arro. Who would want to hurt you?"

I'd been racking my brain for weeks trying to figure that out for myself. "I can only think of people like Duncan—people who I've had the odd confrontation with. A girl I went to college with, a project manager at the start of my career … but that's grasping at straws. Everyone has had a confrontation with someone in their life."

"I want names," Mac demanded.

I opened my mouth to argue when Robyn said bluntly, "Guy."

It was like my heart leapt at the name, and I glowered at my sister-in-law. Not that Guy hadn't crossed my mind, but I knew men like him. They were bullies who fed on the weak, and he'd have moved on to someone he thought was weaker since he knew he couldn't best me. Besides, it was a moment in my life I'd still not quite gotten to grips with emotionally. And there was the small matter of Mac not knowing about it, and I didn't want him to know about it unless necessary.

"No." I glowered at Robyn.

She grimaced apologetically. "Arro, I know not everyone knows, but I think he's worth looking into."

"Why?" Mac asked, and I couldn't look at him.

"Who is Guy?" Arran asked.

"Arro's ex-boyfriend," Lachlan explained. "He was the chef at the estate, but …"

Looking at my brother as he silently asked for permission to tell the story, I shrugged off the shame that was desperate to crawl over me. Even though I knew what Guy had done wasn't my fault, I blamed myself for not seeing the bully in him. I wanted to hide from my mistake, but it was my story to tell. I still didn't think he had anything to do with this, but Mac, for one, wouldn't leave it alone until he knew.

"We dated for about three months. It was fine. We were fine. But gradually, Guy started acting jealous over other men." I couldn't look at Mac because it wasn't over other men. It was over Mac, specifically. The night of the ceilidh, Guy lost it after watching Mac and I interact. I shouldn't have been flirting with another man while seeing Guy, and I owned that, but I hadn't deserved what happened to me.

"One night we got into a fight about his jealousy, and he …" I took a deep breath and exhaled slowly, shakily. "He knocked me about."

"He beat the shit out of her," Lachlan bit out angrily.

"He did what?"

The room grew still, wary, beneath the weight of Mac's quiet rage.

I couldn't not look at him.

"Why the fuck wasn't I told about this?" he asked Lachlan with calm fury as his gaze swept over to me. I felt pinned to the chair by it. Guilty. Like I'd betrayed him. What the fuck? "Is that why he left? How the hell did you hide this from me?" Why had I hidden it from him was his real question.

"I stayed away from you for a while and wore makeup over the fading bruises."

"Why?" His breathing was harsh.

Why didn't I tell him?

I couldn't find the words. I'd kept it from him, thinking he loved me and that he'd kill any man who tried to hurt me. But now, I didn't know what to think.

Mac had proven that he loved my brother and this family more than he'd ever loved me. If he could hurt me like he had, then maybe he wouldn't care like I thought he would.

But that was a lie I told myself right then, because his reaction confused me all the more.

Mac looked like a man who would kill anyone who hurt me.

Fucking arsehole.

"Why didn't you tell me?" Mac barked impatiently.

"For fuck's sake, Mac." Lachlan scowled. "We didn't tell you because you'd not long been stabbed, and we all knew if you found out, you'd kill Guy and probably open up your stitches doing it."

"Did he do anything else?" Mac's expression was stark.

"No," I hurried to answer, knowing what he'd feared. "Nothing like that."

"Arro fought him off."

"And where were you?" Mac directed his anger at Lachlan. "What the fuck did you do about it?"

"Dad," Robyn warned gently.

Lachlan narrowed his eyes at Mac. "Want to come at me again?"

"Lachlan." Robyn switched her warning to her husband.

"No." Lachlan stood and Mac followed suit, while my pulse raced madly as the tension escalated. "You want someone to hit for this, Mac, is that it?"

"Stop it." Robyn marched between them. "Now."

Lachlan stared past his wife to her father, who only looked old enough to be her big brother. "I'm not the person you want to take down for this, Mac, so don't fucking come at me with your accusations and rage."

"I just want to know why I wasn't told about this! Not just then." He glowered at me now. "But now! An ex-boyfriend beats the shit out of you, then he's pretty high on our suspect list."

"Why?" His anger was boiling my blood now as I stood too. "He's just a bully who couldn't get the better of me. Someone like that needs a weaker target than himself."

"Uh, true," Robyn said, sounding wary. "But there's more to it than just him hitting you, Arro. Lachlan punched him." She patted her dad's shoulder and tried to defuse the tension by joking, "Hope that makes you feel better."

Mac shot her a half-annoyed, half-tender look that caused a pang of unnamed emotion in my chest.

"And he fired him ... but here's the kicker—"

"I ruined him," Lachlan finished, staring at his wife in dawning realization. "I put the word out in the industry not to hire him. He couldn't get a decent job anywhere. Fuck!"

"You did what?" I whispered, suddenly filling with dread. "I didn't know that." That changed everything.

"He could be after revenge," Thane said grimly.

"I'll look into it." Mac stared reproachfully at me as if I'd wronged him. Well, screw that! I lifted my chin, refusing to offer any kind of apology for keeping this from him. I didn't bloody know the important part, did I?

"I'll find out where he is."

"But you won't do anything," Robyn ordered. "Right, Dad?"

Mac stared down at her and eventually sighed. "I won't do anything, wee birdie." His voice was gentle, the way it only ever was for Robyn. Then his expression hardened again as he lifted it to meet mine. "But the prick just made it to the top of my suspect list."

15

ARRO

I hated to admit it, but I bloody loved the new Defender. It had all the bells and whistles, and its computer was awesome. Biffy Clyro's "Instant History" had never sounded so good on a sound system. It was more comfortable and luxurious, and it handled the road so much better. In my older model, I had to slow way down into corners for fear of rolling. This one was a Dynamic, and my God, did it take corners like a dream.

Bloody Nora, I wanted to keep this car.

I'd succumbed to its seduction with embarrassing speed and experienced more than a flicker of guilt as I pulled up outside the Portakabin at our Lairg site. I couldn't get rid of Dad's Defender. But Lachlan was right. We needed to put it in storage. For too long, I'd let sentiment win.

I climbed the steps to the cabin and unlocked the door. It was barely light out, and I was the first one on-site, arriving a few hours early. But sometimes, I liked to get here before everyone else so I could answer emails and plow through my administrative jobs, enabling me to fully concentrate on-site when everyone else showed. Marcello was always an hour early to work, so that meant I had to be even earlier if I wanted alone time to get through a good portion of tasks.

I pushed open the door, hit the light switch on my right, and froze.

Fear flushed through me, hot and instantaneous.

My desk, computer, and the walls surrounding it were covered in Post-it notes.

Marcello's desk behind mine was untouched.

I knew what was written on them before I even took a step toward the Post-its.

Why won't you see me?

SLAMMING THE DOOR BEHIND ME, I hurried to lock it, my fingers trembling around my keys. Then I fumbled for my phone, peering out the one small window in the cabin at the dark forest beyond the parked Defender.

I hit Lachlan's name, and it only rang three times before my big brother picked up. "Morning, sweetheart. This is early."

Something inside me soothed at his voice. "Lachlan, I've just arrived at the Portakabin at my site in Lairg. There are Post-it notes all over my desk."

There was a moment of a silence before, "Fuck. Call the police right now."

"No. No police. Lachlan, this is my job. I can't have this being a crime scene. I can't bring this into my work. Please, can you come or send Robyn?"

"We need to tell the police, Arro."

"Robyn *was* the police. Please."

"Arro, we can't be foolish here. This is serious."

Indignant, I snapped, "Do you not think I know that? This is happening to me. But I worked hard for this job, and I won't have my position here affected by this shit. I won't let this creep have the satisfaction. This stays between us."

Lachlan sighed heavily. "Are you alone?"

So alone. "Yes."

"I left for Inverness at the crack of bloody dawn, so I'm too far away, but I'm sending someone over now."

"Not Mac."

"Why?" Lachlan bit out. "What's going on between you two?"

"Uh, nothing. I just … I don't want to worry him," I said lamely.

"Too late. I texted him as soon as you called. You'll stay on the phone with me until he arrives. I'm texting him as we speak to inform him you don't want the police involved. I'm sure that will go over well."

Wonderful.

"Is it the same words?" Lachlan asked quietly.

"Yeah. 'Why don't you see me?'"

My big brother muttered a curse under his breath, then vowed, "We will figure out who's doing this, Arro."

I stared out at the darkness, my pulse racing as I imagined someone watching me. "I believe you," I whispered.

Only five minutes later, after making small talk to distract me from my fear, Lachlan hung up when I told him Mac had pulled onto the site. A different apprehension filled me as the tall, powerful figure of Mackennon Galbraith cut across the muddy yard. I opened the door and then retreated into the cabin as he hurried up the steps. He was so tall, he had to duck his head to enter. His gaze moved to me first, his shoulders relaxing. "You're okay?"

"As good as anyone can be in a situation like this."

His features turned to granite, and I suddenly pitied the poor bastard who was doing this. Between Mac and my brothers, whoever this was, they were really taking a chance with their life.

Mac's attention cut to the Post-it notes, and as he approached them, he pulled on a pair of disposable latex gloves and unfolded a large Ziploc bag. He reached for a Post-it, scowling at it before he put it in the bag. "I'll have my friend in forensics look at them for prints, but I doubt we'll find any." Mac took every single note off my desk, computer, and wall, and put them into the bag. "When do Marcello and the team arrive?"

"Marcello will probably be here in about half an hour. I come in early every morning to do admin."

Mac zipped the bag closed. The cabin was clear, every inch free of Post-it notes.

Free of the crime.

If only I could say the same about myself. Anxiety wearied me, wondering who the shadow at my back was.

"I'm putting security on you," Mac announced.

I bristled. "No, you bloody are not."

He took a step toward me, and I had to stop myself from retreating. "Arro, the next message your brother received arrived along with a deer carcass."

I flinched.

"If you won't involve the police again, then I need security on you and …" He straightened, his expression set, determined. "It'll be me. I'll talk to Lachlan. We'll put Jock in charge at the estate so I can guard you."

The very thought of being forced into proximity with Mac for the foreseeable future made my palms sweat. "No."

His nostrils flared like a goddamn bull preparing to charge. "I'm one of the few men on our team with bodyguard experience, and I trust me with your safety more than anyone else."

"Well, I don't," I snapped. No way was I spending day in

and day out with the one man who made me feel out of control. "It's a hard no."

"For Christ's sake!" Mac's famous patience abandoned him. "Put our shit to the side and let me take care of you while this is going on."

"Our shit?" My body propelled forward with growing rage. "Our shit?" Is that what we were calling the devastation between us?

"You know what I mean." He raised a hand, palm out defensively.

"No, I actually don't know what you mean because I can't encapsulate the life-changing trials of our entire relationship into something as demeaning as 'our shit.'"

Mac took a breath and stared deep into my eyes. "Don't. Don't warp what I'm saying now to suit how you want to see the situation between us."

"I *want* to see?" My God, did he *want* me to kill him? "No, what happened between us isn't how I want to see it, believe me. If I could erase that entire night from my memory, I would, and unfortunately for you, Mac, it happened the way it happened. End of story."

"Not end of story," he said with far too much calm, patience, and far too much dejection in his countenance.

And something in me broke.

"I know what I did that night was wrong," I whispered harshly. "But I don't know why it was wrong. I keep going over and over it in my mind." My fingers trembled as I pressed them to my mouth, trying to find the words.

Mac's anguished expression only angered me.

"Did I read too much into every moment between us? Was it all in my head? Did I assault you?"

Shock flared in his eyes and he stepped toward me. "No, Arro. Fuck, no."

"Then why?" I tried to pierce his gaze so I could finally

understand what the hell was going on in this man's head. "Why did you reject me like I was a stranger to you? You couldn't have humiliated me more. Why?" I suddenly raged, everything swelling up and out of me as I shrieked, "Tell me why!"

"Because I was in fucking pain!" Mac roared.

I flinched back, shocked into silence.

He took a shuddering breath. "You were hurting me, Arro, and I just needed you to leave."

"Hurting you?"

A hard darkness shadowed Mac's face. I'd seen that brooding look before, but rarely. Until that moment, I'd never understood what put that look on his face, but as he spoke, I began to understand. "You can't see what I am," he said hoarsely, "but I know what I am, Arrochar. Maybe there isn't a man out there worthy of you, but I know ..."

Mac drew closer until I had to tilt my head to keep his gaze. "I know for a fact that it isn't me. Lachlan would probably get over it if you and I claimed each other, but it wouldn't take you or him long to realize I'm not who you think I am. I'd disappoint you. And then I'd lose you both. Something I can't risk. And you coming to my home, pushing me, offering me the thing I want most and can't have ... it killed me."

His eyes were bright with emotion, and it was physically painful to witness. "It hurt finding the strength to say no. It hurts keeping my distance from you in that way. But it's better than you despising me."

I shook my head, confused. "And you thought humiliating me would, what? Endear me to you?"

"Arro—"

"I'm not some cold icon of feminine perfection, Mac!" Somehow his confession was worse, the bold truth worse. "I'm real! I'm flesh and blood." I pounded my chest. "I'm flawed and brutal and weak and strong and sorry and fucked-up like every other person who's spent more than two seconds on this bloody planet!" Tears streamed down my face before I could stop them as my voice dropped to a near whisper. "I deserve more from you. I deserve more than to be put on some lonely, god-awful pedestal, to be used as an object for your self-flagellation and repentance for God knows what in your past. When someone tells you they love you, you don't get to say, 'I don't deserve your love,' and think that somehow exempts you from the consequences of rejecting them. You're not exempt, Mac. No matter your reasons, you rejected me like I was nothing and nobody to you, and you spit in the face of my love and did it in a way that made me feel small. Wrong and guilty." I ignored the horrified devastation on his face and whispered, "You hurt *me* to save *you*."

"Arro ..." A tear slipped down his cheek, and it almost broke me, but I couldn't let it soften my determination to face the truth between us.

An exhausting grief swept over me as I stared at this man I'd loved but no longer trusted, at least in the way I had before. "So I suppose you're right ... you don't deserve me because everyone deserves someone who loves them through everything. Through *anything*. And maybe it's an impossible wish, but I want to be loved by someone who would die before deliberately hurting me."

"It wasn't deliberate," Mac argued, a little of that fire, that fight, returning to him. "I did it to protect you. It was the wrong move. I was wrong, Arro. I admit it. I made a mistake. But it wasn't deliberate."

"Too little, too late." I swiped at the tear tracks on my cheeks because tears were of little use to me. To either of us. The pain of knowing why he'd hurt me didn't change the truth.

"I don't believe that," Mac said, just as we heard a car pulling up outside. "I refuse to believe that."

"Don't." My expression softened a little. "It's too late for us. But not for you. Don't keep making this mistake, Mac. Whatever is eating you, whatever is poisoning your mind, go talk to someone so that the next time a woman tells you she's in love with you, you can say it back." Even then, in all my conviction, the very thought of him with another woman made me die inside.

Mac shook his head slowly and answered with a quietness that haunted me. "Unless that woman is you, I'll never say it back."

Before I could scramble to find the words to address what was an inadvertent declaration of love, Mac's gaze moved beyond my shoulders, and he sighed. "Marcello's here."

He straightened and like he hadn't just set off an emotional bomb between us, said, "I'm going back to the estate to talk with your brother, and then I'll return. Until we figure this out"—he gestured with the bag of Post-its—"I am your shadow from the moment you leave the house until the moment you get home and lock the door behind you. I'll work out a system with the team so someone is watching your house at night. No arguments, Arro. This is happening. I'll be back soon."

And before I could protest, he stormed out as Marcello walked in.

"Good morning to you too!" Marcello yelled over his shoulder at Mac in sarcasm. Then he turned to me and said, "Who pissed in his coffee?"

I couldn't answer. I could only stare out the window as Mac jumped into his SUV, swung it around, and drove out of sight. As much as I wanted to shrug off his implied words of love or the realization that the guilt and shame Mac carried regarding his relationship with Robyn was much deeper than

I'd thought, I couldn't. In fact, his lack of self-worth was shocking. Destructive. It had ruined us.

And I wanted to fix it. I wanted to show Mac how wrong he was. To make him see his good.

But with so much anger still between us, such broken trust, I was smart enough to know that I couldn't be the one to make him see it when right now, I could only see the worst he'd wreaked on my life.

Out of nowhere, the dam I'd built broke, and a loud sob burst forth before I could stop it. Uncontrollable sobs racked through me, and I heard the vague rumble of Marcello's surprise before his arms came around me.

For the second time in as many days, I let a friend hold me through my heartbreak.

16

MAC

Leaving my car in a multistory car park, it took me less than five minutes to walk to the building on the banks of the River Ness. I hated being this far from Arro, but Jock was guarding her, and there had been no further incidents these past few days.

Still, I was concerned by the escalation, considering the perpetrator had left the last two notes within less than forty-eight hours of the other. That Arro would barely talk to me wasn't helping. I'd discovered she'd blocked my number on her phone and was reluctant to unblock me for security purposes. She'd done it, though. But it fucking hurt that she'd blocked me in the first place.

Which brought me here.

I'd never have considered something like this, but Billy's advice plagued me for weeks. And during our many long conversations since she'd come hurtling back into my life, Robyn had talked about her experiences with therapy. She considered therapy something ongoing that helped her stay in a good place mentally and emotionally, and she had regular video conferences with her therapist back in

Boston. It was therapy that had helped her face her fear of facing me.

Arro's words at the Portakabin were the final push I needed.

Because it finally hit me that what I'd said in return was true. I'd never love anyone like I loved Arro, and if I was to make things right between us, I had to get my head sorted.

I looked at the main door, at the entrance buzzer with the therapist's name beside it, and despite my determination, I wavered. I considered walking away.

Yet *her* expression filled my vision. Arro. Her torment. Shame. Rejection. Pain.

All of it, I had caused.

Everything I felt, everything I'd never wanted to put on someone I loved, I'd left those emotions with her. I couldn't go on this way.

Even if Arrochar never forgave me, I couldn't go on this way.

I pressed the buzzer.

Not long later, I found myself in an office that wasn't overly large with views toward the River Ness. My therapist introduced herself and asked me to call her Iona. She was a little older than me and had a quiet, soothing voice and a relaxed way about her.

It didn't help.

I wanted to escape. I wanted to turn around and get as far from this building as possible.

My jacket was too warm over my jumper and the jumper too tight across my chest.

"Would you like to take a seat?" Iona gestured to one of the twin sofas opposite each other in the center of the room. Ignoring the one she pointed at, I took its mate because it faced the exit.

Iona smiled pleasantly and sat down across from me. I

wasn't expecting her to dive right into psychoanalysis. "Can I ask why you chose that seat?"

It wasn't her fault I was desperate to get out of here, so I answered politely, "I don't like sitting with my back to a door. I was a police officer, then moved into security—private bodyguard, head of security on a private estate ... just programmed to know where the exits are and to be aware of them."

The counselor nodded. "That makes sense, Mackennon. Though, I should assure you, you don't have to do your own psychoanalyzing just yet."

I smirked. "I knew where you were going with the question."

She nodded again.

"And you can call me Mac."

"Okay, Mac." She settled more comfortably, crossing one leg over the other, a digital tablet on her knee where she'd already scribbled something down. "So ... I have the information you sent over when you booked the appointment, but can you tell me what brought you to therapy?"

"Why I'm here?" Fuck, I didn't even know where to start, and the thought of spilling it to this stranger made that tightness heavy on my chest again. How the hell did Billy and Robyn do this? I'd spent my whole life dealing internally with my own shit, except for the times I'd confided in Lachlan and Arro. And that was only because I trusted them both with my life. To unleash all that, all that darkness buried underneath the Mac everyone thought they knew, to a stranger?

I'd competed and won the US National Jujitsu Championships, chased down some of Boston's worst criminals, guarded Lachlan with my body against threat, faced the daughter I hadn't fought hard enough for, and been stabbed three times in the gut.

Therapy was scarier than all that combined.

"I'm not sure I should have come." I made a move to stand, and Iona gestured me back down.

"Sit, please. I understand it can be more difficult for men to come forward and talk about their feelings. Especially men of your generation. Not a stereotype, but a fact. So I won't badger you to tell me how you feel right now. Just talk to me, like you would a friend, and tell me what *circumstances* led you to come here today."

That tightness crawled up my throat, but before I could give up, walk out, wrap my pride around myself to keep me warm at night, I admitted, "I broke the heart of the woman I love."

I winced as the words echoed between us, not just for their painful truth but because it seemed a betrayal of myself and Arro to voice something so personal to this stranger.

Iona studied me for a moment and observed, "It can feel very odd at first. To confess intimate details of your life to a stranger, but think of it as an opportunity, Mac. I am the one person in your life who has a completely unbiased perspective. I'm not here to judge. I'm here to be the ears you need and to help you understand how you ended up on my couch. And once we understand that, we can work on strategies to help you move forward with your life."

I unclenched my hands, not realizing how badly I'd fisted them. The white of my knuckles colored again. "I ... uh ..." Where did I start? "I've done things, things I'm not proud of, and I think she deserves better than that. Arro. Her name is Arro. But I hurt her trying to keep her away, and I'm ... I'm concerned I can't fix things between us."

"All right. Would it be okay if we went back to the beginning? Can you tell me how you met Arro?"

So I did. I told her how we met when she was only fourteen because I was Lachlan's bodyguard. That our friendship didn't cement itself until her father died when she was in her midtwenties and I helped her through it. How we kissed on New Year's Eve all those years ago, and it changed everything between us ... and nothing. Because I wouldn't allow it.

I told her about Robyn, about our estrangement, about the Lucy Wainwright case, about Lachlan falling for Robyn. I spoke more than I had in God knows how long. To my shock, it all just bloody poured out of me. But these were merely facts. I didn't tell her how I felt about any of it.

"So you're concerned about losing Lachlan's friendship, which is complicated by the fact that he's now married to your daughter?" Iona asked when I paused.

"Well, when you say it like that, it sounds almost incestuous," I joked.

"No." Iona chuckled. "But complex. Like many families. Do you think there are really these obstacles standing in the way of your overall satisfaction with life, i.e., the happiness that being with Arro would bring you? Or is the real problem your sense of self-worth?"

I considered it and answered honestly, "Maybe both."

"Why don't we go back into your past even further? How does that sound to you?"

"Uncomfortable. Painful."

"Then we should definitely go back and discuss why that is. We'll take our time. We'll go at your pace, and we'll pause when you need to."

I shifted, my gaze flicking to the clock.

For Arro, I reminded myself.

Looking back at Iona, I nodded. "All right, then."

"Okay. Let's start with your early years, Mac. Tell me about your parents."

"My mum wasn't in my life, and I suppose you could say my dad wasn't really either ..."

SCHEDULING the therapy session before my jujitsu class seemed like an efficient idea, but in hindsight, probably not the best. I was nothing short of shell-shocked as I walked into the sports center where I'd been teaching martial arts for years. The club was run by former Scottish champion Hayley Jones, and I'd agreed to teach her adult beginner's class on Thursdays. I taught the white belts until they were ready to move on to Hayley's classes as a blue belt. It meant mostly teaching them guard work, but now and then, Hayley needed me to cover her senior classes if I was available.

I enjoyed teaching.

But tonight, I wanted to go home to the quiet of a dark room.

That wasn't an option. I still had to relieve Jock of his guard duties at Arro's. Somehow I got through the class on autopilot, though a student or two asked if I was all right. I'd shrugged off their concern, finished up class, and finally got on the road back to Ardnoch. The hour-long drive home finally gave me the quiet I needed.

However, I couldn't decide how I felt about the therapy session with Iona.

I definitely knew it was uncomfortable as fuck.

I'd told the woman things about my childhood only Lachlan and Robyn knew. Things I hadn't even told Arro.

She asked me if I thought they were things Arro *should* know about me if I felt about her the way I did.

Why hadn't I told Arro?

For a moment, it stumped me.

Iona told me to really think about it.

Arrochar's eyes flashed across my vision. In my mind, she wore an expression that hadn't crossed her face in weeks, the one she wore every time she'd looked upon me—until that night.

What was that expression?

"Hero worship," I murmured.

She looked at me like I was her hero.

Fuck.

That was why it was so difficult to tell her about Robyn. It was why I tried to keep the shittier parts of my past from her, because I didn't want her to stop looking at me like that. Like I could fix any problem and battle any demon for her.

But she didn't stop looking at you that way after you told her about Robyn.

The truth didn't scare her off.

My lies had.

Hands clenched around the wheel, I focused on the drive, feeling far more drained than I could've imagined. If this was therapy, it was brutal.

The sight of the Welcome to Ardnoch sign was a relief; even more so was Arro's cul-de-sac and her bungalow.

Her home made me smile. Arro was never about flash, but about comfort and space. She'd told me she bought the bungalow because it was big enough for all her books and the knickknacks Lachlan had agreed she could take from the castle. My smile transformed to a frown, however, when I saw not Jock's vehicle out front but Robyn's.

Where the hell was Jock?

Parking on the street, I hurried up Arro's front walk. Her curtains were drawn, so I couldn't see anything but faint light between the cracks.

Robyn answered after I rang the doorbell.

"Robbie," I greeted, confused, peering past her into the hallway for Arro. "What are you doing here? Where's Jock?"

My daughter leaned against the doorjamb, casual, relaxed in posture, but there was something calculating in her eyes.

"Jock's fiancé is sick, so he had to go home to take care of him and his son. I said I'd guard Arro until you got back."

I scowled at that. "Putting you both in the crosshairs. Wonderful."

She smirked. "Yeah, Lachlan wasn't too happy about it, either, but I reminded him that just because I married him doesn't mean I stop being who I am. And we both know I can handle myself."

It wasn't said with arrogance. It was a statement of fact. Pride swelled inside me. While I'd always worry about Robyn, as was a father's prerogative, how she'd handled herself with Fergus and Lucy soothed those worries. Robyn was strong, capable, and well-trained.

And suddenly it dawned on me, making me feel stupid for not having recognized it sooner, but that was what Arro needed. I'd been so set on being the one to protect her that I hadn't recognized what she really needed was to feel like she could protect herself.

"You're letting the cold in." Arro appeared in the doorway beside Robyn. She flicked me an annoyed look I'd almost grown used to. Anything was preferable to the devastation in her expression when we'd argued in the cabin. "Mac."

"Arro. I'm just back from my jujitsu class, and I've decided you're coming with me every Thursday from now on."

Her face clouded over. "I'm not uprooting my schedule for this shit. If you need to be somewhere, you be there, and I'll be here."

"Not so I can keep an eye on you," I answered with more patience than I felt, "but to train. It's time you learned how to defend yourself."

This seemed to shock her into silence for a few seconds before she replied, "Well, I'd rather train with Robyn. I've been meaning to, anyway, since last year."

Robyn pushed away from the jamb, looking between us

167

with that same intelligent gaze that seemed determined to uncover our secrets. Whatever she saw in my eyes caused her to reply, "Nah, you're better off with Dad. He knows what he's doing."

Arro looked like she'd been betrayed. "But … Regan said if it weren't for your training, she'd never have gotten away from Austin."

"Yeah, but that was defensive groundwork stuff, and a lot of that comes from jujitsu," Robyn explained. "Which Dad teaches. Specifically to beginners. Besides, he's trained in RBSD—reality-based self-defense. Close combat. It's what you're looking for."

"I don't think so," Arro answered mulishly.

Robyn opened her mouth to respond, but I beat her to it. "Do you want to feel in control right now or rely on other people to protect you?"

"Fuck you," she snapped.

"Whoa." Robyn stepped outside to stand in front of me like a shield. "I don't know what's going on between you, but one, you don't talk to him like that—"

"Robbie—"

"No, Dad." She shook her head, glowering at Arro. "I know you're having a hard time, but just no. You don't talk to him like that. And two, take the damn lessons. For all our peace of mind. It would be good for us all to know you can handle yourself."

Arro stared blankly at Robyn and replied tonelessly, "One, I've been in Mac's life for a long time and you have no idea about our relationship, so I'll talk to him however I damn well please, and two, I do want to train but not with him. Can't someone else do it?"

"No." Robyn lifted her chin stubbornly. "You'll train with Dad every Thursday. Maybe it'll help you work out whatever problem you have with him."

"You're not the boss of me, Robyn Adair. I'm technically your elder, you know."

"Then act like it and take up an offer that could save your life."

The grim reality of the truth in that statement made my heart lurch. When a flicker of fear crossed Arro's gaze, even more so, I wanted to reach out and hold her.

"Fine," Arro snapped angrily, then looked up at me. "*You* can't come in. 'Night, Robyn." She slammed the door in our faces.

We were silent a moment and then I let out a long exhale as I squeezed Robyn's shoulders. "You don't need to stick up for me, wee birdie. I can handle myself, and I don't want to come between you two."

Robyn looked up at me. "You're my dad. I don't like anyone hurting your feelings, no matter who they are."

God, what the hell did I do to deserve her?

I pulled her into my arms, kissed the top of her head, and then set her back gently before I slipped and broke down about everything. "Let's get you home." I walked to her car and waited as she strolled after me.

Robyn didn't get in. She leaned against the driver's door and studied me thoughtfully. "What's going on, Dad?" she asked in soft concern.

"I ..." I looked back at Arro's house, that familiar ache growing sharper and more jagged in my chest every day. "I ... let's just say I hurt her feelings. Badly."

"Dad ..." Robyn frowned sympathetically. "You know I *know*. And Lachlan does too."

"You know nothing," I said gently.

A flicker of something like hurt crossed her face, and I bit back a curse.

And then blurted out, "I saw a therapist today."

Her head jerked back in surprise. "What? Really?"

I instantly regretted telling her. What if I couldn't return to the sessions? What if I couldn't endure putting myself through that again? Would Robyn see that as a failure?

"Hey …" She touched my arm. "First session is rough, huh?"

Surprised, I nodded. "You too?"

"Oh, yeah. It was really hard. Telling a stranger everything I felt without censoring it to make it more palatable the way I did for the people in my life … yeah, that was like I was slowly scraping off the layers of my skin. Excruciating."

Something in me eased. "So that's normal, then?"

"Yeah, it's normal."

"How did you push through it and return for more?"

"Because the pain I was carrying around on a daily basis was a million times worse, and I wanted to find a way to move on without it," she answered.

Pain I'd caused.

"Don't, Dad."

I nodded, swallowing the bitter emotion. "That's one of the reasons I bit the bullet and went. To deal with how I feel about not being there for you. I want to"—I heaved a massive sigh, trying to alleviate the pressure on my chest—"I want to do better. I fucked up with you, and we can't ever get those years back. I don't want to keep repeating that mistake."

"We went over this. What happened between us wasn't just your fault. Mom had a hand in it too."

I would never lay the blame for my part in it at Stacey's feet. Yes, she'd done wrong, but she'd done it because I'd hurt her. She'd loved me, and I'd never really loved her back. If I hadn't stayed in the relationship because she fell pregnant, I wouldn't have led her on, and maybe things would've turned out differently. "I stayed away because I thought you deserved better, and all I did was hurt you more."

Emotion brightened Robyn's eyes, eyes she'd inherited

from me. "Do you know why I forgave you for all that and decided I wanted you in my life as my dad?"

I shook my head—I'd never really understood that kindness. Was only grateful for it.

"Because I know that as much as it hurt me, I think it hurt you just as much. I see that. I feel it. I've always been an action-over-words kind of person, and from the moment I came back into your life, you have been there for me every step of the way."

She squeezed my arm again as I choked down the emotion. "I'm glad you're going to therapy because you need to work this out and start seeing yourself for who you really are. I don't want you making that same mistake over and over again either. I don't want my dad to end up alone when there's"—her attention flickered to the house and then back to me—"someone who loves him like he deserves."

I pushed words out through the constriction in my throat, "She might never forgive me. I might never have that with her."

She raised an eyebrow. "But you're ready to try?"

"Well, the therapy is a starting point. I know I'm useless to her as I am, but maybe if I can get my head screwed on straight, it might work between us. *If* she forgives me."

"I think that's great."

Apprehension filled me. "I hate to ask, but can you not mention this to Lachlan yet? I want to be the one to discuss this with him when I'm ready."

"You got it. I won't say a word," she promised.

Overwhelming love filled me. "I'm so grateful for you, wee birdie."

Robyn reached out to squeeze my hand. "Back at you, Dad."

Dad. That one word was a balm to so many wounds. When Robyn first arrived in Ardnoch, I was Mac. When she

171

started calling me Dad, it was the best goddamn gift in the world.

I'd fought my demons to be a better father to her.

I'd done it.

Gazing at Arro's house, feeling a pull toward it as I always did toward her, I tasted hope on my tongue.

Because if I'd fought my self-destructive thoughts once before, I could do it again.

17

MAC

"Do you think perhaps, Mac, that your mother abandoning you after you were born might be the source of your feelings of worthlessness?"

I swallowed hard at the question. Session two of therapy, and while I'd found it easier to open up about the past this time, I still grappled with Iona's probing questions. "Possibly."

Iona leaned forward slightly. "You've developed what we call a negative thought pattern. Part of the work I do here is cognitive behavioral therapy. An element of that is learning to recognize negative thought patterns and then help you turn them into positive thoughts. You see, your brain is wired to turn a problem or incident in your life into 'your fault.' And surely you know, Mac, that your mother leaving you was not your fault. You were a baby."

"She didn't love me enough to stay," I answered gruffly.

"Not your fault," Iona repeated. "And *her* loss. As for your dad, from what I can tell, you had a fairly close relationship with him, despite his addiction."

"That's true. We tried our best to help him kick his heroin habit, but nothing ever worked with any permanence. He couldn't stand the withdrawals. Even so young, I woke up every morning prepared to find him dead. And that's exactly what eventually happened."

"And how do you feel about his addiction?"

"What do you mean?"

"What were your feelings toward him?"

Confused, I shrugged. "I loved him. I was sad for him."

"And? Remember, you can say anything here, Mac."

"I ... what does it matter? He's dead."

"It matters."

Heart beating a little too hard, I glanced out the window toward the river.

"Be honest with yourself."

"Honest?" I clenched my teeth and then looked at her, irritated she was forcing me to say it. "Honestly? I was raging at him." The words echoed around the room and came back to smack me in the face with guilt.

Iona nodded in understanding. "Can you tell me why?"

"B-because ..." I heaved a sigh. "This ... och, it isn't rational, and I know it."

"Doesn't matter. Feelings don't always need to be rational, Mac, and rarely are in my experience. Why were you furious at him?"

"Because I wasn't enough," I bit out, tears after all these bloody years burning my fucking eyeballs. "I wasn't enough to make him kick the habit. To stay. He left me just like she left me. But I know that isn't fair. I know he couldn't help himself."

"Hold on to that." She leaned in again. "Because that last part is the truth. As much as you feel abandoned by him, addiction is a disease, and he didn't leave you because he wanted to. Did he tell you he loved you, Mac?"

174

I nodded, the tears falling before I could stop them. Embarrassed, I wiped swiftly at them. "All the time," I choked out. "He said it all the time."

"Then believe him over his addiction. He loved you. He didn't want to leave you."

He didn't want to leave me.

He didn't want to leave me.

He. Didn't. Want. To. Leave. Me.

"FROM THE MOMENT your friends assaulted Craig, you tried to stop them?"

After all these years, I could still hear the pounding of feet and fists, of grunts, aggressive taunts and the egging each other on. Cutting through it all was the sound of Craig begging them to stop. "Tried and failed."

Iona tilted her head and studied me in that way I'd grown accustomed to. "Did you want to kill Craig?"

My head jerked back like she'd punched me. "Of course not."

She held up a calming hand. "Did you hit him?"

"No. Like I said, Billy and I tried to get them off. We even fought our own lads, but with our backs turned, Nairn stabbed Craig. Then we ran like fucking cowards."

"But you and Billy found a phone box and called the emergency services?"

"Aye, but we ran. We should've stayed to help him. Maybe if we had, he'd still be alive."

"You were only fifteen, yes?"

I nodded. "Barely."

"So you were a child."

"Nobody was a child on the streets of Govan that year."

"Well, that may have been how you felt, Mac, but physically, mentally, and emotionally, you were barely a teenager. Did you have first aid training?"

Frowning, I shook my head. "Not then."

"So how did you expect to help Craig? You would have impeded the efforts of the paramedics and then found yourself arrested for something you tried to stop."

"I shouldn't have been there in the first place. We'd spent that entire year acting like thugs."

"A mistake. A boyish mistake. I know this because you've proved it by how you've lived your life from that point on, leaving Glasgow to start over and making a living protecting people. That says a lot about who you truly are, Mac, so why are you so focused on using this one incident to determine your identity?"

"I …" I was stumped for an answer because, when she put it like that, it sounded irrational. "I just can't let go of the guilt over not helping him."

"But you *did* help him. Instead of focusing on not staying behind with him, focus on the fact that you put your life in jeopardy by fighting your own friends to protect a stranger. Then, when you couldn't, you made sure the right people got to him. His death is not on you."

"Whoever is coming after our group doesn't believe that."

"If there is someone focused on revenge, Mac, they're mentally unwell, blinded by their grief. You cannot allow those kinds of feelings to manipulate the truth. And the truth is that you tried to do the right thing, and that's all any of us can do."

"I SHOULDN'T HAVE STAYED with her. When Stacey fell pregnant with Robyn, I should have been there for her without being with her."

"Again, Mac, what age were you?"

"Sixteen."

"Say that again and really think about it. Think about how you see a sixteen-year-old now that you are a grown man."

"I was sixteen," I repeated slowly, and a surprising sadness fell over me as I thought about how young a sixteen-year-old is. Still a bairn, really. "I was only sixteen."

Iona nodded slowly. "You weren't even an adult yet, Mac. You might have been very mature for your age, but in other ways, there's no way you could be. You stayed with Stacey because you thought it was the right thing to do."

"But I hurt her so badly that she stood in my way with Robyn. And I let her. Out of guilt."

"Perhaps staying with Stacey was the wrong thing to do. You made a mistake in a relationship, which most of us have done. But you cannot blame yourself for not loving Stacey the way she loved you. We aren't responsible for other people's emotions or actions, Mac. We're only responsible for our own actions, our own responses to their actions, and how we treat them. Were you ever cruel to Stacey? Did you cheat on her? Were you an inadequate father to Robyn when she was a child?"

I shook my head, feeling my chest tighten as the weight of how fucking wrong I'd gotten it came over me. "No. I was a good dad, despite how young I was. And I never betrayed Stacey. I'm not that man. I ... I only ever hurt her by not loving her back in the same way she loved me."

"And that's not a crime. We can't control who we fall in love with any more than Stacey could control falling in love with you. What she could control was her reaction, and placing blame on you, using Robyn as a weapon in your relationship, was wrong, Mac. You need to know she was wrong."

"But do you not understand how I feel?" I asked impatiently. "We've sat here talking about my feelings of abandonment, and I fucking did it to my own kid. It doesn't matter what Stacey did."

"Well, the situation is not so black-and-white as that. But okay, should you have tried harder to see Robyn? Yes."

I blanched but relaxed back into my seat at Iona's confirmation of what I already knew to be true.

"However," Iona continued, "we cannot ignore the causality in this situation, Mac. The causality being that by the time you and Stacey entered this tug-of-war for Robyn, you were already hardwired to believe you didn't deserve good things. Your parents, Craig's death, and your guilt over not returning Stacey's feelings—these all contributed to your negative thought patterns. Now you tell me you and Robyn are in a wonderful place, that you gave her away at her wedding, and she's been very supportive of you coming here to talk with me."

The thought of Robyn filled me with unending pride. I could bloody burst with it. "She's tremendous. I don't know what I did to des—" I cut off.

Iona gave me a small smile. "To deserve her, you were going to say."

I nodded.

"We need to work on this idea that you're deserving or you're not, Mac. We'll get there." She leaned back on the sofa and continued, "My point is, Robyn has offered you forgiveness and understanding."

"Aye, she has."

"Does that forgiveness mean anything to you?"

I frowned, irritated. "Of course it does."

"But you still feel undeserving of her love?"

Sudden intense emotion made it difficult for me to draw breath.

Iona tilted her head to the other side, studying me for a few seconds. "Is Robyn someone who offers third and fourth and infinite chances to most people? Does she see the good in everyone? Too trusting?"

I smirked at the thought, my airways opening up again. "Robyn is a detective at heart, even if she lost the passion for the job."

"Meaning?"

"She's slow to trust, but perceptive as hell. If she accepts someone in her life, then there's little doubt that person is trustworthy and kind. Robyn wouldn't stand for anything else."

Iona offered me a smug smile I didn't quite understand. "Listen to what you just said, Mac. Repeat the words to yourself."

I did, and understanding dawned. "It's different," I was quick to answer. "I'm her father. There's a familial pull that can blind you."

"Blind her to what? Were you cruel when she came to Scotland to find you?"

"Of course not."

"You refused to make yourself vulnerable to her in order to make headway in mending your relationship?"

Remembering the day we'd finally had it out, the way I'd broken down as my wee girl cried over losing me, tears stung my eyes all over again. "No ... I told her how sorry I was, how much I'd missed her, how much I love her."

Iona nodded. "And have you stayed in her life since she came back into yours?"

"I see her almost every day."

"And when she needs you, are you there? If she calls, do you pick up?"

I nodded. "I will never leave her again. I'll die first."

Iona gave me an almost affectionate smile. "Surely, it

179

stands to reason Robyn sees all of that in you, Mac. And that is why she has forgiven you in order for you to move forward. We can't take back the past. We can't go back. But we can change our future, and it sounds to me like that is what Robyn has done. And if she, the person wronged in all this, can forgive you, Mac, then the best gift you can give to her is to forgive yourself."

Her words pierced my chest like a blade, and I scrubbed my hand over my mouth as I stared out at the river and nodded my agreement.

"Every time you have a negative thought about your past with Robyn, I want you to immediately remember something positive that occurred between you, from either the past or the present. Pull up a good memory of the two of you together, one where you're there for her. I want you to do that every time. Every time. And eventually, hopefully, you'll start to see yourself as the father you've become. A good father, Mac."

"WHAT MAKES you so loyal to Lachlan?"

I shrugged. "He was the first person since working in private security who treated me as an equal. He was this upcoming movie star, a few years younger than me, young enough that shit should have gone to his head. And it never did. He was always thinking about home, about his family, about Arro. Everything he did was for them. Soon enough, because we shared a similar sense of humor, views on the world, liked the same sports, movies, music, we became great mates. And it didn't take long for me to realize Lachlan viewed me as his family too. Every discussion about the future, about transforming the estate into what it has

180

become, I was always in those plans. He never forgot about me."

"He didn't abandon you," Iona surmised.

"He never abandoned me," I agreed. "He was the first person in my life who didn't."

"And how did you feel about him starting a relationship with Robyn?"

"Angry at first. But I didn't believe I was entitled to feel that way."

"Did you feel betrayed?"

"No …" I shook my head. "I knew right off that there was something different about the way he was with her. I've watched Lachlan go through many women over our years together, and I'd never seen him act that way … he was completely gone for her. No, it wasn't betrayal that made me angry, it was fear. I was afraid he'd fuck it up and hurt her, not just because I hated the idea of her hurting, but because if she'd wanted me to make a choice between them, I would have chosen her. I would have lost my friend to make amends with my daughter. So I was angry that he'd put me in that potential position."

"Rightly so. But you obviously have come to terms with their relationship?"

"I trust him. I knew, for the sake of our friendship, he wouldn't have pursued Robyn unless he had genuine feelings for her. And I know that he'll be there for her always, because that's who he is. And I want that for her."

"Do you not think Lachlan would want the same for you? For Arro? Do you think he would stand in your way?"

"I think we need to talk about it when the time comes, but no, I don't think he'll be a problem."

"And you want the time to come, Mac? You want to pursue a romantic relationship with Arro?"

I swallowed hard, my pulse throbbing at the thought. "I do. But I … I need to know that I won't hurt her again like I did. I need to know that I'm the best possible version of me before I go to her."

Iona nodded thoughtfully. "And why do you love Arro?"

I raised an eyebrow, not expecting the question. "Why is it necessary to know that?"

Used to my questioning her questions, Iona's lips twitched. "Well, mostly because you feel guilty for loving her, and sometimes that kind of darker emotion is so over-whelming, we lose sight of the actual love itself."

Elbows resting on my knees, I clasped my hands together and bent my head. Staring at the floor, my breathing shal-lowed as I struggled to make sense of the complicated emotions surrounding Arro.

"Mac …" Iona's voice was gentle. "Forget all those other feelings. Forget the guilt, forget the notion that you don't deserve her … forget everything and just concentrate on Arro and why you love her."

Memories, one after the other, passed through my mind. "She … at first I didn't even notice her, beyond the fact that she was Lachlan's wee sister. He adored her, and so she auto-matically became a person I vowed to protect." I thought about the moment it all changed. "When their dad died, Arro was there. She wasn't even twenty-five years old when he died in her arms at the beach. Heart attack. She … she blew me away with her strength. I don't think she even under-stands how strong she is. And by that, I mean she knew she needed her family around her. I think of when I lost my dad, and I felt so alone, and that loneliness was almost a wall. I was convinced no one else could understand what I was going through, so I pushed my gran away. I fell in with lads who most definitely didn't want to talk about fucking feel-ings … and it was the worst thing I could have done.

"So when Arro let us be there for her, I admired her. I admired her openness. We started spending a lot of time together, walks on the beach, day trips here and there to take her mind off things. She came to me for advice about work, and we fell into a friendship as easily as Lachlan and I had. Arro always seemed more mature. I was nearly thirty-seven, and the fact that we could talk for hours made me forget her age sometimes."

"What did you talk about?"

"Our days. Our views on politics and culture, places we'd been, places we wanted to go. Music, art, the village gossip, her worries about her family. We could debate without arguing, and it was fun. It was easy in a way I'd never experienced with a woman."

"Did you ever talk about your family? Your upbringing?"

"I told her the basics. But not how they made me feel."

"Why?"

"Because I liked the way she looked at me. Arro always looked at me like I was indestructible, like I'd take care of everything, like I *could* take care of everything. I think I became addicted to how she made me feel because deep down, I felt the opposite. I felt like such a fucking failure, and she made me feel ... she made me feel like I was *more*."

Iona was quiet a moment, and then, "Do you think you've confused loving her with that feeling, Mac?"

"No," I bit out, shaking my head. "No, if that were true, I wouldn't be here. I'd have walked away the moment she screamed she hated me."

"She said that?"

I nodded, her words ripping through my chest. "After ... after that night in my house."

"Let's go back to your feelings for Arro, then. It sounds like you became very good friends."

"Aye. We did."

"Were your feelings romantic then?"

"I definitely noticed her as a woman. I lied to myself for a long time about it, but Arro ..." I smiled. "She's innately confident and sexy. She could walk into a room wearing a bin bag and you'd notice her."

"But you tried not to ..."

"Aye. Then the New Year's Eve we opened the club, I was having a bad night about Robyn. It had hit me I was back in Scotland permanently, and she was farther away than ever. I just wanted to be alone, but Arro found me and ... I'd known for months how she felt about me. She couldn't hide it. I wanted to ignore her, but that night, seeing that look in her eyes, I told her about Robyn. To make her see that I was actually a piece of shit, and she could do better."

"But Arro didn't see it that way?"

"No. She refused to think badly of me even knowing the truth, and I wanted to believe her. And when she kissed me, I wanted to drown in the way she saw me, so I kissed her back. And then I did my usual and pushed her away."

"Did you know you loved her then?"

"Not then. A few months later. She avoided me after that, and I hated it. I missed her. We bumped into each other on the beach one night, and she brought it up, and even after I lied and told her I didn't feel that way about her, Arro was kind and understanding, even in her disappointment. So different from Stacey. That's when I knew I was in love with her. That I would never love anyone the way I love her."

I looked up to meet Iona's gaze. "Which makes it so unbelievably fucked up that I could hurt her like I did. I led her on and then I *punished* her for coming on to me. The things that came out of my mouth ... She's right. I treated her like she was a strange bloody woman who'd broken into my house. I humiliated her. How do I come back from that, Iona?"

"First, as always, we look at causality. Most of us say and do hurtful things we don't mean because of something else that's going on underneath. For you, we've already concluded, it's the negative thoughts wherein you've decided you're unworthy, that you don't deserve, that you hurt the people you love. These were the reasons you rejected Arro the way you did. It wasn't out of cruelty, it wasn't deliberate. Can we agree on that?"

I nodded. "But I tried to explain that to Arro, and she said it doesn't absolve me of what I made her feel."

"She's right. It doesn't. But *I* need *you* to know where your actions stemmed from in order to prevent it from happening again. You can't use that night to build a case against yourself anytime you feel overwhelmed by negative thoughts or the belief that you don't deserve Arro. Because you will have those moments, Mac. This, what we're doing here, is ongoing. You will have to be self-aware and redirect negative thoughts into positive thoughts. Just like with Robyn, anytime you and Arro have an argument or one of you hurts the other's feelings—which happens in even the healthiest relationships—you can't dredge up the night in your house to prove you shouldn't even be with her. You hold on to the good—how you were there for her when her father died, how you've upended your entire life to protect her against this current threat, how you've been there any time she's called upon you to be there for her. Can you think of a time when Arro asked you a favor and you didn't come through for her?"

Searching my memory, I realized I couldn't. "No."

"Actions speak louder than words." Iona smirked. "Yes, a cliché. But there's such truth in it, Mac. The good you've brought to Arro's life can outweigh the bad. Now, going forward, it is up to Arro to forgive you for that night, and she may or may not. However, I suggest you give her the entire picture. She needs to know you came to me, even though it was one of the hardest things you've ever done. She needs to know this because she needs to know that you're willing to do the work, Mac."

18

MAC

Jock pulled up in front of my car outside Arro's. The days were longer now as we entered the first week of summer, though it remained cold this far up the coast. It felt like early spring, except for the light. It was eight in the evening and still light out and would be for another hour.

I got out to greet Jock and update him on the quiet day. Arro had been working from home for the last few weeks on a new project, and when we did venture out, she was good at ignoring me. It stung, but it didn't feel as hopeless as it once did. I'd been going to therapy every week and could not believe how much better, how much more optimistic, I felt.

Which was why I'd decided tonight was the night I needed to talk to Lachlan.

Jock looked grim as he got out of the car.

"Everything all right?" I asked, approaching him.

He shook his head. "Sorry, Mac, but I don't know how much longer I can do these night shifts. Will understands and wants to help Arro"—Will was Jock's fiancé—"but raising my boy has been left to him for over a month now, and it's not fair to him or to Adam." Adam was Jock's son from a previous relationship, and he had full custody now.

Knowing what it was like to raise a small child when you were doing night shifts, I sympathized fully. "I know."

"Nothing has happened in weeks. I'm starting to think this was a prank, that having seen how much police involvement there is and the protection we've put on Arro has scared the shit out of whoever it was."

There had been no new notes. The police returned Arro's Defender and unsurprisingly told us they had no leads. Unsurprising because we were probably following the same information as they were during our private investigation, and until today, we'd had no leads either. My PI had tracked Arro's scum of an ex-boyfriend Guy Lewis down, and he was living his life, working as a chef in a wee café near the Lake District in England. I'd had someone watch Guy, but there was nothing about his daily routine that suggested he was remotely interested in Arro. Good for him, because I'd like any excuse to scare the shit out of him for what he did to her.

For now, he was not a suspect, though I wanted to monitor his movements. I'd hired the ethical hacker we kept on retainer for the club to register Guy's vehicle so she'd get any hits on the license plate if he entered Scotland. As an ethical hacker, Nylah regularly attempted to hack our security systems and pointed out any issues or flaws. That was her primary job. But she also moonlighted as our unethical hacker because we never asked her to do anything illegal that might harm an innocent. Morally ambiguous, aye, but weren't we all?

The PI had also provided information on Lucy's loudest and most active fans, who believed her incarceration part of some conspiracy. However, a few lived in the States and the other in mainland Europe, and not one of them had traveled to Scotland or seemed to have any immediate connections here.

But today, I'd received information that changed everything and more than likely proved there was a threat.

"I hope you're right," I hedged, not willing to share outside the family for now. "I've been so focused on Arro that it hasn't been fair to put all these shifts on you—"

"I did volunteer."

"I know, but I doubt you thought it would go on this long. I'll talk to Lachlan tonight about giving the boys at work a bonus to guard Arro on rotation. How does that sound?"

Jock exhaled with relief. "Perfect. I can't take another argument with Will."

"Sorry about that."

"Not your fault. Totally mine for not thinking the whole thing through."

I clamped a hand on his shoulder and gave it a squeeze. "I'll have this all sorted out tomorrow, but know you don't need to come back on night shift for this tomorrow night. Take the rest of the week off, and we'll get you into the rotation from next week."

"Och, you don't have to do that, Mac."

"I do. You earned it. Spend some time with your family."

He gave me a grateful, tight-lipped smile. "Thanks."

Getting back into my SUV, I gave Arro's bungalow one last long look. Lights glowed behind the living room curtains. I wondered what she had on the TV and if there would ever be a time again when she cuddled into me on the sofa to watch a film. Something I'd indulged in, taken very much for granted in the past. Ignoring the familiar ache that flared in my chest, I pulled away.

Not even ten minutes later, I drove down the narrow country road toward the water in Caelmore, toward the Adair homes by the sea.

Pulling in behind Lachlan's Range Rover, it did not surprise me when his front door opened and his body appeared as a haloed shadow from the light flooding out behind him. I'd texted him earlier to say I needed to talk.

"Everything all right?"

"We've got a few things to discuss."

"Coffee?" Lachlan asked as he stepped aside to let me in.

"Please. Decaf."

As I walked down the narrow corridor that widened into an impressive open-plan living space, Robyn jumped off the couch and strolled toward me. "Dad."

I hugged her harder than usual, more thankful for her than ever after these last draining weeks of therapy. Robbie had been the person I talked to about it afterward, the person who understood.

"How you doing?" she asked as we dropped our embrace.

"Good," I promised her. "Really good."

"I'm so glad."

"Is there something I'm missing?" Lachlan asked from the kitchen, peering at us with a crease between his brows.

"Uh—"

I cut Robyn off before she had to lie to her husband. "I'm seeing a therapist."

Lachlan looked up from the coffee machine, both eyebrows raised. "Seriously?"

"Seriously."

He seemed a bit dazed, and I fought a twinge of embarrassment. While I might have been wary and uncomfortable as fuck going into those sessions, the entire experience had opened my mind. Not even my friend could make me feel ashamed that I'd needed to talk to someone.

"Lachlan." Robyn's tone held a warning.

"No." He held up a hand, waving her off. "I'm not being

judgmental. I'm just surprised." His gaze met mine. "You've never been one to talk about things unless you're drunk."

I snorted. "Perhaps that was the problem."

Lachlan studied me. "You actually look different. It's going well, then?"

"Aye. I mean, it's difficult and ..." Harrowing, heartbreaking, and I'd been in tears more in the past four weeks than in my entire fucking life, but it was also ... "A relief. I feel better. It's hard to describe."

"That's great, Mac. I'm happy for you."

Appreciative, I nodded my thanks.

"Can I get you anything to eat, Dad? We have some left-over pasta from tonight."

"You know, that would be great, actually. I haven't had dinner."

"You got it." Robyn walked into the kitchen and as she passed Lachlan while he made the coffee, she pressed a tender kiss to his biceps before moving to the hob. He flicked her an equally tender look over his shoulder. I envied them.

We settled around the dining table so I could eat, and I explained why I'd come to see them. I told them about the real reason my gran had sent me to Boston as a young teenager, about the murder of Craig Kilmany. Though it was difficult, it was nowhere near as difficult as it might have been before my sessions with Iona. I also explained what Billy had told me, and that today, I'd gotten word from my police friend, Lisa, that Lee Kilmany, brother of Craig, had just been arrested and released on bail for running a chop shop.

The kicker was they'd found the car that ran over Bryan McNab in that chop shop.

"Why didn't you tell me any of this before?" Robyn asked, looking upset.

"It's not something I ever liked to dwell on."

Lachlan said nothing because he was the one person who already knew about Craig. He'd never condemned me for it, which should've made me realize, as Iona had, that Craig's death wasn't my fault. I'd made mistakes running around with those boys, but Billy and I *had* tried to do the right thing. I could see that now, and I understood more than ever why Billy had suggested I talk to a therapist.

I had a thank-you email to send to Australia.

"So have you talked to Iona about all this? I think you should," Robyn said.

"I have. It helped a lot."

"Good."

"Aye, very good." Lachlan nodded a little impatiently. "But what isn't good is this threat against you, Mac."

"What if it isn't just against me?" I shared the information they'd found on Lee's computer. He'd investigated me and the Adairs and had saved links to newspaper articles about Lucy's trial.

"You think he's behind the notes?" Robyn asked.

"It's a bit off-piste," I admitted, "but he's looking like the obvious suspect."

"Shit." Lachlan sighed. "I was hoping with things being so quiet, maybe we'd overreacted."

"If it is Lee, Lisa assures me the charges brought against him will mean he's back in prison for a long time because it's his third offense." I then explained what Jock had said about his night shift issues, and Lachlan agreed to offer my security team a bonus for adding Arro's guard duty to their rotation. "Good," I said. "I'll make up the schedule and email it over to the team. However, could you discuss it with them? I would, but I have to take over guarding Arro early tomorrow morning so Jock can get home."

"Of course," Lachlan agreed.

Pushing my empty dinner plate away, I mentally drew

myself up. "There's something else." I looked at Robyn. "Would you mind, wee birdie, if I spoke to Lachlan alone?"

Curiosity sparked in my daughter's eyes, but she stood without argument. "Of course not. I've got some things to finish up in my darkroom, anyway."

"Now?" Lachlan frowned.

"Yeah."

"I hate you out there at this time." He referred to the small building they'd built on the side of their land to accommodate an office and darkroom for Robyn's photography business. She'd accumulated a fair number of social media followers for her landscape photography and was kept busy with a steady stream of orders and commissions.

"Lachlan, the sun hasn't even set yet." She kissed the top of his head and smiled at me. "Come say goodbye before you leave."

"Will do."

Lachlan followed her movements as she strode through the bifold doors and down the deck, out of sight. "Why the hell did I not just build a side extension so she could walk directly through the house into it?"

My lips twitched. "And I thought I was overprotective."

He scowled at me. "This whole thing with Arro has me on edge."

Taking a deep breath, I replied, "What I have to say might put you more on edge."

"Do I need a drink for this conversation?"

"I don't know," I answered honestly. "I don't know how you'll react."

"Just get to the point, Mac. You've got me imagining all manner of things."

My mouth was suddenly dry, and I gulped down the dregs of my now-cold coffee before blurting out bluntly, "I'm in love with Arro."

Ignoring my racing heart and its echo in my ears, I waited as Lachlan stared at me.

Just fucking stared.

"Well?" I snapped.

Instead of answering, he pushed back from the table and strolled into the kitchen. Irritated, concerned, I followed him with my plate and put it in the sink, watching Lachlan as he poured himself a small whisky.

"I'd offer you one, but you're driving," he said before he tipped the contents down in one gulp. He pressed a hand against his chest, and I could practically feel the burn.

"Is it really that bad?" I asked flatly.

He shook his head, placing the glass on the counter before he turned to me. "It's not that. I'm now just wondering how long you've both felt like this and have done nothing about it because of me? I think I convinced myself that you were just attracted to her and that if you loved her, you would have done something about it by now. So I'm wondering if I'm the arsehole who's been standing in the way of your happiness this whole fucking time?"

"No." Relieved he wasn't pissed off, I replied, "*I'm* the arsehole who's been standing in the way of my happiness this whole fucking time."

Lachlan scrutinized me. "Is Arro the reason you went to therapy?"

"She was the catalyst."

His face clouded over. "You hurt her, didn't you?" He took an instinctively aggressive step toward me. "What did you do?"

I held up my hands in appeasement. "I said some things to her I didn't mean."

He studied me carefully, searching for the truth. "They must have been pretty bloody awful, Mac, because it has escaped none of our notice that she hasn't talked to you in months."

"I fucked up," I confessed. "So much that I might never get another chance with her." The thought ripped through me, and I looked away, battling against the pain of it.

"I'm sorry to hear that." He frowned. "Another chance? Do you mean to say something has already happened between you? Is this another Thane and Regan situation?"

Uncomfortable discussing this with him, I shrugged. "I'm not going into the details because that's fucking strange, for both of us, but I can say that, no, it isn't like Thane and Regan. Arro and I have never had an affair."

"I thought so." He nodded in contemplation.

"It really wouldn't matter to you if Arro and I got together? She's thirteen years younger than me. She's your sister."

Lachlan scoffed. "I'm ten years older than Robyn, and she's your daughter. Do you really think I'm a hypocritical prick?"

I snorted and shook my head. "No, I know you're not."

"I mightn't have been happy about it before Robyn. I'll admit that." Lachlan leaned back against the counter, crossing his arms over his chest. "It's hard for me to see Arro as anything but a wee girl. I was more father than brother to her."

"I know."

"But Robyn made me realize you can't help who you love, Mac. I realized then you were a better man than I am because you didn't stand in our way, and I knew if it had been the other way around, I'd have tried to keep Arro from you. And that would've been wrong."

I wasn't sure what to say.

"I might even have still tried," Lachlan admitted.

That surprised me.

"Come on, Mac. I know you better than anyone does. You've got everyone else fooled that you're Mr. Can Handle Anything. But I know you. I know you have demons. And I didn't want that for Arro. So knowing that you're doing something about it … has eased my concerns somewhat. And anyway, she *is* a grown woman, and it's not my place to make those kinds of decisions for her."

"Why didn't you ever say anything?"

"Because it's none of my business how you deal with your own shit. It would only become my business if it affected Robyn or Arro. But you never let it affect Robyn. I suspected you let it affect Arro, and you've just confirmed that."

"I am trying, though."

"I know, that's what I said. Have you told Arro how you feel about her?"

"Not in so many words. She isn't exactly making it easy to have a chat these days. I tried to get her to come to jujitsu, and she's somehow avoided every class for weeks."

"Do you think telling her will fix things?"

I bloody wished. "I don't know. I hope so. But … it might not be enough."

Lachlan's expression hardened. "What *did* you say to her?"

My tone implacable, I replied, "That's nobody's business but hers and mine, and I know for a fact she wouldn't want it bandied about among her family."

"Then that means it was pretty bloody shitty." He pushed off the counter. "Fuck, Mac."

"I know." I glanced away. "Believe me, multiply your anger by a million, and that's how much I've got directed at myself. But I'm trying." I looked back at him. "It wasn't easy for me to walk into that therapist's office, but I did it for her. I did it for her, but I stayed for me. For both of us. I needed to know that I wouldn't hurt her again because of my own fucked-up way of thinking."

We were silent a second or two, and then Lachlan asked quietly, "What happens next, then? You tell Arro, she forgives you, you stop going to therapy or ..."

"Robyn said for her, it's a way of life."

"Aye, she still talks to her therapist. So you think that'll be you? Seeing this woman for the foreseeable future?"

I nodded. "Even if Arro can never forgive me."

Lachlan smirked.

"What?" I frowned.

"Arro ... Arro has only held a grudge a few times in her life, and it never lasted, except for Lucy and Fergus. So unless you stalked her brother and stabbed the man she loves, I'm thinking she'll get over it."

I didn't smile at his teasing because I wasn't so sure. It wasn't just a case of hurting Arro's feelings. She didn't look at me the same way anymore. The hero worship, the tenderness ... the trust. It was gone.

And that scared the shit out of me.

Seeing my expression, Lachlan sobered. "Talk to her, Mac. Tell her how you feel. But know I won't stand in your way, and I doubt my brothers will either. I always worried about who Arro would end up with, even more so after that prick Guy Lewis beat the crap out of her. But if I knew she was with you ... well, I could rest easy at night knowing that."

Emotion welled, and I swallowed hard against it, giving him a gruff nod of thanks.

He grinned suddenly. "Though what a bloody confusing family tree. If we have a kid, and you and Arro have a kid ... what does that make them to each other?"

I thought about it and groaned in amusement as I replied, "Well, they'd be cousins, but mine and Arro's kid would also be your kid's either half uncle or half aunt because Robyn would be my kid's half sister."

Lachlan rolled his eyes. "We could start our own reality

show." Then his gaze sharpened, causing my laughter to die. "You'd want kids, Mac?"

The thought terrified me.

But it also filled me with hope.

"I think so. If you'd asked me weeks ago, I'd have said no. But ... maybe I wouldn't be so bad at it after all."

He nodded with a small smile. "You're already a good dad, Mac. Never doubt it."

19
MAC

"If you could have any of the things you think would improve your life, what would they be?"

The answers seemed obvious. "To know who is threatening Arro and end it for her. To spend the rest of my life with her."

"Is that it? No winning the lottery or owning an Aston Martin?" Iona teased.

I chuckled. "I have all I need. I've always known, as Lachlan has always known, despite his fortune, that true wealth lies within the health and happiness of the people we love."

Her expression softened. "Then you've already won. It can take people entire lifetimes to come to that realization. Others never do."

"Then they're fools."

"And you're certainly no fool. So ... what could make your life worse than it is now?"

"Christ." I sank back against the sofa. "The list is endless."

Iona slowly nodded. "Exactly. Most of us are programmed to think about negative possibilities over posi-

199

tive possibilities, and that's because usually when we stop and think about our current situation, we realize there is so much more to be positive about than negative. That's not always the case for everyone, especially when we're grieving or going through a difficult period. But if you only listed two things that would improve your life right now, Mac, then you must be pretty content with what you have."

"I have a good life. I know that. That's never been the problem."

Her eyes glittered with what looked like triumph. "So if you believe you have a good life not because of the fancy security job or the money or the connection to famous people … if you believe you have a good life because you've surrounded yourself with good people, then doesn't it stand to reason that those good people have stayed in your life because they believe you are a good person too? That you *are* a good person too?"

Emotion thickened in my throat.

"I can see this has affected you, Mac. Why? What did I say that makes you so emotional?"

"Because it's so obvious when you say it like that," I answered gruffly. "Why couldn't I just see that? Am I a fucking moron?"

"It's not about intelligence. In fact, in my opinion, you are very emotionally intelligent and intuitive about others. The problem is how you see yourself. It's about a lifetime of only seeing yourself through a false lens, fabricated by feelings of abandonment and worthlessness from the moment you understood your mother left you. Today you're seeing your-self more clearly. How does that feel, Mac?"

My voice shook with how it felt. "Freeing."

20

ARRO

I suspected that if Mac hadn't been my constant shadow during the day and hadn't had one of his men sitting outside in a car watching the house at night, I might have forgotten about the threatening copycat notes and gotten on with my life.

Tomorrow would be four weeks to the day since I'd slammed the door in Mac's and Robyn's faces. Not very polite or mature, I know, but her defense of him aggravated me. And I'm grateful that their relationship was such now that she would defend her dad. Clearly, my feelings toward the bastard continued to be as complicated and confusing as ever.

While I'd gotten pretty good at avoiding conversation with Mac while he was on guard duty, I was feeling stifled. Maybe if someone else shadowed me, I'd be fine. Thankfully, we'd finished work at the Lairg site, and I was working from home on preliminary plans for replanting in Aberdeenshire and harvesting in Fearnmore, which was not far west of Caelmore.

Mac guarded the house, and I felt bad that he had to sit

out in the car the whole time, but any guilt I was feeling was obliterated when he shadowed me in the village. When I went to Morag's to buy lunch, Mac at my side, she'd told us that everyone was talking about the fact that Mac and Jock were guarding me. "Is there something going on that we should be concerned about?" she'd asked. And, of course, Morag wasn't a gossip and was genuinely worried about me, so having to lie made me feel like a dick.

"This can't go on," I griped as Mac and I walked out of Morag's. "I need my life back. I hate lying to people."

Mac opened the passenger side of his SUV, and as I hopped in, I said, "There's no point worrying anybody else if this turns out to be a prank. Which is looking more and more likely." I waited for him to round the vehicle and get into the driver's seat. "There's been nothing in three weeks. This"—I gestured between us—"can it stop now?"

Brows furrowed, Mac swung the SUV out of its spot in the car park outside the Gloaming, but instead of turning left out of the village, he drove right. Toward the beach.

"Where are we going?"

"We need to talk."

Indignation rushed through me. "I'm hungry, and I want to eat my bloody sandwich and get back to work."

He shot me a look of disappointment that pissed me off. "Please, Arro. There are some things I need you to know."

Something in his voice gave me pause. "About what?"

"A few different things. I thought we could have our lunch out by the beach and talk. Like old times."

Like old times.

We weren't the people we were then, though.

Still ... something in Mac's tone made me loath to say no. Moreover, I was wearied of being angry at him. It did me little good to hold on to such anger. I might have been hurting Mac, but I was also hurting myself.

"All right," I agreed.

Mac's shoulders seemed to drop with relief, and we drove the rest of the way in silence. While he parked at the edge of the lot on Gordon's caravan site, raised up over the sand dunes, windshield framing the sea, I settled the coffee we'd gotten from Morag's into the car cupholders in the central armrest before unwrapping our sandwiches. I handed Mac his once he switched off the engine and removed his seat belt.

"Thank you."

I nodded and took a massive bite of my ham salad sandwich. Gesturing with one hand, I gave him a wave that said, "Go on, then."

Mac studied my face so tenderly, it made me self-conscious. Swallowing my food, I huffed, "Don't watch me eat. Just tell me whatever it is you brought me here to tell me."

He smirked and took a bite of his roast beef and pickle sandwich instead. I'd ordered it without asking him, I realized, because I knew that's all he ever ordered at Morag's. I knew some of the tiny details about him that a girlfriend would know. But not all.

My bitterness rising, I looked out the windshield and stayed silent, waiting for him to talk.

"I started seeing a therapist."

The food in my mouth wasn't broken down nearly enough when I jerked in shock at his words, and the damn bite got caught in my throat. Choking, I fumbled for my coffee.

"Are you all right?" Mac patted my back in concern.

I waved him off as I took a drink of the hot coffee and let it wash the choking hazard down. Coughing, eyes watering, I shot Mac an accusing look. "Warn a person before you make an announcement like that."

His lips twitched. "Apologies."

Once I'd fully recovered, I asked. "Are you serious?"

"About therapy? Aye." Mac took another bite, and my gaze dropped, watching the muscles in his jaw and then the bobbing of his Adam's apple as he swallowed. Why was everything about him still so physically fascinating? *Focus, Arro. Therapy, remember.*

"You, Mackennon Galbraith, willingly visited a therapist? Not a physical therapist, but a counselor?"

"Who specializes in cognitive behavioral therapy, especially for men."

Holy shit, he was really seeing a therapist.

A swell of hope baffled me.

So I ignored it.

"Why?"

Mac raised an eyebrow. "You even have to ask?"

"Are you ... are you saying you did this because of what happened between us? You actually took my advice?"

"Of course I did." He turned in his seat to face me. "Arro, what I did was wrong. Everything between us. Pulling you in, pushing you away. Over and over. My fault. My mistake. And it's not an excuse, but I have an explanation for it now."

Blood whooshed in my ears because my heart raced like mad. "Because you think badly of yourself?"

"I've always known I didn't like myself very much, but the therapy is making me realize my past has clouded my self-perception. Has skewed my version of events in my past. With you, what I did, it happened like some self-fulfilling prophecy, not because I am who I thought I was."

Stunned, I slumped back in my seat.

Mac studied me thoughtfully and asked, "Can I tell you why I am the way I am, Arro? Will you allow me that?"

Tears threatened, but I forced them down. And because,

despite our history, I knew he was a good man. "You can tell me anything, Mackennon."

He squeezed his eyes closed, a look of such torment, a part of me wanted to forgive him anything and everything. But I couldn't. Not yet.

However, I could listen.

And as the rain pitter-pattered on the car roof, I did just that. I listened as Mac not only told me about his mum abandoning him as a baby and his father's heroin addiction, but how those events had made him feel. He told me a story he'd never entrusted me with before, about being in a youth gang and witnessing a boy's murder. How he'd carried that guilt and sense of failure with him his whole life. How there was no one left but the murdered boy's two brothers to admit his wrongdoing to. "There's more to that, and I'll come back to it," Mac said.

Then he talked about Stacey and Robyn, and while we'd talked about some of this before, it became apparent that a lot of his feelings he'd kept to himself. And when he told me why, that he was trying to protect this image he thought I had of him, I wanted to tear my hair out in frustration. It was exasperating that he thought I only wanted to see him in a certain light.

Yet somehow, I found the will to stay silent. To listen. To process the progress he'd already made with his therapist. How she'd helped him see the person he really was and provided him with mental techniques to help keep him on the path to be the man he'd always wanted to be.

"And it's work, Arro. I didn't realize how many times in a week I have these thoughts about myself. But I'm learning how to turn them on their heads."

I gaped in amazement at him because no one would believe it if they met Mac. He was this big guy, this masculine bodyguard who oozed charisma and flashed wicked, flirtatious smiles at women just to make them feel good. He came across as this confident, easygoing guy who never let a thing bother him. And it was all a lie. A cover for the mess beneath.

At my silence, Mac looked away, the muscle in his jaw working for a second before he said hoarsely, "I realize that all of this means I'm not the man you fell in love with. But that man wasn't good enough for you, and not because of who he was, but because of who I *thought* he was. I am trying to be a better version of him." He looked at me now, expression filled with so much, too much. "So that whatever happens between us, I will never hurt you like that again."

I forced myself to ask, despite my fears, "What is it you hope happens between us?"

"I ... I love you, Arrochar."

Words I'd longed to hear for so long. I looked away, biting back tears, not wanting him to see them.

"I love you, and I want to be with you."

The tears leaked free, and I swiped at them in vexation.

"Look at me."

I looked back to him, so angry I couldn't bear it. "Why couldn't you say that to me months ago? That night ... it changed things, Mac. Not this"—I gestured between us—"I'm proud of you for speaking to someone, for recognizing this was impacting your life, but I can't change this seed you planted that night. It changed ..."

"How you feel about me," he finished, staring sternly out at the sea.

My gaze caressed that aquiline profile I knew as well as I knew my own face. I wanted to reach out and touch him. I wanted to forgive the past and throw myself into his arms and kiss every inch of his mouth and taste him on my tongue and drown in all the love that still existed within me for him. The love that swam through my blood like millions of tiny pieces of metal filled with atoms seeking their northern poles and knowing they could only find them within Mac.

Fingers twitching, ready to reach out and abandon the hurt, I suddenly seized upon the awful memory of that night and the paralyzing mistrust that came with it.

I lied to him to protect myself. Even as I cursed myself as a hypocrite, the words, "I'm sorry," tumbled out of my mouth.

"Don't you be sorry." Mac turned to me. "You have nothing to be sorry for. But do you think … do you think you might ever change how you feel?"

"I don't know," I offered honestly.

Determination flashed in his gorgeous hazel eyes. "Then know I'm not going anywhere. I'm not ready to give up on the idea of us. I've told Lachlan the same thing."

My breathing hitched at the idea of a Mac who fought for us rather than ran. "You spoke with Lachlan?"

He nodded. "He won't stand in our way."

"He approved?"

"He wants us to be happy."

"Uh …" I let out a grunt of disbelief. "I'm not sure what is happening."

"I'm fighting for you."

"O-o-okay."

"Yeah?" He smiled slightly, a sexy, lopsided expression that crinkled the corners of his eyes and made my fingers itch for a different reason. "Okay?"

"I can't promise you anything," I felt the need to say.

Mac grinned now, wolfish and wicked and very dangerous to my heart. "That's all right. This is good enough for me."

Feeling that familiar flutter of butterflies in my belly, I wrenched my gaze away and took a bite of my forgotten sandwich, even though I was no longer hungry.

"Is that it?" I asked a little belligerently. "All you wanted to discuss?"

Mac's expression sobered in such a way my spine straightened with tension. "There's something else. Craig, the boy who my friends killed?"

"Yes?"

"Billy, the friend who was with me when we tried to stop them, he contacted me a few months back and told me that the others involved in Craig's murder had died under unusual circumstances. He was concerned someone close to Craig was coming for their revenge."

Fear shot through my heart at the thought of anyone hurting Mac. "But you tried to stop them from hurting Craig."

"And I hoped that was the reason they'd left Billy and me unscathed. He moved to Australia with his wife and has had no troubles. But there's a possibility I have had troubles." Mac stared pointedly at me. "We can't rule out that the notes are about me. I thought there was no connection, which is why I never mentioned it, but yesterday I got a call from a contact high up in the Glasgow police, and she told me Craig's brother, Lee, has been brought in for questioning regarding the death of one of my old friends. Bryan McNab was run over outside his house, but the person reversed back over him, suggesting it was deliberate. The police didn't have a lead because the car used in the crime had been reported stolen a few days before, but Lee's been under investigation for running a chop shop. And they found that car in the garage he's running it out of."

"Jesus ... but w-what does that have to do with me and the notes?"

Mac took a shuddering breath. "They found information on us all on a computer they confiscated from Lee's office in the garage. There was stuff about me, where I work, links to articles he'd saved about Lucy's murder trial, and there were photographs of you and me, Arro. He had someone follow us months back."

"But why not target Robyn, then? She's your daughter."

"Perhaps because Robyn seemed like too strong a target, just as we discussed before."

I considered this and let out a string of curse words. "Did you tell Lachlan?"

"I told him and Robyn last night before I spoke with him about …" He gestured between us.

"So what now?"

"We wait and see if the police can provide us with any more information, but until Lee is in prison, I can't suspend your security detail. And you have to stop finding reasons not to come to jujitsu. I want you there tomorrow."

Processing it all, I nodded slowly. "Okay, agreed."

"This could all be a good thing, Arro." He pressed a reassuring hand to my shoulder and for the first time in weeks, I let him touch me. "If this is Lee, once he's behind bars, everything can go back to normal."

Well, not really, I wanted to say. Normal was when Mac brushed off our feelings and my advances.

The normal Mac now spoke of involved a possible future of waking up to him in my bed every morning.

A dream I'd once longed for.

A longing, if I was honest with myself, that still existed somewhere within me.

Except a pesky, painful thing called fear wouldn't let me reach out to turn the longing into a reality.

21

ARRO

"I understand this must be a strain on you," Ada observed as she drove us toward Inverness so I could attend Mac's jujitsu class. Ada Renshaw had been on Mac's security team at Ardnoch for almost as long as the estate had been open for business. I knew—because I'd badgered her with questions years ago at a party she was on duty for—that she lived north of Ardnoch in Helmsdale with her cats, Horace and Holly. Ada had fascinated me at the time because I'd never met a female security guard. Moreover, she was the most content bachelorette on the planet and had said she unequivocally would never give up her autonomy for a relationship. I admired her sense of self and the way she lived her life, not giving a damn what anyone else thought.

Thinking of her comment, I sighed. I'd avoided Mac's jujitsu class for the last few weeks, finding one excuse after the other not to attend. Last week I babysat for Thane and Regan because they'd asked me to weeks ago, and I refused to back out. Robyn came over to babysit with me, but she was, in actuality, guarding me.

As much as I dreaded Mac teaching me martial arts, I had

to admit, it might be nice for my family to view me as capable of looking out for myself. Besides, I didn't dread it so much now after our talk yesterday. I was nervous to see him again. I'd barely slept last night, going over and over in my head what he'd said, considering all the work he was doing to better himself. It had put a pretty big dent in my anger toward him.

In fact, I wasn't even sure I was still angry.

How could I be? He'd laid himself bare yesterday. It was a wee bit like payback for the fact that I'd literally laid myself bare to him.

That didn't mean I trusted him like I once did.

"It's suffocating," I finally answered. "The constant guarding. But there are worse things than being loved so much by your family."

"Absolutely. Doesn't mean it isn't a pain in the arse." Ada had a rather plummy English accent, and I loved the way she said *arse* like *ahrse*.

We shared a grin just as my phone rang in my purse. Pulling it free from the junk I needed to clean out, I smiled at the sight of Brodan's name. "Hello, you," I answered happily. While we'd texted and I knew my middle brother was worried, we hadn't spoken often lately. He'd been busy filming a new movie while doing press for another due out in a few weeks.

"How is my favorite sister?" Brodan asked without preamble, speaking loudly over voices in the background.

I snorted. "You know that means something now because you have a new sister in Robyn."

"And as lovely as she is, you're still my favorite."

"Charmer. Where are you? It's loud."

"On set. We're taking a break while they work out the camera sequence for the next scene. I just wanted to check in."

"I'm fine. Ada's driving me to Inverness to do Mac's jujitsu class."

"Why isn't Mac driving you?"

"He's busy in the city before his class." At his therapy session. Pride filled me, and I couldn't ignore it. It was odd to feel proud of someone and at the same time wary of them.

"Tell gorgeous Ada I said hi."

"Brodan says hi," I passed along.

Ada smirked. "Tell him his last movie was fucking awful."

Laughing, I repeated it, and Brodan barked his laughter. "She's lying, but I appreciate her trying to keep my ego in check."

"Modest much?"

"I'm a damn excellent actor, and we all know it."

We did, but I teased, "Your arrogance is a problem."

"My distance is a problem," he said with an exasperated sigh. "I'm scheduled to do a few TV interviews in a couple weeks for the new film, and I'm going to make sure we squeeze in a quick trip home. I need to know for myself that you're okay."

"Brodan, I'm fine, I promise. I'm guarded twenty-four seven." Plus, hopefully Lee Kilmany was the reason for all this, and it would be over as soon as he was back in prison.

"I still need to see for myself."

"You didn't come home when it was Lachlan."

"Because we're in the public eye, we deal with obsessed fans and threats regularly, and it never occurred to me that the threats I'd received were connected to his. I never expected it to turn out the way it did. I'm not that naive anymore, and I'm going to be there when my family needs me."

I could hear the guilt in his voice. The truth was, Brodan should have come home, and he didn't, and even when he did eventually show up, he wasn't himself. He still wasn't himself. Something was going on with him, and no matter how many times I asked about it, he shrugged me off. That hurt. Not just because he didn't feel he could confide in me, but because I hated the idea that one of my siblings was dealing with something difficult on their own.

"Are you okay?" I asked for the millionth time in as many months.

"I'm fine, sweetheart. But they're shouting for me to get back, so I'll check in later. Stay safe."

"You too. I lo—" The line went dead before I could finish the sentiment.

Silence filled the car until Ada asked, "Are you all right?"

I sighed, leaning my head back against the headrest. "When we were younger and Dad was always hiding in his office, we were left to ramble around that drafty old castle. I was so close to my brothers then. Lachlan and Thane were different—Lachlan always was more like my dad, and Thane, my protective big brother.

"But Brodan and Arran were only a few years older, so they were my pals, my buddies. They told me everything, even things I didn't want to know, about the girls they got off with in random and often not very private places. Even when they went to uni, now and then I'd go stay with one of them at the weekend. They'd call me every week to tell me about their school or girl problems." Emotion brightened my eyes. "I don't know when that changed. I don't know when I lost them."

Ada was quiet a moment and then said, "You haven't lost them, Arrochar. Brodan wouldn't be calling you in the middle of filming a multimillion-pound movie if you'd lost him. If you'd lost him, Arran wouldn't have stayed while this threat looms over his sister."

While I knew that was true to an extent, I also knew that something had changed. "It's … it's deeper than that. Something changed in them both … they have secrets. Remember last year when Brodan was in bar fights that were splashed across the media? His crazy behavior stopped, but he never really explained why it happened in the first place. It was so unlike him. We never used to have secrets from each other."

"I'm sure that goes both ways. Aren't there things about you they don't know?"

Mac.

I watched the world pass by as I realized Ada was right.

Maybe the distance between Brodan, Arran, and me wasn't just coming from them. Maybe, without being cognizant of it, I'd put distance between us, too, to protect my secret feelings for Mac. And maybe, now that Mac had put everything out in the open with Lachlan, that would filter down to Brodan and Arran … and maybe my freedom to be honest with them would signal to my brothers that they could tell me anything in return.

I hoped so.

THE ROOM MAC taught the class in was too big. It wasn't even a room; it was a basketball court, by the looks of things. His class didn't even take up half of the space.

Mac greeted me as soon as I walked in, and I tried not to seem as nervous as I was when I returned his welcome.

"Are you okay?" He squeezed my biceps, and I nodded.

He gave me a reassuring smile. "Why don't you take off your shoes and go stand with the others?"

I nodded and watched as he walked away to his place at the front of the class.

He wore a T-shirt so tight, the broad muscles in his back shifted as he strode across the room. While the navy trousers of the gi hung loosely on many a man's arse, Mac's clung to his rounded, muscular cheeks. He picked up the jacket of his gi and secured it with his black belt. Mac seemed to feel my gaze and stared back at me. Powerful, beautiful ... repentant.

I flushed, looking away. *The man is unfairly attractive*, I grumbled inwardly as I kicked off my trainers and walked across the cold court floor to join the back row. Most of the students, except for two others, were in traditional white gis with white belts. I wore sports leggings and a sports tank.

A few students were limbering up, doing stretches I remembered from PE class back in the day. Just the thought of high school PE made me want to grab my shit and get the hell out of there. The only thing keeping me from bolting was that I truly had intended to join Robyn's training sessions with Eredine and Regan, but had never gotten around to it. Now that this was my only option, I was determined to learn as much as I could, even if having Mac as my teacher was a bit like tempting fate.

But being close to him here wouldn't change my mind. I wasn't ready to let Mac back into my heart after one conversation. No matter how profound the conversation had been.

As I bent my knee, pulling my foot to my arse and trying not to wobble on one leg, my resolve wavered as I watched a woman, perhaps my age or a little younger, approach Mac to ask him something.

He bent his head to hear her, and she leaned closer. Her body language and the way she smiled flirtatiously up at him screamed, "I'm ready and available!"

Remembering the brunette at the beginning of last year, a fiery flush of jealous possessiveness scored through me. If the brunette was anything to go by, Mac made a habit of sleeping with his young, attractive students.

Really, what the hell did that actually say about him?

Nothing good.

Hardening myself against him, I decided he could shag the entire class, and I couldn't give a damn.

I was, of course, lying.

And I also knew Mac would not tell me he loved me if he was sleeping with a student.

Get over yourself, Arro. But my eyes refused to move from Mac and the woman.

The young woman returned to her place in the front line, and Mac faced the class to address us. He searched the students until he found me in the back. "Arro, can you come to the front, please?" He looked at the young man before him. "Luke, do you mind letting Arro take your spot?"

"Not at all." The guy was amiable and smiled at me through the others before he headed to take my place.

Hesitant, I passed him with the most grateful smile I could muster and took his spot right smack bang in front of Mac.

Wonderful.

Feeling attention on me, I glanced to my left to see the young woman who'd just flirted with him eyeing me with curiosity.

"Right." Mac clapped his hands. "Let's warm up."

Everything went all right for a while. I mean, compared to my fellow beginners who had been taking the class longer than I had, I needed to limber up a bit. But Mac didn't focus on me for most of the stretching session, walking around the group, adjusting other people's form. In fact, it lulled me into a false sense of security. I thought maybe he'd stay away because he understood his presence confused me.

We finished up stretching and sat almost cross-legged, except Mac instructed us to press the soles of our feet together. The goal was to stretch the muscles at the top of the inner thigh, but I didn't understand how until ...

"You want to press your knees toward the floor to

increase the stretch," Mac's quiet voice rumbled in my ear. Ignoring the answering goose bumps, I stiffened at the feel of his heat at my back before he pressed his large palms to my knees and gently pushed down.

The muscles immediately burned.

"Feel it now?" he murmured, his lips brushing my earlobe.

My breasts tightened, followed by an erotic flip deep in my belly. Holy crap.

I gritted my teeth and said through a fake smile, "Yes, now get your fucking hands off me."

To my irritation, Mac chuckled, a rumbly, sexy sound that, combined with his hands on my legs, caused further inappropriate tingling at the apex of my thighs.

Bastard.

He eased away and instructed, "Keep pushing those knees down."

His departure allowed me to breathe and concentrate again.

Honestly, by the time we'd finished stretching, I felt like I'd had a full and proper workout and was ready to go home.

"Right. We're going to go back to some basics today, since we have a few new students who missed the closed guard lesson. Guard is any position where we find ourselves bum on the ground with our legs in front of or wrapped around our opponent. You have closed guard, full guard, half guard, and open guard. Closed guard is a fundamental guard type in jujitsu, and tonight, I'll demonstrate with our new student Arro, and then you'll work in pairs, taking turns as the opponent."

I barely heard the end of his sentence, because all that kept repeating in my head was "I'll demonstrate with our new student Arro."

"Uh ..." I let out a grunt of disbelief. "I'm not sure what is happening."

217

"I'm fighting for you."

Oh, I understood now! The bastard was playing dirty because he knew I was so physically attracted to him, it would distract me from all else.

"Arro, will you join me on the mat, please?" He wore a bland smile, but I saw the glitter of mischief in his eyes as he strode past me.

Trying not to glare, I followed him and caught the young woman, whose name I'd overheard as Annie, glower sullenly as I passed her. One other new student, a woman in her mid- to late-thirties, gave me a sympathetic and bolstering smile.

I joined Mac on the mat, hoping the look in my eye communicated the many ways I was fantasizing about evis-cerating him.

By the wicked laughter in his, I assumed he knew exactly what I was thinking.

"Okay, Arro, lie on your back, please."

At my hesitation, the laughter in his expression died. "This is useful. Please."

With a sigh, I laid down on my back, staring up at the high ceiling with its harsh strip lighting.

"Right." I heard Mac say, and I dropped my gaze to watch him as he towered over me, directing his words to the class. "We need to know how to do this for competition, but this is also useful training if you ever find yourself in a real-life attack. We'll go into that after we demonstrate the grapple." He stepped toward me and lowered himself to his knees. It was suddenly a little too hard to breathe as he took hold of my thighs and instructed, "Wrap your legs around my waist and lock your ankles."

My cheeks heated at the suggestion because my body seriously loved it. "What?"

Mac held my eyes as his voice rose for the class. "For closed guard, you wrap your legs around your opponent's waist and lock your ankles behind their back to maximize your leverage."

He waited.

Finally, with a sigh, I looked up at the ceiling while I wrapped my legs around him and locked my ankles. Mac leaned into me, his hard stomach pressing between my thighs, causing several types of frustration.

I startled when he grabbed the front of my tank top with both hands.

His expression was reassuring as he murmured, "We'll get you a gi for next week." Then louder, he explained to us all, "There is a center area of control here. We're both attempting to keep our arms inside the other's. Inside control equals dominant position. Everyone understand?"

There was a murmuring of yeses as I tried to ignore the feel of Mac's stomach muscles flexing against me as he moved. "So my arms are inside Arro's, but Arro needs to get her arms inside mine. Your job, Arro, is to break my grip so you can get a dominant grip on me. Raise your arms, elbows bent, palms out … good. Now, the hand closest to your upper body is the grip you need to break first."

Concentrating on his instruction helped me forget our intimate position because, feeling his weight on me, I realized how powerful this information was, now more than ever. If an assailant as big as Mac attacked and got me on the ground, I wouldn't know how to get out from under him. The thought was scary as hell.

"Now, you want to break my grip by pulling that arm up and out toward my fingertips. Take your opposite hand and grab hold of my wrist."

I did that.

"And then slip your other hand under my wrist to steady yours."

Once I did that, Mac nodded, pleased. "Good. Now push my wrist upward—and stop."

I did with his arm raised and stretched out toward my head.

"When you release me, you can push my arm away with the hand that was holding your wrist, and this brings your arms inside mine, exactly where you want to be."

Once we did that, Mac made me repeat it several times until the movement was fast and fluid. Then he had me grab the lapel of his gi and bring my knees forward, which brought his face against my chest. That broke my concentration more than a bit as he turned his cheek to talk to the class. My heart was pounding, and I knew he must hear it.

Don't think about it, don't think about, don't think about it.

If Mac felt my entire body tense, he didn't react to it. He continued his instruction with professional aplomb. He told me to adjust my hips slightly to the side to bring my leg on top of his back to help keep him down. The lesson seemed to go on for ages until eventually, Mac had taught me how to free myself from him and get back on my feet. We repeated it until I could do this smoothly, and a surge of pride and self-sufficiency flooded me.

Still, as the class paired off to practice, I muttered so only he could hear, "You had to choose me, aye?"

This time, Mac's expression wasn't teasing. "Aye, because more than anyone else in this room, I need to know you can do it. I need to know that if anyone comes at you, you can handle yourself. I care if my students learn self-defense. But you're not just a student. You're the woman I love. And if you can't protect yourself against an attacker and something happens to you, I'll spend the rest of my life in prison. Because I'll kill the fucker."

That shut me up.

Because I knew deep down, he meant every word.

22

MAC

Annie Stuart had been frequenting my class for two months, and while I took her flirting as harmless, I should have seen it coming when she lingered after class.

Arro waited for me while I'd changed back into my street clothes. I usually showered at the center, but I didn't want to keep Arro waiting too long. She'd taken to the lessons with determination, despite the discomfort my proximity caused her. Discomfort because she might currently mistrust me, but her body definitely did not. When I first pinned her, I saw the flare of arousal in her eyes and the flush on her skin. Her shallow, sharp breaths gave her awareness away.

Resolved to ignore the enticing sight of her beneath me, I compartmentalized the realization of a long-held fantasy and tried to think of her as any other student. It wasn't easy, but I got through it. Mostly because I was serious when I told Arro that I needed her to learn this stuff now so I could live without the constant fear of something happening to her.

Teaching her self-defense wouldn't ease those fears entirely, but it would make me feel better. Moreover, I knew it would make her feel more in control. I saw the hard satisfaction in her expression when she grappled and got out from under me.

On a personal note, I had hope that yesterday might've knocked down some walls between us. I needed her to remember how much I loved her, and I believed maybe she finally did.

When I returned to the reception area, Arro was sitting on the floor scrolling through her phone.

Annie leaned against the opposite wall, also waiting. Unlike most of the other students who'd all left still wearing the gi, their traditional uniform, Annie had taken off the jacket. Her cropped tank top left little to the imagination.

Approaching Arro, I tensed as Annie walked over to us with a deliberate swing in her hips.

"I just wanted to say thanks again for another great class." Annie stopped before me, ignoring Arro.

The woman wasn't my type. Too immature. Too self-involved. And she treated the other women in the class as a threat, as competition. She always paired off with one of the few men and continually offered to partner with me. It hadn't really bothered me … until this moment.

"You're welcome," I said, sounding stiff even to my own ears.

"So … are you free right now, maybe? Thought we could get a drink?"

"No." It was blunt. Far blunter than I'd normally be, but Arro was right next to me, and I didn't want her getting the wrong impression.

Annie's eyes rounded in surprise. "No?"

"I'll see you next week," I said, not wanting to engage in this conversation any longer.

She screwed up her face, morphing her pretty features into something ugly, glanced at Arro, huffed, and then stormed out of the reception area. We heard the bang of the front entrance doors slamming behind her.

Sighing heavily, I looked at Arro, her expression worryingly blank. "Come on," I murmured, leading her toward reception. There was one class later than mine, so the receptionist was still on duty. He took the keys to the court, and I thanked him.

I'd been planning to ignore the moment with Annie, but as we walked toward the exit, Arro said, "I wouldn't bet on her coming back next week."

"I'm not." Studying her, finding her expression blank and completely irritated by that, I assured her, "Nothing happened between us. She flirts, I ignore it."

At Arro's snort of disbelief, I caught her arm, drawing her to a stop by the door. "I mean it. I don't sleep with my students."

She gently removed her arm from my hold. "I know for a fact that's not true."

"What the hell does that mean?" Anger brewed in my gut. We had our differences, but I hated being accused of lying under normal circumstances, never mind by Arro.

Her blue gaze washed over my face, her disappointment so evident, it made me want to punch my fist through the wall. "I came here at the beginning of last year. You'd brought a picnic to my work, and I thought it was such a romantic gesture, it had to be a signal to me that you were ready for more."

I blanched at the bitterness in her words and the reminder that I'd been a selfish, confusing bastard to her.

"Anyway, I decided to surprise you after your class one night and waited out in the car park. You left with a brunette around my age, and by the way you kissed her up against her car, it was obvious you two were fucking." Arro laughed softly, hollowly, the sound almost as bad as the knowledge she'd witnessed me with someone else. "Guy had been asking me out for weeks … and that was the moment I gave up on you and said yes to him."

She blew out a long breath. "But then, of course, you sent out a bunch of mixed signals months later, and I found myself back at square one … wondering how many of your young students you'd been shagging while pretending I was too young for you." She gave me a strained smile, like she didn't care.

We both knew she cared.

And I hated myself all over again for hurting her. "That woman, Pippa, she wasn't a student. She taught a spin class for a while here at the center. I don't sleep with my students." And because, for Arro, I could swallow my pride, I confessed, "I haven't been with another woman since Pippa."

She looked visibly surprised.

"It was empty. I've grown tired of empty sex."

The words hummed between us.

"I'm sorry. All the mixed signals. It … it wasn't intentional."

After what seemed like forever, she nodded slowly. "I know. I heard you yesterday, Mac, believe me. I'm just … I need time to figure out how I see our future, if we have one." She looked away and pushed open the door to exit. I watched her walk ahead for a few seconds and experienced that familiar hard pull toward her that forced me to follow.

I'd just stepped out of the building when I heard the harsh squeal of tires and followed the sound to a black car with tinted windows racing through the car park—

Heading directly for Arro.

"ARRO!" I roared as I ran toward her, shoving her out of the way seconds before pain slammed into my side and I was up in the air, rolling across the car's bonnet. Years of training kicked in a split second, and I tucked my head and rolled as I hit the ground.

"Mac!" Arro screamed, and I raised my gaze as tires squealed against tarmac and the car reversed in my direction. I lunged out of the way just in time.

Suddenly, the vehicle sped away again, and I took a mental snapshot of the license plate as it barreled out of the car park. Hurrying toward Arro, I grabbed her biceps and lifted her onto her feet. "Are you all right?" I asked as I hastened her into my vehicle.

"I'm fine. Are you okay?" she asked, her voice trembling.

Too focused on getting her out of there in case the perpetrator came back, I didn't answer. Instead, I jumped into the driver's side and instructed, "Seat belt on!"

"Mac, you just got hit by a bloody car!" Arro yelled. "Tell me you're okay."

I couldn't feel a damn thing except urgency, but I gave my body a cursory once-over and determined, except for an ache in my right ankle, I was all right. "I'm fine," I assured her.

Seconds later, I was flying out of the car park.

"What the hell just happened?" Arro whispered in shock.

"Call 999," I barked at my car.

The next few minutes, I patiently explained to the police what had happened, despite the terror thrumming through my veins. Arro had almost been hit. I gave them the registration plate and explained I was driving to safety. The police dispatcher asked if we needed medical assistance, but I could deal with the aches and pains on my own.

Once we'd hung up, Arro opened her mouth to ask another question, but I said to the car, "Call Lisa."

It rang five times before she picked up. "I'm assuming this is an emergency," she answered wryly.

I then explained everything all over again and continued,

225

"I need you to make sure the police are taking this seriously. We could catch this bastard, Lisa, right now."

"First, are you both all right?"

"We're fine, we're fine."

"Okay, then I'm getting off the phone and straight onto my colleagues at Inverness to make sure they're on this."

"Thank you, Lisa, I appreciate it."

"Not a problem." She hung up, and a tense silence filled the vehicle.

I looked briefly at Arro. "You sure you're all right?"

"I'm not the one who just got hit by a car, Mackennon!" Arro cried in outrage.

"I told you, I'm fine. My ankle hurts a bit, that's it."

"Wait until the adrenaline wears off." Out of the corner of my eye, I saw her shaking her head in exasperation. "It's that Lee bloke, isn't it?"

"I assume so. I'm sorry." Feelings of failure and guilt threatened to overwhelm me.

"Hey." Arro reached out and rested a hand on my knee. "Not your fault."

Weeks before, her words wouldn't have penetrated, but now I let them remind me of what Iona had asked me to do: flip the negative on its head, and think of the positive.

What was the positive here?

I glanced at Arro.

I'd saved her from being hit by that car.

I chanted that over and over in my head until it sank in. "I know," I eventually responded. "Thank you."

Unfortunately, she removed her hand from my leg. Still, I could feel her there like a phantom touch.

"Who is Lisa?" she asked tentatively.

As much as I didn't want to remind her I'd been with other women, I was in my forties, and my sexual history was fact. Besides, it wasn't like Arro hadn't been with other men.

I was almost certain she'd slept with Grayson Evans at Lachlan and Robyn's wedding. The prick. "I met Lisa years ago when Lachlan was still acting. She was just a police officer in Glasgow then, and we had a casual affair."

"Oh?"

"We've remained friends, and she's flown up the ranks since. She's a chief constable now."

"Very good."

The sharpness in Arro's tone almost made me smile. She sounded jealous, and while I hadn't intended to make her jealous, it did mean she still had feelings for me. And I'd take what I could get.

AFTER UPDATING LACHLAN, I assured him, despite Arro's quiet protests, that I would sleep on her couch. There was no way I was just sitting outside her house. I needed her close. No arguments.

We'd barely let ourselves into her bungalow when the patrol car pulled up and parked. I went to the door and ushered the two constables inside. They asked us questions about the incident outside the sports center, and I explained there was CCTV at the building entrance that might provide useful footage for their investigation.

"You do know this is more than likely part of a bigger investigation?" I asked.

The female constable, PC Bell, nodded. "We've been briefed on the situation."

They asked a few more questions, but when they repeatedly grilled Arro about if she was sure the car had tried to reverse over me, I broke in, "She said she's sure. And like I said, there is CCTV at the sports center. Don't you think that's where you should focus your time?"

The male constable threw me a look, but nodded.

Minutes later, they departed with promises to update me.

"I don't think you did us any favors losing your patience. It isn't like you, Mac," Arro said behind me.

Turning from the closed front door, I shook my head. "I have no patience for the suggestion you're not intelligent enough to know what you witnessed."

She sighed, nodding her head. "Aye, I was seconds away from biting their heads off too." With a shrug, she gestured to the living room. "Go sit. I'll make us coffee and grab snacks. You must be hungry."

As I moved into the living room, however, my ankle throbbed and my ribs hurt from the impact with the car. Limping a little, I stopped to pull up my trouser leg and have a look. My ankle was swollen.

Arro sucked in a breath, and I brought my head up. She watched me from the kitchen doorway. "Are you sure it isn't broken?"

"I don't think so. If it is, we're talking about a minor fracture. Nothing to worry about."

"Take off your shoe and sock," she ordered, marching over to the armchair to grab its cushion. Then she piled all the sofa cushions with it at the end of the sofa. "Sit, elevate that foot." She gestured to the plush stack. "I'll get ice and paracetamol."

Not one to be fussed over, I'd usually protest, especially after the mind-numbing recovery after my stabbing last year. Yet, I quite liked Arro fussing over me. I always had.

By the time she returned to the living room carrying a tray with supplies, including our coffees and snacks, I was sitting up on the couch with my legs outstretched, foot elevated on her cushion tower.

Arro tutted as she studied the red, swollen ankle before

applying a tea towel filled with ice. The frigid touch to my hot skin made me involuntarily jerk.

"Okay?" She looked at me.

I stared into those stunning, pale-blue eyes and felt relief and peace settle over me. She was here, and she was safe. "It's good, thanks."

Something in my voice, or perhaps the way I studied her, caused a telltale flush on the crest of her cheeks, and I tried not to feel too smug about it. Tearing her gaze from mine, she wrapped the ends of the tea towel around my ankle so the ice pressed up against the swollen area without me having to hold it.

"You're an angel," I said as she handed me a coffee and a wee plate of snacks.

Arro straightened and looked down at me in a way I didn't quite understand, until suddenly, I recognized her expression. It was a look I thought I'd never see again. "I'm not the angel, Mackennon. You pushed me out of the way of a car tonight. If it had hit me, I wouldn't have been able to land like a bloody ninja like you or get out of its way fast enough when he came back. I'd probably be dead. You saved my life. Thank you."

Emotion clogged my throat. "You never need to thank me for that, Arro."

She chuckled, blinking back tears. "Actually, Mackennon, anytime you save my life, I'm going to thank you. It's just bloody polite, you know."

Arro's eyes lit up at the sound of my laughter, and for a moment, I felt a prickle of hope.

But as if realizing the pull between us was stronger than ever, she abruptly stopped smiling, grabbed her own coffee, and sat primly in her armchair. "I wonder what's on telly," she said, her voice a little too high as she reached for the remote.

ARRO

WITH A GROAN, I flipped off my duvet, threw my legs over the side of the bed, and sat up. Exhaustion clung to me as I buried my face in my hands and remembered the events of the night before.

I still couldn't believe Mackennon had pushed me out of the way of a moving vehicle.

And since when was he Mackennon again? I scowled.

Since he saved my life.

That sort of thing softened you toward a person.

Damn the man! I could actually feel him in the house, I was so aware of his presence. It had taken ages to fall asleep because of the adrenaline, and now the morning light pouring through the crack in my curtains had woken me at the break of dawn.

Coffee.

I needed coffee.

And to check on Mac. He couldn't have had a decent sleep on the couch. I'd told him to take one of the kids' beds in the guest room, but he said the living room was a better central point for him to keep guard.

Hopefully, soon the whole need for a guard would be moot when they found the arsehole behind this craziness.

Glancing in my mirror to make sure I was decent, I considered changing my sleep shorts into jogging bottoms but decided if my attire made Mac uncomfortable, he'd have to deal with it. It was just a pair of shorts. And my T-shirt was decent, except for the lack of bra.

I should put on a bra.

Pee first, then bra.

That decided, I opened my bedroom door and stepped into the hall, about to cross to the bathroom when its door opened.

Mac froze at the threshold when he saw me and then relaxed. "Morning. Sleep all right?"

Of course, he was awake at the arse crack of dawn.

And he'd showered.

His hair curled by his ears, droplets dripping onto his bare shoulders into a glistening trail down his naked chest, over his hard pecs, past the three scars in his upper torso, zigzagging over his muscular abdominals before disappearing beneath the waistband of his jeans. His jeans hung low enough to reveal the defined V-cut of his obliques.

The fucker.

Mac raised his arm, and I noted the towel in his hand before my gaze was drawn to his flexing biceps as he dried his hair.

The bastard.

The man was godlike in his proportions.

"Ugh!" I gestured at his body in frustration before stomping down the hallway toward the kitchen.

"Arro?" I heard him ask in confusion.

"Fucking saving my life, using my shower, walking around half-naked with a body like a cast member of bloody *Magic Mike*," I muttered angrily under my breath as I clanged angrily around my kitchen.

"Eh, did I miss something?" Mac asked from the doorway.

"Put on a shirt, Mackennon," I snapped without looking at him.

He chuckled darkly and replied, "Only if you put on a bra, Arrochar."

Glancing sharply down at my chest, I noted my nipples poking through my T-shirt and let out a stream of murmured expletives. Whirling around, I glowered at him and marched across the kitchen, intending to hurry past him. But when I reached the entry to the hall, he blocked my path, maneuvering me against the wall.

I was fairly tall, but Mac still had a good eight inches over me, and I felt every one of those as he raised an arm above my head and leaned in. I smelled my shower gel on him, my shampoo in his hair. Suddenly, the idea of us sharing toiletries was intimate in a way it never had with anyone before.

My gaze drifted from his hard-earned body, past lips I could draw from memory, and up to his eyes, but I found him staring at my breasts. My nipples tightened into harder points beneath his interest.

Mac let out a grunt of masculine desire as his eyes flew to mine.

Breathing shallow, I tried to unjumble my thoughts and searched for equilibrium and rationality as part of me yelled I should stop whatever this was.

But the throb between my legs was louder, the pounding of my heart fiercer. The need coiling deep inside was very much screaming at me.

"Mackennon?" I whispered, my attention dropping to his mouth.

He raised his other hand to cup my cheek, and I tilted my head into his touch, squeezing my eyes closed at the rasp of calluses against my skin. Goose bumps prickled all over at the thought of those hands on my breasts, on my thighs, his long fingers sliding inside me—

I shook myself, pulling away from his touch. "Mac—"

His head descended for mine, his lips just brushing my mouth, when the doorbell rang through the house. Mac retreated with a muttered curse, his eyes blazing, his expression promising me this wasn't over.

My lips tingled.

Oh, boy.

Literally saved by the bell.

"I'll get it," I squeaked, sliding out from between him and the wall.

But he caught my arm to halt me. "I'll get it. You … might want to put on a bra."

Ah, right, of course. I nodded and hurried toward my bedroom.

The sound of male voices filtered toward me as I pulled on a robe. I knew those voices.

My big brothers.

They'd cockblocked Mac without even knowing it.

The thought made me chuckle as I strode out to greet them. Lachlan, Thane, and Arran were all in my living room, up at dawn to check on us.

As I accepted their embraces and listened as they all spoke gruffly over one another about their worry, I attempted to put the confusing incident with Mac in the kitchen behind me and just appreciate all the familial love in this room.

Once we'd all had coffee and the boys were preparing to leave for work (well, Lachlan and Thane were), Mac's phone rang.

He crossed the room to pick it up, and I noted he was no longer limping. His ankle looked much better today. It was hopefully just a sprain, then. "It's Lisa," Mac told us before he answered.

We listened to the one-sided conversation on tenter-hooks. Inwardly, I prayed that they'd caught the perpetrator, that it was Lee, and we could put this mess behind us for good.

When Mac hung up, his eyes came to mine as he conveyed, "They caught him. Patrol car caught Lee on the A9

233

near Blair Atholl. They questioned the sports center receptionist and he hadn't seen anything, but the CCTV footage corroborated our story. They've got Lee in custody but haven't questioned him yet. Lisa says the evidence is pretty cut-and-dried. And this time, he won't be released on bail." Mac slumped as if the weight of the world had been lifted from his shoulders. "It looks like this might be over, Arro."

That stifling feeling that had suffocated me these past weeks melted away, too, and it was like I could breathe properly again. I accepted more hugs from my brothers and agreed to join them for a celebratory dinner later in the week.

I watched Mac as Lachlan hugged me again, and though I was relieved we were more than likely in the clear, I was more confused than ever about Mackennon Galbraith.

23

ARRO

T he sound of Arran's laughter mingled with the kids' giggles and Eredine's low chuckles. Such joyous sounds filled me with a sense of peace. Regan sat beside me at her kitchen island while Eredine, my brother, and my niece and nephew played out in the garden.

"They're at that age where they want to go on playdates with friends on the weekend, but ever since Arran moved into the annex, they love hanging out with him instead," Regan said, giving me a soft smile. "He's so good with them."

A flicker of unease ran through me, bursting my bubble. I worried about how the kids would react once Arran left. It was surprising he was still here, now that the threat hanging over me (and Mac) was over. The police had formally arrested Lee Kilmany. He'd been charged with the suspected murder of Bryan McNab and the attempted murder of Mac (Lisa told Mac her detectives were trying to find evidence that linked him to the crimes involving his other old friends), and those were separate from the charges of conspiracy to handle stolen goods.

While Lee denied sending the notes to me, he'd also

denied running over Mac and killing Bryan McNab. We'd had a family meeting, and all felt pretty sure we had our suspect. Mac thankfully agreed I no longer needed private security, i.e., him shadowing my every step. It was hilarious to me that six months ago, I would've thoroughly enjoyed having Mac breathing down my neck every hour of the day, but now I was glad to have some space from him for a while.

I ignored the little voice in my head that said I'd missed him this past week. While it might've been a wee bit true, the bigger truth was I needed time to process everything that had happened between us since March.

"Where did you go?" Regan's voice cut through my thoughts.

I gave her a bland smile and fibbed, "Just wondering how long Arran will stay. I'm surprised he's still here."

Regan leaned into me. "He and Thane talked last night, and it sounds like he's staying permanently. Apparently, Gordon is retiring and thinking of selling the Gloaming."

Shocked, I gaped at Regan. Gordon had owned the Gloaming since before I was born. The hotel, bar, and restaurant were part of Ardnoch's identity. "It can't be true."

She nodded. "He came to Lachlan to ask if he might be interested in buying it. Lachlan said he'd give it some thought, told Arran about it, and Arran showed genuine interest in running it. I think he's considering taking his piece of the Adair inheritance to split the cost with Lachlan. Go into it as partners."

My heart raced at the thought. In a good way. A slow, hopeful smile creased my cheeks as I looked out toward the garden, where I caught flashes of Arran racing after the kids as they played football. "Then he's really staying?"

"I hope so."

Lewis got hold of the ball, his little face scrunched with determination as he dribbled it toward their imaginary goal lines. Eredine moved to intercept him, but Arran wrapped his arms around her waist and lifted her out of Lewis's way.

"Not fair!" Ery laughed, looking happier than I'd seen her in a while. "That's cheating!"

Arran barely released her when Eilidh jumped on him too. He fell to the ground, laughing as Eilidh climbed all over him, tickling him in punishment.

I dragged my attention from the scene to smile at Regan. "I think, despite my earlier worry, he's been good for Ery."

Regan nodded, but with raised brows. "I wonder how Brodan will feel about their friendship when he gets back."

"Brodan doesn't get a say," I said a little too sharply.

Regan made a face. "Okay, Mom."

"Sorry. It's just … Have you noticed how every time he's home, he watches her and flirts with her, but then he buggers off again, forgetting she even exists? I'm sorry, but Eredine deserves better. I don't care if he is my brother."

"And considering Mac kind of played you that way for a while, I can see how you'd feel sympathetic toward Eredine."

I gaped at her for the second time. "How do you know about Mac?"

She grimaced. "Was I not supposed to say anything? I thought because he talked with the guys, it was all out in the open now."

"I knew he spoke to Lachlan, but I didn't know he'd spoken to Thane and Arran. Why haven't they mentioned it to me?"

"Because we are all giving you space to figure out what you want. Though nosy busybodies"—she gestured to herself—"are extremely interested to know where you're leaning on the whole Mac thing. Personally, I think you guys are great together."

"Regan," I pleaded.

"Sorry, sorry." She pretended to zip her lips shut. "Not

another word." Then, "Though I agree with you about Brodan and Eredine. But I'm not sure she has anything romantic in mind with Arran. They argue a lot."

"It's called verbal foreplay, Regan. And a sure sign that something is going on. Eredine is usually shy with men, including Brodan. With Arran, she's ... sassy. Like she's comfortable with him or something."

"You sound worried."

"It wouldn't be the first time my brothers have fought over a woman. The two of them are best buddies, and when they were sex-mad, moronic teenagers, they shared everything, including women. It was never a problem for them, the scoundrels, until Arran slept with ..." I realized I was about to divulge information I was pretty certain neither of my brothers would want me sharing. "Let's just say someone he shouldn't have. It caused a rift, and even though those two can never stay mad at each other, I do not want history repeating itself with Eredine. She's ..."

"A complicated mystery," Regan finished my sentence.

"Even to me, and I've known her almost as long as Lachlan and Mac have."

Regan looked pensive as she stared out at the garden. "Can I tell you something?"

"Of course."

"I recognized Eredine when I first met her."

I jerked in shock. "What do you mean?"

"I thought I recognized her as this social media influencer and dancer from YouTube. She had a few million followers, millions more views on her videos. Her name was Cadenza. And I am ninety percent positive she was the spitting image of Eredine. She stopped posting years ago. I mean, I was only a teen when I followed her videos. I guess I forgot about her after a while because there's always someone new to follow, right? Anyway, here's the strange part."

Regan leaned into me again, her voice low. "I tried to find those videos, and they were gone. Completely wiped off the internet. I tried googling *Cadenza*, and nothing. So, I set a Google Alert last year for her, and a few weeks ago, this conspiracy theorist had written an article about this group he thinks exists similar to the Illuminati. He mentioned all these people who had mysteriously disappeared, and he mentioned Cadenza. I don't believe the creepy omniscient global power group theory, but I was relieved because for a second there, I thought maybe I had imagined it all. When I went back to look at the article, it was gone."

A sense of dread, of something ominous looming over us, caused goose bumps to prickle my skin. "Have you tried googling Eredine?"

"Yeah, but we all know that's not her real name."

True enough.

"I googled her, her profession, where she works, and there is zero mention of her on the web. Don't you think that's weird?"

"There wouldn't be." I shook my head. "Lachlan doesn't advertise anything about the estate. In fact …" I narrowed my eyes. "They use an ethical hacker to test their security systems for flaws, and she built a program that alerts them to online articles about the club. Mac's team sifts through them and asks his hacker to delete any that mention details they don't want known."

"Isn't that illegal?" Regan smirked. "I thought you said she was an ethical hacker?"

"Not my point. She *removes* posts and articles off the web for them."

Regan's eyes widened before her gaze flew out toward the garden. "They're protecting her?"

It would appear so. Not that I was surprised. Deep down, I'd known that all along.

"But from what?" Regan whispered.

I looked out and watched Eredine shove Arran with a mischievous laugh as she commandeered the ball. "Leave it alone, Regan," I ordered sternly. "If she's hiding here, then there's a good reason, and it's our job as the people who love her to let sleeping dogs lie."

Regan nodded determinedly and promised, "I'll let it go."

24

MAC

"It's been a tough week."

Iona tilted her head to study me. "Why is that?"

"Arro's avoiding me. Last week, I understood. But another week has passed, and she hasn't reached out. She hasn't returned to my class either."

"And how does that make you feel?"

I sighed impatiently. "Irritated."

"And?"

"Agitated."

"Mac"—Iona's lips twitched—"what's beneath the agitation?"

Leaning forward, elbows on knees, I stared out at the River Ness. "I let myself hope after we'd had an honest conversation. I thought maybe there was a chance. But her avoiding me just preys on all my ..." I hated even saying the word. "Insecurities."

"Have you been practicing the techniques we discussed?"

"Aye." I looked back at her. "They help. But this week, I've had a lot of moments when I had to catch myself from falling back into the bad habit of convincing myself she's better off without me."

"But you caught yourself? The techniques helped?"

"Aye, but it's tiring."

"It is," she agreed sympathetically. "And worth it. Now … how do you know Arro's avoiding you?"

I frowned. "Because I haven't seen her."

"Has she not been taking your calls?"

"Eh, I haven't called her."

Iona shrugged. "Why not?"

"I thought she needed space to think about everything."

"Did Arro tell you she needed space?"

"She said she needed time."

"Time and space are related, but they're not the same thing. Arro might well be able to process your relationship while still spending time with you. If you'd like to see her, Mac, all you have to do is ask. She might not agree to it, but at least you'll have taken a step to move things forward."

I'D ALMOST FORGOTTEN how busy the club could be during the summer months. Last summer was quieter than usual because of the chaos Lucy had wreaked on us all. Lachlan had canceled his annual summer solstice ceilidh, but it was going ahead this year, and there were people completing tasks all over the estate to prepare for it. Club members who owned private residences had flown in to spend their summers here, and the castle was soon to be near full capacity. Most members couldn't stay longer than a few days, but they'd all flown in for the ceilidh.

I'd been in the kitchen talking to the estate chef, Rafaella, because her sous chef was convinced supplies were missing from the pantry and fridge. We went into her small office off the kitchen to discuss the possibility one of her staff was stealing, and I told her we'd check the kitchen's security camera footage. I further offered to speak with Lachlan about installing a discreet camera into the pantry and refrigerator area.

Lachlan called at that moment and told me he needed me down at Loch Ardnoch, a private loch on the estate where Lachlan had built several cabins, one of which Eredine ran her Pilates, yoga, and mindfulness classes from.

I strode past the great hall, glancing into it, so used to the grandeur of its sweeping staircase, stained glass windows, and medieval fireplace that I barely noticed it now. Except on days when it was busy like this. A few members chatted on the chesterfield sofas by the unlit fire, while the company Lachlan had hired to decorate were up on tall ladders, taking measurements along the galleried balcony.

Housekeeper Sarah McCulloch, granddaughter of local farmer Collum McCulloch, and another housekeeper named Mallory were on hands and knees working a stain out of one of the expensive red carpets.

I was about to slip down the corridor to our offices and through a side exit door that led directly across the golf course toward the loch when my path was blocked by Hollywood actor Iris Benning. Halting, I raised an eyebrow at her sudden appearance.

She'd only recently become a club member after garnering her second consecutive Oscar nomination. Tall, athletic, apparently talented (though I wouldn't know because I hadn't seen any of her films), the brunette held herself with a confidence that belied her years.

And considering I knew her to be only twenty, the look in her eye made me a wee bit uncomfortable.

"Ms. Benning, is there a problem?" I kept my tone neutral, professional.

Her dark eyes glittered with a come-on that was as unnerving as it was unmistakable. She stepped into my personal space, uncaring if anyone was watching. "Please, Mac, call me Iris." At my silence, she smirked. "You know, I've been here for four days, and I've been watching you, but you've been too polite to watch me back."

I wasn't even aware of her existence beyond her name on our member roster.

"Ms. Benning, I'm on my way to a meeting. Is there something you need? I can call on Wakefield."

She frowned at my continued flatness. "Okay, maybe I need to be more forward with you Scottish guys. I think you're hot, and I want to fuck you. When can we do that?"

I blinked, surprised anything could still shock me. Not that women hadn't spoken plainly to me like this before or that club members (of all genders) hadn't tried to slip their room cards into my hand ... but Iris Benning was barely out of childhood. It was disturbing.

Using the same bland but diplomatic tone I'd used with previous members who'd wanted to sleep with me, I said, "Ms. Benning, as head of security for Ardnoch Estate, that would not be appropriate. Have a good day." I moved to walk past her, but she wrapped her hand with her long, spiky nails around my forearm. Fuck.

"No one needs to know, Mac." She closed the gap between us again, her too-sweet perfume irritating. "Please." Iris pouted in a way I assumed she thought was seductive. "I have all these daddy fantasies running through my head I'm dying to act out with you."

Shuddering in horror, I pulled my arm from her grip. "Aye, nope. Not going to happen." I shuddered involuntarily again and strode away.

"Ooh, playing hard to get," Iris called loudly enough for anyone to hear. "I like it!"

I grimaced.

Save me from bored film stars.

Taking a deep breath, I marched left down the narrow staff corridor and toward the side exit. I burst into the humid summer air and tried to forget about the odd interlude as I made my way down to Loch Ardnoch.

Less than ten minutes later, I spotted Lachlan on the pathway at the top of the loch. The sun glinted off the placid water, and its stillness created a calm. Eredine's studio was in cabin one, and I could see her walking past the gabled end window.

"What's happening?" I greeted Lachlan.

My friend raised an eyebrow. "You took your time."

I sighed, crossing my arms over my chest. "Iris Benning accosted me."

"What?" Lachlan scowled.

"Ach, it was nothing either of us hasn't dealt with before." I considered that. "Okay, this was a wee bit more upsetting than usual."

"What the hell did she say?"

"She was … blunt."

"Need me to have a word?"

"'Course not. I've just added her to my 'know when they're here so I can avoid them' list."

Lachlan chuckled and turned back to the water. "Angeline Potter still on that list?"

"Still top." The British actor tried to corner me almost every time she visited the estate.

"Oh, how awful it must be," my friend teased, "to be wanted."

His words hit with deadly aim. After taking Iona's advice, I'd tried to call Arro, but it went straight to voice mail. So I'd texted her this morning instead to ask if she'd like to meet for coffee tomorrow. No response. Fucking crickets.

"Sorry." Lachlan studied me. "Didn't mean to piss you off."

I told him about Arro.

He sighed heavily. "Give her time. And don't let her catch an oversexed starlet barely out of high school flirting with you."

"That would require Arro to be in the same room as me." I glowered.

Lachlan opened his mouth to reply, but agitated, I decided I no longer wanted to discuss his sister. "Why did you need me here?"

"Oh, right." Lachlan gestured to the loch. "I think it might be nice to create a party area here for the ceilidh. Somewhere quieter, romantic. Light lanterns across the loch, have a deejay play mood music, have a bar here, that sort of thing."

"And?"

"And I thought we could set off the fireworks here instead of up at the castle, but I wondered if that would affect the anti-drone perimeter?"

"The fireworks shouldn't be a problem, but maybe there's an alternative to fireworks ... though, the cost would be exponentially higher."

"What are you talking about?"

"Drone displays. We'd need to make sure the display was well within the perimeter so as not to set off the anti-drone system, but they're more environmentally friendly, and I know you're working toward making the estate greener."

Lachlan tilted his mouth in consideration. "I've seen them. They're quite effective. How much are we talking?"

I shrugged. "I don't know offhand, but easily six figures."

He cursed under his breath. "For a light show?" But I knew Lachlan's expressions enough to know that the idea intrigued him. "Maybe I know someone who can get me a discount."

"Maybe."

"I'll look into it. It would be something different, and you know I'm always looking for ways to keep the members surprised and satisfied. I could ..."

My phone buzzed in my jacket pocket, and Lachlan's voice faded into the background at the sight of Arro's name on my screen. I clicked on the notification.

I can do coffee. Flora's tomorrow at noon?

I felt so fucking euphoric, you'd think she'd just agreed to marry me. I quickly typed back I'd meet her there and that I was looking forward to it.

"Arro?"

Glancing up from my phone, I found Lachlan smirking at me. "What?"

"She texted you back?"

"Aye, how did you know? Also, I don't know about you, but I still find it strange discussing this with you."

"Well, get over it because if she forgives you, this will be our lives moving forward. And I knew because you're grinning like a Cheshire cat." He smacked me on the back as he strode toward the castle. "You're a lost cause, man."

I followed him. "Says the man *owned* by my daughter. She bought you a leash yet?"

Lachlan threw his head back in laughter. "As her father, I'll save you the horror of answering that question."

"Fuck off."

The bastard only laughed harder.

"Keep laughing, and I won't tell you what I really think about your plans for the loch."

Lachlan stalled and looked back at me. "Go on, then."

"It's a bad idea. Right now, the members respect the grounds. Turn Loch Ardnoch into a party area, and they might think it's okay to go down there whenever they want for a knees-up. Besides, the cleanup will be a pain in the arse.

247

All those water lanterns, the inevitable rubbish and damage to the land ..."

"You've got to give the members some credit, Mac." Lachlan frowned, his gaze moving past my shoulders, and I could tell my concerns were sinking in.

"Never mind the fact that they might think it's okay to do the same at Loch Evelyn." It was a smaller loch down by the coast, named after Lachlan's ancestor. "Drunk people do stupid shit, Lachlan."

He nodded, heaving an exasperated sigh. "I just wanted to do something different this year."

"Then do it on the castle's main grounds. Save some of that budget for the drones. Just leave the loch alone. I think Eredine and the staff who live at the loch will appreciate that too."

"Fuck, of course. I wasn't thinking."

Knowing the real cause, I assured him, "The members aren't going anywhere. This estate is more than fancy events that offer unique moments. The uniqueness here is privacy in a place of outstanding natural beauty, and that has always been the attraction, Lachlan. Stop worrying so much. If memberships decrease, then you worry."

He nodded, following me back to the castle. "We grew up land rich but cash poor, and I always assumed once I had some real money, I'd stop worrying about financial security so much. But it never goes away. The worry is always there, and as our family grows, it makes me think about it all over again."

I understood, and I knew I would probably never be able to shift that way of thinking for him, but for now, I could reassure him. "Ardnoch is thriving. Try to enjoy the ceilidh, Lachlan, for what it is—your first one with a wife."

He grinned. "Considering our activities at the last two ceilidhs we attended, I think I will."

"You're such a dirty bastard."

Lachlan's loud laughter followed me as I marched ahead of him to the castle. "I'm really enjoying being your son-in-law!"

I gave him the middle finger before I disappeared inside, the door cutting off his renewed amusement.

I COULDN'T REMEMBER EVER FEELING nervous about meeting a woman. Flirting, saying the right thing, that had always come easy to me for the purpose of getting a woman into bed. My whole life I'd been spoiled for choice, and I knew that made me a lucky prick.

However, I was apparently utterly shit at the relationship stuff.

And I'd never wanted to be more capable of something in my whole life than exactly that as I walked down the street toward Flora's Café. I passed neighbors and nodded hello, but I was barely aware of them. All I could think about was saying the right things to Arro, so I didn't push her away. The pressure was unfuckingreal.

My attention caught on the public car park outside the Gloaming, and I noted Arro's new Defender there. I was relieved she'd retired her dad's old vehicle for safety reasons, but I knew it couldn't have been easy for her, and I hated we hadn't even discussed it. We would have done so in the past.

The reminder that I could say the right thing to Arro—because I'd done it for years as her friend—made me feel a wee bit better as I approached Flora's.

There she was.

Sitting at a table by the window, her hands cupped around a cappuccino, staring down into the coffee with a

249

frown puckering her forehead. Her long hair fell over her shoulders in soft, blond waves.

Heart racing harder, I picked up my pace and strolled into the café. I didn't even greet the owner as I always did. I only had eyes for Arro.

She looked up as soon as I walked in.

"Hi," I said as I pulled out the chair across from her and sat. She wore a pale-yellow T-shirt with a censored naked banana on it, and I tried not to smile, and failed. "I like your T-shirt."

Arro smirked. "Regan bought it for my birthday."

I took in her face, and everything in me went calm and still, the chaos inside finally slotting into place like a puzzle, its restlessness fizzling out with relief. She'd caught the sun these past few weeks, freckles glowing on her cheeks and sprinkled across her nose, her skin a soft golden tone. It made her eyes an even paler blue. Arro was beautiful, but beyond the kind of beautiful you experience when you look at an attractive person. She was beautiful to me in a way that burst from the inside out. The kind of beauty that caused this rising, aching sensation. The kind of beauty that reminded me why life was worth living.

Fuck, I loved this woman.

Arro's eyes widened a little, as if she could read everything on my face. She probably could.

"Mac, you didn't say hello." Flora, the café owner, broke the moment between us as she approached our table. It was only as I looked up that I realized the café was filled with customers, the tables all full. I hadn't even heard their chatter until now, I was so focused on Arrochar Adair.

"Flora, morning. Can I get an Americano, please?"

"Um … yeah, of course." Her head bobbed like she was confused. "I'll just bring that over." Her expression flattened, and she stomped away.

I turned back to Arro. "What was that?"

Arro raised an eyebrow. "Mac, you usually flirt with her. It makes her day."

Ah. Right.

Flora Macdonald was an attractive woman around my age, but she was also very married. Mick Macdonald was a bus driver and a dry sort. I didn't think he did much flirting with his wife. I flirted with her because it was second nature, but I would never flirt in earnest with a married woman.

And now … I didn't want to flirt with anyone but Arro. I never wanted her to mistake it for something it wasn't or be hurt by it. I'd inflicted enough pain.

"I'm not going to flirt with another woman in front of you."

"It's never stopped you before."

I grimaced. "We both know it was just out of habit. But … things are different between us now. I would never do that to you."

"Mac, we're not …" Arro shrugged unhappily. "I don't know what we are. I came here because I want to at least try to be friends again, for our sake and everyone else's, but anything else … You shouldn't change yourself for me."

I mimicked her unhappy shrug because I was already changed. There was no going back.

"Your Americano." Flora reappeared and dumped it on the table. "Anything else?"

At her snippy tone, I inwardly sighed and smiled up at her. "No, Flora. Thank you very much."

She softened a little and muttered, "No problem."

Once she'd left us, Arro's mouth twitched with laughter.

"What?" I asked, unable to drag my attention from her lips.

I watched them move as she replied, "You can't help yourself. When you smile at someone. It's … affecting."

251

"I only care that it affects you."

Arro shook her head. "Are you going to say things like that to me all the time now?"

"Aye."

She chuckled, and the sound made me smile, made me itch to touch her. "Well, at least you're honest." Tilting her head in thought, she asked, "Speaking of which, how is ..." Her gaze darted around the café as if to make sure no one was listening, and then she leaned in to continue quietly, "How is therapy going?"

Taking advantage of the need for privacy, I lifted my chair and placed it right beside hers so that when I sat back down, our knees touched. Ignoring Arro's raised eyebrows, I leaned in, inhaling the floral perfume she'd worn for years. "It's ongoing. Iona is great. And the methods are working, I think. It's tiring sometimes. But I definitely feel different. Better. Lighter."

As if she couldn't help herself, Arro wrapped a hand over my forearm and squeezed. "I am proud of you, Mackennon."

Her words were a pleasurable burn in my chest. "That means a lot. Thank you."

At my gruff reply, she gave my arm another squeeze and then withdrew.

"How have you been? That wee prick at work still giving you a hard time?"

"No, I've barely seen Duncan. I'll probably see more of him as we move ahead with the new project, but that won't be for another few weeks yet."

We made small talk for ten minutes or so, but then Flora approached to ask if we needed anything else. Ordering two more coffees and a couple of scones, neither of us missed the way Flora's gaze deliberately bounced between us and the fact that I'd moved my chair closer to Arrochar.

"That's all," Arro said pointedly.

Flora lifted her chin haughtily and walked away. Glancing around, I noticed a group of older villagers near the front counter gawking at us.

"For fuck's sake," I muttered under my breath.

Arro noticed the villagers' attention.

I sighed. "Maybe I shouldn't have sat so close."

She snorted. "Yeah, for my peace of mind. Not for theirs. Let them look. Bloody busybodies."

Arro grew up in this village, and I knew she was used to everybody meddling in one another's business. She'd long decided the only way to get through it was not to give a shit what they thought or said about her. I'd always admired that attitude and shared it.

"I can move," I offered.

She shook her head. "No, not for them. Even if having your leg pressed against mine is extremely confusing."

"Why?" I leaned closer.

Irritation flashed across her face. "You know why."

Need tightened in my gut as the air thickened between us. My eyes dropped to her mouth, and honestly, I couldn't give a fuck who saw us.

But as my head dipped toward hers, she spoke, halting my progress. "You know what hurt the most, Mac?"

I jerked back, dread filling me at her despondent tone.

Her gaze moved over my face, something indecipherable in it. "I don't think it's your rejection that still bothers me. It was how desperate I'd felt at that moment. Desperate for you to love me." Tears glistened in her eyes, and a thick, painful lump rose in my throat. "I never ever want to feel that way again. That's not who I want to be. I'm not that woman."

Terrified by what that might mean, I grasped for her hand. "Arro, think about what's behind that, though. Is it really to do with me, or did that come from something else?"

She yanked her hand away and hissed under her breath,

"Of course, it was about you. You pulled me in and then pushed me away so many times over the years, I was so confused and mixed up about you."

Flora suddenly appeared, her expression disapproving as she placed our coffees on the table. "I'll be right back with the scones."

We sat in tense silence as we waited for Flora to return. She hovered a second too long until I gave her a flat stare. Clearing her throat, she wiped her hands down her apron and walked away.

"We shouldn't talk about this here," Arro murmured.

I studied her downcast countenance. "Aye, I sent out a lot of mixed signals that didn't help any ... but, Arro, think about it. You grew up with four brothers who loved and adored you. What you have with them is more special than you realize. And I think it only emphasized the fact that your dad *wasn't* there for you." I leaned in, my voice low as she lifted her tortured gaze to mine. "A dad who didn't tell you he loved you until he was dying. Of course, that fucked with your head. And along comes me"—emotion made me hoarse —"the first man you've ever romantically loved?"

She gave me a brittle nod.

"And I make you feel like I love you back, but I never say it. Don't you think that's why you felt desperate that night? Because that moment with your dad haunts you, and you never want to have a relationship with someone you love like that again ... where the love comes too late."

A tear escaped, and she looked out the window, swiping the drop from her cheek.

I curled my hand around hers. "I love you."

Her eyes flew back to mine.

"And no matter if you decide to give me a chance or not, know that I will always love you."

I could see her struggling to keep in the tears, and I squeezed her hand harder.

"Everything okay here?" Flora startled us.

Fuck off, Flora. I glared up at her. "We're fine."

Arro scowled at the woman but nodded.

Once she'd left again, Arro bent her head to mine and whispered, "If she comes over one more time, I'm going to tell her to fuck off."

I barked my laughter since she'd mirrored my thoughts, and the tension between us eased somewhat.

We sipped our coffees and then Arro observed, "You always were so perceptive, Mackennon. It amazes me your self-perception is so skewed."

"Aye." I heaved a sigh. "Life's ironic that way, eh?"

She gave me a compassionate smile, and I experienced that pleasurable burn again.

Arro wasn't running. She might not have agreed to give me a shot romantically, but she wasn't running.

There was still a chance for us.

25

ARRO

Lachlan had outdone himself this year.

I strolled into my family's ancestral home, my attention drawn upward to the expansive ceiling now camouflaged by tree branches, leaves, and blossoms. Four mammoth, very real-looking, faux trees stood in each corner of the massive reception hall, their branches arching toward each other across the ceiling to create the canopy. Strings of LED lights dripped from the branches, shining like thick strands of golden diamonds.

Blossoms in pinks and greens and purples and blues brought color to the canopy, and fairy lights had been wrapped around the large tree trunks. Flowered garlands draped the galleried balcony above and all the way down the stair balustrade. The scent of jasmine filled the air, and there were oversized vases filled with flowers and more twinkle lights. Waist-high tables had been strategically placed for people to gather around and talk while they drank champagne and ate canapés served by waitstaff. A violinist wearing a formal evening gown played music from her spot on the landing.

It was fantastically overwhelming to the senses.

"This is amazing," Regan said behind me.

I glanced over my shoulder at her and Thane. He was so handsome in his kilt, Regan stunning in a golden-green dress that made her copper-red hair pop. Eredine, to everyone's surprise, had offered to babysit the kids alone. It was the first time since Regan's stalker, Austin Vale, had knocked Eredine unconscious to kidnap Eilidh and Lewis. I shuddered thinking about it.

Having been told the story, Arran had decided at the last minute he didn't want to attend the ceilidh and would stay behind to watch the kids with Ery. I didn't believe the decision was a last-minute one at all, and while I might question his motives, I was grateful to him for keeping her company.

"Is it always like this?" Regan asked as she ventured farther in among the glamorously attired guests.

"No, he's definitely gone all out this year," Thane murmured, taking it all in. "Sometimes it's hard to remember what this place used to be like."

"Do you miss it?"

"Yes," we answered in unison.

Regan gave us a sympathetic look, but I shrugged. "Lachlan did what needed to be done to save it. It's just ... it holds so many memories for us."

"And it always will."

I spun around at my big brother's voice to find Lachlan, Robyn, and Mac standing before us. Smiling at Lachlan, I reached out to embrace him. "The castle looks tremendous."

"Thank you." He hugged me back. "That means a lot."

I pulled away to hug Robyn. "And Mrs. Adair looks stunning, as always."

Robyn chuckled, shaking her head. "It's still weird being a Mrs."

"Not as weird as being a mum, I'll bet," Thane murmured, pulling Regan to his side with a tender look.

"Are you pregnant?" I gasped.

Thane chuckled as Regan shook her head frantically. "No, no, no."

"Then what …?"

Regan looked at Thane, teary-eyed, as she smiled tremulously. "Eilidh called me *mum* tonight." She shrugged, but I saw the complex emotions roiling in her gaze. "Just casually. 'Mum, can I go to bed later tonight since I can't go to Uncle Lachlan's party?'"

I looked at Thane, wondering how he felt about that. As if reading my thoughts, he said, "It feels right. Eilidh knows and will always know about Fran, that she was her birth mum, but Regan loves her like a mother, and Eilidh loves her like a daughter. It feels right."

Robyn, sensing the heightened emotion, drew Regan in for a tight squeeze, and I heard her murmur, "You okay? You happy?"

"Extremely," Regan choked out. "But I'm close to bawling like a baby, so maybe some champagne?"

"On it." Robyn gave Thane a small smile and took Regan's hand to go find champagne and probably talk a little more about the momentous occasion.

Lachlan approached Thane to do the same, and so I had nothing else to do but finally acknowledge Mac. He looked extraordinarily sexy and handsome.

He'd never dyed the grays that had started growing in around his hairline in his midthirties—that just wasn't Mac. He couldn't give a shit. And honestly, that and the dusting of gray in his stubble gave him a rugged, distinguished air. His hair was so long at the moment, it curled behind his ears.

Thick, silky hair a woman could really get her hands into, if you know what I mean.

Damn the man.

I shivered at the heat in those ever-changing hazel eyes as they dipped down my body and back up again.

Mac wore his kilt well, a black, fitted jacket and waistcoat with the family tartan—a dark green plaid with red, black, and white accents. His long black knee socks accentuated muscular calves formed from the daily hours he spent in the estate gym.

While I appreciated Mac in a kilt, he made it very clear he appreciated me in this dress.

I wore a simple but sexy blush-colored gown—pencil-thin straps, a plunging wrap-front bodice, a figure-hugging silhouette, and an exaggerated hem. The strapless push-up bra I wore under it was doing magical things for my average-size breasts. And the pièce de résistance was the high slit on the right side. Nude strappy high-heeled sandals completed my outfit. I'd done my hair in a loose, thick fishtail braid that hung over one shoulder. Diamond stud earrings I'd inherited from my mum sparkled in my ears to match the elegant necklace that had belonged to her too.

Mac took a step toward me as if compelled to. "You're beautiful."

A flush of pleasure prickled my skin. "Thank you. You look very handsome."

And we might have been stuck like that for hours, staring at each other, if a server hadn't approached and offered us drinks. I took a glass of champagne while Mac turned it down. He didn't drink the bubbly stuff.

He offered me his elbow. "Want something to eat?"

"Sure." I slipped my arm through his, feeling his hard muscle beneath my fingers. A heightened spark of awareness rushed through me, and I attempted to maintain some distance.

Mac pulled me tighter against his side, refusing to allow it.

I wanted to be irritated.

But the truth was, I was a tactile person, always had been. I loved to be touched and cuddled and showered with affection. Mac publicly acknowledging he wanted me as close as possible spoke to that part of me that had always longed to touch him and be touched by him.

Damn it.

Since our conversation in Flora's last weekend, my resistance began to wane bit by bit. Probably before then, if I was honest, but more so this week. Mac texted every day to check in, called me a few times too. I'd forgiven him when he'd apologized and told me about his therapy. Now, though, I was growing toward trusting him again. I didn't know if I ever really could, but something was shifting, changing inside me. Thursday night, we'd watched a thriller on Netflix together over the phone, discussing it, laughing at the plot holes Mac pointed out, until I'd grown too tired to continue. The way he'd wished me good-night, in that deep, rumbly voice, seeped into my body, and I'd dreamed of him.

And now here we were, and he was looking at me like ...

Well, to be frank, like he wanted to devour me.

The thing was ... I was no longer sure I didn't want to be devoured by Mackennon Galbraith.

FURY AND JEALOUSY, two of my least favorite emotions, churned in my gut as I watched a young woman monopolize Mac while I danced the "Highland Barn Dance" with Thane. Mac and I had been having a great time, despite the sexual tension, talking, laughing, and eating from the massive buffet in the dining room. Lachlan had opted for a lavish selection of party food instead of a sit-down dinner. The rest of my family soon joined us, and not long later, the ceilidh dancing started.

I hadn't really thought anything of it when Grayson Evans approached to ask me to dance. I'd actually been relieved he didn't hate me after our last encounter, but as I glanced back at Mac, his face was like thunder.

And I realized he didn't know I hadn't slept with Gray.

Before I could return to explain, another guest kept me on the dance floor for "The Dashing White Sergeant." None of these dances, FYI, were easy in four-inch heels. It was then I'd noticed Mac had been left alone, but not for long. A woman (more like a girl!) who seemed vaguely familiar and wore a cutout dress she looked far too amazing in, approached Mac. She'd gotten physically closer to him within the last minute.

And despite my jealousy, I knew Mac well enough to know he was uncomfortable. He always looked extra stern when he was in a situation he didn't want to be in, his lips pressed into a thin line, brow furrowed, shoulders stiff.

After hopping and skipping sideways from Thane, and then back toward him as part of the steps, my big brother pulled me away from the dancers.

"What are you doing?"

"You're going to break something craning your neck to see what's going on with Mac," Thane replied dryly. "Just go over there."

I immaturely stuck out my tongue at my brother, but he chuckled and gently shoved me toward Mac.

As if sensing me, he looked up. Annoyance flashed across his face. And jealousy. I saw it. It made me feel a little better about my possessiveness.

Our complicated situation aside, he was my friend, and as a friend, it was my duty to rescue him. Approaching Mac, I sidled close, and despite his irritation, he rested his hand on my hip. I placed my hand on his flat, hard stomach in a claiming gesture and cuddled into him. Heat flushed through me, and I felt the telltale tingle between my legs.

Distracting me from my sexual awareness of Mac, the familiar young woman sneered at me. "Excuse you."

I raised an eyebrow at her churlishness. "I'm sorry. I don't believe we've met. I'm Mac's date."

"Uh, I don't care who you are. We were talking, and you rudely interrupted. Do you not know who I am?"

I chuckled at the cliché arrogance. Sometimes it was hard to believe people like her existed, but I'd witnessed outrageous superiority complexes at university when I met a particularly entitled son of a British lord. While many of Lachlan's club members seemed nice enough, there were the odd few who thought themselves God's gift to mankind. "Sweetheart, I don't care who you are."

The girl dragged her gaze down my body and back up again. "Does Lachlan know someone let the riffraff in?"

Mac tensed against me. "Ms. Benning, your continued membership to this club is contingent upon your good manners. You do not insult Ms. Adair, period, never mind inside her ancestral home."

Ms. Benning. Ah, now I recognized her. Iris Benning.

Och, damn it. I'd liked her in her last movie too. See, this was the problem with Lachlan running a club for Hollywood people. Sometimes it ruined the illusion. This was why the old saying "Never meet your hero" was often true.

Her chin snapped back, but that disdain never left her face. "Oh, right. Sorry. I didn't know you were, like, Lachlan's sister."

It annoyed me she kept calling my brother by his first name. She hadn't earned that intimacy as far as I was aware.

"Well, now you do. Enjoy your evening." I offered a saccharine smile.

"Yeah, whatever. I'll catch you later, Mac." She winked before stalking off.

Fucking winked.

Like it was a code I couldn't decipher!

Hearing his beleaguered sigh, I reluctantly released him. His fingers curled into my hip as if to stop me, but then he caught the gesture and let me go.

"What the hell?" I scowled up at him. "What is she? Twelve?"

Mac glowered. "Twenty. And a pain in the arse. I don't see her lasting long. We've already had one staff complaint about her poor attitude."

"Is she harassing you?"

He shook his head, staring down at me with such tenderness, such—

Want.

Mackennon Galbraith didn't just love me ... he wanted me.

Suddenly, it was difficult to draw in a full breath.

My dress, bra, even the straps of my sandals felt too tight.

"So ... Grayson Evans?"

Thankfully, there was no judgment in his tone, or I might have killed him. But the twitch in his jaw told me he hated the idea of me and Grayson.

I could've been a right cow and gone down the revenge route by allowing him to think I'd had sex with the actor.

But I wasn't the tormenting kind. "Nothing happened. In fact, that night I burst into tears in his room, and he held me until I fell asleep."

Mac's eyes filled with regret. "Darlin', I'm so sorry."

I knew that.

I believed it down to the depths of my soul, and while a

263

lingering voice in my head warned me to be careful, a bigger part of me who had loved Mac for so long wanted to ease his pain and remorse.

Seconds from throwing myself at him, I drew in a sharp breath. "I need some air," I muttered, hurrying away before I did something I hadn't thought through.

The room was packed with so many guests, I had to push my way among them to reach the corridor that led into the staff area. It was off-limits to guests, but not to me.

Hurrying down the carpeted hallways, desperate for the breezy sea air, I pushed out of the emergency side exit and stepped onto the gravel driveway that surrounded the entire castle. My stiletto heels hated the stuff, but I got across it without falling. It was only as I moved onto the forked path that I could enjoy taking in a cleansing breath. A soft wind ruffled my hair and whispered cooling kisses across my skin.

Unbuckling my sandals, I carried them as I took the path leading to Loch Evelyn. It wouldn't surprise me if people were celebrating at Loch Ardnoch, since it was larger and occupied by some of our staff. I'd more than likely find privacy to gather my thoughts down at the smaller loch.

It took me ten minutes to walk there, and by the time I reached the loch—black in the night, except for the moon glow glinting across it—my skin had cooled. I threw my sandals down by the edge and considered pulling my dress up to dip my feet in. Lowering myself to do so, the snapping of a branch behind me drew me to a startled stop.

Fear froze me.

And then melted away in an instant as Mac appeared on the path, marching toward me, kilt flipping upward with his powerful stride.

"You shouldn't be out here alone," he lectured, the moon illuminating the determined hardness in his expression.

I opened my mouth to protest, but suddenly Mac was

upon me. He hauled me against his body as his lips crashed down over mine.

Gasping in shock, more than a little aroused by his hungry kiss, I allowed myself barely a few seconds to decide whether to kiss him back or push him away.

But then his hand slid down over my arse, pulling me deeper against him, and just like that, my desire overcame rational thinking.

I moaned into Mac's kiss, licking at his tongue with mine. His other hand tightened around my nape as he groaned with a need that rumbled down my throat and made my nipples harden behind my bra.

I wanted nothing between us.

Years of pent-up longing burst forth, and I pushed at his jacket. Mac broke his hold on me to shrug out of it and then I started on his waistcoat.

"No time," he panted against my mouth as he took me to the ground.

Cool grass prickled my upper back, the scent of soil and salt air mingling with Mac's aftershave as he bracketed my head with his hands, covering my body with his. His lips moved from my mouth, his stubble scratching my skin as he kissed a trail down my throat to the rise of my breasts. I stared up at the evening sky in a daze, the stars watching as my body hummed and throbbed with a need unlike anything I'd ever felt. Every inch of me experienced his touch, his scent, his taste, heightened in a way I'd never encountered. There was a surrealism to it.

Years.

Years I'd dreamed of this moment.

"Fuck," Mac bit out, and I brought my gaze down to his head as he scattered reverent kisses across my cleavage. His eyes flew to mine, a savage edge glinting in their darkness.

Damn if that didn't excite me.

"Mackennon," I whispered, arching my hips into him.

Something triumphant flickered in his expression, and he tugged the front of my dress down, taking the bra with it. His breaths grew shallow as he tugged a little harder until both breasts were free. My nipples peaked in the cool coastal air. "Beautiful," Mac murmured hoarsely, cupping me in his large hands.

I whimpered, arching my back, and he squeezed, brushing his thumbs across my nipples.

"Yes," I said, pressing his hands firmly to me.

Mac squeezed harder until a pleasure pain shot through me and I moaned. He grunted and seconds later covered my right nipple with his hot mouth.

Streaks of arousal darted through my body, centering between my thighs as Mac sucked my nipple, licked and laved and tormented it while he caressed and fondled my other.

Wet heat dampened my underwear.

Just from him touching my breasts.

"Fuck me," I murmured thickly. "Mackennon. Please."

His head jerked up in surprise.

I panted beneath him, even as I pressed my hands to his stomach, wishing he were naked but too impatient to have him do anything about it. "Fuck me. I'm empty. I'm so empty without you."

Those words broke something in him. The control he'd been holding on to by a thread snapped. He sat up on his heels and slipped his hands beneath the slit of my dress to grab my thighs, forcefully spreading me. My body responded viscerally, my arousal increasing tenfold. I was more than ready for him as he ripped off my underwear, and I gripped my inner thighs to his sides as he came down over me.

Our lips brushed in tingling butterfly kisses as he held my

gaze and fumbled beneath his kilt, shoving his underwear down to free himself.

Then he was hot and throbbing at my center.

"I love you," Mac said against my lips, and I saw all that love in his expression.

Before my fears and confusion could yank me from the moment, Mac thrust into me, and I cried out as his thick, hard heat stretched me.

It took me a second to adjust.

Then he slid back out, the friction sending lightning bolts of sensation to the coiling tension deep in my womb.

Oh my God. I gasped, throwing my head back as he consumed me.

Gripping my left hip beneath my dress to anchor me, Mac pulled me into him as he thrust inside, harder this time. My breasts bounced with every drive, drawing his attention, and Mac took my nipple in his mouth again, sucking, grunting around it as he fucked me faster, deeper.

I could do nothing but hold on to his upper arms, my nails biting into his shirtsleeves as the pleasure overwhelmed me.

We were primal. Grunting and moaning under the moon, the madness of long-suffering lust possessing us.

"Mackennon," I huffed out as my orgasm hovered closer.

Mac released my thigh to pin my arms above my head, his upper lip curled in a snarl as he neared his own climax.

His kilt fluttered over my torso as I arched my hips off the ground, tightening my thighs around him to move in perfect rhythm with his thrusts.

"Fuck," he panted, pleasure tightening his features even more. "Arro, Arro, fuck—"

With one last thrust, that tightening pleasure inside me exploded, and I threw my head back, eyes shut in euphoria as I cried out my release.

Mac kept moving inside me, my climax rippling around him in delicious tugging waves.

His drives stuttered, and then he bellowed my name into the night sky as I felt the heat of his orgasm, his cock throbbing inside me, his hips shuddering between my legs.

Panting, Mac rested his forehead on my breasts and released my wrists, only to caress my arms in soothing strokes. Slowly, I came back to myself staring up at the night sky, body thrumming, heart racing, skin sweat-dampened and slick. And Mac, still inside me.

Finally, he lifted his gaze to meet mine, his features slack with satisfaction, but his expression blazed. "Best sex of my fucking life, and it still wasn't enough of you."

Aftershocks of my orgasm pulsed around him at his confession, and he squeezed his eyes closed in pleasure, giving an involuntary thrust inside me. I moaned, pulling him down for a kiss. It was heady and slow, and it delayed the inevitable discussion that needed to be had.

Finally, Mac reluctantly broke the kiss and pushed up as he pulled out of me.

I whimpered at the sensation, and something like dark satisfaction etched his face.

I glimpsed his cock before he tucked himself away, and while it would have been easy to be distracted by his size, I felt the wet on my thighs with a startling jolt.

"We didn't use a condom." I gaped up at him.

He frowned. "You're still on the Pill, right?"

"How do you know that?"

Mac grinned. "I know a lot about you, Arrochar Adair. Including now that you're a screamer, and it feels like heaven to be inside you."

Flushing with excitement at his words, I pushed up from the grass, tugging on my bra and the dress straps as I tried not to let his sexiness sway me. "Mac, we should've used a condom."

"I know *I'm* clean." The nonquestion hung in the air.

"I'm clean," I promised. Guy had been my last lover, and I'd had a health check since then.

Mac shrugged before reaching for his jacket and pulling the square handkerchief out of its breast pocket. "Let me."

Trying desperately to ignore the renewed sizzle of arousal as he wiped the cloth between my legs, I bit my lip against a moan.

Mac's knowing gaze only made me hotter. Finally, he stood and held out a hand to help me up. "I promise we will use one next time, until we're ready not to."

"Next time?"

He stepped into me, wrapping his arms around my waist to cuddle me close. "Aye, next time. Unless ..." His grip on me tightened. "You don't want a next time?"

Before I could answer, bagpipes playing "Flower of Scotland" drew our attention back to the castle, and coordinated, moving lights in purple and green filled the sky over Ardnoch Castle.

"What the ...?"

"Drone display. Instead of fireworks," Mac murmured. The drones came together to make a gigantic three-dimensional thistle in the sky. It was so cool to watch that it took me a minute to realize what time it was. Lachlan always held the finale at midnight.

Wasn't that when Cinderella's dress changed back to rags, her carriage to a pumpkin?

Glancing away from the beautiful light show, I studied Mac's handsome face as he looked up at the thistle. Hearing the searing cry of the pipes, I knew, despite the niggling fear, that I didn't want what happened between us to just be a memory.

26

MAC

Sliding my arm around Arro's waist, I eased her back down onto the grass by the loch so we could watch the display. The drones' colors changed to blue and white as they moved into a new formation—the St. Andrew's Cross flag. To my relief, Arro didn't struggle or bolt. In fact, she rested her head on my chest and let me slide my fingers between hers to hold her hand.

I couldn't quite wrap my head around what had happened. When she'd left the party, I'd intended to follow to keep her safe, but seeing her in the moonlight, looking like a stunning loch nymph, years of wanting had driven every thought from my mind.

Anyone could have come across us, but I'd genuinely lost sight of anything other than Arro and the need to be inside her.

If I was honest with myself ... maybe even the need to claim her.

As she had claimed me. Branded me. Hers. Forever. No woman would ever compare.

Which was the reason I'd lost my mind and done something, as head of security, I'd either fire someone else for doing or have Lachlan warn a guest over.

Somehow, I couldn't dredge up enough guilt about it—and definitely no regret.

The drones formed a Highlander in his kilt, then the Loch Ness monster, and finally returned to the thistle, ending the display. We heard the cheers of guests in the distance.

"I can't go back in there." Arro lifted her head. "My dress is covered in grass stains." She laughed softly. "Everyone will know what I've been up to."

I grinned, feeling more than a little satisfied by the reason for those grass stains. "You can wait at the door while I have a car brought around."

She studied me. "I'm going home alone tonight, Mac."

My stomach dropped. "All right," I replied. "Does that mean you don't want to give me a chance?"

Tears brightened her eyes as she tugged her hand from mine. "I don't know what to do. I'm terrified of walking away from this, but I'm also scared that if I give you a chance, I might realize I can't trust you, and then I've just messed you about."

"Arro." I grabbed for her hand again, holding it tight between both of mine. "Let me take that risk. I'm willing to take it. Just try ... We'll go on dates, we'll spend time together, we'll see how it goes. And if you decide after that, you don't want to be with me, I'll abide by it. No questions, no pushing you. I just want a chance."

Her mouth, swollen from my kisses, trembled. "I don't want to hurt you."

Heart pounding, I answered hoarsely, "Any time I get to be with you—a day, a week, a few months—it'll be worth it. I'd rather have a moment with you than nothing at all. It'll last me a lifetime."

Arro's eyes turned smoky with tenderness and desire.

"Sometimes you say the most perfect things, Mackennon Galbraith."

Relief trickled through me as I tugged on her hand, bending my head to hers. "Go on a date with me, Arrochar."

She nodded slowly. "Okay."

My grin was so big, I was sure I looked like an idiot, but it made Arro's laughter light up the night, and that was all I cared about. "Come on." I helped her up. She held her shoes in one hand but reached for mine with the other. "Let's get you home."

When we reached the castle driveway, I swept her into my arms.

"Mackennon!" she cried, half fright, half laughter, as she clung to me.

I grinned at her. "You can't walk barefoot on that gravel."

"I could get used to this," Arro teased. "You're very strong, Mr. Galbraith."

Suddenly, an image of carrying her across the threshold of a honeymoon suite hit me hard, and I had to force myself to reel the fantasy back in. It became easier when we rounded the corner of the castle and found Lachlan and Thane outside, talking.

"Oh, fuck," Arro muttered.

"Aye," I agreed with a sigh.

I knew by the time I lowered Arro onto the smooth slabs of the portico beside her brothers that they knew.

"You've got grass stains on the back of your dress," Lachlan told Arro conversationally, but there was a glint in his eyes I couldn't work out, even after all these years of knowing him.

Arro gave her brothers a quelling look. "And those stains are none of your business."

Thane nodded, seeming a little green. "I'd prefer it to stay that way, to be honest."

"So …" Lachlan glanced between us. "Is it official, then?"

I turned to Arro as she turned to me, and she said, "We're … going on a date."

"Bit late for that, isn't it?" Thane said dryly.

"I thought you didn't want to talk about it." Arro raised an eyebrow. "But we can if you like. We did it by Loch Evelyn—"

"Arro." Amusement and horror filled me.

"Best sex ever," she continued. "There was this moment—"

"Stop." Lachlan glowered at her.

"Where I thought—"

I covered her mouth with my hand, drawing her back against my chest. She laughed, feeling the vibration of my own laughter. "You're evil." I chuckled.

She pushed my hand away and glanced up at me, eyes sparkling with humor.

Fuck, I loved her.

As if she could hear those words, she melted against me.

Thane cleared his throat. "So … are you going back inside?"

Arro shook her head. "Of course not. Everyone would know what we've been up to."

Lachlan pulled his phone from his sporran and swiped the screen a few times before lifting it to his ear. "Dave, can you bring a car around for Ms. Adair? I need you to take her home … good. Thanks." He hung up. "Dave will be here in a few minutes."

"He can drop me off at mine too," I said.

Lachlan grunted.

I glared at him. "Have him report to you if you'd like. Arro wants to go home alone."

"Why? What did you do?" Thane demanded.

Arro groaned. "Oh my God, either you don't want to know what happened between us or you do."

"Arro …" Thane warned.

"I'm not five anymore, Thane. I'm not obligated to tell you my business, but since I'm afraid you might torture Mac as soon as you get him alone, if you must know, it happened in the heat of the moment. But for now, we're taking things slow."

"Jesus Christ, is this how it'll be?" I huffed. "Detailing every second of our relationship to you two?"

"Not every second," Lachlan grumbled boyishly.

"Aye, not the bloodcurdling parts," Thane agreed.

"Bloodcurdling—" Arro moved as if to shove her brother, but I held her back.

"Let's just agree that is all you get to know about it for now," I said sternly.

They considered this for a few seconds, then Lachlan said, "Fine. And you have my best wishes."

"Mine too." Thane nodded.

I relaxed into Arro, and she grabbed for my hand, as if sensing my tension deflate. Lachlan and Thane were my family, too, after all. I didn't want to ruin our friendships.

Then Lachlan eyed me, his expression grim, and he warned, "Hurt her, and I'll kill you."

"And I'll find a magical shaman to bring you back to life just so I can kill you harder," Thane added with absolute seriousness.

Lachlan cut him a look. "Always got to one-up me, eh?"

27

MAC

In search of privacy, I'd chosen this particular restaurant for my first date with Arro because it was a good twenty-five minutes north of Dornoch—and also because it was her favorite. We brought her here on her last birthday, before I ballsed everything up between us. And she'd mentioned that night she wished she had more excuses to come here.

An Aberdeen business friend of Lachlan's built and owned the restaurant. He had several fine-dining establishments around the country, two of which had garnered Michelin stars. This one, North Star, was situated on a piece of land just off the A9 outside Brora. It perched on the coast with spectacular views across the North Sea.

To be honest, I was more of a burger-and-steak kind of man. Not playing into any stereotype—it's just the truth. But Arro loved seafood, and this place offered the best menu in the area.

"You didn't have to bring me here, Mackennon," Arro said under her breath. I held out a chair for her at a small table by the window. "It's too much."

"Hush," I admonished with a smile and took the seat

across from her. We were so close, our feet touched. I imagined her gorgeous legs beneath the table easily enough since she'd worn a tight skirt that stopped at mid-thigh, showcasing said amazing legs and cupping her magnificent arse. Her short-sleeved silk blouse in a striking pale blue matched her eyes.

"And this table." She widened her eyes at me comically before looking out at the sea. It was still daylight, but the sun was beginning its descent toward the horizon, its colors streaming across the water toward us. "How did you get this table? It's one of the best in the restaurant."

"Do you think Lachlan's the only one with some pull?" I teased.

Arro shook her head, smiling. "Apparently not." Her amusement died slowly, and I understood when she said, "You really didn't have to make a gesture like this. I would've been happy with a bag of fish and chips on the beach."

And that was one of the reasons I loved her. "I know. But I didn't want our first official date to be a bag of fish and chips on the beach."

She took a deep breath, her hand fluttering near her chest. "Whoa, when you said that, it still feels so surreal. We're on a date. Me and you. After all this time. It's hard to compute. I spent all day with butterflies in my belly."

Tenderness filled me. "I've been nervous too."

"Really?" She seemed pleased by that.

"Absolutely. You matter, Arro."

Last night as Dave drove us to our respective homes, I asked Arro to go out with me the following night. I didn't want to waste any time. Thankfully, she'd said yes.

I was glad we didn't wait. I would've been an impatient mess until the date.

"I didn't think you got nervous about anything. Well, other than Robyn."

"The two most important relationships of my life."

"Ours? Our relationship?"

How could she not know that by now?

"Even over Lachlan?"

Ah, now I understood. Leaning across the table, I told her firmly, "Your brother is family to me, always will be, but going forward, you will always come first, Arro. Always."

Emotion brightened her eyes, and she nodded.

"May I get you anything to drink before you order, Mr. Galbraith?" The server appeared at the table, breaking the moment.

Conversation eased between us over the course of the meal, and we talked about our usual, everyday stuff as we ate and watched the sea grow steadily choppier.

I told Arro about Robyn and how she'd been rooting for us for months. This surprised and pleased her, and I felt stupid for not realizing that, of course, Arro might be a wee bit concerned about my daughter's response to us.

"How do you think the village will react?" Arro asked a few hours later as I held her hand and led her across the restaurant's small car park to my SUV.

"I couldn't care less," I replied bluntly.

"No, me neither," she assured me. "But you saw how they were in Flora's when they thought something was going on between us."

Holding the passenger door open, my gaze dropped to her legs as she hopped in and smoothed down the short skirt that stretched across her thighs. Heat coursed south as I imagined those legs wrapped around me. "I don't care about their reaction, Arrochar," I murmured thickly, studying her body, lingering on the silk where it clung to her breasts before meeting her eyes. Her cheeks flushed, expression bright with arousal. "It would take an army to hold me back now."

Her lips parted, and I couldn't help myself. I leaned into the car and kissed her. It was meant to be soft, reassuring, but as soon as she opened her mouth, I took her like a starving man.

She tasted sweet from her dessert.

I pulled back but stayed close, my nose almost touching hers. I could see every striation in her eyes as she held my gaze. "Let's promise to keep this about you and me. No outside interference."

Arro nodded. Voice a little hoarse, she said, "I promise."

BLOOD RUSHED in my ears as we stepped into Arro's house.

Because I knew what I wanted. What I needed. And I didn't want to waste any time in my pursuit of it. That had been the longest drive of my life. Every time Arro shifted in her seat, my attention moved with a will of its own to her thighs.

Arrochar Adair had done something I hadn't known was possible anymore. She'd turned me into a horny fucking teenager. I was a man reborn.

"I'll make coffee," Arro said as soon as the door locked behind us.

No, I wanted to say. *I just want you.*

But she'd already kicked off her heels and strolled through the living room to the kitchen. I followed her in, my gaze on her perfect arse in that skirt that had fascinated me from the moment she got in my car.

My trousers tightened as all the blood in my body rushed to my dick.

"I was thinking we could go for a coastal drive next weekend. It's been ages since I've been around the NC500," she called from the kitchen.

I'd take her anywhere. I walked into the kitchen. "Aye, sounds like a plan."

She kept her back to me as she moved about, filling her coffee machine with water before placing it back on its holder.

"We could stop by Morag's and grab stuff for a picnic, maybe find a nice spot to have lunch."

"Absolutely," I murmured.

"And I was thinking—oh." She startled, turning her head to look up at me as I cradled her hips in my hands and pressed her into the counter. Her eyes flared as she felt my arousal digging into her arse. "Oh." This time she said it so breathy, I grew impossibly harder.

Cupping her jaw in my hand, I tilted her head so I could kiss her. Hard. Deep. Until she panted into my mouth with excitement. Grinding into her arse, I groaned at the feel of her undulating against me.

"Mac ..." She broke the kiss for air, her chest heaving.

Still holding her hip, I smoothed my other hand up her stomach, over the silk of her shirt, and I cupped one of her gorgeous tits. Feeling her, caressing her, learning her.

"Mackennon." Arro arched her back, resting her head on my upper chest.

"You make me feel like a boy again," I murmured in her ear. "I'm walking around with a constant hard-on for you. It's ridiculous."

She smiled, a sultry tilting of her lips, utterly smug. "Well ..." She slipped her hand behind her to push between us, rubbing over my cock. "Maybe we should do something about that."

I kissed her voraciously, needing her taste on my tongue as I took both her hands and placed her palms flat on the kitchen counter. I released her mouth to order, "Keep them there."

She nodded, chest heaving with anticipation.

Reaching for the hem of that tight skirt, I smoothed it upward until it bunched around her waist. I stepped back slightly to take in the sight of her lace-covered arse. Her perfect, tight, round arse. I caressed her, her breathing loud and shallow. Squeezing her, I leaned back in to murmur in her ear, "One day, you might let me fuck that glorious arse of yours."

Arro moaned at the thought.

Duly noted.

Raging hot, hard as a steel pike, I peeled her knickers down and stopped them at her knees, enjoying the visual far too much. Then I gently caressed between her thighs, finding her clit. She was slick with arousal.

Fuck, that was satisfying. Understatement.

"Oh." Arro bowed against the counter as I circled her clit, pressing hard, rolling my thumb. "Oh, Mac, oh, oh, God ..." Her nails curled into the counter as she stiffened against me and then cried out in climax.

I released her as she sagged but only to unzip and push my trousers and underwear to my ankles. I quickly sheathed a condom I'd carried in my wallet.

Gripping her hip, I pushed her feet apart, stretching her knickers ... and I thrust into her.

"Argh!" Arro arched her back as her tight, wet heat squeezed around me.

"Fuck." I stilled a minute, already about to blow. "Look at me."

Arro tilted her head upward, her lids low with lust. I kissed her, tongue tangling with hers as I caressed her tit, teasing her nipple between my finger and thumb, all the while throbbing inside her tight channel. Her inner muscles squeezed around me, and I grunted as sensation seized me.

I could wait no more.

I broke the kiss and fucked her as I'd fantasized about doing for far too long.

Gripping her hips in my hands, I yanked her ass toward me and pumped in and out, my balls drawing up with each drive into her.

"Arro!" I panted, my grip almost bruising as I watched my dick move inside her. "You feel incredible."

"Harder," she begged, gripping the counter. "Mackennon, harder."

Her wish was my command.

I fucked her like there was no tomorrow, gritting my teeth against the desperate need to come.

"Arro, come, darlin'," I demanded. "Come for me." I released her hips to reach over her and hold her hands down as I kept thrusting. "It's me and you, Arro," I growled impatiently in her ear. "Together. Like we've always wanted. Come on my cock, darlin'. Come around me hard."

And just like that, she stiffened against my firm hold and cried out as she throbbed around me in the tightest fucking euphoric tugs. So hard, my vision went white as I flooded the condom with the hardest release of my goddamn life.

My whole body hummed.

It was like I was elsewhere on another pleasure plane where all I could feel and smell was Arrochar.

"Mac …" Her voice filtered through, drawing me back to the world. Then her laughter. "Mac, you're heavy."

Realization dawned, and I opened my eyes.

I still leaned on Arro as she propped herself against the counter.

Huffing out a cursed apology, I eased off her and reluctantly pulled out. I pulled up my trousers and underwear but didn't zip.

"You okay?"

Arro turned around, looking a little shell-shocked. "I

think ... I thought my heart was going to explode." She reached down to kick off her knickers and then smoothed her skirt over her thighs. Her gaze dropped to me as I rolled off the condom and tied it. Impossibly, I was still semihard, which held her attention as I crossed the room to bin the condom. "Mac?"

I didn't bother tucking myself back in. I wasn't done. Taking hold of her hand, I said, "Leave the coffee."

"Again?" she asked, wide-eyed, before I led her toward her bedroom.

"It would seem you make my cock think it's eighteen again," I teased. Her delighted laughter made me so happy, I could barely bloody stand it.

Once in her bedroom, I undressed her. She stood before me, half naked, her nipples jutting proudly from her perky tits. Absolutely no shyness in my Arro. I whipped off my shirt and threw it with hers on the floor.

"Mackennon," Arro whispered, stepping into me to caress my arms and then my stomach, which contracted at her touch. "In the kitchen ... that was ... different, right?" She looked up at me, still stunned.

I understood the feeling. Drawing her close, I nodded. "I've never come like that in my life."

"You said things." She bit her lip against a smile.

Grinning, I nodded. "I did. And you enjoyed them."

"I've never ... no one's ever talked to me like that in bed, but ... I liked it. A lot."

Chuckling, I drew my hands around her waist and upward to cup her tits. She moaned, her hair falling down over my arms. "Look at you"—I nibbled at her mouth—"so fucking gorgeous."

Needing her naked, I stripped off her skirt and enjoyed the way she hungrily watched as I removed the rest of my clothes.

"Mac," she said, chest heaving as she devoured me. "You're so sexy, it might kill me."

I gave a bark of pleased laughter and then hauled her nakedness against mine. She was soft and warm against all my hard edges. "What do you want to do next?"

Arro seemed surprised by the question.

I smiled wickedly. "I've gotten my way the first few times. Now it's your turn."

She squirmed excitedly against me. "I want you to let me have my way with you."

"Meaning?"

"Lie on the bed and don't touch me until I say so."

"Fine." I kissed her, hard. "But turnabout is fair play."

"I look forward to it," she promised.

And that was how I found myself being tortured. Lying spread out for her on her bed like an offering. Don't get me wrong—I enjoyed her lips and tongue and soft hands—but the woman had more patience than a saint, and she was tormenting me with her slow pace.

"Arro, come on," I growled, curling my hands into restless fists to stop from touching her.

Having mercy, her hot mouth engulfed my cock, and I let out a satisfied grunt as she sucked it. Hard.

Holding Arro's stunning blue gaze while her lips wrapped around my cock was too much. I'd never cared more; I'd never been so thrilled to have a woman's mouth on me. Her slow ministrations had already built me toward the breaking point, and now this …

"I'm going to come," I warned her in harsh pants.

She released me and despair would have flooded me, but seconds later, I was sheathed in her tight heat.

Her hair spilled across her shoulders, tangling over her beautiful tits, her stomach flexing as she rode me.

Had a man ever experienced anything better than this?

Somehow I doubted it.

"Can I touch you now?"

She nodded, her cheeks flushed.

I gripped her hips in my hands and thrust up into her.

"Ahh!" Arro fell over me, pressing her hands to my shoulders. "Stop, don't. Let me," she begged.

I nodded, teeth gritted.

And she undulated slowly, up and down, her eyes holding mine as I watched her exult in taking her satisfaction from me.

I slipped my hand between us and fondled her clit.

Arro groaned, fingers biting on my shoulders. "Yes," she pleaded.

I explored the bundle of nerves, taking her almost to the edge, and then I stopped. But only to take hold of one of her hands and push it between us. "Feel us," I ordered. "Feel me moving inside you."

She did, and she rode me harder with desperation. Suddenly I was pinned, holding on to her hips as she braced her hands on my shoulders to fuck me.

I got to watch her come, snapshotting the expression of unadulterated pleasure on her face as she rippled and pulsed around me.

That was when I let go, grinding her down on my cock as my hips arched off the bed to climax inside her.

Arro sprawled across my chest, breath puffing hotly against my nipple. I wrapped my arms around her, holding her close. "I love you so fucking much," I whispered into the silent bedroom.

Arro tensed for a second and then turned her cheek to kiss my chest, before settling back against me.

An ache flared in that exact spot.

But I tightened my hold on her, patient, waiting.

I'd wait a million lifetimes for her.

28
ARRO

Heart racing, my skin coated with a light sweat, I moaned as Mac pulled out of me and rolled onto his back.

We laid panting in my bed, gazing up at the ceiling as we tried to catch our breaths.

I'd never experienced anything like the past week.

So much for going slow!

Mac and I had spent every night together since our date at North Star on Saturday.

Now it was the following Sunday, and I swear to God, I had definition in my abs from all the sex.

So much sex.

Like six years of lusting after each other, culminating in a week of so many orgasms, I'd lost count and was possibly suffering the effects of an endorphin haze.

This morning Mac had woken me up to make love. It was slow and gentle and beautiful, but I was also a little sore from last night.

"Last night," I murmured out loud in awe.

"I know," Mac replied, sounding smug.

He should be smug.

We both should be smug.

"We could win awards for last night," I panted softly. "That thing you did when my legs were over your shoulders ..."

"Aye, we'll need to do that again."

"And that other thing. I didn't know my body could bend that way."

"You're satisfyingly flexible."

I preened. "We both are."

"We'll need to do that one again too."

"As much as I'm looking forward to it"—I moved onto my side to face him—"I'm a wee bit sore."

Mac turned to me, frowning. "Why didn't you say?"

"Because I wanted sex," I answered. Obviously.

He smirked, but there was still concern in his expression as he slipped his hand between my legs. I shivered as he petted me. Mac touched me with no inhibitions, like my body was as much his as it was mine. Oversensitized, I grew taut as he prodded gently at my opening.

"Here?" he asked hoarsely.

I nodded, biting my lip to stifle a moan.

He moved upward to my clit and circled it with his thumb. "Here?"

I shook my head, pushing into his touch. "We can't." My mouth argued with my body. "We're due at Thane's soon."

"Let me kiss you all better first," he growled hotly, moving down me to push my legs apart. And then his tongue was on my clit, and I couldn't resist. Watching Mac go down on me was one of my favorite things in the world.

But I didn't know if my heart could take much more.

Apparently, it could.

A few minutes later, I'd come again, and Mac kissed his way back upward. He gave my breasts a lingering kiss each before he rolled off the bed and sprung to his feet with a spryness I admired.

"What about you?"

"I'm good," he promised as he pulled on a pair of jogging pants. "I'd suggest a protein shake to get you going, but I know what the answer will be."

"Coffee," we said in unison.

I chuckled, curling on to my side, loving the way his gaze drifted over me. Mac had been here so much this week, he had spare clothes in my wardrobe and his very important protein-shake powder in my kitchen so he could drink it before he left for the gym. He rose at the crack of dawn, and while I struggled to wake up for my workday, Mac would already be at the gym working out before his shift at the estate.

Today was the first morning we'd lazed around in bed. Watching Mac's fine arse stroll out of my bedroom, I squirmed with glee.

Best goddamn week ever. Other than the sex, my favorite moment was actually two nights ago when he sat in my armchair, and I curled up on the sofa, and we both read. Nothing but the sound of our light breathing and pages being turned. I'd looked up from my book, watching Mac's eyes move across the words, and I thought to myself, *I could do this forever*.

The perfect contentment of that moment had scared the shit out of me. Just as it did when Mac told me he loved me. My throat had closed, blocking any possible answer. He hadn't said it to me again since last Monday.

Shaking off my sudden melancholy, I focused on the good. And there had been so much goodness this week, I was like I was floating through life.

But now it was time to return to the real world.

Except for my work colleagues, the only person I'd seen

was Mac. My family had grown antsy, even though it had only been seven days. They wanted us over for Sunday breakfast, an occasional occurrence either at Lachlan's or Thane's. This week, I was a hundred percent positive Mac and I were the reason for the get-together. Our family was nosy and wanted to see for themselves how things were progressing.

I smiled smugly as my gaze fell on a tube of lube on my nightstand.

Oh, if my family knew what Mac and I had been up to, they'd die of horror.

The thought made me chuckle evilly as I reluctantly rolled out of bed to prepare to face them.

———

"READY?" I asked Mac as we rounded his SUV.

He reached for my hand, drawing me into his side as we stared up at Thane's home. "Ready when you are."

Mac didn't look the least bit nervous, so I decided I shouldn't be either. However, it was different from walking through the village together (something we hadn't done as a couple yet) because I couldn't care less what the villagers thought.

I cared what my family thought.

So yes, I was a wee bit apprehensive, even though my brothers seemed happy for us.

Thane's front door opened and Regan appeared, smiling that dimpled smile. "Are you just going to stand out there all day?"

Mac and I shared another bolstering look before we strolled up the steps. He released my hand to step back and let me go in first, but I reached behind me, needing him. Seconds later, my hand was engulfed in his again.

Regan's gaze dropped to where we joined together, and she beamed. "Aww."

"Shut up," I ordered, even as I grinned.

"Everyone's already here. Come in, come in." Regan sauntered ahead of us, walking out into the open-plan living space of their large home.

Everyone sat scattered around the living and dining area.

"Aunt Arro, Uncle Mac!" Eilidh cried out, jumping off Lachlan's lap to rush us.

"I feel rejected." Lachlan looked glumly at his wife.

Robyn chuckled. "Thrown over for my father. How horrifying."

I laughed at my big brother's mock glower just before Eilidh hit me. Mac released me so I could swing Eilidh up into my arms. My biceps strained. "Oof, you're getting too big for this." I chuckled as she clasped my face in her hands.

Eilidh grinned. "Aunt Arro, I missed you. Where have you been? Have you been choppin' down lots of trees because my teacher said we shouldn't chop down lots of trees, and I wanna talk to you about it because I think you might need to be something other than a tree-chopper. You're too good for it." She patted my cheek solemnly, like she was my eighty-year-old aunt.

I could feel the vibrations of Mac's chuckle against my back as I struggled not to laugh, wondering how to explain a forest cycle to a six-year-old and cursing her teacher for clouding the reality of my job.

"Uncle Mac!" Eilidh turned the rays of her effervescence on him. "Hugs!"

I transferred her to Mac before she fell out of my arms with her struggling. Her long legs dangled as Mac held her against his hip.

"How are you, Bonny Blue?" Mac asked her, using the

adorable nickname he'd used ever since she first opened those big blue eyes and stared up at him.

"Uncle Mac, I got star pupil for the third week! Though Ms. McGuinley says I need to"—her voice dropped to a loud whisper—"learn to talk really quiet, but I said"—her voice rose again—"but then no one will hear me!"

Mac grinned at her. "Don't worry about that, Bonny Blue. People can hear you in Inverness at that octave."

Eilidh considered this and cackled loudly, making us laugh.

If there was a God, I hoped he'd give me a kid just like Eilidh Adair.

Still carrying my niece, Mac followed me into the sitting room. I ruffled Lewis's hair as I passed the armchair where he played his Nintendo.

"Hi, Aunt Arro." He looked up with a small smile. "Uncle Mac."

"Hey, wee man." Mac nodded at him. "You doing good, kid?"

Lew's expression lit up. "Made it to Kingdom 15."

Mac replied, "Nice." He lowered Eilidh, who immediately took my hand and pulled me down beside Thane on the large couch.

Arran sat beside him, and both my brothers seemed to study me, their eyes moving back to Mac as he pulled a seat from the dining table and sat next to Eredine. I smiled at my friend before I took in Lachlan, also focused on me.

Minutes seemed to pass in silence, though I'm sure it was only seconds.

"Why is no one talking? You're all staring at Aunt Arro and Uncle Mac." Eilidh's little brows puckered as she snuggled into my side.

I cleared my throat, not sure how to explain our change in relationship to a six-year-old. Or if I should. Glancing at

Lewis, I saw him looking up from his game like he sensed the strangeness in the room too.

Then I took in Mac's solid presence, his calm demeanor, and his expression that said he'd follow my lead. Really giving this relationship a proper shot meant not hiding from our family. Taking the risk. If it fell apart, it fell apart, but the kids were in my life a lot, and I didn't want to stop being affectionate around Mac whenever they were with us.

"Well," I said, exhaling slowly as I looked between my niece and nephew, "Uncle Mac and I are dating now. We're together." At their blank expressions, I continued, "Romantically. We are to each other like your dad is with Regan."

Eilidh wrinkled her nose and pulled away to look up at me in confusion. "But I thought you always were."

"Me too." Lewis shrugged and returned to his game.

Robyn's snort broke the silence. She grinned at her father. "Out of the mouths of babes."

"So?" Eredine sidled up to me in the kitchen.

Arran took the kids outside to play after Thane had told Lewis he'd had enough game time for the day. When Lewis grumbled about it, Arran swept in to distract him. But not before I grilled my brother about the Gloaming.

After we'd settled in, it was wonderful how we fell into a natural rhythm with my family. Arran and Lachlan told us about the offer they'd made Gordon and how they were waiting for Gordon's solicitors to contact theirs to see if he'd accepted it. They had plans to renovate the hotel, bar, and restaurant, with Arran overseeing it all. I was so happy my brother was staying in Ardnoch, even if he still wouldn't really explain why his wanderlust had suddenly vanished— or why he hadn't come home sooner when we needed him.

Lachlan told us Brodan had sent over a digital copy of his new film for us to watch, since the premiere was in Los Angeles. It was too adult for the kids, so we'd wait for them to go to bed before watching.

Conversation was easy. Even when Mac crossed the room to sit beside me, snuggling me into his side after Eilidh vacated the spot.

I'd gotten up to make everyone fresh tea and coffee when Eredine followed me.

"So?" I smiled at her as I moved around the kitchen.

My friend glanced over her shoulder at Mac, who laughed at something Robyn said.

"You both seem happy." Eredine's expression was filled with questions.

"We are. We're taking each day at a time. Though ... kind of at warp speed. We're spending nearly every second together outside of work."

"That's nice." Ery leaned into me. "I'm glad you gave him another chance. Mac's one of the really good ones."

"I know that. And thank you again for being there for me when I needed someone to talk to."

"I'm always here for you," she promised.

I curled my hand around her wrist and gave it a gentle squeeze. "You know I'm always here for you, too, right?"

Eredine swallowed hard, something grim and unsettling flashing across her eyes. Her lips parted, her breathing increasing a little as she said, "Arro—"

"We need juice!" Eilidh cried out as she rushed into the house. "Energy boost!"

I looked back at Ery, but her expression had closed down. "I'll get it, Eils," she said, moving around the kitchen.

Frustration filled me because I suspected my friend was about to tell me something important.

I tried to catch her eye again, but she hurried after Eilidh out into the garden.

Sighing, I forced myself to let the moment go. Once I had the tea and coffee ready, Mac helped me carry everything into the living room.

"Tell us, Mac," Thane said as he sipped his coffee, "any word on Kilmany?"

Mac shook his head. "In jail until his court date. It'll be a few weeks yet until we hear. For now, he's denying all charges. The police still haven't tied him to Frickle, Kenny or Jamie, but they have the car tied to Bryan's murder, plus Arro's and my witness accounts." He looked at me. "I asked to visit him."

I raised an eyebrow. This was the first I'd heard of it.

Mac shrugged despondently. "I wanted to talk to him. To explain what happened."

"He's a murderer, Dad," Robyn whispered. "You don't need to explain anything to him."

"It's for both our sakes," Mac said. "But it's a moot point because he denied visitation as well as the charges. Arro and I will probably be called in to make statements again soon, and then we'll have to take the stand in court."

Something I was not looking forward to, but I would do it to put the dangerous arsehole away for good.

"He still denies leaving the notes for Arro?" Thane prodded.

"He denies everything."

"I still don't understand why he went after Arro instead of directly after you."

"We're talking about someone who is mentally unwell," Robyn said. "Let's not look for reason where there is none."

"And let's talk about something happier," Regan suggested.

"Say, for instance, you getting into the MBA program at

the University of the Highlands and Islands," her big sister said with a proud smile.

"Seriously?" I asked Regan.

She shared a look with Thane, who appeared just as proud if not more so than Robyn. "I want to open a preschool here. There's only one, and it's kind of depressing. The kids don't really seem to get much stimulation there. But I thought I better do the work before embarking on something so significant as opening a business."

Excited for her, I offered without thinking, "You should do it in Caelmore. We own lots of land here. I'm sure we have the perfect spot where you could build something specifically designed for your needs." I stiffened as soon as the words were out of my mouth; I shouldn't have just willy-nilly offered her Adair land without my brothers' input.

However, Thane slid his arm around Regan's waist and glanced between me and Lachlan. "I've already spoken to Arran about this, and he's on board. I just need the go-ahead from you two and Brodan. I want to give Regan a plot of land here, and I'll help her build the preschool."

Regan opened her mouth to protest, and Thane hushed her.

"We have the land," he told her sternly, then looked at us. "You can say no, though."

"Why would we say no?" Lachlan frowned. "Of course, Regan can have it. Arro clearly just offered it."

"And his wife would withhold sexual favors if he denied her little sister this request," Robyn added.

Lachlan raised an eyebrow. "As if you could last a day without me."

"Is that a challenge?"

"Aye, why not?"

"Lachlan," Thane warned.

"Fine." Robyn held out a hand. "Shake on it. No sex until

one of us breaks, and the person who breaks does all the cooking and grocery shopping for three months."

"Lachlan—"

"Done." Lachlan shook her hand.

Thane groaned. "You're a right prat."

Our eldest brother shrugged cockily. "I will not break first."

"Does it matter when this deal means you're not having any sex for the foreseeable future?"

Lachlan considered this and then glowered at his chuckling wife. "Funny, is it? You've got a stronger sex drive than me, woman."

"Can we not discuss my daughter's—" Mac choked on the thought, looking green. "Let's change the subject."

And so we did, but I noticed Robyn didn't look so cocky anymore.

Note to self: never make a no-sex deal with Mac.

We talked more about Regan's plans for the preschool, and then Thane called for takeout. The bulk of the evening was spent eating dinner and playing with the kids. After, the kids showered and Thane put them to bed.

It was late by the time Lachlan set up Brodan's new film, connecting his laptop to Thane's TV. We switched off the lights to make it more cinematic, and I rested against Mac's chest as we lounged back to watch the movie.

Pride filled me at Brodan's portrayal of a man who wakes up in what seems to be a dystopian outback with no recollection of how he got there. The film was about him piecing together his memories as he tried to survive the desert and find his way back to some manner of civilization. It was by far Brodan's best piece of acting. So good, I almost forgot he was my brother.

As the credits rolled, a stunned silence fell over my family.

Then Lachlan said gruffly, "Well … he's a talented son of a bitch."

We all immediately started talking over each other in excitement as we discussed which bits we loved best, where he stunned us with his performance, when we forgot we were watching Brodan and just saw him as the character. We shot him texts to tell him how much we'd loved it, but I made a note to video-call him tomorrow so I could tell him to his face.

After that, we said our good-nights, and Mac led me out to his SUV, opening the passenger door and placing an unnecessary but welcome palm on my arse to help me in. He rounded the bonnet, hopped in, and once he was pulling out of the driveway, I commented, "They didn't make it weird. Us."

"Did you think they would?"

"I wasn't sure. But it wasn't weird. Not at all."

Mac grinned in the dark of the car, the headlights beyond us illuminating his face. "Eilidh certainly put us in our place."

I groaned, but smiled. "God, we must have been so obvious."

His chuckle warmed me from the inside out.

But then he sliced through the amiable mood with, "Do you want kids, Arro?"

The abrupt question shocked me into silence for a few seconds. My heart raced as I fought through the fear of the outcome of this conversation and answered honestly, "Yes." I swallowed hard. "Do you?"

"You know, Lachlan asked me the same thing when I told him how I feel about you."

"And?"

Mac looked at me as he slowed on the narrow country road that led away from my brothers' homes. "I want kids with you. I used to think it was too late—"

"You're still young, Mackennon," I huffed.

"I know I'm not old," he said, laughter in his voice. "But to be a father again ... forty-five is a wee bit later than usual."

"But you want kids?" I hung on to that vital part of what he'd said.

"It scares me," he said. "I don't want to hurt another child like I hurt Robyn—"

"You would never," I cut him off again.

"I know." He shot me another look before turning onto the main road. "Anyway, I just wanted to make sure we were on the same page. Not that ... well, we're not anywhere near there yet."

I deflated a little, coming back to reality. Of course we weren't. I couldn't even tell the man I loved him yet.

"Right," I whispered, lecturing myself about sticking to my plans to take things slowly. "We're not there yet."

Feeling more than a prickle of glum disappointment, I ignored why that was and prattled on about Brodan's film to alleviate the sudden tension between us.

29

MAC

"Arro always wants to stay at her house. I'm worried about that."

"Why?" Iona asked.

"I'm worried she's afraid of going back to mine. She hasn't been there since March. Since that night."

"Have you tried talking to her about it?"

"I'm being a bit of a coward," I confessed. "I don't want to burst this bubble we're in. I don't want to take her back to a place that might make her change her mind about us."

"That's understandable. However, if your relationship is to last, communication is key. Tough discussions can't be avoided. They only prolong the inevitable. Don't you think it would be better to do it now?"

"I don't want to hurt her."

"If she isn't ready to be in your house again, then you can support her in that. But I also think it's important you two talk it through, because it isn't about the house. It's about the trust between you."

ANOTHER WEEK PASSED, but it might as well have been months. That was what it was like to be with Arro. An endless high. I hadn't known it was possible to be this fucking happy. I'd longed for contentment for so long, and I was sure this would eventually ease into something like that, but right now, I was ecstatic. I was in love for the first time in my forty-five years on the planet. All those years without her seemed like a waste, and yet I'd relive every single second—even the worst—if it led me to this moment with her.

It was the third Saturday since our date at North Star. That seemed like a lifetime ago. Time was acting strangely. Having spent our days at work and much of our nights together at Arro's, we'd dodged the village. Spending all our downtime at Arro's bungalow, however, meant there was surely some neighborly gossip about why that was.

But I wasn't hiding our relationship. We'd worked too bloody hard to make a go of it. We still were.

"Are you ready for this?" Arro asked after we'd parked her Defender in the village's main car park on Castle Street.

"I am. Are you?"

Her answer was to curl her arm around mine as we walked toward Flora's. That morning had been a heavy one. Instead of going to the gym, I'd made Arro breakfast in bed.

"What's all this?" she'd said, blinking sleepily as she'd pushed into a sitting position.

I'd placed the breakfast tray over her, and she grinned up at me in delight. "I want to talk to you about something, and I didn't want you to have to do it before your coffee." I smirked at the omelet I'd made. "Then somehow that turned into breakfast."

"Aren't you hungry?"

"I ate as I cooked."

Arro sipped at her coffee. Then, "You look serious, Mackennon. Should I be worried?"

"No." I sat down on the bed beside her. "But I don't know if I should be worried."

"I'm confused." She picked up her cutlery and began eating. A few seconds later, she impatiently swallowed a bite and said, "Well?"

"You don't want to stay at my place," I blurted out.

That concern grew as Arro sat back against her pillows and studied me carefully.

Finally, she sighed. "I didn't want to ruin what's happening between us. I thought going back might bring everything up, and I didn't want to …" She trailed off, guilt flashing across her face.

"Didn't want to what? Arro?"

"Didn't want to feel differently toward you again."

Anxious heat warmed my skin. "Do you think you will?"

Thankfully, she shook her head. "I've forgiven you, Mackennon, I promise. It's just … the trust is still building. I'm worried the memories will mess up that process."

My fears had tried to take hold, but I was done letting them control me. "I want you to come to the cottage today. We don't have to stay long, but I want you to try. We can't ignore these things, Arro."

To my gratitude, Arro nodded. "Okay. You're right."

So here we were, back in the village. But on the drive in, Arro had requested we lead up to the cottage by stopping for a coffee at Flora's. That I could do. It would also mean putting ourselves out there with the villagers, which seemed risky considering Arro might take one step into my house and decide we were forever tainted by the memory of my fuck-up that night.

I was living on the side of hope that it wouldn't be as drastic as all that.

We were great together, and though my demons liked to

argue with me now and then, I knew deep down, Arro thought we were great together too.

Ardnoch was at the height of its tourist season, but we were in the village early enough to find a parking space, and hopefully, a table at Flora's. We passed more strangers than neighbors, but the villagers we passed definitely gave a double glance at us arm in arm.

"There's a table in the back," Arro observed as we approached the windowed front of Flora's.

I opened the door for her, the bell above ringing to announce our presence. Some people looked up; others didn't. A couple of faces I recognized, but the rest were tourists.

Flora came out from behind the counter as I held open the door for Arro. She strode past me, her floral perfume no longer provoking thoughts of desperate, pathetic pining but memories of kissing and caressing every inch of her. I now knew this woman's body as well as I knew my own.

Forcing away thoughts that might get me into trouble, I closed the door behind us and placed a guiding hand on Arro's lower back as I led her across the small café.

"Morning, Flora," Arro said to the owner.

Flora's gaze zeroed in on where I touched Arro, but she merely nodded and welcomed us to the empty table before taking our order. Like last time, I moved my chair close to Arro's so our knees touched. I could tell by Flora's unusual stiffness that gossip had definitely circulated.

I lit a fire under it.

Arro's sip from her cappuccino had left a foam mustache across her top lip. Before I could think about my actions, I bent my head to kiss the foam off. Except, as always, the kiss changed into something a little longer, hungrier. Reluctantly, I broke it, stroking my thumb over her bottom lip, holding her gaze, silently telling her the three words I hadn't spoken in almost three weeks. Because it had grown too painful not to hear them back. As much as I was ready to wait for her, I couldn't take that particular rejection. I'd say them if I thought she needed to hear it, but for now, I hoped my actions spoke those words for me.

That was when I sensed the staring.

Lifting my head, I found Flora gaping over the counter at us like a codfish. Arro groaned under her breath, and I followed her gaze across the room to see Janet Mulree, owner of a tourist gift shop, sitting at a table with her college-age daughter.

Janet Mulree was one of Ardnoch's biggest gossips.

I was aware of her and her daughter leaving five minutes later ... but honestly, I had no idea the woman could work as fast as she did.

When I got up not long later to pay our bill, Flora admonished me with one hand and offered me well wishes with the other. She said as she handed me a receipt, "It's not what I expected from you, but I do hope it'll work out for you both." Flora's tone suggested she thought Arro and I would not last.

I tried not to let that into my head. My immediate thought to myself: *Aye, everyone can see you don't deserve her.* But I choked that thought down and let it dissipate as Arro stood and placed her hand in mine.

"Let's grab a sandwich from Morag's to take back to yours," she said as we stepped out of the café. A summer drizzle wet our hair and skin as we hurried across the street, the sky darkening above. Though we'd been lucky with a very warm summer this year, downpours were still a common occurrence.

I ushered us into Morag's, but before we could make our way to the back to the deli counter, something caught Arro's eye at the end of the first aisle. I followed her as she stopped at a row of magazines, and then walked along the stacks until she suddenly plucked one out of the kids' section.

"Eilidh is obsessed with this." Arro waved a copy of *National Geographic for Kids*. "I bought an issue months ago just for something for her to read in the car, and now it's our thing. I need to get Lewis something, too, though." She scanned the stacks as I looked tenderly down at her, wondering what life might be like with our own kid one day.

If I'd have the energy for it.

I'd find the energy for it.

If it made her happy.

I was vaguely aware of the store door opening, but I was too busy watching Arro, obsessed as I was, to note anything else. Then I heard, "Did you hear, Morag? The Adair family are at it again. That family and the scandal that follows them is atrocious." The voice was familiar.

Arro stiffened in front of me, and I placed a comforting hand on her shoulder as she listened.

That was when I realized the store aisles hid us and the gossiper had no idea we were even there.

"You know I don't listen to gossip, and especially not about the Adairs. They're good people." Morag tried to wave off the male gossiper.

I always liked Morag.

"Och, you won't be thinking that when you hear what I have to tell you. Janet Mulree was just in Flora's, and that security guard was all over the Adair girl. He's twice her age! And there they were, just brazenly kissing. And Janet said it was not an appropriate kiss."

"Mr. Oliphant, for a start, Mac Galbraith is not twice Arrochar's age, and second, it's nobody's business what they do. Now, what can I get you?"

"I'm astonished at you, Morag," Oliphant continued. I knew him. He was a landlord and owned a small portfolio of property here in Ardnoch and in villages along the coast. He'd grown up with Morag's father, who was a Sutherland and had distant connections to the Duke of Sutherland. Oliphant's family didn't date back as far as Morag's or the Adairs, but it was obvious from his attitude that he'd been brought up to believe he was from a superior family. He had always been a judgmental old bastard.

"It's everybody's business what they do. They've turned this village and their ancestral name into a walking scandal. First the eldest transforms his family estate into a Hollywood circus and the village with it, and then he marries an upstart American—"

"Mr. Oliphant—"

"Then, then"—his voice rose with agitation—"his brother had an affair with a woman half his age who also happened to be his children's nanny. It's shameful, I tell you. And we let him get away with it, so now the sister is shacking up with her sister-in-law's father. Have you ever heard anything like it?"

Arro huffed and marched toward the deli counter.

"Arro—"

She waved me off, so I followed at her back to make sure she was all right as she did whatever she needed to do.

"I tell you, they've brought shame on the Adair name."

The deli came into view as we rounded the aisle. And there he was, hunched over his cane, leaning on Morag's counter.

Morag blanched at the sight of us.

Arro stopped behind the old man, and I behind her. "The only shameful person in this village is you, Mr. Oliphant," she said calmly.

He startled, almost dropping his cane as he whirled around to peer at us over the glasses perched on his nose. His mouth pinched into a fine line before he sneered, "I'm only saying what everyone is thinking."

"Not true," Morag said and smiled softly at us. "I say it's about time. I'm thrilled for you both."

"Och, haud yer wheesht, woman." Oliphant stomped his cane belligerently. "Do not encourage this distasteful misconduct."

Morag stiffened. "Do not speak to me like that in my own establishment, Mr. Oliphant, or I'll have to ban you."

"Don't talk nonsense." He dismissed her before saying to Arro, "Well, what do you have to say for yourself?"

Arro stiffened. "I have nothing to say to you, Mr. Oliphant. I couldn't care less what you think of me or my family. In fact, I doubt we've ever wasted a second of our lives thinking about you, and I don't intend to break that habit. Now, if you're done"—she reached back for me, and I stepped up to her side—"we would like to order our food."

The old man huffed and spluttered and opened his mouth to say something else.

"I wouldn't," I warned him, not caring if my tone was threatening and he was just an old man. I didn't want to listen to any more of his bile.

He stomped his cane once more like a fucking cliché and hurried past us, threatening Morag that he would never spend money in her store again.

"Good riddance," Morag said, grimacing. "He always was an unpleasant wee man." She leaned over the counter, smiling widely. "Is it true, then?"

Arro leaned into me. "It's true."

Morag looked pleased, which admittedly felt good. "I really am so happy for you both. You make a beautiful couple."

"Thanks, Morag," Arro said, sounding a little hoarse, as if the comment had made her emotional.

"You just ignore the gossips. They turn things into a scandal where none exists. They'll find something else to talk about soon enough. Now, food? The usual?"

By the time we left Morag's, Arro was subdued. I didn't know if it was about Oliphant or the fact that we were walking down the street toward my row house.

I gave her room to think, and it was a silent walk.

Once we stopped outside my door, I looked down at her and offered, "We can do this another day."

"No." Arro shook her head, looking determined. "I'm not afraid to go in there anymore. I want this, Mackennon. I want to make this work. Subconsciously, I knew that before we came into the village today. I wouldn't have shared you with everyone, putting ourselves out there to be judged like that, if I didn't know I was going to fight hard to be in this with you. A room in a house will not scare me away."

Reassured, I let out a shaky exhale.

Arro gave me a tender smile, took the key from my hand, and opened the door.

I followed *her* in.

And the first words out of her mouth weren't "I can't do this" or "The memory is too awful"… It was, "Jesus, Mackennon, it's bloody stifling in here. When was the last time you checked in?" She marched over to the window that faced the street and pushed it outward, letting warm air into the much warmer air in the house. Grinning over her shoulder, she said, "This way, the nosy bastards can hear everything we're getting up to."

Relief and amusement mingled as I shut the door with my foot and strolled over to her. "Then let's give them something to listen to." I lifted her over my shoulder, her shrieks of laughter filtering out to the street as I threw her onto the couch and came down over her to tickle the life out of her.

Her screams of hilarity could probably be heard down at the Gloaming.

Just like that, the terrible memory was exorcised by who we'd become.

By who *I'd* become. And the forgiveness she gave to the man I used to be.

T he sky was so blue today, barely a cloud marring its perfect gradient from baby blue on the horizon to a warm cornflower at its height. Nothing was quite as beautiful, however, as the shore at the Bay of Sannick, a striking turquoise bleeding into royal blue as the water lapped the golden-white sand of the beach. On a day like this, you might think you were somewhere in the Caribbean.

Even the grass of the surrounding fields looked an unearthly bright green as the sun shone down on us.

Mac settled a blanket on the sand, the beach quiet despite the busy tourist season. He'd agreed to work this Saturday to cover one of his team's shifts, so I'd taken today as a personal day to make sure we wouldn't miss our time together this week. Coming here on a Wednesday meant beating the weekenders, but there were still some folks roaming around. We were just a few miles down the coast from John O'Groats, after all.

"What a perfect day," I commented with a smile as Mac removed lunch from our picnic basket. It *was* perfect. While it was one of the warmest days on record this year, the breeze from the bay was soothing. Though it reminded me to dig into my purse for the sunscreen. I handed it to Mac first.

"I'm good." He waved it off.

"You're wearing a T-shirt that displays your delicious manceps and thick manarms, so while, yes, you're always *good*, you also need to take care of your skin."

Mac grinned but took the lotion. "Manceps? Manarms?"

I looked at said biceps and forearms and said, "On second thought, give it back."

Raising an eyebrow, he did just that while I scooted closer to him. A low chuckle fell between his lips as I smoothed the lotion on him myself.

"Opportunist," Mac murmured, and while we were both wearing sunglasses so I couldn't see the look in his eyes, I knew by his tone that they would be filled with tenderness.

I smiled flirtatiously as I took my time, feeling every sinew and muscle in his arms. "I enjoy touching you. Sue me." Smoothing the lotion down over his hands, I tangled our fingers together playfully.

Mac brought our joined hands to his mouth and pressed a sultry kiss to the back of mine. "Let me do the rest," he said quietly, expression heated, "unless you're into me fucking you in public."

I threw my head back in laughter and promised to grant him mercy after I got the back of his neck. That meant shoving my breasts in his face, to which he gave me a not-so-stern warning to stop.

I scooted back to my spot on the blanket, and Mac handed me the lotion once all his bare skin was covered. "Want a hand?" he asked.

Shaking my head with a smile, I replied, "You better not."

With a smug chuckle, Mac reached for his sandwich instead. Once I was done with the lotion, I ate too. "Has Robyn been here with her camera?" The Bay of Sannick was roughly two hours north of Ardnoch on mainland Scotland's most northerly coastline.

"I think she's been everywhere in Caithness and Sutherland at this point," Mac replied. "Lachlan's taking her to Glasgow in September. They're staying down there for a few weeks so Robyn can explore the central belt."

It still amazed me that Robyn was actually making money as a landscape photographer, and not because her photos weren't spectacular (I planned to commission a few whenever I built my home), but because it wasn't easy making money from artistic endeavors.

"Does that mean you're running the estate again?"

Mac shrugged. "Not like when they were on their honeymoon. Lachlan will work remotely while they're down there. I know Robyn prefers to go off on her photography scouting alone most of the time, so he'll have time to work."

Oh, speaking of photographs … I opened my purse for my phone. "Will you take a selfie with me?" I smiled at him. "I realized there are very few photos of us, and we've hardly taken any since we got together."

Mac's answer was a lift of his chin and moving himself a few inches closer. His arm slid around my waist, and I nestled back into him as I raised the camera. "Smile, and if you can't smile, big guy, then just think of the fantastic things I did with my mouth in bed this morning."

His laughter filled my ear, and I grinned as I snapped the photo.

Mac grasped my chin lightly and turned me into him for a kiss. It was one of the best kisses of my life, even though we'd certainly had more exciting ones. But I could still feel the amusement on his lips, feel the adoration in the sweetness of it. The sounds of the water gently lapping the shore, the gulls crying above, and the laughter in the near distance from those we shared the beach with … yeah, it was a perfect kiss.

And when I later checked the selfie, it was the best photo ever. I'd captured Mac laughing while I grinned, delighted I'd amused him.

As we sat enjoying the contentment of a beautiful summer's day on a wee slice of heavenly beach, I thought of everything I didn't know about Mac and how I so desperately wanted to be the person who knew every inch of him, past and present.

"How are things with Robyn? I feel like I haven't asked you that in a while."

His lips lifted up at the corners. "They're good. Better than I ever could've hoped for."

"Do you talk about her with Iona?" It was silly, I knew, but I was almost jealous of Mac's therapist. She maybe knew him better than I did.

"I do. My past with Robyn is a huge part of why I feel so much like a failure. Talking about it helps me see things clearer. To accept failure where it is, aye, but to recognize my success with her too."

"You should feel only success now, Mackennon. You're a wonderful dad … even if it still feels really weird that you have a daughter Robyn's age," I teased.

But Mac didn't smile. He stared out toward the sea and confessed, "Sometimes I get into these phases where I can't stop thinking about two things. The first is when she broke down crying when she finally confronted me about leaving her. I play it over and over in my head, and I swear to God, it feels like my guts are being ripped out every time."

"Mackennon," I whispered, tears brightening my eyes. I hated that he was haunted by that moment.

"I'm learning to do it less," he promised me.

"And the second thing?"

"Is about her getting shot in the line of duty. That no one called me. That she actually …" His voice cracked. "Died. She died and might never have come back. And never mind that I didn't know and I wasn't there to see her through her recovery … but what if she *had* died? How long would Stacey have waited to tell me? Would I have missed her funeral? I would never have had the chance to make things right between us."

"Mackennon." I rubbed his back in soothing circles. "You mustn't let yourself fall down that rabbit hole."

"I know that now," he reassured me. "You wanted to know if I spoke about Robyn at therapy, and I do. We speak about these things."

"And Iona helps you come up with ways to divert the negative thoughts?"

"Aye. As soon as a thought like that comes to mind, I think of something good that happened between me and Robyn instead."

"And it works?"

"I have to be aware a lot, which is a little wearing, but aye, it works, and it's worth it."

Silence fell over us, and I suddenly regretted taking him to that grim place. Trying to change the subject, I asked, "Do you ever miss all the traveling you used to do? With Lachlan?"

If the turn of conversation surprised Mac, he didn't show it. Mind you, I couldn't see his eyes behind his sexy sunglasses. The man looked like an ad for aftershave. All he needed to do was take off his T-shirt, go into the sea, and then emerge half-naked, brooding at the camera. I shook myself from the fantasy to hear his response.

"No. It was fine, but I started to long for a home base."

"Do you miss Glasgow or Boston?"

He looked at me. "I missed my gran, and I missed Robyn. But not really either of the places."

"What happened to your gran?"

"She passed away a few years after Robyn was born."

"I'm sorry, Mackennon."

He nodded. "She wasn't perfect, but she tried harder than anyone else in my life when I was a kid. You'd think a teenage boy would hate being sent off to another country away from his friends, but I was grateful. To my uncle, too, even though he was reluctant to have me there. He paid for my flight."

"Whatever happened to him?"

"He's still in Boston. Perpetual bachelor. I check in with him every new year, but that's about it. We never had an easy relationship. He keeps his distance from everyone." Mac turned to me again, and I wished like hell I could see his eyes. "I used to worry that I'd end up like him."

Reaching over, I covered his hand with mine. "That will never happen." Then realizing that sounded like a promise for forever, a wee bit of stupid panic made me say, "No matter what happens with us."

His shoulders seemed to hunch up, and he gave me a tight smile.

Fuck.

Why did I say that?

"I mean—"

"It's okay, Arro."

MAC

313

I KNEW she felt guilty and I pulled my hand from under hers, but only to hold it in mine, reassuring her.

Her answering hold was so tight, I grew concerned. "Arro?"

"I'm sorry I'm so messed up about all this," she whispered.

"Hey." I moved closer, nudging her with my shoulder. "Don't apologize. Go at your own pace, darlin'. I'm happy to do that."

We sat in tense silence for a while, watching the unusual calm of the water, a family who'd obviously come from Duncansby Head strolling down from the dunes, and the towering sea stacks that were believed to have stood for over six thousand years, slowly being eroded by the staggering force of the North Sea. I considered Arro's footwear and whether a walk might break the tension.

Then Arro said, "Did you know I had a crush on you from almost the beginning?"

Surprised, I shook my head. "No."

"How would you?" She shot me an amused smile. "I was only eighteen when I really noticed you. Too young for you to notice me."

I didn't know what to say because it was the truth. She'd just been Lachlan's wee sister back then.

"God, I loved having a crush on you." She chuckled, as if remembering. "It excited me anytime you came to the castle for a visit, and I enjoyed fantasizing about what our life together would be like if you ever noticed me." The laughter in her voice faded, however, as she continued, "Though deep down, I didn't think you'd ever notice me."

Emotion made my pulse race hard as I studied her profile. I didn't know what to say. Part of me still didn't feel like I deserved that kind of steadfast affection.

"It changed when you and Lachlan came home after Dad died. My feelings, I mean. But you know about that." She glanced at me. "You offered me friendship, but I wanted more. And while a crush was fun ... loving you for so long, unable to speak about it, was this agonizing weight on my chest. So much pain that no one knew about." A tear slipped down her cheek, and I reached to swipe it away, afraid to speak in case my emotion overcame me.

To the depths of my soul, I regretted every second of pain I'd caused her.

"When we had our falling-out, something happened. Something shifted, and it was like the anger closed a door on the pain. But that's where all that love is, Mackennon. It's behind that door with the pain. And I'm afraid. I'm afraid to open the door."

Pulling her against me, she rested her head on my shoulder. I kissed the top of it in reassurance as she tightened her hold on my hand.

Strangely, while her words hurt, they filled me with hope.

Arrochar Adair loved me.

I was certain of it.

And one day, hopefully soon, she'd feel safe enough to open the door again.

ARRO

Nothing existed for me but him and sensation.

The thick hotness of him inside me. His tight hold on my hips. The musky smell of sex in the air. The cool metal of my bed frame growing hotter in my hand, the softness of the mattress beneath my knees. My gasps and pants. His growls and grunts between pleasure-hazed commands for me to take him as hard as I could. The coiling lust tightening deep inside with every powerful drive into my body as Mackennon took me from behind.

My chin dropped to my chest as my grasp on the bed became such it rattled with every thrust.

"Mackennon!" I cried, feeling that coil tense to near explosion.

His grip on my hips was almost bruising as he demanded I come in that deep, rumbling voice of his that turned me on no matter where we were. Needing to see his face, I glanced over my shoulder at him. Mac's eyes glinted with fierceness I coveted. He always looked like a conquering Viking when he was close to release, and that turned me on too. Everything about this man made me mindless with desire.

"Mackennon," I whimpered, holding his eyes as I pushed back against his thrusts.

Suddenly, I found myself pulled upward, forced to let go of the bed. My back now rested against Mac's chest, his arms wrapped around my torso, one hand slipping between my thighs to circle my clit. His pumps into me slowed, sexy and languid as I rested my head on his shoulder and undulated against his arching hips. His lips caressed my ear as he told me how beautiful I was, how perfect I felt around his cock, that I was everything, how his body was made for just this moment.

It was too much.

The tension inside me shattered into a million pieces, and the strength of my release was such Mackennon grunted with surprise as my inner muscles clenched around him, wrenching his own from him.

Once reality returned to me again, I tilted my head back to look up at him. He bent his to kiss me. When we released one another, I smiled at him, dazed.

Truly amazed at what existed between us.

We'd shared six of the best weeks of my life.

Mac cupped my cheek in his hand, his expression adoring. "I love you so much, Arro."

He hadn't told me he loved me since the beginning, and a part of me had dreaded it as much as I yearned for it. That confusion hadn't worked itself out yet, and so a response caught in my throat once more.

Disappointment dimmed the light in Mac's eyes, and I felt like the biggest arsehole in the world as he gave me a quick kiss before pulling out of me. I thought he'd walk away, go lick his wounds elsewhere, but I should've known better. Mac got out of bed and reached under me, lifting me into his arms. I wrapped mine around his neck as he carried me like a bride on her wedding night into the bathroom.

There would never be a wedding night for us, I realized glumly, if I didn't get past this stumbling block. What the hell was wrong with me? Could I really still fear him hurting me after all this? Surely, I understood by now that Mac would rather die than hurt me again? He saw his therapist every week without fail, and she'd even suggested I come along to a session with him in the future, something Mac was totally comfortable with.

He turned the shower on and gently lowered me into it. "You shower first, darlin'. I'll make you a coffee."

Those three words bubbled up inside, but he'd already left the bathroom by the time I got the *I* out.

Damn it.

The rest of the morning was tense. I knew Mac was trying to work us through the tension with small talk, but I kept waiting for my moment to tell him I loved him. The words just wouldn't come out; I kept telling myself it had to be a perfect moment.

Instead, we readied ourselves to leave the bungalow to collect Eilidh and Lewis. I'd offered to take them into Inverness for back-to-school shopping to give Regan and Thane some time to themselves.

"Got everything?" Mac asked as he grabbed the car keys off my sideboard.

It might as well be our sideboard, I thought, as I nodded and followed him to the door. We were practically living together. And doing it well! I thought it would be an adjustment to give up my autonomy, but Mac wasn't like any man I'd dated before. Perhaps it was his age, but he was a million times more mature than any of the men I'd dated. He told me when he was having a bad day, when he had to fight a little harder against the doubts in his mind that he wasn't good enough. He always asked about my feelings, and I knew he genuinely wanted to know.

Plus, Mac could compromise like nobody's business. Nothing was a hassle for him. He didn't make the small things into big things. And bonus points—the man was tidy! Years of looking after himself meant he cleaned up at his back. There was no fighting over dirty laundry or dishes or anything silly like that. The only thing we "argued" over was what to watch on television, and honestly, I didn't care. I just enjoyed teasing him. Life with Mac was easy, this miraculous, complex mix of serenity and explosive passion.

And the thought of him not being in my house filled me with dread.

Mac opened the door and stepped outside.

I had to tell him.

"Mac, I—"

A low bang sounded in the distance seconds before Mac grunted, his right shoulder flying backward.

Then he whipped around, face pale, expression haggard with fear as he threw himself over me. Confusion slowed my thoughts, my understanding. There was another bang, and his body jerked against mine. Suddenly, I was flying back into the house, my head rattling off the hallway floor as Mac collapsed over me.

"Fuck!" he gritted out as he used his long legs to slam the door shut. "Stay down and crawl into the bedroom hallway!"

I could only watch as he locked the door, and then suddenly, there was a shattering sound and the glass pane at the top of my door rained down over Mac's head.

"Mackennon!"

Understanding dawned.

We were being shot at.

We were being fucking shot at!

Mac was shot.

Terror filled me. "Mackennon!"

He slumped down behind the door, his color worryingly

pale, his features etched with pain. "Arro, make sure the doors are locked, but stay low."

"I'm calling the police." I fumbled in my purse.

"Arro, doors!"

"I can do both." My hands shook as I grabbed my phone. "We need to slow the bleeding."

He nodded calmly. Too calmly. "Doors first. You can't help me if you get shot too."

That had me moving. Staying low, I called the police as I scrambled into the kitchen toward the patio doors. A reassuring dispatcher assured me police and an ambulance were on the way and told me to find somewhere to hide. I couldn't. My mind reeled.

Mac. Who was shooting at us? Why?

I'd just locked the kitchen door when my kitchen window blasted out behind me. I stifled a fearful shriek as it lodged in my throat and huddled against a kitchen cupboard, hiding.

Then I heard a click and an exasperated curse. Another click. Another curse.

Was the shooter's gun empty of bullets?

In retrospect, it was sheer stupidity, but all I could think about was Mac bleeding in my hallway. Rage filled me as I stood to look out the window, and I saw someone in a black ski mask staring furiously at the house, gun dropped at their side.

At *her* side.

That was definitely a female figure in the tight black clothes.

What the hell?

I raced for the patio doors and unlocked them. And as I stepped outside, our attacker looked over at me in shock ... but then raised her gun.

"I know you're empty!" I snarled like an animal and flew at her.

It was almost comical the way she reared back in fright. Not so tough now without her gun.

But me? The fury inside me was equal to a loaded weapon.

The shooter ran around the corner of the house and I gave chase, shrieking my wrath like a woman gone mad. She was fast, but I was bloody faster. Once she hit my front garden, I launched myself at her back, my teeth crashing against my top lip, the taste of blood on my tongue, as I hit her with my full weight. Her garbled shout died as I slammed on top of her. She tried to wriggle free, but I pressed my knee into her back. "Stay down!" I yelled. The gun had scattered out of reach.

"Arro!"

I looked up to see one of my neighbors racing across the street toward me. A quick glance told me a few had come out of their houses at the noise.

Paul Wiley, a teacher at our small high school, lowered beside me and helped hold the shooter down. "What the hell?" he asked, eyes behind his glasses round with shock.

Suddenly, the whole situation hit me, and my tears welled. "She shot Mackennon. I need to check on him."

Paul turned green but nodded before shouting over his shoulder. "Ronnie! Here! We need you!"

Ronnie, another neighbor, was a recently retired computer engineer. Older, but a big man, and he loped quickly across the street to help, holding down the screeching bitch beneath us as Paul took my place without losing his hold on her.

"Have you got her?" I double-checked, already walking backward toward the house.

"Yes, go get Mac."

"What on earth?" I heard Ronnie ask as I fled around the side of the house and inside.

"Mackennon!" I called out as I grabbed towels and hurried back to him.

He'd moved away from the door. Blood smeared my hallway walls.

Hysterical tears threatened, but I forced them down as I raced over to him.

The dark navy of his T-shirt was soaked from a shot to the shoulder. But there had been two shots fired. "Where else are you hit?" I demanded, shaking as I pressed a towel to his shoulder. So much blood. It coated my hands.

"The shooter?" he asked, the words too faint in my ears.

"We've got her. My neighbors have her pinned in the garden. Her gun ran out of bullets or jammed or something."

"Her?"

"I don't know who it is yet—ski mask. Mackennon, other wound?" I caressed his face, trying to get him to focus on me.

His eyes met mine, but they weren't right. They were glazed over, the light in them dimmed. Tears fell before I could stop them. "Back," he told me.

He'd been shot in the back.

Because he'd covered me with his body.

"Mackennon." I leaned down and kissed him, my tears falling onto his chest. "Stay awake, Mac." I pressed harder on his wound to stem the blood, and he grunted. "Sorry." I scattered wet kisses along his jaw. "Please."

"Arro," he whispered, just as his eyes closed.

Frantically, I searched for his pulse. Too slow. Thready.

"Where is that ambulance?" I cried.

As if in answer, I heard the sirens in the distance.

But Mac's pulse was fading beneath my fingertips.

"No! Mackennon." I sobbed over him. "Don't leave me. I love you. Please don't leave me. Please. I love you." Time held no meaning as I begged and pleaded with him, hoping he could hear me, hoping he would fight. The world bled out as

I lived inside my fear. Not another man I loved. I couldn't watch another man I loved die in my arms. "Mackennon!"

"Miss, out of the way."

"Miss?"

"Get her out of the way."

Hands grabbed at me, pulling me from Mac. I raged in fury at the shadowy figures holding me back until the picture in front of me started to make sense.

Paramedics moved quickly over Mac.

"Still got a faint pulse. Let's go."

I watched as if through a piece of warped glass as they struggled to get his big body onto a stretcher. I saw the blood all over my hallway floor and smeared across my walls. Mackennon's blood. Sounds grew muffled in my ears as I followed them out into the garden.

Men, policemen, blocked my way as I tried to get into the ambulance with him.

Questions, they had questions.

Fuck their questions!

Then my neighbors were there, and two other police officers had the shooter in their hands. Her ski mask had been removed.

A young brunette I didn't recognize glared back at me with all the hatred in the world.

"I hope he fuckin' dies," she snarled. "His lot took ma Craig, and naebody else gave a fuck. But we did. We never forgot whit happened. And I hope the bastard dies fur it."

I flew at her.

I think I broke her nose before they hauled me off her.

It wasn't enough.

At that moment, I wanted to kill her for what she'd done. I didn't care about her pain. All I felt was fear and rage. In fact, I'd never experienced rage like it.

I heard the threat coming out of my mouth, the words

that I'd end her if Mackennon died.

In all my fury and viciousness, it was no wonder I ended up in handcuffs right alongside the bitch.

3 2

MAC

It didn't seem that long ago I was in this hospital with stab wounds. Now I'd been fucking shot. Thankfully, they'd gotten both bullets out in surgery.

Concerned, I watched Arro as she slept in the armchair beside my bed. She was there when I woke up for the first time during the night, while the nurses explained what happened to me and assured me the doctor would be in first thing to talk to me. The doc had arrived fifteen minutes ago, and Arro had slept through the whole conversation.

Still in a lot of pain, I wanted to reach out for her, but every time I did, it hurt.

Apparently, I'd been out after surgery for a whole day and night. I'd sluggishly demanded answers from Arro last night before exhaustion pulled me under again.

The shooter was Lee Kilmany's girlfriend, Roisin Bankman. She was also Craig Kilmany's ex-girlfriend. They'd been working together to avenge Craig. I still didn't know if she'd been aiming for me or Arro, or both. All I knew was they were both behind bars now, and Arro was safe.

A noise brought my head up from watching Arrochar

sleep. Robyn hurried into the room with Lachlan at her back. Remorse filled me as my brave, strong girl's face crumpled, and she burst into quiet tears as she reached for my hand.

"I'm okay, wee birdie," I promised, tightening my hold. "I'm right here."

Lachlan rested his hand on her shoulder as Robyn sat down on the free chair at my other side and tried to gather herself.

"I was so worried." She swiped at her tears, her gaze roaming over me. "Dad, you gotta stop doing this to me."

I chuckled and groaned as pain shot through my back.

"What? What's going on?" Arro jolted awake, her face adorably sleep-creased as her wide eyes flew around the room. She relaxed at the sight of Robyn and Lachlan, but tensed as soon as she looked at me. "Are you okay?"

"I'm fine, darlin'," I promised her.

Arro stared at me, haunted.

I wanted to kill Lee and Roisin.

"I'm okay," I assured her.

"Are you okay, Arro?" Lachlan asked her.

"He's still furious the police arrested you," Robyn said. "We all are."

Confusion and anger filled me. "What the fuck?"

"I hadn't told him yet." Arro shot her brother and my daughter an annoyed look.

"You got arrested?" I demanded.

She shrugged wearily. "I fought with the police about not getting to go in the ambulance with you, and then Roisin said some things … I just flew at her."

"Broke her nose," Robyn added proudly.

I raised an eyebrow at Arro.

But she didn't smile. She shrugged again, dark shadows in her eyes. "I would have killed her if I'd had the chance."

Realizing how terrified she must have been, how much

trauma it must've brought back from her father's death, I held out my palm to her. Arro slipped her hand into mine, her lips trembling as she refused to look at me.

Fear niggled in that place where all my demons laid in wait.

"What happened?" I asked.

"Arro called me. I called my lawyer, and we both arrived at the police station to ream them. They had witness statements from her neighbors. They told me they were keeping her there to calm her down. Oh, aye, fucking arresting my sister after her boyfriend gets shot is one way to keep her calm." Lachlan's voice rose angrily with every word.

Robyn hushed him, reaching up to soothe him.

Looking back at Arro, that niggle wouldn't leave me alone.

She still wouldn't look at me, even though I silently begged her to. I squeezed her hand, but she merely tightened her grip.

Robyn cleared her throat, drawing my attention and I saw her watching us with a furrowed brow. Ever so perceptive, she released my hand to stand up. "Lachlan and I will get us all some coffee. Can we get you anything, Dad?"

"Water, if I'm allowed."

"We'll check with the nurse."

I gave her a grateful nod as she led Lachlan out of the room to give us privacy.

"Talk to me," I demanded.

Finally, Arro lifted her gaze to meet mine. And promptly burst into tears, racking sobs that gutted me.

I tried to reach for her and hissed in pain, which only made her cry harder.

Fuck!

"Arro, please, darlin'."

And then suddenly she was clinging to me, resting her

327

head on my stomach as she cried more tears than I knew a woman had in her.

It was awful. I'd give anything not to have to witness her like this. Emotion tightened my chest as I caressed her hair and waited for her to calm.

Finally, she whispered, "I was terrified. So terrified of losing you."

I squeezed her shoulder as I brushed her hair behind her ear. "I'm sorry if it brought things back up about your dad."

"Only you would know that."

"Anyone who loves you would know that. I'm sure your brothers are worried about it too."

"There was so much blood, Mackennon," she whimpered.

"It was just a scratch," I assured her.

Arro lifted her head, expression belligerent. "Just a scratch? Try two more wounds on top of the three that are already my fault."

"These weren't your fault, Arro. This was my shit that got us into this mess. And the other three weren't your fault, either, for Christ's sake. Fergus was unwell."

"But you covered me." She grabbed my hands. "As soon as that first bullet hit, your first thought was to cover me."

Of course it was.

Understanding filled her eyes along with something like awe.

"I'm here, and I'm alive," I reminded her. "I'm not going anywhere."

"There was so much blood." That haunted look flashed across her face again. "Your pulse was fading beneath my hands. And all I kept thinking ..." Fresh tears scored her cheeks. "All I kept thinking was that I'd spent the entire morning trying to figure out a way to tell you I love you too ... and I was terrified I was too late."

I gripped her, pulling her toward me, the cardiac monitor

picking up the sudden racing of my heart. "I know you love me. I knew it then, and I know it now."

"But I never said it, and I'm so sorry."

"Don't be sorry, Arro."

"I love you, Mackennon." She leaned gently over me to press a kiss to my lips. "I love you so fucking much, I think I would burn down the world for you."

I kissed her harder, ignoring the pain for the pleasure. "I love you too," I promised. "And I'm not going anywhere. I've got too much to live for. You. Robyn. Our family. You're stuck with me for life, Arrochar Adair."

She studied my face, her eyes and nose red with tears. She was the most beautiful thing I'd ever seen. "Move in with me. When you get out of the hospital. I know it's fast ... but we fit. Don't we? It feels right."

Joy filled me, obliterating any anger or resentment I felt toward Kilmany. "Aye, I'll move in with you." I grinned against her lips as she kissed me with happy pecks. "There's definitely no getting rid of me now."

"Good." She kissed me harder.

"Okay." Robyn's voice cut loudly through the room. "That stuff can wait until you're healed up."

Arro smirked as she broke the kiss, but promptly slid off the bed to take her seat beside me.

I might have been lying in a hospital bed recovering from gunshot wounds, but watching my daughter, once estranged, fuss over me with worry and love, while a woman I'd adored from afar sat by my side with open love between us ... well ...

I actually was like the luckiest bastard out there.

33

MAC

It impressed the doctors how quickly my body was healing, and it looked like I'd be out as quickly as I had been for my stab wounds. Still, a few days in, and I was already restless as hell to leave.

"Everything is looking good," Sheila, my nurse, had said that morning. "I'll talk to the doctor, and we'll see about getting you discharged today or tomorrow. It'll be up to the doctor, mind."

A few hours later, the doctor still had not come in to see me. The wall-mounted TV aired one asinine midmorning show after another. I'd forced Arro to return to work to give her some normality. Until her windows were fixed, she was staying at Thane's, for which I was glad. Even though I knew she was safe, I didn't want her to be alone while I was recovering.

Sheila had just popped back in with more water and to ask if the doctor had been in yet when my phone buzzed on the bedside table. My nurse promised to search out the doctor and left as I picked up the call.

From Nylah, the club's ethical hacker.

The rhythm of the beep on my heart monitor grew faster.

"Nylah?" I answered abruptly.

"Mac, hope you're well," Nylah said, having no idea I was lying in a hospital bed since I hadn't spoken to her in a few weeks. "Look, I know everything was tied up with the Kilmany bloke, but I thought you might like to know that I just got a ping on a license plate for Guy Lewis. You wanted me to let you know if he entered Scotland. A security camera picked up his car at a petrol station in Inverness early this morning."

Foreboding crashed over me.

Lisa said Lee Kilmany had denied leaving Arro those notes. And I just assumed because he'd denied everything else ...

"Fuck! I have to go, Nylah. Thank you."

"Aye, no—"

I hung up on her and immediately dialed Arro. She didn't answer. Shit!

Sitting up, I began pulling at the equipment attached to my body as I called Lachlan, and my bloody phone rang out.

Finally, Lachlan picked up. "Mac, are you—"

"Where are you?" I barked.

"I'm at the castle. Why?"

"Guy Lewis." I shoved off the bedcovers. "He's here. Nylah picked up his license plate in Inverness this morning."

"It could mean anything, Mac."

"Get to Arro now. She's not answering her phone. I'm on my way."

"You're in the hospital. You stay! I'll go."

"Just find her and call me as soon as you have."

The door to my room burst open just as I stood, and the doctor stared at me wide-eyed. "Mr. Galbraith, I'll need you to get back into that bed right now."

331

I straightened to my full height and watched him swallow warily as I warned, "And I'll need you to get out of my way."

34
ARRO

Thane kindly allowed me to take over the office at the front of his house while I stayed with them. The windows in my bungalow were standard size, so Lachlan had pulled in a favor with a company to get new ones fitted at the beginning of next week. He'd already sent in decorators to repaint my walls and his flooring guy to rip up the ruined planks and replace the hallway flooring. There would be no remnants of what happened to Mac, and as always, I was thankful for my eldest brother's efficiency.

And as much as I loved my family and enjoyed being around the kids, I was looking forward to returning home. Mac would be home with me by then. We needed to pack up and move his stuff.

Was it too soon to ask him about building a house in Caelmore?

Since the shooting, I'd had to fight the urge to fill our lives with everything we wanted right away. The panic hadn't receded. I didn't know if it would until Kilmany and Bankman were sentenced. Or even then. It was like this agitation that kept kicking my heart rate up every time I didn't have work or something else to distract me.

I needed Mackennon home. That would surely help.

My phone beeped by the computer I stared at dazedly. Flipping it over, I opened a text from Marcello.

Meet me at the new site. We need to talk. I'll be in the Portakabin.

We hadn't even started work at the new site. Confused, I texted back, *Is everything all right?*

Minor emergency. No need to panic. Just need your help.

I sighed. Well, I could use a distraction. *On my way.*

Grabbing my purse, I threw in everything I needed before striding into the kitchen to where I'd left my car keys.

Regan was already in there, emptying the dishwasher. "Hey, I was just about to come in and ask if you wanted another coffee?"

I shook my head as I grabbed my keys off the island. "Marcello texted, and he needs me at the new site at Fearnmore. It's not far, so I won't be long. Do you want me to pop by Morag's, grab us a sandwich for lunch?"

"Oh, yeah, please. I like her chicken salad wraps."

"No problem. See you in a bit."

A few minutes later, I swung out of Thane's driveway, looking back at the land along the coast and thinking of a future home there with Mac. Would he be as comfortable living next to his daughter as I was living next to my brothers? Hmm. Maybe we could build a little farther down the coast for more privacy if it was an issue.

Stop planning Mackennon's future without him, I admonished as I drove down the country lane toward the main road.

Fearnmore Forest was about thirty minutes west of Caelmore, and I used that time to think about Mac coming home.

When I called him this morning, he said the nurse mentioned the possibility of him being discharged today. Hopefully, my visit this evening would turn into a pickup. I knew he was restless in that hospital bed, and his wounds this time around were actually less severe than the stab wounds had been.

The thought of how much he'd suffered in the last year made me shudder.

Nothing else was going to happen to that man.

He was mine to protect now.

My hands tightened around the wheel at the mere thought of anyone trying to hurt him.

Ten of those thirty minutes to Fearnmore were taken up by the single-track road all the way to the site. It was a devil to deal with for our larger vehicles because it had some fierce bends. I'd been granted permission from the Highland Council to bring the vehicles in down a straight single-track road to the west of the woods and create a new road in from there. We were set to start work on that at week's end, so for now, I was stuck with the old road to where we'd begun setting up the site.

Finally, I pulled into the clearing where we'd already built our modular cabin. We'd brought it in pieces on smaller vehicles before building it on site.

The car parked outside of it wasn't Marcello's.

What on earth was going on?

I hoped what Marcello had to tell me wasn't anything too dramatic. I'd had enough drama to last me a lifetime.

Crossing the yard, muddy from last night's rainfall, I hurried up the cabin steps and burst in. "I hope this—"

I froze. Everything in me froze.

Written across the back wall of the cabin in what looked like dripping blood:

> You were once so very dear to me
> But now so very dead to me

THE NOTE LACHLAN RECEIVED from Lucy and Fergus, along with a deer's carcass at Ardnoch last year.

It hadn't been Lee Kilmany tormenting me.

I whipped around to run from the cabin and a scream choked in my throat at the sight of the man standing in the doorway.

Everything in me recoiled in horror.

Guy Lewis, my bastard ex-boyfriend, sneered as he stepped inside and slammed the door shut behind him. I watched as he turned the lock and I stepped back, eyes darting everywhere for an escape, a weapon, anything.

"You know, I didn't think this day would come," Guy said conversationally as he followed me in. "When I started sending the notes, I honestly didn't think you would take it that seriously. But of course, I underestimated your protective big brothers and that arsehole Galbraith."

He *had* sent the notes.

Robyn had been right.

"Why?" I asked, even though I couldn't give a shit what his excuses were for tormenting me. The psychopath.

I needed to stall while I tried to think. *Think.*

I'd left my phone in the car.

What a moron!

"Why?" Guy stopped, staring at me like I was a moron too. "Your brother ruined me, Arro. For fucking around with his precious sister, he ruined my reputation. No good restaurant in this country will have me."

"Then why stay?"

"That's not the point," he snarled. "He fucking ruined my life because I dated his sister. Where's the justice in that?"

336

"We both know that's not why. And like I said, you could have returned to Australia."

"That's not the point!" he repeated furiously.

Something dawned on me. "You can't go home, can you? What happened, Guy? You make too much of a habit of beating up women whose families want to kill you for it, and now home is no longer an option?"

"You know nothing!" he spat. "I won't be chased out of an entire country because of a piece of snatch!"

I flinched at the word, glowering back at him. Fear thrummed through my blood, my heart, my body trembling with it, but like hell would I let him see. "You're a coward who beat me up for no good reason. It's not my fault you pissed off Lachlan because you beat on his sister."

The punch was so quick, I had no time to move or block it.

Pain exploded across my face and then my back. Ringing filled my ears, and it took a second for a sense of reality to return. Cheekbone and eye throbbing, I looked up from where I was now sprawled on the floor beside Marcello's desk. My lower back ached where it had hit the desk corner.

I glared up at Guy as he loomed over me, and I forced myself back to my feet as the room spun, my hands searching the desk behind me for any weapon.

"You know my dad was a brute," Guy said. "He used to smack us around for the slightest thing. I vowed never to be like him, that I'd let the small stuff go. But the big stuff ... I just can't let that shit go." Guy studied me, his expression filled with hate. "I loved you, Arrochar. I loved you from the moment I saw you. Why couldn't you love me back?"

Before I could think of an answer that might calm him, he continued, "And I almost felt bad about what happened between us that night of the ceilidh. I thought maybe I was

337

imagining this thing between you and Galbraith. Even after Lachlan fucked up my entire career, there was a small part of me that wondered if I'd deserved it for hurting you like that.

"But the voice in the back of my head kept telling me you were a slut, and you deserved so much worse than what I did to you that night. And I was right." He grinned maliciously. "I mean, I tell you, when I asked Duncan to leave those notes, I thought maybe I was overreacting—"

"Duncan?" Wait? What?

"Oh, yeah, didn't you know? I have family in Scotland. Marcello's assistant is my second cousin. He thinks you're a cunt, too, by the way. Happy to help me. Stole Marcello's phone this morning so he could text you to come here."

Shock froze me again.

"He was also the one who told me you've been fucking Galbraith, and that I was right all along. Vindicated!" he roared, and I recoiled. "But Duncan was worried because you were never alone, that dirty bastard Galbraith watching you every second. So I told him to pull back. But then he told me you two were public now. You stood there that night and told me that my jealousy was all in my head, but it wasn't, was it? You've been spreading for Galbraith for years."

"Wrong," I snapped. "I never cheated on you."

"Right," he huffed.

"I don't cheat," I said, and it was probably foolish, but my hatred took over as I sneered, "But if Mackennon had crooked his finger at me, I would have dumped you in a heartbeat."

Guy bared his teeth and lunged.

And I brought my knee right up between his legs as hard as I could, my shriek of outrage filling the cabin.

Guy bellowed in agony as he crumpled to his knees, and I skirted around him for the door.

However, a hard tug on my ankle brought me crashing to

the floor, my chin jarring off the floor. Pain ricocheted through my head, but I fought through it as Guy's hand climbed higher on my calf, attempting to pull me to him. With a shake of my leg, I loosened his grip long enough to turn to face him. He was purple with rage.

I drew back my right knee to my chest and drove my foot down to his face, smashing it hard into him. He howled in pain, collapsing off me, and I stumbled onto my feet. Guy grabbed my ankle with a bestial roar, and I shook him loose, kicking him in the head again.

Adrenaline charged through me as I hurried to unlock the door, curse words falling from my panicked lips as I yanked it open and ran down the cabin steps, almost tripping as I hurried toward my Defender.

Weight slammed into my back, shoving me into the front of my car, my breath momentarily stolen as Guy imprisoned me with his body.

He gripped my hair painfully, yanking my head back to murmur in my ear, "When I heard someone shot Galbraith, I knew this was my chance. My only chance to get at you, to punish you. I was going to kill you, Arro. Blunt trauma to the head, or choke you, maybe, whatever seemed right in the moment. Got all the cleaning supplies in my trunk to wipe everything in that cabin clean just in case you pissed me off and it got a little messy. Well, you pissed me off, gorgeous." He pushed his hips into me, and I was nauseated at the feel of his arousal. "And actually, I think I'm going to teach a lesson a little slut like you needs … and then I'll kill you.

"In fact"—he licked my throat as his hands dropped to my hips, and I gritted my teeth as I squirmed, trying to find a break in his hold—"I might even choke you to death while I'm fucking you."

"Arrrgh!" I shrieked, snapping my head back into his, feeling the throb of his chin crack off my skull. He stumbled back, loosening his grip just enough to give me room to slam my elbow into his gut. With another scream of fury, I twisted around with a jump and backhanded his face with the force of my momentum. He stumbled, hitting the ground, and I ran around the car, hauling myself into the driver's seat.

As I switched on the engine, Guy staggered back to his feet.

I revved the car as he swiped blood from his nose, and then I reversed, trying to find space to swing the car around so I could race out of there.

He marched menacingly toward my car, determination and murder etched into his features.

I threw the car back into drive, yanking the wheel to turn it as I stepped on the accelerator. The SUV jolted forward on a turn, clipping Guy hard enough to send him crashing into his own car.

He slumped to the ground.

I waited.

There was no movement. His eyes were closed, blood trickling from his nose and mouth.

I got out of my vehicle just in time to vomit up everything inside me.

The sound of engines sent renewed fear through me, and I glanced beyond the car to see two black Range Rovers careening onto the site.

A sob of relief burst from me as Lachlan jumped out of the first SUV. Running to him, I threw myself into his arms and clung to him like he could make the last thirty minutes disappear.

"You're okay." Lachlan held me hard. "I've got you, you're okay." Over my head, I heard him order, "Check that fucker for a pulse. And someone call an ambulance." To me he whispered, "The police are already on their way, sweetheart.

Regan told us where you were. You're okay now. But you have to tell me if you're hurt, Arro."

I hurt everywhere.

But mostly my soul ached for what I'd just been forced to do to another human being.

"Arro? Talk to me, sweetheart. Arro? Arro?"

I hurried through the hospital corridors, ignoring the ache from my wounds as one task consumed me.

Get to Arro.

By the time I'd bullied the doctor into sending security away and discharging me, I got the call from Lachlan that Arro was safe but in shock. She was already in an ambulance on her way to Inverness, following the ambulance that carried Guy Lewis.

She'd hit him with her car.

I needed to know what else had happened.

I needed to know if she was okay.

What could have happened haunted me as I charged through the hospital. I wasn't there to protect her. Had I failed her? Did I deserve to know if she was safe?

Don't, an internal voice fought me. *You're wounded from protecting her.*

No one saw this coming, right?

Or had I just been so relieved to enjoy the idea of a peaceful future with Arro that I'd grown lax and dropped my hold on professional paranoia?

I blew through double doors and was in the loud, controlled chaos of the emergency department. Searching the waiting area for faces I recognized, I spotted Robyn standing against the wall, glaring anxiously around her.

Hurrying toward my daughter, I drew her gaze, and her lips parted in surprise. She stormed toward me. "No, you should be in bed."

"Where is she?" I snapped impatiently.

Robyn raised an eyebrow. "Dad, she's fine. But you're recovering from bullet wounds, and since I know how that feels, I also know you shouldn't be running around like a madman."

"I need to see Arro, Robbie, so help me or get out of my way, wee birdie."

She sighed. "This way."

Following her, heart racing in my chest, every second seemed like an hour before she led us to a nurse.

"Hey, we spoke earlier. You checked in my sister-in-law, Arrochar Adair. Can you tell me where she and my husband went?"

The nurse glanced behind Robyn at me. "Immediate family only. She's with a consultant."

I stepped forward belligerently, my usual calm and patience gone. "I'm her—" Fuck! *Boyfriend* sounded so juvenile and impermanent. "*Hers*," I decided with a glower.

The nurse gave me an unimpressed look, and Robyn raised her hands, palm out. "Apologies for my dad. He's actually recovering from bullet wounds and just got discharged to come find his ... Arro." She shrugged.

"Wait." The nurse cocked her head. "Arrochar Adair is your sister-in-law, but she's also your father's girlfriend?"

"That better not be judgment I hear." Robyn looked up at me. "Did you hear a tone of judgment?"

"Oh, no, not judging, just fascinating." The nurse studied

me thoroughly. "To be fair, you don't look old enough to have fathered this one." She gestured to Robyn.

"Arro," I bit out impatiently, like a fucking caveman. Then, because I had much respect for health care workers, I added, "Please."

"Right, right." She nodded. "This way. The doctor might not let you in, though."

As we followed her, Robyn shook her head. "I swear, the next person who tells me you don't look old enough to have fathered me, I'm gonna pop their head right off."

"I heard that," the nurse threw over her shoulder.

I was barely listening. "Robbie."

"Dad, she was fine. A little banged up, but fine. Stop panicking."

"If it was Lachlan, how would you feel right now?"

"Yeah, okay, point taken."

The nurse stopped at a door and knocked before entering. "Dr. Braemyre—oof!"

I barged past the nurse, zeroing in on Arro, who sat on a bed, her legs dangling over the side. She had a blood pressure band around her biceps, a cut lip, and her left eye was almost swollen shut.

If Guy Lewis wasn't dead yet, he was about to be.

"Sir!" the doctor protested, but I ignored them all and rushed to Arro.

She grabbed onto me, pulling on my T-shirt in desperation until we had our arms around each other. Her trembling body fired my rage.

"Leave them be." I heard Lachlan say behind us. I hadn't even noticed him in the room.

After a while, the doctor said, "Sir, I really need to continue examining Ms. Adair."

Reluctantly, I released her, but at the haunted look on her

face, I stayed beside her, leaning against the bed as I held her hand.

The doc glanced back and forth between us and then sighed before he finished taking Arro's blood pressure.

"You said you hit your back too?" the doc asked.

Her back?

I frowned as she nodded and lifted her shirt. Glancing behind her as the doc did, I hissed at the large bruise on her lower back. The doc examined it and shook his head. "It doesn't appear to be anything to worry about. But if you notice any blood in the urine, I want you back here immediately."

Arro nodded quietly. Too quiet.

The doc touched her chin, tilting her head up as he shone a penlight in her eyes. He switched it off and gave her a reassuring smile. "No sign of concussion."

"What about earlier?" Lachlan asked, and I noticed him for the first time. He looked haggard and pale, his features tight.

That put me back on alert.

"Arro was practically catatonic when I got to her."

"Shock does that." The doctor looked back at Arro. "Your blood pressure is low, which happens after an adrenaline crash. The shaking and dizziness you said you experienced is low blood sugar." He looked to Lachlan and Robyn. "A wee bit of chocolate might not go amiss."

"On it." Robyn slipped out of the room.

"I'm really okay," Arro finally spoke, and everything in me relaxed with relief. "It was just shock," she reassured Lachlan. Her lips trembled. "Is … do we know how Guy is? Are they going to arrest me?"

I squeezed her hand harder. What the hell had happened out there?

"No," Lachlan bit out angrily. "No, they'll have to go through me and the ten thousand lawyers I'm about to hire."

"Lachlan …" Arro gave him a sad smile. "You can't protect me from everything."

"He tried to murder you," Lachlan hissed. "There is no way anyone is arresting you for defending yourself."

"He's right," I added, pulling her close. "It'll never happen."

"I will note every one of your injuries," Dr. Braemyre added, his tone kind, his gaze maybe a wee bit too soft on Arro for my liking, but I'd forgive him for it. "I'll make sure it's comprehensive enough that the police get a real picture of what you went through today."

"Doctor, are you able to give us an update on the bast—on Lewis?" I asked.

He gave me a regretful shake of his head. "I can only give that information to immediate family. Now, I'm afraid the police have asked to come in and speak with you after my examination."

"It's fine." Arro nodded, but she squeezed my hand until it was almost painful. I gently slid my arm around her, pulling her to my side.

We waited in silence for the police to come into the room. By that point, Arro nibbled the chocolate bar Robyn brought her, but just barely, like she didn't have the stomach for anything.

Throughout the police interview, it took everything I had not to march out of that room and hunt that piece of scum Lewis down.

"So you fought him off and got into your vehicle?" the female constable asked gently.

"Yes. I was trying to reverse, swing the car around, and I clipped him by accident as I tried to drive out."

"What was Lewis doing before you hit him?"

"He was coming for me."

"So he was still in pursuit?"

"Yes."

"Do you—" The male constable was cut off by his colleague when she said, "I think we have all we need."

He pressed his lips tight and nodded in agreement.

The woman gave Arro a once-over, something flickering in her expression. "I'm sorry for what you've been through today, Ms. Adair. We'll be in touch."

"Can you tell me if he's okay?" Arro asked, tears brightening her eyes. "I just want to know that I didn't ..."

The constable gave her a sympathetic nod. "Mr. Lewis has sustained some injuries, but the doctor said he'll recover. He's under arrest. We have constables stationed in his room. That's all I can tell you just now."

"Thank you," Arro whispered, slumping with relief.

"Aye." I reached out to shake the woman's hand. "Thank you." She'd been kind, not drawing out the questioning or coercing Arro into admitting some kind of blame for what had happened.

She shook my hand with an abrupt nod, and the constables left us alone.

Lachlan held Robyn by his side as he exhaled slowly. "Let's see about getting you discharged and home. I don't know about all of you, but I could do with a rather large whisky."

I just wanted to be alone with Arro, but I understood that being around her family was probably what she needed. Nodding, I stood and helped Arro off the bed. She winced from some invisible hurt, and I forced myself not to think about the fact that Guy was in the hospital. Arro was what mattered. Not murdering that bastard. Though I'd like to, and I would without compunction ... if it weren't for her. She (and Robyn) needed me not to be in jail.

Sliding my arm around her slight shoulders, I held on to

Arro as we searched for the doctor. It seemed to take too long to get her discharged, and as we waited, she leaned her entire weight into me and whispered, "Can you take me back to yours? I just want to be with you."

Emotion thickened my throat as I pressed my cheek to her forehead and whispered, "Anything you want, darlin'. I'll give you anything you want."

LATER, despite the protestations of her overprotective big brother, Arro and I found ourselves alone in my house, lying in my bed, arms and legs entwined. I kept a tea towel filled with ice pressed to her swollen eye as we held each other. For a long time.

And then her voice cut through the silence. "You can take this off for a while." She covered my hand holding the ice to her face. "The doctor said to ice it every twenty minutes or so."

I nodded. "Need fresh ice, anyway." I dropped the wet towel on the floor. I'd deal with it when I got up.

"You better not take any of this on yourself, Mackennon."

"I'm not," I promised her. It was difficult because it was second nature to see it as a failure, but I wouldn't let those kinds of thoughts come between us. "I'm proud of you," I told her gruffly. "You have so much strength in you, Arro. So much fire and fight. I've never been more thankful for it."

She drew in a shuddering breath. "I'm glad that's who I became at that moment ... but I don't know if I'd feel that way if I'd killed him."

I lifted my head as she tilted hers up to meet my gaze. "If you'd killed him, it would have been self-defense. And I wouldn't be sorry for it."

"Have you killed anyone, Mackennon?"

I nodded. "When I was a police officer."

"I'm sorry," she whispered tearfully. "I hate that for you."

"It was self-defense. Kill or be killed. Doesn't make it any easier, but it's the one thing in my life I won't take the blame for. He put me in that position when he fired his gun at me. Just like Guy put you in that position when he attacked you. Be at peace with it, Arro, because if it had turned out differently, if he'd …" I couldn't bear thinking about it. "If he'd *hurt* you … I would have killed him."

Her gaze sharpened. "You don't mean that."

"Do you remember the rage you felt when faced with Roisin Bankman?"

Understanding dawned. "Yes."

"Then you understand how I feel right now and how I would've felt if he'd stolen my future with you."

She nodded slowly. "But I'm here, Mackennon. I'm here. And I'm not going anywhere." Humor suddenly lit her expression. "Unless, of course, there are more skeletons in the Adair closets, just waiting to terrorize us."

I groaned. "Don't, you'll jinx us."

Arro laughed lightly, the sound a bright relief.

Then, "What happens now? There'll be a trial, won't there?"

"Aye. Another one."

"We're going to be experts at this soon."

"Hey." I tilted her chin back up. "We won't live our lives with this hanging over us. There will be a trial, and we'll deal with it as it happens. But for now, we're moving on. Together."

"I want to build a house in Caelmore with you," Arro blurted out.

My lips twitched. My Arro, impatient and passionate. "Oh, really?"

She sat up a little, countenance brightening, and I was glad for the distraction. "What do you think? We could choose a plot a little farther down the coast from the boys. Design it exactly to our specifications. We could put in a gym so you don't have to get up so early to use the one at the castle. Sea views. A proper library for all our books where I can finally host our book club."

I grinned at her growing excitement. "Our book club?"

She nodded, already far away, building the house in her mind. "I've always wanted a proper chef's kitchen too." Arro's gaze turned back to me. "Maybe a shower big enough for sex."

"Oh, I like that idea." I caressed her hip as she seemed to slump, battling the exhaustion the attack had left her with. "We'll talk about it later, darlin'."

"But you want to?"

"I can't think of anything better," I promised, brushing a soft kiss against her lips.

She let all her love shine out of her. "Maybe two kids' bedrooms?"

The thought filled me with equal amounts of terror and anticipation. "Sounds like a plan."

Arro relaxed against the pillows, eyelids drooping. "I didn't just fight for me today," she confessed softly. "I fought for that. Our future. Us."

I settled in closer, the ache in my chest a pleasure pain. "I know."

"I love you so much."

For once, I didn't question whether I deserved to be loved by this extraordinary woman. Instead, I allowed myself to feel nothing but awe and gratitude that I was.

"I'll love you forever," I promised, pulling her close, feeling her melt in love and trust in my arms, allowing sleep to drift over her with me to guard her and her dreams.

EPILOGUE

ARRO

"I think it would be better to have a partition wall that was also our bedhead and then behind the bed, a walk-in closet and then behind that, a spacious bathroom," I said as Mac and I stood over Thane's shoulders while he drew on his computer.

Drew us our dream house, that is.

"What do you think?" I asked Mac.

He shrugged. "I think I like whatever you like."

Thane chuckled. "You always were very wise, Galbraith."

They shared a laugh, and I gently shoved Mac, my engagement ring flashing in the light. Mackennon had wasted no time proposing after my ordeal with Guy, and Lachlan couldn't argue it was too fast because he'd married Robyn within only a year of knowing her.

"I'm serious," I huffed. "This is your house too."

"Darlin', I got my gym and I've designed the security.

Those are really my only points of interest other than how big our bed is."

"That's enough," Thane cut in. "No one needs to hear any more about my sister's bed."

I rolled my eyes. "Your wee sister has sex. Whoop-de-doo."

Mac shot me a disgruntled look. "There's a bit more to it than a whoop-de-doo."

Lips twitching, I agreed. "Last night there were several whoop-dees and multiple doos."

"Fuck this." Thane pushed back from the computer, and Mac and I had to scatter out of the way.

I grabbed at my brother's arm, laughing. "I'm sorry, I'm sorry, I'll stop."

Cutting us a dark look of warning, Thane replied, "Regan and I need everyone in the living room, anyway. We'll return to planning your *sexless* dream home afterward."

"I guess it's too late to mention the red room of pain, then?" Mac teased.

Thane looked at him in horror. "How the fuck do you know about the red room of pain?"

"How do *you* know?"

My brother scowled. "Regan made me watch the films."

Mac raised an eyebrow. "Made you? Oh, aye, I'm sure that was *hard* for you."

"Fuck off." Thane stalked out of the room.

"I know it was hard for me when Arro made me watch them," he called after him.

"You're a bastard," my brother answered back.

Laughing, I fell against Mac as we followed him out of Thane's office. "That was cruel."

"But so worth it." Mac snorted.

We were still laughing like schoolchildren when we wandered into the living room to find everyone—Robyn,

Lachlan, Arran, Eredine, Thane, Regan, and Eilidh and Lewis
—settled around.

Robyn made a face at us. "You two are so sickeningly
adorable."

"Adorable." Mac tugged playfully on her ponytail. "I've
never been called *adorable* in my life."

"Well, you are." Robyn grinned at him, so much love in
her eyes. I knew she was happy for her dad because she'd
told me several times it overjoyed her to see him so content.

"So, what's going on?" Arran asked. "Not to be rude, but
we're waiting on a call from the solicitors to let us know our
payment's gone through."

He referred to their payment for the purchase of the
Gloaming. It had been weeks of checks and surveys and
back-and-forth with Gordon's solicitors, but they'd finally
agreed on a price, and the contracts had all been signed. By
the end of today, my brothers would be the proud new
owners of one of Ardnoch's most beloved haunts.

It was much talked about around the village because, of
course, Gordon was also beloved by our community. Some
felt like the Adairs owning such an important business was
only an invitation for us to buy up more and more, while
others seemed to think it was fitting that Gordon passed the
reins to my brothers since he and his wife had no children of
their own.

Again, the Adairs were giving Ardnoch much to discuss.
Word had spread quickly about Guy's attack, and since it had
been right on the back of Mac's, we were all anyone was
talking about. Members at Lachlan's club who ventured into
the village during their stay had confessed it was one of the
joys of Ardnoch that the villagers gossiped more among
themselves than about the Hollywood stars living only a few
miles from them.

Not fun for us, really. People gawked at me for weeks

after Guy's attack. But I was feeling much calmer about the incident months later, even proud of how I'd fought back. It hadn't taken long for the trial against Guy to go ahead. Thankfully, because of the cameras I'd forgotten were installed in our modular cabin to protect our computers from theft, there was no question about Guy's intent that day. Moreover, the disturbing items—several knifes, ropes, and heavy-duty cleaning products—discovered in his car that day only served as further evidence. It hadn't been easy to watch that footage from the cabin. I think it affected Mac worse than anyone.

But it was footage we needed. While Guy was sentenced to fifteen years for attempted murder, I was cleared of all charges. Guy, from prison, had filed a civil suit against me for hitting him with my car, if you could believe it. My solicitor wasn't worried a damn bit, so I wasn't either. I was just relieved that Guy's criminal charges meant he would likely never be allowed to set foot in Scotland again. His creepy cousin Duncan was fired and charged with harassment (for leaving the notes) and theft (for stealing Marcello's phone). He'd probably end up with a slap on the wrist but I really only cared he was out of my life.

As for Lee Kilmany, he awaited trial for suspicion of murder on multiple counts and attempted murder. Roisin Bankman awaited a separate trial for conspiracy to commit murder and for attempted murder. There was no doubt in any of our minds that they'd see the inside of a prison cell and stay there for quite some time.

As Mac wanted, we moved on with our lives without letting the shadows of the past hang over us.

Thane sat down beside Regan, who had the kids snuggled beside her. Eilidh's excited bouncing in her seat drew my attention to the purpose of our gathering. What was going on that made Eilidh look ready to burst? Her bright blue eyes met mine, dancing with delight, the secret trembling on her lips.

"Someone better tell us why we're here, or Eils is going to do it," I warned, laughing.

"Can I?" Eilidh turned to Regan and Thane. "Please?"

The couple shared a look, and then Regan gave Eilidh a dimpled smile and a nod.

In an instant, Eilidh jumped off the couch, arms and legs stretched like a sea star, and announced with an excited shriek, "Mum and Dad are getting married, and I get to be a flower girl again!"

The room erupted in joyful shouts of congratulations and tearful hugs of joy.

As I hugged Regan, she whispered, "I hope this doesn't seem like it's stepping on your toes."

"Not at all." I pulled away to tug at the hand she'd been hiding from everyone. Her engagement ring was stunning and as perfect for her as mine was for me. While mine was a solitaire with a simple platinum band and pear-shaped diamond in a prong setting, Regan's was a little flashier. Thane had chosen an emerald-cut ruby with a diamond halo and diamond band.

"Do you love it?" I asked, staring at it, a little in awe.

"Um, yeah." She gaped at it like it was her first time seeing it. "He nailed it. And the stones are ethically sourced, so I can feel good about that."

"I think you can feel good about a whole lot," I said, looking around at our family, watching Eilidh regale Robyn about being a flower girl twice over.

"Hey, this is just a thought." Regan's words brought my gaze back to her. "And we totally understand if you don't want to, but Thane and I want to have a simple wedding, nothing over the top ... and we thought maybe that sounded right up your alley too."

"What are you saying?"

"Do you want to have a double wedding? I kinda like the idea of it being this big family thing, you know. Of sharing that with you. But," she rushed to say, "I totally get it if you want the day to yourself. You and Mac have waited a long time."

We had waited a long time.

But the thought of sharing my wedding day with my brother actually made me emotional. Tears stung my nose. "I'll talk to Mackennon, but I love the idea."

MAC

WE'D BARELY GOTTEN home and through the front door when Arro jumped me.

She'd been eyeing me in the car all the way from Thane's, and I knew that look.

We'd celebrated Thane and Regan's engagement with a family dinner, ordering takeout and calling Brodan on Face-Time to fill him in. He was finishing up filming and promised to be home soon. I wouldn't hold him to it. Brodan Adair had gone from being the biggest homebody I'd ever known to a man who acted like he was being chased from Ardnoch by the devil himself. At least his uncharacteristic bar brawling had stopped.

He seemed happy enough for his brother, though, and when we hung up, we fell into chaotic conversation, juggling several subjects at once in a way I'd grown used to as part of this family.

The joy of the evening had aroused Arro.

She'd caught my eye across Thane's dining table, and I knew that heated expression and what I had to look forward to when we got home.

Nothing quite prepared me for Arro's impatience, however, and before I knew it, I was sprawled on the hallway floor, still fully dressed, being ridden hard.

"Fuck," I gritted out between clenched teeth as Arro ground down on me, her hands on my shoulders for purchase. I gripped her hips to feel the motion of her frantic undulations. Jesus Christ, this woman would be the death of me. And what a way to go. "Take off your top," I commanded harshly.

Her expression said she was reluctant to slow down, but Arro quickly threw off her light jacket, top, and bra, and I sat up to take a hard nipple in my mouth.

Arro gasped at the movement, arching into me as I sucked and laved, taking turns on each perfect breast. She began to move on me again, and I growled around her nipple with pleasure.

"Oh, God." Her fingers bit into my shoulders as she braced her knees on either side of my hips and gave me all she had.

"Fuck ..." I released her breast, but only to crush her mouth beneath mine as she tried to wrench my very soul from my body. The woman could move. We broke apart, panting for breath as I held her gaze. Her lids sat low over her eyes, desire turning them a darker shade of blue. "That's it," I murmured thickly against her lips. "Take it, darlin'. Take it all."

"I'm coming," she gasped. "I'm coming!"

"Come hard on me, Arro," I growled, my hold on her tightening. "Give me everything."

Her loud groan of release echoed off the walls as her inner muscles squeezed around me in fisted, tight waves that

357

drew my balls up. I bellowed with unearthly fucking satisfaction as my release flooded into her.

Holding her close, rubbing soothing circles on her naked back, I waited until she'd come down from her high before I made a move to lift us off the floor.

Arro clamped her legs down around mine to stop me.

Amused, I brushed her hair off her face and asked, "Do you want to stay here all night?"

She shook her head, chasing my fingers with her lips. I cupped her face in my hands, loving the way she bussed into my touch. "I want to ask you something."

"All right?"

She caressed my face with her eyes as she said, "Regan and Thane would like us to have a double wedding."

Wondering if she was conflicted about her answer, I said, "I'm sure if you don't want to, they'll be okay with that."

"I do want to," she hurried to say. "But only if you want to. I don't want you to feel like our wedding was hijacked. I will not be one of those brides who takes over everything. This is *our* wedding."

Grinning, I cuddled her closer. "Arrochar Adair, if it were up to me, I'd march you to the nearest justice of the peace and have them marry us on the spot. All I care about is being your husband and you being my wife. When I proposed, I didn't care how we made that come about ... but do you know what? I think getting married alongside your brother and Regan sounds exactly right for us."

Her eyes brightened with happy tears. "Family," she murmured.

"That's it. It's all that matters." I grinned at her mischievously. "And it'll give this village more to gossip about, what with the complicated family tree we're creating."

Arro threw her head back in a wicked cackle that made me laugh. "I love it! Yeah, we're doing it. Double wedding."

"Double wedding," I agreed.

Her expression softened into such love, it made me hard again. "Just so you know, I'd marry you anywhere too. All I care about is us. I don't care about the trimmings and trappings."

"That's why we're perfect for each other."

"We are, aren't we?" She did a little shimmy on me that made me groan. She chuckled with delight. "It took us a while to get here, but we got here eventually. And soon"—she lifted her left hand to flash her engagement ring—"we'll be forever."

I shook my head as I used my training to take me to my feet without losing my hold on her. Arro wrapped her arms around my neck as I carried her into the bedroom and promised, "We already are forever." I threw her on the bed, shrugging out of my jacket, preparing to show her what I planned forever to look like.

With her hair spilling across our pillows, her cheeks flushed with desire, and eyes bright with adoration, I honestly thought my heart might burst with gratitude as my future wife whispered fiercely, "It's always been you, Mackennon. It always will be."

ACKNOWLEDGMENTS

Some characters pull you in just that wee bit deeper than others and Mackennon Galbraith was one of those characters. Writing his and Arro's love story has been a pure joy and their journey will stay with me always. I hope you enjoy reading about their epic and hard-won love as much as I enjoyed writing it.

For the most part, writing is a solitary endeavor, but publishing most certainly is not. I have to thank my tremendous friend Catherine Cowles for reading early versions of Always You and providing wisdom and advice that helped make Mac and Arro's story as authentic as possible. You are an amazing light of support and kindness in the book community (and beyond!) and I'm so very grateful for your friendship!

Of course I have to thank my amazing editor Jennifer Sommersby Young for always, *always* being there to help make me a better writer and storyteller. Thank you for loving Mac as much as I do!

Thank you to Julie Deaton for proofreading *Always You* and catching all the things! You have an amazing eye for detail. And thank you for loving Mac, too! It's a Mac lovefest lol.

And thank you to my bestie and PA extraordinaire Ashleen Walker for handling all the little things and supporting me through everything. I appreciate you so much. Love you lots!

The life of a writer doesn't stop with the book. Our job

expands beyond the written word to marketing, advertising, graphic design, social media management, and more. Help from those in the know goes a long way. A huge thank-you to Nina Grinstead at Valentine PR for your encouragement, support, insight and advice. You're a star!

Thank you to every single blogger, Instagrammer, and book lover who has helped spread the word about my books. You all are appreciated so much! On that note, a massive thank-you to the fantastic readers in my private Facebook group, Sam's Clan McBookish. You're truly special and the loveliest readers a girl could ask for! Your continued and ceaseless support is awe-inspiring and I'm so grateful for you all.

A massive thank-you to Hang Le for once again creating a stunning cover that establishes the perfect visual atmosphere for this story and this series. You amaze me! And thank you to Regina Wamba for the beautiful couple photography that perfectly encapsulates the longing between Mac and Arro.

As always, thank you to my agent Lauren Abramo for making it possible for readers all over the world to find my words. You're phenomenal, and I'm so lucky to have you!

A huge thank-you to my family and friends for always supporting and encouraging me, and for listening to me talk, sometimes in circles, about the worlds I live in.

Finally, to you, thank you for reading. It means the everything to me.

ABOUT THE AUTHOR

Samantha Young is a *New York Times*, *USA Today* and *Wall Street Journal* bestselling author from Stirlingshire, Scotland. She's been nominated for the Goodreads Choice Award for Best Author and Best Romance for her international bestseller *On Dublin Street*. *On Dublin Street* is Samantha's first adult contemporary romance series and has sold in 31 countries.

CPSIA information can be obtained
at www.ICGtesting.com
Printed in the USA
LVHW091927190522
719221LV00012B/1470